CONTEMPORARY AMERICAN FICTION

AMONG BIRCHES

Rebecca Hill grew up in Mississippi and Illinois and graduated from Grinnell College in Iowa. She received a master's degree from Harvard. Her first novel, *Blue Rise*, available from Penguin, received a Friends of American Writers Award and the Literature Award from the Mississippi Institute of Arts and Letters. Married and the mother of two daughters, she currently divides her time between Minnesota and Georgia.

Among Birches

REBECCA HILL

PENGUIN BOOKS

For Jude

PENGUIN BOOKS
Viking Penguin Inc., 40 West 23rd Street,
New York, New York 10010, U.S.A.
Penguin Books Ltd, Harmondsworth,
Middlesex, England
Penguin Books Australia Ltd, Ringwood,
Victoria, Australia
Penguin Books Canada Limited, 2801 John Street,
Markham, Ontario, Canada L3R 1B4
Penguin Books (N.Z.) Ltd, 182–190 Wairau Road,
Auckland 10, New Zealand

First published in the United States of America by
William Morrow and Company, Inc., 1986
Reprinted by arrangement with William Morrow and Company, Inc.
Published in Penguin Books 1987

Grateful acknowledgment is given for permission to quote *One Writer's Beginnings*
by Eudora Welty, published by Harvard University Press.

LIBRARY OF CONGRESS CATALOGING IN PUBLICATION DATA
Hill; Rebecca.
Among birches.
(Contemporary American fiction)
I. Title. II. Series.
PS3558.I442A8 1987 813′.54 86-21188
ISBN 0 14.00 9852 6

Printed in the United States of America by
R. R. Donnelley & Sons Company, Harrisonburg, Virginia
Set in Baskerville

13 April 1926. Virginia Woolf at home in England writing to Vita Sackville-West, who travels abroad in Russia with her husband: "I will tell you about Anna Karenina, and the predominance of sexual love in 19th Century fiction, and its growing unreality to us who have no real condemnation in our hearts any longer for adultery as such. But Tolstoy hoists all his books on that support. Take it away, say, no, it doesn't offend me that AK should copulate with Vronsky, and what remains? . . . Put yourself that question on the Steppes with the owls hooting and a melancholy wolf slinking behind the everlasting birch trees."

I

Unity

The events in our lives happen in a sequence in time, but in their significance to ourselves they find their own order, a timetable not necessarily—perhaps not possibly—chronological.

—EUDORA WELTY, *"Learning to See"*

CHAPTER ONE

Finally after dinner they sat around the fire in the living room with the last of the wineglasses balanced on knees and end tables. The plum-colored modular sofa formed a box canyon at that end of the room facing the fireplace, and Aspera sat at the outlet, handy for liquor glasses or coffee spoons or the telephone. This was her favorite part of the evening, after the tableside duties of getting food and drink into people and conversation out of them: the reign of peace and digestion when stories would be traded for the privilege of not moving.

She glanced round the circle one more time. Old friends—though time and place had meshed so imperfectly over the years that some of these old friends of Will's and hers hadn't met before. Tonight they bridged all gaps; birthday parties were good for that.

In the dining room the table setting had established a tone, black linen napkins gently folded and laid on a cream damask cloth. An echo of the wallpaper, where above the high oak wainscoting black swans floated on a cream background. This formality felt right; she was rested these days by elements that offered shape and definition instead of asking for them. Old friends helped that way. They agreed on notions of cause and effect, or at least would disagree charmingly, a range she counted on. They'd laugh at the same things. With new friends added, they would not try one another beyond what might be endured in silence.

From where she sat, Aspera could see the mahogany table

where the company had left a genteel debris of silver, black linen, china. Dinner scraps rested lightly on the plates, and each plate still had a separate identity, seemed still to belong to one particular guest. They had not yet become part of the after-clutter and last labor, had not yet become dirty dishes.

She pushed deeper into the sofa back. Around the fire, the circle of acquaintance would gather itself in. How she wanted that harmony—one of the classic mistakes. Require the goose to lay golden eggs. She took one careful breath, rubbed the little bones beside the bridge of her nose. The stories would begin. Everybody would tell about themselves or about children, stories told before to other people, but that was to the good. Rough edges had been polished off, all the ease of telling and being listened to and telling again.

Next to Aspera, Dena crossed her legs. Her stockings gave up a silken sigh. "Guess who had a run-in with the police in Houston," she offered.

The chorus of interrogators went after details. Dena's daughter Angie and her boyfriend were taken from a bar to a Houston police station and booked. The charges were loitering, creating a public nuisance, disturbing the peace. Told they'd spend the next three nights in jail if they demanded a hearing, they pleaded guilty. It turned out the station had received a complaint from that particular bar the night before, and the patrolmen had settled on picking up two "drifters" there—

"To make things come out even," Dena finished. Her frown, printed on petite features with restraint, was to show she had her emotions under control.

Aspera sat back. She wanted to go on listening, and noticed then that everyone else sat forward or back, according to temperament or maybe angle of digestion.

"Can they get legal redress?" Bunny asked, leaning forward.

"Not if they pleaded guilty," Will said. "How old is—how old are the kids now anyway?" Sober, he would have remembered the names along with the ages, would also have remembered that with Baby Kevin here with Vicky, age ought not to be addressed.

Dena covered. "Both Angie and David are nineteen. They both finally had jobs in Houston. What they were most afraid of was losing their jobs." Her voice quavered the merest shade.

"So now they'll have a police record." Dalton rested his head on the sofa back.

"But in *Houston,*" Bunny countered. "Like a police record in Selma a few years back. Or Chicago. Special conditions—"

"Mean zip," Dalton pronounced quietly. His eyes closed for several seconds, as though the issue had been settled. This impatience with Bunny's politics appeared weary and customary. Aspera marveled that he argued at all. Did he expect Bunny to stop looking for loopholes in the way of the world? Unless she'd changed since Aspera knew her, Bunny saw the world as an open target. The private sphere was where she moved in silence. "A police record means next time you don't get hired," Dalton said to his wife.

"I'm about to become a corporation," Bunny reminded him. "I can decide what disqualifies and what doesn't." She turned to Will, placed a hand on his arm. "You'd hire a clerk with a Houston police record, wouldn't you?"

Will grinned. "I'd hire Angie," he hedged.

It was Vicky who returned the conversation, reeling on its political flywheels, back to Angie and her boyfriend.

"It shakes you up, doesn't it? They're so vulnerable." She spoke to Dena with their shared knowledge of motherhood, and with her hand aligned the sharp creases of her pants legs. Beside her Baby Kevin seemed to be staring at the ashtray on the coffee table, his fine fresh coloring up, his nostrils open as if to pick up the correct scent. He placed a hand on Vicky's knee as though he'd comfort her.

Vicky blinked, registering the presence of his hand, registering also that for this company she knew this Kevin and his warm hand were in error.

Will cleared his throat, and Aspera saw the vector of attention leap guiltily off Vicky's knee and come to rest on his face.

"I still remember how tiny Angie was when she was born," he said. "Scared the devil out of me."

"You and babies," Dena exclaimed. "Did I ever tell you what Will said? After he found out I'd had a girl, he said, "Well, you'll want to get a gun, got to keep off the greasers."

The group startled into laughter.

"You can't start worrying too early," Bunny said soberly. "We finally put Brookie into a girls' boarding school this year."

A beat while the logic was patched in.

"How old is your daughter?" Dena inquired.

"Fourteen," Dalton said, at the same time Bunny answered, "Almost fifteen."

While Aspera was trying to register this difference, the conversation veered.

"Good idea," Will said. "Lock 'em away."

"Is there something you want to tell us about teenage boys?" Vicky asked him.

"My memory is too good." Will grimaced and crossed his legs. "I can still remember when it was a big deal to defoliate a virgin."

Vicky moaned, covering her eyes.

"What? Oh," Will said. "Well, it used to be deflowered, but times have changed."

"You've had a lot to drink, Will," Bunny said in her little-girl voice.

He frowned in thought, and Aspera held on to the sofa cushion. "*Beholed,* a virgin!" he said. He spelled it for them.

Dena rolled her eyes. "Somehow I'm sorry all this started with Angie."

Kevin began to say something, but Will held the floor, talking over him. "Besides!" he called out. "Angie's always been fast. There was the time Aspera and I had her with us in the Townsend Cafe, downtown? You know that little place here in Bracken? No more than eight stools around the lunch bar, and six of them full, six Minnesota farmers in for their morning coffee. Angie was just a squirt, maybe five, and the guy on the next stool said something to her. Said 'Candy, little girl' or something. And she turned to me and said in this sweet clear voice, 'Uncle Will, that man said hello. He has a penis, doesn't he? Daddy has a penis, you have a penis, Aunt Aspera has a bagina'—now the kid starts going around the room pointing—'he has a penis, she has a bagina, he has a penis, he has a penis, and *I* have a *little, tiny* bagina—right, Uncle Will?' "

Will was still holding the finger signs for *little, tiny* while the room rocked with laughter.

Dena fluttered her fingers from forehead to mouth, her face flaming crimson.

"Nothing wrong with checking your elemental facts," Vicky said.

Aspera turned and peered out the living room windows to see once again how the last light of September rose from the trunks of the paper birches. The light was afterglow, making of the trees a staggered wall of ghostly tusks shooting up along the curb. An excess of elementals—the phrase rose like a ghost. She shook her head to dispel her mother's voice. Still, through the glass the vision was arresting, whitenesses at their irregular intervals, birches leaning and reaching in the dusk.

The group around her exploded into laughter. She turned her head to it without thinking. Next to Dena, Vicky and Baby Kevin were still snugged thigh to thigh, Dalton and Bunny split round the right angle, then Will of course opposite herself. To her wifely ear, his latest remark had come muffled by doors and cabinetry, while the shrill of Bunny's response carried clear as water. Hotline was the word that had brought the laughter.

Aspera found Dena's eyes aimed at her own, a stark bird-look that said, Such behavior! This look normally had eyebrows to go with it, but Dena was one for the soft pedal in public. Which was precisely her recommendation to everybody else.

Dalton meanwhile was doubting aloud that Angie would ever have cause to be one of Bunny's clients. As his words trailed off, Dena's eyes snapped forward. "Bunny—it's all right if I call you Bunny?—these referrals for pregnant teenagers, are they part of your degree work?"

Bunny straightened in the sofa. She brushed away a lock of glossy hair that had strayed into her line of vision. "My telephone service takes the place of a thesis. Back in Sacramento, women's studies focused more on action. Which suits me."

"You're a feminist then, yourself?"

Bunny shrugged, a loose motion involving a single shoulder. Her voice came out small, little-girlish. "Not that I want to wear sandwich boards—they don't travel well." She smiled at Dena, dimples deepening.

Will pounded the thick glass of the coffee table, which caused several metal objects to dance upon it. "Time for dessert!" he announced. "You're a dessert man, aren't you, Dalt?"

This time as he swept them all toward diversion, Aspera felt relief. Lately she was unsure if Will did what he did by design, or by some instinct that just happened to make her jumpy.

Dalton had turned to her. "What's on the dessert menu?" he asked.

She smiled at him. For Dalton, the question was tardy. Faced with the prospect of a meal, he needed to hear what would be served so he could plan his intake. Options were limited and alternatives had to be managed. From the time he walked in the door, Dalton normally wanted to know whether he should go long on salad or short on French bread, whether he ought to take his allotted pats of butter with the brussels sprouts, or save them for a possible fettuccine Alfredo.

"Would you settle for a calorie count and fat rated in grams?" Will put in, leaning around Bunny. Prankishly he blocked her view as he added, "Or are you carbohydrate-loading tonight?"

"I'm ignoring your husband," Dalton said to Aspera. "I strongly recommend that you do the same. Now, is this serious, about dessert?"

She smiled at him. "Dessert is always serious. Tonight we're having—"

"Birthday cake," Will said. "Big surprise."

Everyone laughed.

"*Special* birthday cake," she amended. "Since tonight we celebrate not only my birthday but the autumnal equinox—"

"Homemade apple cake!" Will trumpeted. "We found green apples at the stand outside Bromley. You know that last bend on Highway Six? We've been going there for years."

His interrupting rattled her. She felt an anger yeasting up, anger that would have to be punched down. Such wifely and violent notions occupied her mind lately, occupied in the military sense. Will's style as host was to stir people up, chafe them into combat, and it was bad luck that she was after peace these days. She had a job just holding on to continuity.

"Not green apples, but the first of the Minnesota Haralsons," Aspera told Dalton. "I stopped on my way home from Cold Spring."

Dalton listened. His academic's mind would fix on the variety of apple and the name of the town; she was grateful. She needed help establishing order in things. Words were important; they stamped down images in people's minds, and right now she wanted her *I* made distinct from the *we* that Will was trying to absorb it with. She wanted Dalton or even Bunny to pick up this difference and ask Will, "Oh, did you both go?"

From the tray of hors d'oeuvres left on the coffee table, Will reached for a disc of cucumber. "We get our honey from that place too," he added. He lifted the cucumber to Bunny's mouth; she bit the circle neatly.

"This must be the royal We," Vicky kidded him.

So Vicky knew how hard she found it when Will spoke for her. When he told not only his stories but her stories, when he finished her sentences and in general behaved as though she were not competent to hold up her end of a dependent clause—no secret after all. Was there a single secret in the entire room?

Dena smoothed the moment over. "It is very good honey," she affirmed. "I don't know quite why it's so special, but it is. Perhaps the apple blossoms."

"*I* think it's special," Aspera said, rubbing the bridge of her nose where tension rode like a wire. "Will doesn't care for honey at all."

"What an unnatural creature you are, Will," Bunny chided. She lowered her head and pouted at him, a motion that somehow implied more.

"I know, I know," the unnatural creature confessed. He had brought a wineglass up to his mouth, had spoken into its half-empty chamber.

"A man that doesn't go for honey!" Bunny kept it up, catching Aspera's eye. "At our house I practically have to keep it under lock and key."

Will wiped his lips with the back of his hand. "That's what I thought," he sympathized, eyeing Dalton. "He's an animal, isn't he?"

Bunny giggled. Aspera would have thought the entire company had felt the conversation slip those several notches, but Kevin entered in as though the ground were still solid.

"I'm trying to think what they call those deals they serve honey with?" he asked Vicky. He made a circular motion with his hand.

She shrugged, smiling at him.

His unclouded eyes swept the company. He rested them on Aspera. "Do you know the thing I mean?"

"We've got one of those things," Will answered.

"A honey-dipper," Aspera said to the young man, whose eyes had not moved. He seemed sweetly focused on her, asking for clarification and yet in some way offering it. She made a circular motion with her own hands, floundered for words. "It's an odd-looking device, like a dipstick—"

"But it works," Will finished. He leaned over and nudged Bunny. "We've got one of those dipstick devices and it works great."

Bunny dimpled and made pointing motions at Will. "Ignore this man," she told Kevin.

Will chortled. Nobody had managed it yet.

In the kitchen Aspera waited for the water to come to the boil. It was nearly there, even on low heat, and she had no wish to speed the process. Coffee mugs on a tray, seven separate clicks. Only mugs—no one in this crowd used sugar or cream anymore.

Dena appeared in the kitchen doorway. She carried a basket of cheese and fruit, which she showed to Aspera like a hall pass. Then she walked forward and stood beside her hostess. "Didn't you tell me Will introduced Bunny to Dalton fifteen years ago?" she asked.

"True."

"It's been going on that long." Dena ran her fingers over the grapes, then set down the basket. "And you're letting both of them back into your life?"

Aspera took in the uptilted eyebrow. "They're back in Minnesota," she answered. "Both of them."

"And only an hour away," Dena mused. She lifted the lid off the kettle and looked inside. "Not far enough."

Aspera settled the lid again. "Look at the bright side. Bunny might find some lonely professor for you among Dalt's colleagues."

"And you imagine there'd be something left of him?"

Aspera went to the sink and rinsed her hands, hiding the smile. Dena was trying to help. Some years ago the two of them had dropped the preambles, all those hesitations gracing a risky opinion: I hate to say it but, this may sound harsh but. In general society women couldn't do without reluctance and qualification, so in private they practiced efficiency. Brave words in the kitchen.

"She's not that dangerous, Dena."

"She looks bored to me." With her hands Dena smoothed

the feathering of her red-gold hair at the nape of her neck. "Married women are very dangerous when they're bored."

"That's just Bunny."

Dena wrinkled her nose. "Bunny. She actually lets people call her that? Grown-up people?"

Aspera made a wry face at her friend. "With a name like Aspera, I try to give everybody else a wide berth."

Dena opened a cupboard and located the plastic wrap. "But surely. Isn't she going to be running a feminist referral service? Of course she doesn't exactly call herself a feminist. She knows *about* feminism. The way entomologists know about bugs."

Aspera's laugh came out louder than she expected, and she covered her mouth. Treachery from a distance made up for so much. In the living room the jokes could be made by somebody else, but twenty feet away in the kitchen, she and Dena could stand ankle-deep in movie blood and no harm done. In a sudden vision she saw red stuff rolling down the passageway from the dining room, foaming like the Red Sea dotted with tiny Egyptians. Yet on the sofa Bunny would go on flirting with Will, unaffected as Fearless Fosdick.

"A real expert," Dena giggled.

"I guess we're razor-sharp out here," Aspera whispered, beginning to find a straight face. "OK. The last thing I want to be tonight is dull."

"Or blind," Dena said. She set the wrapped fruit and cheese on the counter and reached for a paper towel for her hands. Then she added, "It's just that Bunny is such a challenging name for an expert." She placed a single cool finger on the inside of Aspera's arm. "Don't you think the word hotline might make her mind wander?"

"Geez." She shrugged off Dena's touch.

"It's the breasts, don't you think?" Dena went on airily. "What would you guess, size forty-two long?"

Aspera bit her lip. When she could, she said, "That's not nice. Hers aren't so much bigger than yours."

Dena regarded her coolly. "It's difficult to tell. I don't wear mine loose around my waist." She preened, pressing her large and firmly brassiered bosom forward. "A number of things about her could stand shaping up, and I mean aside from her—conversation."

Vicky shouldered through the swinging door with the last

two wineglasses in her hands. "Whose conversation? I can't get a word in edgewise between Bunny and Will. Had to take these away from them."

"Shhhhhhhhh!" Aspera told her, watching as the door beat shut.

"Isn't Bunny an interesting name for a pregnancy referee?" Vicky went on. "Dena, what are you doing all puffed up and chesty like that?"

"She's waiting for a call on her hotline," Aspera said. She was surprised when they both laughed, and then she laughed with them. "Now put those down," she said to Vicky.

Vicky set the glasses on the counter with ceremony.

"Kevin is absolutely charming," Dena said to Vicky, taking a step nearer. Four fingers came to rest on Vicky's shoulder. Ancient practice, touching one that you envy to dispel the evil. As the fingers fluttered and were withdrawn, something registered with Aspera, times she had felt undefended against Dena's decisions to touch. Dena could be so funny, but her touch never soothed, and without thinking Aspera put another paper towel into those hands. Then tried to cover. "Did you know Dena mixed the salad by hand?" she asked Vicky. Those long fingers, tumbling croutons among the glistening greens. Aspera paddled her own hands in the air. "Dressing and all?"

"Fingers simply work so much better," Dena sighed, now languorously applying the towel as though some trace of oil remained. Aspera glimpsed the lacquered nails large and pinky-iridescent, like scales on a carp. Wearying, the way sensuality was forever at issue.

"You don't simply look to tell if the leaves are coated," Dena went on, "you get the feel of it, down to the bottom. Delightful textures, really." Taking in Aspera's expression, she bubbled a laugh. "Get your kicks where you can."

"Wish I'd known," Vicky said. "Thing about Dena's hands, you never know where they've been." She and Dena grinned at one another. Vicky winked at Aspera, and the warmth was very welcome, indeed. Aspera felt herself relax, felt the world around her come back into focus.

Dena had folded both her paper towels together and now laid them on the counter. She took a breath and sighed, a long sigh that undercut the ease in the room. With her palms she smoothed her skirt, some nuzzly fabric in rose and brown, over her hipbones. Was Dena all right these days? The gestures made arguments of their own.

"Smashing outfit," Aspera told her.

Dena smiled. Even perfection didn't mean you could do without reassurance, and her eyes swept briefly over Vicky's black sweater and pants. For that moment Aspera believed she saw what Dena saw, noticed the way dark shades made the few sparkles of gray stand out in Vicky's hair.

The dark clothing was left from the old days, before fifty pounds had come off Vicky's small frame. A heart condition had moved her to rigors she'd never have endured just to be attractive, something hard for Dena to understand; harder still that Vicky, widowed the same year Dena divorced, had then become the magnetic pole at which unexpected compasses aimed.

"Are you going to tell us where you found that charming young man?" Dena asked.

Vicky made her small eyes go shrewd. "Under which cradle, you mean?"

"I want you both out of here," Aspera said.

Vicky set her hands on her hips. "What's the rush?"

"Give me a break," Aspera pleaded. "I just turned forty today, I can't take stress. Vicky, get going. Dena, take those dessert plates with you before anybody else out there gets restless."

"We don't take orders," Vicky replied. "We've been forty for years." She gave Dena's smooth skirt a pat and then strode through the kitchen and around the corner.

They heard her shut the bathroom door.

The paper towels on the counter had come unfolded, and one flap waved in the air. Dena pressed it down again. "You're the restless one tonight, my dear," she told Aspera gently. She put up her free hand and with her long nails rearranged the feathering of Aspera's bangs. "Will is just being Will."

Aspera put her concentration on the oblong of toweling. She took it up, turned and dropped it into the wastebasket behind her. She settled the lid. "Just what was it I used to like so much about him?"

Dena turned and carried the stack of small plates toward

the swinging door. As she turned to back through it, she extended one finger. "Don't let Will's behavior interfere with your pleasure. And mind your manners."

They both heard sounds of Vicky emerging from the bathroom. Dena fixed Aspera with sharp maternal eyes and the one finger, then backed through the door.

"What did I miss?" Vicky moved into the kitchen from the other doorway. She hunched her compact frame and put one stubby finger between Aspera's eyes. Vicky's body had become muscular and taut, almost slender. But stubby fingers were stubby fingers, and this broad imitation of Dena was the more comical.

Aspera smiled. Vicky would be making this joke even with Dena there; that was her way. Still, Aspera considered it chancy to go against the central vein of a friend's character; you didn't tell Dena she had to reveal naked truth, and you didn't tell Vicky she had to cover it up. Somewhere between the two, she saw herself uneasily perched.

"Look into my fingernails!" Vicky whispered huskily. Her hand made a chubby claw, the bitten-down nails hovering bluntly over the bridge of Aspera's nose. "You are getting advice," she droned. "I am Madame Vampira and you are getting bad advice!"

Aspera batted the hand away. Though more and more it did seem they'd arrived at middle age for just this: to give each other bad advice.

She turned and checked the kettle now trembling on the burner, turned the flame still lower. It was true, she was the restless one. And if life strategies are formed at age three, then by forty it was natural they all knew how to put words to them, could hand out wisdom like pearls.

Vicky put her fists on the counter and leaned on them. "My dear married person," she said. "You are surrounded by friends, and your friends see that your husband is spilling wine and most everything else in Bunny's direction. Will is going to be very entertaining in about half an hour, you know."

"I know." Aspera opened the silver chest and picked up a bundle of dessert forks. She started toward the swinging door.

Vicky followed. "It's your own fault. You never had the heart to—" She stopped short as the door opened from the other side and Will pushed through.

"What's taking so long out here?"

Vicky put one hand on her hip and finished her sentence. "—tell him the female eardrum isn't a sex gland." She winked at Will, then seized the forks from Aspera's hands and brushed past, leaving the two of them alone.

"Sex gland?" Will repeated. "Is that what you women talk about?"

Aspera felt her face burn. She turned and busied herself about the kitchen. "I'm just doing things till the coffee water's ready," she said over her shoulder. She rinsed the cheese plate and fitted it into the dishwasher rack. She dribbled olives back into the tubular bottle.

"It's not ready yet?" When she didn't reply, he said, "OK, I'll get this." He reached up and with a groan lifted the cake from atop the refrigerator. As he set it unsteadily on the counter she pretended not to watch.

"Three-point landing!"

She poked artichoke hearts back into their squat jar. These she carried to the refrigerator. She pulled the plastic bag of carrots out of the vegetable drawer and from the snack tray she took up a handful of celery and carrot sticks that had begun to dry and curl.

The edges were whitened where the pieces had been cut. She examined them closely, tried to see if she could actually spot a depleted vegetable cell.

When Will's hand grazed her back, she thrust the sticks into the plastic bag. He seized her shoulders, nearly knocking her off her feet.

"Kettle's boiling," he sang. "You can't stall out here any longer." He turned her swiftly around and she spun, bringing the carrot bag with her.

While he pressed her to him and she breathed his winy breath, Aspera pulled a carrot out of the bag and poked it deep into his abdomen. Will held her away, looked down to the carrot, and then into her face.

"I just thought you might like to know how it feels to be a woman," she told him.

He threw back his head and whinnied. "Criminy! So that's why women are so angry."

He gave her cheek a double pat and turned to take the kettle off the burner. Out of the corner of her eye she watched him.

Her husband, dressed with casual precision in a faded shirt with vented breast pockets, cuffs he'd rolled at the wrist, the final delicate wheat-yellow of the cotton contrasting with his ruddy skin. Married to this man for twenty years? His back was to her now, and her eyes also took in the waist drifted over the belt, the ample posterior firmly rounded.

She slid the tray of cups from the counter. "I'll take these out now if you've got the coffee."

"Don't leave without me." The kitchen filled with steam and the aroma of fresh coffee as he poured the stream of water into the Chemex from a showman's height.

Aspera heard the stream cease as she set her heel to hold the swinging door for him. The door opened on an L-shaped passage lined with cupboards, pantry-fashion, that led to the dining room, which room opened in turn on the living room. The house had been built by Will's parents in the twenties; strangely enough Aspera felt the presence of her own mother most palpably in this narrow passage, between kitchen and dining room, with its glassed-in birchwood cabinets.

Why do we consort with dangerous people, entertain them in our lives? Ah, but we are each of us dangerous to one another; we stare through eyes glassed with evil. So Elvira had taught her. The rest went: But evil is natural, just as in Lake Erie—just as in Lake Erie the lamprey is the natural companion of alewives. Yes. Then: We can still hope not to feed it with ourselves.

Will passed through the doorway, and by the time Aspera reached the living room he was setting the Pyrex pot on the edge of the coffee table. She put the tray of cups down and lifted the pot enough to slide a cork trivet between glass and wood.

"This party is unsafe," Will announced to the group at large. "Forty candles tonight, and I caught the birthday girl out there taking the smoke alarm off the hook." He poured the coffees and peered at Aspera over the thin channels of steam that rose between them. "I want to warn you, Dalton—you too, Kevin, he remembered to add, "look out."

"What now?" Dalton inquired.

"Women don't like vegetables. That's how it is."

"Vegetables?" Dena laughed.

"Furthermore they want to be called persons. You can read about it in the papers. When a man does something, it says so. When it says person—then a woman must have slept her way to the top. Ready to eat cake? Men and persons too?"

"Willllll," pouted Bunny, tilting her head again.

Having seen this move before, Aspera wondered at the effect. Did women with large breasts use that outthrust lower lip to point at themselves, or was it more complicated than that?

Will shook a finger. "Language is important, Bunny-girl. The way to a man's heart turns the stomach. Come out to the kitchen and help me with the cake."

Bunny gave a down-turned smile and got to her feet.

On some mission of her own, Vicky stood up and walked to the dining table. Reaching the place where she had sat at dinner, she carefully smoothed out her napkin, folded it. Aspera thought some communication was intended, but her friend was absorbed, preoccupied. Appearing to act on one more afterthought, Vicky picked up the thick black linen rectangle and brought it back to the living room. She sat next to Kevin again and arranged the napkin on her lap as though some etiquette still required it.

Baby Kevin glanced up and caught Aspera's eye.

Baby Kevin. She flushed and looked away. This time the nickname had come automatically; it was no longer funny, she and Will would have to stop calling him that.

Taking her own place on the sofa next to Dena, Aspera marveled at the web of treacheries. Somewhere the concept of loyalty had been muddled, but all the same it was a way of keeping order. With Will she could joke about Baby Kevin; with Dena she could make fun of Bunny; she could allow Vicky to call Dena Madame Vampira and to ridicule Will's lust-incited or at least liquor-incited displays. It didn't seem fair at the same time that it was utterly just. Isn't that what parties are for? You invite all the people you know, all the keepers of your separate identities, and you put them in a room together to see how it works out.

Meanwhile, it followed that any two guests in that company could get together and make wonderfully illuminating remarks about her. She knew it was true and looked around the circle, longing to know what revelations might be had. What part of her life was ridiculous? Her generosity, or lack of it? Her accommodations to Will, or lack of them? Her silences? Her periodic inability to maintain those silences, her slipshod management of surfaces—that area where Dena so excelled—so that at times in exasperation or pettiness nobody's secret measured up to the effort she expended in keeping it?

Shouts of laughter came from the kitchen.

There were things she ought to attend to; the tapers on the dining table had become slender vanilla stubs; she noticed how they burned unevenly in the draft, one no longer the double of its onetime mate and twin. She could get up and snuff them. At the thought her thighs tensed to bear her weight upward, but the table was in the next room, the candles not much after all.

Dena was murmuring to Dalton about the fire, and Vicky had settled in next to Kevin, still fingering the black napkin on her lap. By some agreement they all eased into their places and sipped coffee, content to gaze together at the glowing spikes of flame in the fireplace, so right for this early fall night. That silence felt to Aspera like communion at last, a needed space sliding between things. Peace, and yet some edge stayed caught in that odd gesture of Vicky's, the way she held on to her bit of linen: something firm to touch with one's hands.

Aspera's own hands suddenly felt conspicuous and empty. She folded them together and looked at what lay before her. Nobody smoked anymore, yet the bronze and pewter ashtray remained centered on the coffee table, because it was beautiful, because it matched the tobacco canister, the lighter, the cigarette box. These objects were part of this room. They picked up a portion of the light and gave it back in a way she had become accustomed to. She'd never thought of breaking up the set, though it would offend her deeply if anyone, say this Kevin, misunderstood and opened the box, lit one of the aged Lucky Strikes and laid ash in the ashtray.

In this way one's life became populated with relics. A smile crept to the corners of her lips. She understood it now; the geometric shape of experience concerning Vicky's napkin, concerning Elvira's world of superstition and sentiment. People had trouble throwing away the clothes of the too recently dead, that was all. When things have been animated by a sense of being necessary, disposing of them with a show of clarity and logic felt indecent. Fetishes and relics—because there was nothing objective that was worth saving. People hung on to an object or a person until they were through, and that was that. Aspera's smile faded. Let no one say that life can be lived without superstition and sentiment; life without superstition and sentiment will not even get you through a dinner party with your friends.

They lie beside one another and without real intent listen as the infrequent cars pass on the street below. The window is open, the night air still cooling inside and outside, enough moisture to make the sounds carry and blend. Like the pedal held on a piano: Sustain.

Time one of them spoke.

He draws a breath, hesitates. Then, "Do you know how passive you are?" The question lies on the air gently, as though it were not a question at all but a minor point of information, perhaps a reminder to breathe all she needs to.

She takes her time, lets the surprise, mild as it is, fade back.

"No."

And this one syllable too seems to last, to fill for some time the need for sound inside the room and out.

Bunny reappeared in the passage with dessert plates and forks.

"Where are the lights?" she called, and four outstretched arms pointed the way. She turned down the dimmer in the panel beside the living room doorway, leaving them peering at one another in the suddenly inadequate light of the fire and the two candles on the dining room table.

At last Will paraded in, bearing aloft a fiery apple cake. The glow preceded him down the passage from the kitchen, and a hush fell over the group as he came into the dining room. The scene could have passed for a vision: a bearer comes by solemn torchlight to the tribe assembled in silence. Fire can throw a spell, can change the nature of boundaries. Will reached the living room and held the cake above Aspera. She looked at the shadows jumping on the walls.

"And you thought we'd lose count out there," he said. With

a flourish he brought the cake down and set it before her with its four ranks of flaming candles.

"This is an epic moment," Dena urged.

"Epic," Dalton said, taking up the word. "What's the myth of the month, Aspera?"

She turned to him amazed. They hadn't used this code since college days when she had steeped herself in classical mythology. She'd done what medical students do with their textbook case histories—lived the stories she read, examined her life for symptoms. She had spent whole weeks as Cassandra, as Eurydice. It became a standing joke between Dalton and her—coeds back then needed standing jokes with the roommates of their steadies, needed something neutral to say while they changed places for the afternoon or for the night. The amazing part was that just lately she'd begun to do it again, to live day to day inside one myth or another.

"Ariadne," she confessed. She looked at Dalton as though there were something important about him that she had forgotten.

"Spider Woman," Will said.

She wanted to take back her answer. Ariadne laid out thread for her hero to find his way out of a labyrinth; that was the myth, and what Aspera was thinking of these days was finding her own way out. While she still had enough string.

"Do you think the three of you have changed since you were in college?" Vicky asked Dalton.

Dalton furrowed his brow as he considered.

"I think Dalt feigns intelligence better than he used to," Will said.

As the small group groaned and shook their heads, Aspera said, "We're all still children."

"All those candles are turning into stubs," Bunny said in her small voice.

The group sang "Happy Birthday" with hearty dissonance. Then Aspera took a painful breath and leaned close to the cake, her face showing orange above the glow. She blew rapidly and systematically. Some of the tiny flames proved stubborn; for a brief moment she suspected a trick. Her chest contracted with effort, and when she began to sputter she was one row and several scattered candles short. Amid the cheers she felt a steady breath against her face, glanced up to see that from across the table Kevin was helping her. His brow was unfurrowed beneath the locks of smooth dark hair, mischief in the eyes. As she looked at him he winked, and she motioned with both hands for everyone to pitch in. In a great rush of common breath the candles went out, their thready smoke plumes shifting with the varying currents of air.

A shout of victory went up, and as Aspera gazed at the faces leaning in around her, showing now in the firelight, she felt a buoyant rush of love. Here were her dearest friends, the people who cared for her.

The forty candles still smoked as Bunny brought the dimmer up and Will reached over Aspera to dip his finger into the pale frosting. "Not bad," he said. "But we get chocolate on my birthday."

Vicky picked up the cake knife, handed it to Aspera. "Any weapon-bearing women in your myths?" she asked.

Aspera shook her head. "Very few."

"And historically speaking, that's one reason we don't worship women." This in a flat tone from Dalton, so that they turned to him in some surprise. He looked at the ring of faces and said, "Well, we don't, do we?"

"Come on, Dalton, this is Roman Catholic Minnesota." Will's tone was broad. "You have to hand it to the serpent," he said; "that was fast thinking, telling Joseph that Mary was still a virgin."

Aspera winced in confusion. "That was an angel who told him," she decided. "You're thinking of the serpent in the Garden of Eden."

"I get these supernatural guys mixed up," Will said. "Wasn't the message the same: *Try it, you'll like it*?"

Sinusy sounds of laughter made their way round the room. Aspera cut the cake. As the small plates passed from hand to hand, murmurs of appreciation followed. She lifted her fork to signal them all to begin, and saw Will snatch a candle from Bunny's piece of cake and suck off the smear of frosting that stuck to it. As the others lifted forks, Bunny reached to retrieve her candle; Will seized the hand and pulled it under the coffee table.

Aspera chewed cake. She could not see whether the hand was taken back, hated herself for looking.

"I could go for ice cream with this," Will said, far too loudly.

Aspera thought he addressed her, that his picture of her might be: somewhere out in the kitchen. Naturally he would raise his voice to speak to her from where he sat in the living room with Bunny.

Her body seemed to be contracting down to some hard limit. She used to be able to counter feelings like this by thinking of larger perspectives—history was good that way, good for famous solutions: a war to end all wars. Mythology was good too: Ariadne. Spider woman.

Don't let his behavior spoil your pleasure. But Aspera's body reported lubrication gone out of sockets that now rubbed bone on bone, and for no cause she could name; nothing new. This flirtation between Bunny and Will was so old it had sprouted chin whiskers, the way women do when the estrogen runs dry. Will played Bunny's sex-object stuff for laughs, and Bunny played up to Will for proof of her standard assumption: Men were entirely manageable so long as you didn't reject them sexually. Sweet-talk them and flirt, touch their arms when you asked them to take out the garbage, and chances were good they'd refrain from their normal pursuits of rape and murder.

Aspera knew all these things. Soft and inviting, that was the ticket.

"Aren't you having any?" Dena spoke to Dalton, who sat with his cake pushed away, his fork in place.

"Hey, Dalt, it's OK," Will urged. "This is just sugar; we don't keep it locked up here, at least not for company."

Dalton swept a hand down to display his trim torso, the product of evident discipline. "It's the tortoise over the hare at last, old buddy, old roommate. The last laugh."

But it was in fact Will who laughed, wringing humor out of Dalton's vanity. "It's priorities," Will said, tipping back his chair and slapping his hands on his ample hips. "Takes a big hammer to drive a big nail."

While everyone was still choking on cake Aspera tried to think if there wasn't something else that needed doing in the kitchen.

Will rode the moment. "I'm just telling you the facts. After all, I know you guys a lot better than Angie knew those German farmers in the Townsend Café." He pulled a face. "Just the elemental facts, ma'am."

"I can add a few," Aspera said. "It wasn't the Townsend Café where Angie said that, it was the truck stop on Route 47 outside Minneapolis, and she'd just turned three. I was teaching tenth-grade Latin and I had my library-science course work on the counter, and since you were working downtown, Will, you weren't there at all."

The room fell silent in the way that it can after an antipersonnel bomb has been dropped. The walls jumped forward, showed themselves unaffected. In that silence Aspera heard the hard edge of her own voice, felt the instant backwash of regret as Will's face lost its reckless happiness and tried to find something more suitable to wear.

"Of course I was there!" he protested. "God, I can see it! Every detail!"

Aspera remembered now about the fabric that supported them all like a fireman's net; above her head a rent hung flapping, but she ought not cause others to fall through.

"You got most of them right," she said lamely. Her eyes burned and she tried to look out the windows but the vision of birches was gone; what showed back against the blackness was a double of the room she was trapped in.

"It's a blessing to have a memory like yours, Will." Here Dena's voice entered with a finished roundness, promising to deflect the energy of straight lines. "History can always be improved upon."

"Details changed to protect the innocent." The offhand suggestion was Kevin's as he sat weighing in his hand the lighter from the coffee table. His very mildness helped mend the moment, helped them all retrieve accord.

"Dammit, Aspera," Dalton said, "Will's getting on, going to be forty himself soon!"

Aspera closed her eyes and opened them. She spoke in answer to the plea and warning in Dena's eyes. "All right, all right, I give."

Three or four more cars pass. At length he rolls to one elbow to look at her directly. The move is nearly silent. The cotton sheets, gone pliant in the saturated air, conform to his motion, damping sound. The shift in pressure on the mattress makes her turn to him.

"I guess I am going to say this," he says.

His breath on her face something between salt and cereal. Full on like this, his eyes have color again, are not the discs of translucent gray she has wondered at.

"You are much too passive."

He waits, solemn. "Not for me but for you."

She searches the colors as they form again in his eyes. Morning will be here. Greens, browns. The next time he speaks the tone is urgent. "You have to go after what you want. Just go get it. Take what you want."

"I am taking what I want," she cries. Emotion makes her voice sound too loud. She tries to whisper. "Look at me. I'm here. I'm taking it as fast as I can figure out what it is."

He rolls off the elbow and lies flat again next to her. She hears him exhale into the paling dark. She is learning from him, she knows that.

"It's a matter of wanting," she explains, noticing as she speaks that she is also learning from herself. "I haven't wanted anything for a long time. It's remembering how to want something."

CHAPTER TWO

Time for champagne, and presents. On the occasion of her fortieth birthday: a bedpan, a walking stick, a tooth glass, a jar of facial depilatory, the *Tibetan Book of the Dead* and, in the traditional place, taped inside the rim of the bedpan, a furry jeweler's box. Aspera had to put her hand inside and feel under the rim to locate it. By feel she also located something flat taped next to the box but left that where it was.

The velvet box held pearl earrings of a delicate pink cast. She tried them on and while the party admired them Bunny tapped a finger on the bedpan. She said, "Say, what about the letter?"

Will had initiated the letter three years ago, when Dalton had turned forty. Written on funeral-parlor letterhead, it proposed methods of interment. It had passed from Dalton to Dena to Vicky and now to Aspera.

"Be a sport," Will urged.

"Being a sport," Dalton said, "is probably not a female-correlated trait."

"She doesn't have the testosterone for it," Will explained to the group. "Dalton had the same problem."

"We all did," Vicky put in. "Given the letter's innuendos on 'Stuffed Like Trigger' and the rest."

"Dalton gave *me* 'Refrigeration in Meyer's Meat Market,' " Dena reminded him. "Things have toned down a little," she promised Aspera.

Will tore the letter from its tape. Opening it, he announced,

"Let's hear it for Interment Method Number Four: 'Dehydrated à la Mosquito!' "

Aspera didn't feel like being kidded about her funeral on her birthday. The great secret of being kidded, however, was not to have feelings. She sat down heavily on the sofa next to Kevin.

He turned and looked at her, lifted an eyebrow.

The look was not one she could read. He was well intentioned, she felt, and yet out of step with everyone else in a way that seemed almost stubborn—that much she had taken in. She shrugged, tried smiling at him.

He rubbed his cheekbone with the edge of his hand. He said to her, "Forty is dead?"

Will held up his hand for silence. " 'This budget method employing native-bred mosquitoes,' " he read aloud, " 'may apply should you survive till early spring. Your body will be laid out in a typical Minnesota backyard at sunset for approximately twenty minutes. Some distortion of features could ensue, but think of the improvement.' "

Laughter. Questions about SPCA regulations. Warnings: Will turned forty next, then Bunny.

The letter would go on making the round of birthdays—Aspera concentrated on linkages—like the passing of a baton or a curse. The pattern of energy was circular, wound tight. But one of her clenched hands was seized and warmly patted by Vicky. Aspera looked up and caught Dalton's quick wink. Dena leaned over and scrutinized the pearl earrings with a professional eye, declared them perfect for her friend's pink complexion. Kevin's steady gaze seemed to confirm, and the complexion grew pinker. For these expanding gestures of comfort Aspera loved each of them.

Vicky and Kevin made the first move to leave. Aspera felt the lesion begin as they stood; everyone else would depart in their wake—parties worked that way.

Unreasonably, she wanted them all to stay the night, wanted a pajama party, the way children did it: popping corn and lighting candles as children would light them, for horror. If she could have one wish, go back—"We live time backward," Elvira had told her once; "that's why we feel guilty learning what we know we shouldn't have forgotten."

Aspera felt guilty now. With her friends about to depart, she wanted protection against the things all of them ought not to forget. Staying up and watching through the night would bind them against loss. Friends forever. But at forty she couldn't ask that the birthday candles be lighted and blown out again, as a real child might. And she ought not make a scene when her friends had to go home.

At the front entry hall she and Vicky gave one another quick tight hugs, and, because it was awkward to leave him out now, Aspera hugged Kevin too. English lavender was what she was thinking as she next hugged Dena, but the thought must have been left over from Kevin, a slow verbal translation of what had flown to mind when her cheek had rested against his. For Dena smelled lemony, as she always did.

"Are you sure you won't stay over?" Aspera asked her. "It's such a long drive back to Minneapolis."

"I'll be fine."

"Dena, you sexpot, when are you getting married again?" Will demanded. He seized her in the bear hug that always made her squirm.

"Now, Will," she gasped, wedging an elbow between them and readjusting the angle of her beret, "I've already told you. Marriage is an addiction. It has to be given up cold turkey, like drugs or alcohol."

He squinched his face to make a show of calculating. "The cold turkey part sounds right, but I can't relate it to real pleasures like booze. Explain it to me again?"

From behind him Dalton took a sizable pinch of Will's waistline. "Maybe I can help," he said. "It has to be given up, like white bread."

"OK, OK, now I get it." Will released Dena. "Although you know, white bread has its uses. You can put it in window cracks to stop the draft, it's soft and cuddly in bed at night—"

"Soft and cuddly in bed?" Dalton asked.

Will put an arm around Aspera. "Well, I admit it chafes a bit when it's toasted."

Laughter, groans. Last hugs, happy birthdays, another tussle at the door with Bunny, a final round of farewells shouted into the sobering shock of fall night.

* * *

They finished clearing up, Will carrying dishes in from the dining room, Aspera stacking the dishwasher, running water into the sink to do the crystal and the silver by hand. She dribbled soap into the water; the forced stream from the faucet made sudden billows. Spontaneous generation.

"We should do this more often," Will urged, his largesse another effect of liquor. "Entertain, get everybody together. It's great having Bunny and Dalt around, eh?"

"Fine. Your birthday is coming up."

"Let these vultures pick my bones? Ha."

"No party?"

"Nope. Anyhow, that's December. We don't want to wait that long to invite Bunny and Dalt again, do we?"

"You keep giving me this *we* stuff." Aspera again heard her own sharpness, used the next remark to blend it back. "You can see them on your own, you know."

"You know I never enjoy things without you."

Aspera's shoulders collapsed with her sigh. Will moved behind her to rub the shoulders, and she braced her arms on the sink.

"One flesh," he reminded her, leaning to speak into her ear, his touch lingering.

She moved to rinse two crystal cocktail glasses, gripping the brittle rims.

"Some of our flesh could dry." She pointed at the towels on the rack.

He gave her shoulder a pat and cheerfully plucked up a towel. In this mood he was mellow, eager to please, easily deflected. The grounds for anger vanished when she needed them. Who could complain of such a man?

"I think everybody had a wonderful time," he declared.

"I wonder. We're an odd blend."

"Baby Kevin?" Will's voice grew hollow as he left the kitchen and spoke to her from the hall. "Hang on," he called. She heard the bathroom door click shut.

Baby Kevin. All right: cruelty at play here. Baby Kevin at twenty-six was a sweet baby, well behaved, clean, mannerly. He was not the embarrassment they all feared. Still, twenty-six was young for this group. They were fully a decade into their postromantic period, and it was proving an uncertain time.

They tried to avoid the obvious traps, tried to hold to the channels that would route them between chaos on one side and ossification on the other. And still they came up hard against categories, against the language itself. Nomenclature was a problem, for names must be given to new categories. Yet the old ones didn't give up their hold; they had all of history behind them and they insisted.

A younger lover introduced into this group was certain, she knew, to excite malice; a younger lover with the same name as the deceased husband was more than could be borne with grace. What were she and Will to call him—they whose standard use of the name Kevin called up Kev Varney, sight and sound and smell? Kev of the eccentric bow ties and redolent pipe and the silent, stealthy laugh. He would stand beside his wife, laughing at Vicky's antics until his shoulders shook and still no sound escaped, as though it were a contest between them. And of course Vicky was fat when Kev was alive, round and funny and Kev Varney's wife, not a sexual being whose choices people had to accommodate.

How many men in the world named Kevin? What odds—? Aspera set a glass carefully on the counter. Any awkwardness that could be reduced to mathematics was fundamentally comic, so she and Will had determined to see the joke in this one. Surely it was a joke that they remained so possessive of Kev's memory and of Vicky herself when clearly life had moved on, established a new category. Between themselves they'd tried their hands at nomenclature. Tried Young Kevin, Other Kevin, Little Kevin, Kevin Junior. Finally it was Baby Kevin that took root and flourished—why? Because it was the least kind? Because it diminished him past their having to take him seriously? Yes. Because hovering at age forty, the three things they most feared were death, divorce and younger lovers.

This evening they had sat with those very elements gathered at their table. Dena divorced from Charles, Kev Varney dead and Kevin Stowe taking his place beside Vicky. These were facts, and Aspera thought she and Will acknowledged them. What they didn't acknowledge was the feeling that a tainted energy had been released into their small circle, and that it was not finished. Their precautions had become superstition, the crudest magic. Baby Kevin was the best they could do to stave off the third demon of the decade, and they meant to do their best. They called names in private, while in company they acted at being kind; they stood and waited for Baby to screw up, to do something resoundingly stupid. With any luck at all, he would do this thing publicly and specifically in their presence, so they'd turn to one another and see the lesson home. *See? You see how it is? Category closed; there is no hope in youth and inexperience. You see?*

Will walked back into the kitchen and picked up his drying towel. Aspera seemed to be staring at him. "My hands are clean!" he joked.

She looked up at Will's half-smile, which awaited something from her. She drew a breath. "Sometimes I think we talk to each other in code."

He blinked hard, acting out perplexity. "You mean, the way people do who have been married a zillion years?"

"I think I mean all of us," she stammered, "the whole show. Hasn't it gone too far, all this forty-is-dead stuff?" She stirred her hand into the water in the sink and brought up odd pieces of silverware. "A stranger couldn't make out what we were on about."

"Like Baby Kevin?" Will said.

"Let's not call him that anymore."

Will dropped a butter knife into the water where she groped. "What do you suppose he's up to? The guy is what, thirteen, and his biggest worry is what's in his lunchbox and who's going to butter his little sandwiches for him."

Aspera dumped the hot silver, hot from scalding rinse water, into a fresh linen towel and wrapped it tightly. She dropped the bundle onto the Formica so that the metal clattered and rang. Fork-tine melodies.

"Vicky's forty-two." She flipped open the towel on the glitter of silver. "You think forty-two is that old?"

Will moved behind her again, pressed against the length of her body with both hands holding her shoulders. "Forty is young enough; you can butter my sandwiches anytime."

One of his hands was still wrapped in the drying towel, and Aspera felt the dampness through the cloth of her blouse, felt the warmth of his groin pressed to her hips. When they were alone he was like this, close and vulnerable. He was her husband who needed her, and for whom she felt only the most sporadic and clouded desire.

In contrition she turned to kiss him, veering for his cheek at the last moment when she caught the sharp chemical scent of his breath. He tightened his hands.

Mistake, giving away little pieces of herself. Pieces don't satisfy; they whet appetite, excite predators. One bite and there is that scent, fresh blood, flesh with the life so recent. One piece and the whole is desired, deserved.

Didn't Will deserve her love? And he wanted her, his fingers moved on her back, displacing a single layer of cells with each stroke. She did love him but something was wrong, a mistake had been made. She had given up that piece, those first few cells were enough really; raked from her body in this way they had given up the merest scent.

She pushed back against his chest, shut her eyes.

"Will, I feel bad about the Angie story," she whispered. "For embarrassing you. I never know what to do when these things happen."

The moment stood carved in relief. Then he released her and stepped away. He took a stance next to the wall. Aspera watched him, seeing that he could not deal with two of her at once: the wife whom he desired and the wife who caused such discomfort. She imagined they had separate preserves in his mind—like the fairy-tale split of mother and stepmother. What to do? Stop reading Grimm and take up Freud to hear the rest of the story.

Will locked his knees against the door frame. "I do these things in total innocence," he complained, "but you really nail me for it."

"Every time, total innocence?" She pulled her fingers over her eyes. "I don't know how to handle it!"

"Why don't you save it, tell me afterward?"

The fingers split and she looked through eyes that felt dull as pottery. "Last time I told you afterward. About the same story."

"I don't remember that."

"When you're drinking you forget."

"Yeah? Then I can hardly wait. Tomorrow I might not remember this." He broke from the wall, took three rapid steps and halted. "I think you embarrassed everybody. I think we were all just ready for some laughs."

She looked at the man who stood leaning now against the counter, his buttocks resting on hands he inserted in his back pockets. At his collarbones the second button strained open over his throat, clean of hair like a baby's. Pants creasing across solid thighs. A careful attractive man with a serious face. Serious and sober, cheeks faultlessly clean-shaven, this man she so rarely desired.

"I'm sorry," she said.

He stood a moment looking at the floor before her feet, rubbing his chin lightly with the top knuckles of four fingers. He held the fingers and palm loosely, cupped, as though they might hold a pencil, as though the next motion would be to jot down some thought. Everything he did was so familiar, and familiarity cannot be the wellspring of contempt, she decided, not at all. In some way she loved him specifically for every familiar thing; the familiar is indeed what saved her from hating him. If he were some new man who broke into her life and tried to sink a thirsty taproot—

She didn't like to think that way. It was important that she be able to love her husband, not see him as a stranger. As a stranger he would no longer command anything from her. She observed him with care to see all that she knew, all that bound her to him.

He looked up as though she had spoken aloud. "Are we done in here?" he asked. "I'm beat. Let's go up."

"There's just this," Aspera replied, taking up the bundle of silver. "I'll take care of it. And I think I'll walk before I come to bed."

A few more motions at cleaning up in concert, and then in the generosity of ritual he kissed her brow good night.

"Happy birthday," he offered, as though it were an apology. Apologetically she smiled, in generosity holding herself to be kissed.

CHAPTER THREE

On the front steps Aspera felt in her jacket pocket for Kleenex. The air made her eyes smart, her nose run. Only the equinox, but that hard bite of frost in the air. Cover the tomatoes. No: turn the hose on them.

How was it? The air underneath the spray is held above the freezing point—something traded off, some exchange bound into immutable laws.

She sighed a horsey plume of vapor into the air and laughed at the evidence—making four or five more volleys of warm breath promptly challenged by the cold air. Heat transfer. It sounded abstract enough to ignore; yet here was physics before her very nose, she would have to plunge right through it. In the deep of winter this stuff would freeze on her eyelashes, freeze on the knit-hairs of her muffler. Nothing abstract about that. Everything in the world lay ready to be changed into something else.

Looking up she saw the fixed maps of Orion, Pegasus, Cassiopeia—all that firepower, so far away. Every clear night that past summer Mars, Saturn and Jupiter had glowed in a bright close triangle. A collaboration to what effect? She ought to know. Like the tomatoes, some law she ought not forget.

She could explain the tomatoes, though. Laws take advantage of a disposition to behave predictably. Water droplets turn to ice in freezing air, their heat thieved away like so many picked pockets. Keep the air temperature busy chilling down a tireless supply of water drops, and tomatoes are spared. Diversion pays off.

Her face pushed into the hard prickle of cedar while she reached behind the shrubs, located the handle of the water spigot. She turned it, the webbed disc pressed flat into her palm. She heard screw threads whining, then the ballooning rush of water into the hose. In the dark she could not see the sections jerk erect in their coils, but at the corner of the house she stood, still feeling the cold of metal transferred into one palm, and waited for the tick-tick-tick of the activated sprinkler.

Kevin's hand on Vicky's knee. Out of place because in this group trust has eroded to where touch itself is a cynical act, overlaid with politics? Points and counterpoints laid into that long mosaic of evening turned radioactive in her mind: Vicky removing her napkin from the table. Kevin's hand. That look of Dena's, meant to pierce resistance, the repeated failures of the hostess to let things ride, ride, ride.

Aspera walked down the long slope to the water from the house. Three short blocks and the river lay black and smooth in its banks, mist rising in patchy drifts as if the Mississippi too practiced at breathing when nobody was about.

She continued along two blocks of park road with its converted gaslights, then turned off along a short alley with garage lights mounted glaring into the dark. Though she shielded her eyes from them nearly every night, these struck her as out of place in Bracken. The town did not nourish fear, no more than hope.

She took a path up and around the new apartment buildings and condominiums. She walked this route regularly, noting as a matter of course whether Vicky's lights were on, observing the silencing effect of drapes pulled behind sliding glass doors, of glass doors latched behind the wrought-iron rail of the lanai. Security. A quaver of guilt here, envy: what would it be like, a new life handed you?

She lifted her glance to the triad of bright planets dimming in fog that gathered along the river frontage. Astrology was no less tenable than the Bethlehem star—her mother's argument, and now twenty years later Aspera conceded the point. When you wearied of the way stimulus and response paired off and regimented themselves, when behavior wore predictably into its groove, you could harbor a great yearning to arrange matters on some other cross, some other wheel.

At the equinox Virgo gave over to Libra, and the virgin with the sheaf of corn took to weighing things in her own hands. She required new props: scales and a blindfold. Purity changed in favor of balance, one small step for astrology, one giant step for womankind. Mother, may I?

Aspera pulled her trenchcoat tight, clutching it together at her throat. She could have used a hat, even gloves. Her fingers felt raw holding the stiff cloth, and yet she stood gazing up beyond Vicky's second-floor balcony. No thoughts ran in her head, and she ignored the instinct of her body: Move.

A distant rumble of glass doors prefaced a voice. Vicky's voice, sliding down in the cold air, a low call that left a margin of silence for those who slept.

"Aspera!"

Aspera came fully to, lifted her hand toward the dim figure above.

"Is that you? Come on up."

"Oh. No—"

Vicky answered the tone and hesitation. "Nobody's here," she said. "Come on."

The warm air of the foyer rushed out to meet her as Aspera pulled the heavy downstairs door open, and seconds later Vicky had buzzed her in. Up the stairs and down the hall, the door to the apartment ajar. She went in and closed the door behind her. Her fingers ached and fumbled at coat buttons.

Vicky moved in the kitchen where the red dot of the coffeemaker glowed. She came out into the light, took the coat and pressed her cheek to Aspera's.

"Freezing!" she exclaimed.

To Aspera the contact was sudden heat and surface, as if she'd grazed her cheek against hot parchment, a glowing lampshade.

Vicky hung the coat in the closet. "I thought you might walk tonight," she said over her shoulder.

Aspera rubbed her hands together. "The way ghosts walk?"

"If you don't express yourself, you walk after you die. Yeats said so, but how would he know? Coffee in a minute."

Aspera let herself drop onto the sofa. Household hint: A bag of groceries can be safely dropped from most any height if all it contains are paper products. She pulled the wool afghan over her shoulders, blinked up at Vicky's face while her thoughts swam circles.

"You're tired," Vicky told her. "You ought to be home in bed, but it's too threatening, right? You prefer freezing to death." She turned and disappeared into the kitchen. A muffled slam of cupboards. Vicky would be rushing the coffee-maker, holding first one cup and then the other under the drip-spout.

Aspera could not help but feel alive here. Vicky's force was contained, applied. It frayed the casings but left the wires; nothing to damp the moving current. She put her feet up on the thick glass of the coffee table. This living room was the place she felt most at home, not a home remembered but one desired. Furniture new and spare and white, and yet a forgiving softness to the room. The sculptured couch, wheat color of the carpet and drapes, whipcord fabric covering the walls. Spots of color glowed in paintings over a dining area and in rough wool weavings that hung like exotic birds' nests along the wall that separated the kitchen from the rest. Aspera closed her eyes and let the color spots reverse out in retinal purples and greens.

Vicky walked in carefully, holding a mug of coffee in each hand.

Aspera rubbed her hands over her face. "Will and I had words after everyone left."

"Any new ones?"

A pause.

"I guess not."

Vicky stopped in the middle of the carpet. "You know what? I'm sick of coffee. I want something else, hot milk maybe. That interest you, or you want this stuff?"

"Milk," Aspera said, surprised.

"Come sit in the kitchen while I make it. One of my kitchen stools would improve your posture."

Vicky's tone brought Aspera sharply awake. With some effort she rose from the low sofa and followed into the kitchen, still wearing the afghan. Vicky dashed the coffee into the sink and rinsed the mugs in hot water from the tap. Steam rose briefly. Aspera watched in silence as Vicky set the mugs on the counter, then turned and snapped off the coffeemaker, turned again and squared her body toward Aspera.

"Look. You sit around your own birthday party with this long-suffering face and then you come here and long-suffer some more. I listen to the sad stories and the deep sighs, and I think the world is made out of glue and we're just bugs trying to yank a leg or two free before the stuff hardens."

Without moving her eyes from Aspera's she slapped the cupboard door shut next to her face. The door bounced once, then clicked shut on its magnets.

"Now that's crap, and I don't believe it for two seconds except when you're here. Out of loyalty I'm supposed to believe you're sincere, that you're trying, that goddamn, the world turns out to be glue after all."

Aspera gaped for words to answer.

Vicky stood with her arms folded in the blue flannel robe. "Dammit, Aspera, you key into a part of me that wants to lie down and die. I can't afford it."

Abruptly she turned and took milk from the refrigerator, filled the cups. Aspera watched in stunned concentration as the hands moved with cinnamon, nutmeg, honey, vanilla. Set the mugs inside the small white cavern of microwave oven, set the timer, punched the switch.

Vicky glanced back. "I'm being too hard on you, right?"

Aspera shook her head.

"Stop doing that!" Vicky exploded. "Stop behaving so well! When somebody hits you *blam* you don't have to soak it up like Miss Damp Mop."

"And if I don't soak it up I make an ass of myself! That already happened tonight."

"You sideswipe him on old stories, congratulations." Vicky put her hands on her hips. "Maybe it's a step in the right direction. Did you follow through? Did you tell him, Look buddy the next time you piss on my foot it's a punch in the nose? No, let me guess. You said—" she paused, came out with—"Gosh, hon, dunno why I say such things."

Aspera hung her head. "Bingo."

The timer rang and made this a joke. Vicky grimaced and pulled the mugs out, then dropped a spoon into her cup.

"Some couples, it's like they can't keep their hands off each other in public. I always figure that's strictly for show, to cover for how they never touch each other when they're alone. You know?"

Aspera chewed her lip. They both knew Dena and Charles used to do this, and that it got worse after Charles filed for divorce. Hands all over each other then.

"It looks like the same category to me," Vicky said. "You and Will do your fighting when people are around because you don't do it any other time. Afraid to try it without the referees?"

Queerly frightened, Aspera nodded. "I guess."

"Frankly I don't like being used that way. If you're going to ask for my time at a dinner party, I'd appreciate it if you'd do your fighting either before or after. Is that unreasonable?"

Vicky stirred her cup vigorously, spoon clanking against ironstone. "There's such a fog of dishonesty."

Not looking at one another, not talking, they both stirred their milk. Aspera watched brown flecks of spices float up through the foam as she stirred it, speculated on telling them apart: fine cinnamon dust; heavier, darker silt of nutmeg.

She and Will did not fight. Their disagreeing was done covertly and with shame, the way everything illicit was conducted. They had become so afraid of losing what they had that they swaddled it in layers of cotton batting as if it were porcelain or—

Aspera was twisting her ring violently around her finger; she looked down and was surprised to see a wedding ring when what she had been thinking of was Will's too-large high school ring. She'd worn it on the same finger, as Bracken girls who went steady did, wrapping the inside of the circlet with tape. Will had helped her fill and seal the wrapping with paraffin to make a close fit. Such labor! How important it was, this ring that clearly belonged to him, customized for her—that was high school, all right. She smiled thinking of what had followed: how her finger had developed a vivid rash, had itched and flamed! Together they'd dismantled the paraffin and tape, and for years the ring had swung plain on a chain around her neck. She never took it off. She remembered the proud cold rhythmic thump at her breastbone as she walked the halls of Bracken High.

After college they were still at it, wearing their matching wedding rings around Minneapolis where Will struggled in a downtown architectural office to keep himself in shopping-mall contracts, and she taught Latin to unwilling teenagers. Nine years of that, and she'd begun to spend nights and summers at the university picking up courses in library science. He lingered nights in the office, sampling imported beers as he worked up floor plans. Even in the months when he had no work he stayed up in the office, all glass and altitude, putting dreams into lines and angles drawn in ink on fine paper.

Back in Bracken, Hancock's Best Lumber had carried on. Then Will's father died, and abrupt changes occurred in Will. He wondered why he and Aspera spent so much time apart. He wondered, as if he'd never considered the idea before, about making a living in a small-town lumber business. He stayed at home and talked more and drank less, and soon she had given up notions of a degree in library science. They'd be together all the time; they'd have the house on Birch Circle and the store and each other.

Nine years of togetherness in Hancock's Best Lumber in Bracken, and now Aspera wanted out. She desired it more with each day that passed, just the way Will desired another store. This difference proved something, and neither of them wanted to know what. The matter had run up between them like a seam in flesh, around which scar tissue formed a double furl. No feeling around the wound.

Aspera didn't want to talk to Vicky about this no-feeling. Where Will was concerned she felt a pull of loyalty like an undertow. Married women talked freely when their husbands were dead or divorced; the past tense was noisy with interpretation. But this was the present, and she didn't want to talk. Not because Vicky wouldn't understand, but because she might grasp everything immediately and leap ahead, faster than Aspera could bear to go. Dena could be relied upon to circle round and leave you where you stood, but not Vicky. Maybe dishonest was as good a word as any for the way Aspera wished to steer the talk around the shape of what was withheld. She might say things she'd be unable to forget, logical things, obvious things. Words that would not be unsaid once they spilled into the world, took life and purpose of their own.

The silence grew heavier between them. They sipped their milk.

"Should I go?" Aspera asked. "I don't know what to say. My God, it's nearly one. You probably want to sleep."

"You done talking?"

Aspera pressed the bridge of her nose. "I'm afraid to start. What if I apologize again?"

Vicky half grinned, then mockingly rubbed the bridge of her own nose between fingers and thumb. She let the hand fall to the counter. "In a way I want you to go. Just to have the satisfaction of kicking your candy-ass out. And in a way I want to keep you here and yell at you some more. Some friend, eh?"

"You are my friend. You're the best—"

"Look at me." She set her cup down, spread her hands. "I've spent my adult life kicking bad habits. I don't drink, I don't beat up on little kids, I don't eat myself to death. Kev died, so I don't take care of an alcoholic any more. I don't want to take care of anybody, not you, not Will or Dena or Kevin or anybody. I think I ought to have it made, but I have this feeling; I look around me and every relationship I've got looks like one more bad habit."

Aspera returned the steady gaze. References to this stark history of Vicky's always shut her up, seemed to leave nothing worth saying. How to connect this past to the strong woman she knew?

Vicky sighed, ran her hands through her dark hair. "I probably qualify for sainthood—I sure am unfit company for the living. God, Aspera, it must be me. If I'm sick of everybody at once, it must be me, right?"

"Are you sick of everybody?"

"I'm pissed at you because I expect you to make sense, and when you don't I start to feel crazy. It's you or me, right? I've decided it's you." Vicky turned and shook a finger in Aspera's face. "It used to be the store but now Will's on line with that and you're still half gone. I'm done treating you like a convalescent; carry your own weight."

She began to pace. "The truth is, I'm also sick of myself. I'm sick of this tight little circle of ours; we suck in the same air over and over—cheese breath, Listerine and beer farts—

and let me tell you, I don't consider Bunny and Dalton an improvement. They have the same smell about them, strictly stale air."

"What about Kevin?"

Vicky stopped dead, wheeled to face her. "Kevin?" she challenged. "Which one?"

Aspera shut her eyes. "The one you brought to my house tonight."

"Kevin Stowe. Very dangerous."

Aspera waited.

Vicky shook her head. Her eyes traveled the line of the ceiling. "He's not a real person, you know. More like a spring where you can go fill your cup."

"He looked pretty special."

Vicky shrugged.

"Did something happen—I mean, that he isn't here tonight?"

Vicky's full mouth crimped into a smile. "It's not like going steady in high school, Aspera."

Aspera shook her head, as though the action would dislodge some thought pattern. "I don't know what we're talking about."

Vicky took her time. She sat down on the other stool. "Damn if I don't miss Kev Varney sometimes. This was our life and he checked out of it, the premature son of a bitch. Here I am, a woman born to wear a size thirty-eight toddler, all slimmed down and no place to go."

"I'm sorry, Vick."

"Any number of warm bodies in the world, you understand, but—" She shook her head slowly, let out a breath. "My body feels like a stone tonight."

Suddenly she leapt off the stool, sent it scudding backward on the tile. "And you just apologized. Why should *you* put up with this weeping-willow dripshit? The truth is that people who need people are boring." She pulled her mouth askew. "Particularly if they need dead people."

Aspera twisted her ring around and around her finger. "You look at things harder than I can stand sometimes," she said. Her voice came out a whisper; she cleared her throat, though that did not move the constriction. "I don't know how you got strong enough or smart enough to take everything on," she whispered. "I want to and I don't want to. But I still learn from you, I want to be around you."

Vicky's face softened. She sighed. "As long as one of us goes flaky at a time, OK. Lately we're not taking turns."

They smiled. Finding accord was such a relief. With Vicky it was usually within reach, even if you had to fight for it. Afterward, this feeling of lightness.

"What we need," Vicky said, pulling Aspera off the stool, "is to go out and find somebody with some fresh juicy energy to leech off of." She linked arms with her friend, led her to the closet. "Unfortunately I sent Kevin home, but dawn has not yet broken. Get your coat and I'll walk you home. First victim we see is mine; I don't like the way you leave suction marks."

Outside, the cold fog had swelled up above the riverbanks. Trails of vapor threaded among poplar branches along the river path, and under the diffused orange glow of the streetlights the spruce and pine looked man-made for a technicolor dream.

"Maybe we should walk to the Greyhound station. What we want," Vicky proposed, her white breath lacing the air, "is somebody with a good stubble, someone in rumpled clothes who will stop watching pay-TV to form a bond with us."

"Somebody who hasn't been unconscious for two months," Aspera said. "I feel it's important that he be able to fog a mirror."

"Right. A live one. I mean, in the single life, vibrators are OK; trouble is, they tend to chip your teeth."

They sputtered and laughed aloud, the sounds ringing cheerfully through the colored air. Despair was a localized phenomenon, like the mist. You could leave it behind. She hurried to keep pace with Vicky, and they walked up the park slope where a giddy breeze began to pick up. Their talk grew loud with the numbed overconfidence of cold and safety.

"That vacuous act of Bunny's is an act, right?"

"You bet."

"Nice change, having somebody say the first thing comes into her head. I don't even mind the echo."

Aspera expelled a cloud of laughter. "Dena minds."

"Dena hates married women who flirt. It's called the Change of Life."

Aspera pursed her lips, but Vicky leaned in close. "Bunny plays her game a bit fast and loose, wouldn't you say?"

Aspera kicked a stone, sent it skidding ahead on the sidewalk. "Nope. I wouldn't."

"Come on."

"Bunny knows precisely what the traffic will bear. Let anybody come within breathing distance of Dalton, and see what happens."

"What about the way she breathes on Will?"

"That's just Bunny." Aspera shrugged. "Like you said, it's all stale. People don't change."

"People get tired."

Aspera met Vicky's eyes. Right. OK.

"People get bored."

Their voices had got quiet. Aspera kicked at another rock, missed. "Funny, that's what Dena was telling me."

"Dena's not dumb. She's horny as a black widow spider, but it hasn't made her dumb. Yet."

"You don't like Dena much these days."

Vicky shrugged. "You're supposed to quit trying to climb in the sheets between Mommy and Daddy, didn't her mother tell her that?" Vicky shoved her hands in her jacket pockets, pulling the leather tight over her hips. "On this late-blooming singles circuit, there're always married men who can be pried loose. Library system: borrow one, put it back when you're done." She glanced at Aspera. "I've tried it. It's like puberty for the unmarried, it takes a while to figure out how the equipment works."

"Sounds a little depersonalized."

"Sex can be less than personal. I hear it even happens to married people."

Aspera winced.

"Sorry," Vicky said. "Something got to me tonight, being with all those people. I got the distinct scent of old scores waiting to be settled."

Aspera turned to walk backward for a few steps. The wind blew against the back of her head as she peered at the gauzy woods along the far bank of the river. At the rim of the slope a gibbous moon slid down among the birches, one great chunk missing from its side.

"I know you don't want to hear this," Vicky said. "But how come nobody likes a clean fight anymore?"

They had reached the halfway point, the corner where by custom they separated and returned to their own houses. Aspera turned her collar up against the cold, keeping the other hand jammed tight in her pocket. After the good nights she turned and spun and waved once but did not linger to see whether her friend had still more information for her.

"Do you think one person can destroy another?"

He is quiet. She watches the green of his eyes go level. "Maybe not without—what's the right word?" He takes his time. "Complicity."

"Mmmm." She wonders if he means to say more. She waits, but the only sound she hears is a television beyond some wall.

"I read something," she begins, and when she sees the green eyes steady on her, she takes a breath and goes on. "That you become fully adult when you deliberately cause pain to somebody you love. Have you done that?"

He restacks the pillows against the headboard, plumps them into position. "You mean, somebody besides my mother?"

She looks at him.

"You really want answers to these questions?"

When he opens his arms to her, she nestles against his chest. "I don't need to know everything," she finally says, "but I want to be trusted with what I ask about."

"Why ask?"

A good question. Her jaw moves against a silky froth of chest hair. A picture has come to mind, and she speaks as though he too can see it. "When I was little I always wanted to watch the needle go in when I got a shot. People always try to get you to look the other way, you know—but that's what makes me scared. I do better watching."

After a minute he says, "I'm the type that looks away. And is this what you want to do," he wonders, sliding the cool skin of his knuckles along her neck, "lie here with me and talk about pain?"

She relaxes to his touch as it slowly descends. "It's what I think about. I don't want to be seduced."

The hand stops. He laughs silently, the bed shakes. "You don't? I do." He stretches and yawns, a lazy sound. "Seduction is nice.

People enjoy it." He tilts her chin up, searches her eyes with his. She wishes her eyes were flooded with that green, that gold. Softly he accuses her. "You couldn't seduce me if you tried, could you? You don't know how."

Seduction. She goes home and, at the Bracken Public Library, looks the word up in three places.

CHAPTER FOUR

She opened windows. Still the bedroom smelled of sour breath as she undressed by the light of the closet bulb, Will's snoring less Katzenjammer than emergency ward, a rasp that caught every third breath with an expiring rattle. She switched off the light. Before she slid along the narrow crevice between the wall and her side of the waterbed she stopped and pulled open the slatted blinds of the west window. She could not bear to wake up in a dark room. She needed that much margin, to begin the day with light already coming in. In fall and summer and spring she calibrated every shade of dawn, morbid grays to briefest apricots, lilacs. She watched to see what arrangements the sun might make with the clouds that day, mindful of how, in deepest winter, morning would come to be defined only by the numbers flipping in Will's clock.

Aspera lifted the edge of quilt over his shoulders. He moaned and turned.

"Jesus fucking gale in here." One blurt of consciousness before the curtains of sleep swung to.

No way to tell whether Will was momentarily awake or speaking from within his dream. Questioned, he turned irritable either way. In their senior year of college they'd taken a statistics course together. Aspera learned to go to sleep as homework problems were fragmented beside her in the bed. She had dreamed numbers in colors and drifting through air like letters in soup, appearing and disappearing. Once, in the middle of the night, she woke to hear him mumbling features of a problem she'd tried to solve. She came alert, but he said nothing more.

She listened to his regular breathing as long as she could bear it and then shook him roughly awake. He stared at her, groggy and furious. But what about the rest, had he solved it? No! Was she out of her mind? She felt perhaps she was.

Her mother's face floated back to her, grim and uselessly shrewd. Elvira sitting at a pearl-gray Formica table with chrome ridging, sitting under a doughnut ring of fluorescent kitchen light which she declared poisonous to the eyes. She sat there nevertheless, and hummed, a sound as atonal as the light itself, or as the mosquitoes that hummed at her bare plump shoulders. They were in the summer kitchen, which is what Elvira called the basement they lived in the year round. Though the tall grass and size of the shrubs surrounding it testified to its age and state of neglect, the rest of the house was sound. Still they lived in the shadow of the stack of the nuclear plant, and Elvira refused to trust anything that rose above ground.

Elvira liked to start off summer evenings wearing a fresh long-sleeved cotton shirt. As the humid nights wore on, she unbuttoned the front and shrugged out of the sleeves, then tied them in a knot over her bosom. The shirtfront was buttoned partway up from the waist, the last buttoning dividing at the cleavage of her breasts, the knot of sleeves failing to conceal this division. Aspera sighed tensely, and listened for cars on their road. Her mother had swung the curtains up and over their rods to invite the possibility of a breeze. Though the tall grass probably served as curtains enough, Aspera could not trust to it.

She stood in the kitchen, noticing odors laid over a smell of basement damp: cooking oil, incense. She watched her mother unwrap a pack of cards from their black silk kerchief, and feared her life would go on forever in this setting, in just these confines. Elvira hummed and sighed and sweated, and laid out the pictures. Knights. Trees. Swords. Bodies pierced and prone. The four vertical lines above her mother's nose, and the two curving deep alongside it, shone in the fluorescent light.

"Do people change, Mother?"

While she waited for Elvira to answer Aspera pulled a chair close to the wall and stood on it. She laid her face along the dark screen of the window, breathed deep. She meant to have it appear that she merely gazed out into the darkness.

"No."

"I mean, as they get older, do they?"

The cicada hum beyond, the cedar and earth scents, the deliberate pat of the cards in their design.

"People don't change," her mother breathed. She cleared her throat and turned more cards over. The rasp of voice added, "They just practice."

Aspera pushed her nose against the screen, breathed the air that came from outside. She would have love. She would not live like this. She would not practice bitterness every day.

To drown out the sound of her mother's answer in her head, she had drummed her fingers in rhythm on the concrete window ledge.

"Will-loves-me, Will-loves-me, Will-loves-me," she sang under her breath, sang and tapped until Elvira used a different voice to make her stop. She gathered herself up stiffly and got down from her chair, left her mother alone under the ring of light.

Lying in bed Aspera thought about the stiffness. She could find the physical locus this very moment: tension in her neck and in a band across her forehead, splayed down her forearms and hands, in her thighs and stomach. She could find the feelings easily, having practiced them so long.

The sound of the cards, the humming, the grating of voice—these were what she had needed to forget, she reasoned now. Whereas the things her mother had said began to make sense lately. All those years pushing tones out of her mind; how could she know she would have use for the words themselves?

These nights her eyes flew open to catch the ghost of one or two as they slid from her dreams. Something about jewelry, a necklace. Could you direct dreams, point them in the direction you needed to go? Elvira said so, though you'd wear your angels out that way.

Propped up on her elbows now she looked out the window. It was almost two now, and still Mars and Saturn and Jupiter burned their way west along the ecliptic. Superman fell from the skies, refugee from a shattered crystal of a world. Brought us Kryptonite, a lesson in how things one has known and been can turn lethal. One shard of wreckage sucks away your strength by mere proximity. Need a lead casket for it.

She sank down next to Will, who turned mercifully away from her in his sleep. A lead pipe would do. Do not think such things.

Her dream when it came was scraps and pieces of a story she had read as a child, one about silk, billows of shimmering silk woven by a Chinese princess of threads so fine that miles of it, a river of silk it seemed in her dream, could be drawn through the eye of a needle. In the story this feat of skill and delicacy was the princess' means of deserving the love of a prince. In Aspera's dream, however, the prince was sewn into the girl's dress, stitched into a broad pocket that fitted from her waist to her hem, and his head stayed between her hands and the loom. A shuttle hung beyond her reach, wedged between warp threads. At her feet a slot opened as broad as the crack underneath a door, and soon it showed one corner of some coarse stuff, fibrous, bristling with dark filaments of hair. These were the color and texture of the princess' own hair. The slot widened between her feet, and she yanked and hauled at this stuff which slicked off in her grip like cat fur.

Awake again, Aspera tried to dispel the dream. Touched her own hair, Will's. She rubbed her finger along the reddish down that now grew along the rims of Will's ears, exactly the kind of down that had once created a haze on his cheeks and chin. The boy she married had become this hard-minded hoary-eared man who sprang up cursing the alarm clock at 6:30, who rammed himself into the shower, who swore a steady stream of abuse every single day as he carefully shaved the whorls of stubble at the lower corner of his mouth and over the notch of his chin.

Loving him from the age of fourteen, Aspera had watched Will match wits with these whiskers, which, once the downy preamble was over and done with, grew in fierce and wiry with utter disregard for the tender facial skin of a young boy. Worse, these whorls in his beard performed like double cowlicks of the face. He'd tried growing a full beard in college, those early-married years. The red whiskers got past the itching stage and then displayed their strudel marks at his mouth and chin.

Strudel: whirlpool. Will's streak of anarchy would have loved an eccentric beard, but the architect in him rejected unruliness.

And it was the architect who shaved each morning with such furious precision.

The architect also determined that they would not dash for the church along with other couples of their high school class, ink smearing from one certificate to another. Will's parents were much relieved. Though Aspera imagined she would do anything to be sure of him forever, in point of technical fact she remained a virgin beyond high school.

Thus for four years and then two more, Will's parents had held their breath and prayed first one prayer and then another. Elvira seized her daughter's right palm from time to time, compared it to her left and rolled her eyes skyward before muttering, "As above so below." The wedding, when it took place, was white and drew relief from all concerned, relief so deep that between the young couple at first it passed for fervor.

She was not a virgin bride. Though in the thick of high school passion, they had observed the niceties of the era. Fingers didn't count. Fingers constituted a technicality where love was concerned; fingers counted in algebra class. And then all the sophisticated lore of college argument descended upon them: one morning in late May, their first year of spring finals, Aspera sneaked early into the dormitory room Will shared with Dalton. She came in panic, owing to the history final that lay ahead at eight o'clock, and in pain, owing to her period that had come during the night. Her periods were inexplicably painful that spring, a heavy flow, cramps that disabled her for fully a day. Did fingers count?

Will and Dalton's room was in the basement of the dormitory. It was a simple matter, they had found, to leave the window open and let her slip in. Dalton, who had free use of the door, courteously slipped out.

That gray dawn she came to Will bearing the safety of her throbbing uterus. She felt it round and liquid within her, like the red center of a dipped cherry chocolate. Dalton dressed quickly while she hid her eyes. He too had the history final; he could use the hour, he said, for review. Myth of the month: Artemis, virgin huntress.

And so Aspera lay on Will's bed with him and he lay caressing her, soothing her. His beard scrubbed her face and neck, his mouth still tasted of sleep's ammonia and chalk. She moaned in misery as he rubbed her back, moaned when he turned her to rub stomach and thighs and before long he too moaned, his palms damp as they hastily made the round of belly to thighs to belly to breasts to belly to crotch. Her panties down, the pull of tampon string—she clutched Will's shoulders.

"It's all right," he whispered, and then he was on top of her, a white blur of jockey underwear whirling off through the air. He did not speak and she did not open her eyes, determining in that way to remain innocent of particulars while at her perineum the grating push grating push grating push sear of pain liquid release.

When her eyes flew open it was in triumph: he was inside her. He, Will. The physical sensation was no more than a rasping of tissue, but the rest was surely desirable. Wondering, her eyes looked into his, which shone back a tenderness leavened with determination.

"Is it all right?" he asked, and she nodded, a confession not of pleasure but of bravery.

"I love you." He moved inside her and before she thought she had dug fingernails into his bare shoulder, again not the communication of pleasure. Inside, she felt scraped and raw, yet wanted him to remain. They both knew what they were supposed to know: it was a safe time of month, no risk of pregnancy; it was reputed to be a cure for menstrual cramping; it was because they loved each other. It. His breath jerked out unevenly, then changed. He lifted his chest from hers, pushed up on his arms as though to spare her as much as he could while below where they were locked together in the swellings of tissue she felt the fluid-staccato pulse of his orgasm.

Her hands traveled the emery of his face, found the skin of his eyelids. She drew him down and kissed his lips. As his muscles relaxed she sensed how he had sheltered her from the weight and imposition of his body. He gazed down from where he held himself above her, his face so flushed and glossy with sweat that had come, so she thought as she held the small of his back with her two hands, upon his entire body like warm dew. They had lain together before, had been naked together, pressing their luck length to length in this very bed and others. It was not naïveté they shared all those times but restraint, and now that too was conceded. He looked at her, a look she came to recognize as inquiry, and the question was whether her body had an answer for his.

No. Inside where he now softened she was abraded and sore, the triumph not in her body but in her love for him which, she concluded, must be located elsewhere.

Will's face went uncertain and he began a forced motion, moving his body up and down. She gasped in clear pain and he froze above her, eyes wide.

"Am I hurting you? Should I stop?"

The truth? She had heard how vulnerable. She clasped him tightly. "It hurts when you move," she whispered. "Just stay with me."

"But I'm crushing you—"

He felt both light and heavy upon her, his pale angular body with rosy skin, its sparse bronzy-red body hair arranged and spaced as though it had been penciled in place. The weight was right, was enough so that he felt real and substantial. The reassurance was what she needed. He was material and joined to her flesh, and the weight and the pain made her believe it.

She had not thought of blood, and when they moved from the bed, from their envelope of white sheets, the red sight of it was a shock.

She wanted to wash the sheets there and then, more galvanized by the evidence than by the event. She pulled at them, saw how the blood soaked through the mattress pad.

"What are you doing?" Will cried. He took the sheets from her hands. "You have to get dressed. Get your stuff, I'll walk you."

He pulled on jeans, a T-shirt. He picked up white socks from the closet floor, turned and saw her.

"Aspera, I'll take care of them. Are you all right?" he whispered.

She nodded yes. Wrapped the useless tampon in wastepaper, expired white mouse, injuries. She tucked Kleenex into her vagina. Gently.

"You have an exam, sweetheart. Let's move."

He found her shoes, grabbed her sweater from the chair, kissed her. She would have clung to him but he hustled her out of the dorm.

"I'll take care of the bed." They hurried through intersections of sidewalks. "Don't worry. I love you. Think about history now." He shivered in the morning cool, handed her a pen from his back pocket while he held the heavy door open. She stepped into the echoing hall, waved to him through the plate glass.

One bluebook from the stack by the door. She found a seat, wrote her name. Wasn't true, sex no cure for cramps. Confusion topped off the grinding jangle of sensation in her body. She felt her head go light. A fact: lovers! Think about history. A sheet of questions was passed back. What was the function of mysteries in Eleusinian practice? Oracles? Vestal virgins? Her brain divided neatly, one half expanded in the lightness of pain in her body, the other half contracted in exertion over rituals of antiquity. She finished. She turned pages backward in the examination booklet, looked at blocks of her small handwriting arranged in so much space on the pages. She thought to read them, but mind would not bend to it. Nor could she walk out of the examination room. For twenty minutes she sat immobilized while the world trickled back, filled in the space around her. Radiators ticking, pens scratching over wood. The room with heads bent, students walking forward and then back with booklets. Clock with rigid hands. Dalton's face turning, inquiring. She blushed hot, remembered Will's sheets. Stains that would not come out, a sudden certainty: Will scrubbing at her blood over his sink. Certainty too about the maids who would come to collect bedding that morning and, who, in a college this size, would easily guess when and how and what and who.

She felt a liquid seep down into her pants, prayed Dalton would this once finish and leave without waiting for her.

In the afternoon light he lies on his back, his arms folded like butterfly wings over the pillow, hands behind his neck. She watches him staring into space. She smiles. He knows she is watching and perhaps he knows she is smiling but he continues to stare.

"Aspera," *he says. As though the word were a small object he had just discovered through racking his brain, or that had turned up among the bedcovers.*

"Aspera." *An insect, a particular kind of insect. One with five legs or seven.*

She waits.

He turns to her, a gravity in his face that yet has the flavor of adventure. She has come to look for these things in his silences. Men like this: were there more of them? Ones you had to wait for, or miss the grace of these eloquent pauses? Men whose rhythms you were careful not to disturb with your own, because from the placid-looking surface some surprise might yet emerge. Wait. Wait.

Enough time, not like Will. Stop thinking of Will. Stop comparing.

"Aspera"—*he speaks her name as though it is a mere word between them*—"*has got to go.*"

She knows it is not time to jump in, one never jumps in. Everything rests in this, not to flood with reaction but match him rhythm for rhythm. She has time. She lets go a breath.

He looks past her shoulder, giving her still more leeway. "I can't wake up and roll over and say, 'Aspera.' I don't even know what it means."

She closes her eyes, lets her head fall back on the pillow. "It's Latin. My mother's translation."

"Latin for what—hope?"

Stubbornly she stays in the slow rhythm now. Yawns, pats her mouth. "Sounds like hope." She keeps her eyes closed. "But it means wilderness."

In second grade Aspera knew what love was. She and Elvira and Chester Heimler had come to Minnesota, to the town of Fridley in their Airstream trailer. Elvira enrolled her daughter in the parochial school, feeling that spirituality should have daily precedence, even Catholicism. Aspera was instantly popular; she believed it was the pink satin ribbon that her mother tied into her hair each day before school. She wore her hair in a side part, the other side serving as the gathering point for a single clump of dark hair that was banded and then adorned with the ribbon. She had not been popular in Indiana, but at the new school prettiness or newness or the pink ribbon seemed to be enough. Each day after school she was met by her mother at the door of the Airstream (it was Chester who called it the Airstream; Elvira called it the trailer) with a kiss, while the one hand that patted her head also slid the ribbon from its station above the rubber band. Elvira took the ribbon to the kitchen sink and rinsed it, then plastered the wet satin band along the splashboard to dry flat and straight for the next morning. Pink went with everything, she said; it was the color of the ray of love. Aspera wore the ribbon to Catholic school every day and to the Methodist church on Sundays. Elvira said spirituality went with everything.

Chester Heimler began marking off the foundation of what was to be their new house. He set stakes into the prairie grass and stretched string between them, wrapping each stake several times. His string outline showed that the house would extend beside the trailer to occupy the center of the lot; nevertheless Aspera pictured it growing up around them with the Airstream as a kind of nest egg.

Then her father began to dig the earth away. As he made the hole grow larger and larger Aspera feared the Airstream would fall in. He worked each evening after he came home from the factory, saying to Elvira he'd have supper cold if it meant losing the light. Some nights after he ate he'd go back to work in the dark. For that he bought a long corded electric lantern, a hook affixed to its top. He called it a trouble light, and Aspera felt better knowing he understood the danger.

It was more than a year before Chester had anything to hook his light to. These things take time, he said. When they could afford it, he paid workmen to come and frame up timbers for walls. The workmen gave Aspera sticks of gum. Their pants were stiff and greasy green, and the wood they put up was sticky with pine syrup.

What they left was another kind of outline, this one of a house upright. The night they finished Chester went out and stayed late into the night with his trouble light hung on a skeleton of yellow doorframe. Aspera watched from the window above her bed cubby in the trailer as he walked around and around. At first he kept to the pretend doorways, then freely wove a path through the pretend walls.

In the weeks that followed he worked late in the yellow light with his hammer and a spotted brown sack full of nails. She remembered words he used: Sheetrock. Countersunk. Firring strips. She remembered silver packets of insulation.

Arguments at the supper table, she remembered. After he had come in to eat supper streaky and sweated, and before he went out again.

"Look at this work," Chester complained to Elvira. All but

weeping, he made them both go outside and look while he ran a screwdriver along a space where the green wood had bowed and an angle did not meet. "No pride. Men who don't care."

The high hard sound the voices had at the supper table. Chester found fault with the way bricks or doorknobs were cast these days. He could build molds, make frames for these things the way his father used to.

"Chester. You wear us all out. The girl will be grown before she lives in a house."

In fourth grade Aspera asked to eat her supper cold with her father. Her mother folded her arms; Aspera ate warm food while those elbows above her head showed yellow-white. Time was the trouble. Bathtime, bedtime. Elvira said it was time the trailer was moved to the back of the lot, at least. As far as possible from the pounding that went on into the night, for the sake of the child's sleep. Dreams were friable, according to the books Elvira read by lamplight. Membranes let certain elements through, left the silver cord at risk. Whole years of time were passing, that was it. Masonry, wiring. Doors that leaned unhung, wanting perfect hinges. Proper tools were wanting: mallets, vises. Houses took time. Aspera added columns of figures and filled in the blanks of spelling workbooks to the sound of her father's wrenches grating on pipe, fell asleep to his mallets tapping into the night like a stubborn heartbeat.

The arguments stopped. Between the sawing before supper and the tapping after supper, almost no sound at all. Forks against plates, the muffled sound of chewing. One evening in late spring, Aspera flung herself in and out of real doorways, her hair flying first into her face and away from it in the stiff breeze that had come up. Chester judged the color of the clouds after sunset. He realigned the handmade bricks that presently held down tarpaulin and sheets of flapping plastic over stacks of sheetrock, and Aspera put down her piece of blue chalk to run and bring him the largest field rocks she could still find in the dusk. When they had finished weighting everything he sat with her on the place where the front steps would be, facing west into the orange-lined purpling clouds. He set one large hand on her shoulder and the crook of his arm cradled her back. Aspera remembered always the warmth, the weight.

The fifth-grade girls had begun to call her Aspirin; and when she wore the pink ribbon, Baby Aspirin. A bad sign, since girls' esteem was factored out of what boys whispered. Mornings she tore the bow from her hair as soon as the yellow schoolbus flapped its stop sign at their driveway. The ribbon lay coiled inside a jacket pocket. She did not dare to throw it away, but at last Elvira let it go unremembered. Too late. On Aspera's way to the pencil sharpener one day she stomped on the broganed foot of Dewy Thorson, expecting he would groan aloud to show off his pain and preferment. But Dewy drew his foot back with a pinched look that she recognized from home. The end of love.

Now Chester drove semis from Minnesota to Arizona, from Arizona to Texas, Texas to the Florida Keys. Aspera saw Florida Keys lined up like piano keys, the merest spaces between them, their geometric cliffs perfect under ivory overhangs. All this driving her father did took time. Elvira marked how it was taken. She got a job in the public school cafeteria, and Aspera was enrolled there. God was everywhere. Elvira said she could have predicted everything about this house pipedream from horary charts before shovel one was put to earth. Chester would never finish what he started, typical Pisces. It was in the stars, and as above, so below.

At first he sent postcards. Aspera read the names that curved inside the winged circles of postmarks: Pensacola, Galveston, Baton Rouge. He came back to the Airstream three times, sitting with his back to the window that would have showed the unfinished house. Then presents came instead. That first Christmas a parcel appeared in the mailbox beside the driveway, its paper wrapping tattered. Dimpled corners of a white box showed through. For Elvira there was an ivory ring; for Aspera a necklace. Add-a-Pearl, the tag explained, and on a thin gold chain was a single starter pearl.

"Ring of bone!" Elvira flared. At midnight she flung the ivory circlet into the prairie grass. But Aspera refused to let the necklace be taken from her neck, and when her birthday came in September so did another pearl. The following Christmas, another.

The summer before seventh grade Aspera found a paperback book tucked into the newly nailed eaves of the house. The roof had just gone on, plywood yellow and fragrant, though the two-by-fours of the framing had weathered to gray. The book belonged to the workmen Elvira had hired, and it was not thick like the books her mother kept. Aspera read the stories. One she read over and over. She felt she was close to understanding this story of a boy near her age whose teacher asked him to stay after school. He was to hold a ladder underneath her while she hung decorations for a Halloween party. This teacher was busy with balloons and streamers and let her skirt slide up, and there was a lot about how she was moving on the ladder to nail paper pumpkins to the bulletin board while the boy's pants bulged, and how the teacher grabbed him inside his pants and told him next time he should let her know *in time.*

Aspera put the book in its place under the eaves in case the workmen came back for it. She knew by all the things that weren't explained what kind of stories these were, as though they didn't need explaining, all that new information and still the lack of it.

That Christmas no pearl came. She and Elvira had moved into the house, settled into its unfinished rooms, sold the Airstream. Aspera sobbed all Christmas afternoon despite the figure skates her mother tried to show her again and again, pink pom-poms dangling from the laces.

Aspera snuffled aloud as Elvira dumped logs into the fireplace. Her mother turned, face fierce.

"Here is love!" she screamed, clutching the loose cloth over her own bosom. She reached down and seized the front of Aspera's sweater, twisted the handful of wool. "You think love comes from the Florida Keys? You think I don't count? Four pearls! Four!"

"I hate you!" Aspera shrieked. She tore from her mother's grasp. "He still loves me and he stays away because of you!" She ran from the room, stayed shivering in her bed for the rest of the night.

In the morning Aspera apologized. For two days her mother's eyes darted from side to side and did not meet hers.

They spent days and nights in silence. Vacation. Aspera read books from the library, stories of heroic deeds, fairy tales. She read how those you loved fell under spells that made them wayward, ugly, invisible. There were things to be done to break the spells. Light candles, knit sweaters from stinging nettles. While Aspera read, her mother consulted esoteric texts full of small print, thumbed through old Christmas catalogs, drew charts and divided circles, wrote letters. She asked Aspera to hand her compasses, an envelope, stamps. The silence between them wore through along with the new year.

Two weeks into January the Christmas pearl arrived. Aspera unwrapped it in triumph, showed it to her mother with hard eyes.

Elvira's face went briefly soft, a wan smile.

"Let's see," she said, sorting in the wrappings. She sighed. "San Francisco. Maybe he's driving a new route, maybe the mails are slower."

Aspera forgave her mother. Both of them came to expect the brief visitations of hatred, notes on the refrigerator to avoid conversation—hard moments that would dissolve. The girl's love for her father was purer, less tainted with complexity. Before she slept at night she touched the pearls at her throat. Her father loved her in ways she could never feel sure of with her mother; love is more convincing when you do not witness its actions every day.

In eighth grade Aspera wore a bra, and Dewy Thorson began calling her on the phone after school. During the day girls and boys looked past one another when they crossed paths in the halls, gazed down at the spatters of aggregate in the floors or at the black rubber flashing that served as a kind of baseboard. Arriving home Aspera checked the mailbox, unlocked the house. This ritual she performed carefully, looking each day for signs of Chester's return, the definite clue: toolbox under the kitchen table, oily jacket on a peg behind the door. Not to look might be a sign, might tip the balance in some way. Dewy's phone calls seemed accidental or in some way a test, two or three hurried sentences about rate problems or geography which she answered absently, her eyes still moving around the empty room.

That June she opened the mailbox on a letter from Boca County, Florida. The printed return address specified the coroner's office. One Chester Heimler had been buried in May at county expense, cause of death accidental; road mishap involving consumption of alcohol on the part of the deceased.

The coroner regretted a dearth of morgue facilities for holding the body. Apologies extended along with a bill.

Elvira paid it and ordered a headstone for the burial plot: "Chester Heimler: A Workman, Approved Unto God." She put the house up for sale.

The sign hung from the mailbox at the road. In midsummer it attracted one of the construction workers who had roofed the house. He stopped in to tell Elvira he had a finished house in Bracken that he'd trade her. He talked about Bracken Hospital, the brewery, the granite quarry. When he described the nuclear power plant with its strobe-flashing chimneys Elvira paid attention.

Aspera pleaded for her father's house; in the loaded car she fingered her necklace and watched the mailbox until it was blotted out by trees and long grass.

Bracken was a prairie town, the meandering river its salvation. The necklace with seven pearls stayed in place when she waded the rocky river bottom, swam in the quarries or the brown lakes; one hand held to her throat, she pulled herself cautiously through the water with the other.

In Bracken High School civics class, a boy was assigned to the seat in front of Aspera. His reddish cinnamon-colored hair grew unfashionably long about the collars of his corduroy shirts before it would be cut too short and too high above his ears. By fiat of alphabetical proximity, he and Aspera occupied the last two seats in the back corner of the room next to the windows. After several weeks a mutual silence was replaced by a whisper of banter slipped into the undertones of lectures on the Battle of Concord and the Louisiana Purchase. Aspera leaned forward over her desk, as though to see the blackboard better, and he would turn in his seat as though preferring his right ear for the droning at the front of the classroom. He began a habit of resting the crook of his elbow or his blue corduroyed forearm or his tense freckled hand on the corner of her desk. The fingers often drummed a rhythm on the wood.

The pair defended themselves with last names, with carelessness each had learned by then to affect.

"Want your quiz, Heimler? Ninety-four, too bad."

"Because I copied from you, Hancock."

But in other classes—home ec and biology, where she did

not see him—she used to write his full name inside her notebooks. Again and again and again she wrote it. She listened hard for this name among the chattered words in the lunchroom, stopped her sewing machine to hear it in home ec. She learned he went to the Lutheran church, his parents ran the lumberyard, he had a retarded brother who had died. She felt an overwhelming sympathy as she labored over bound buttonholes and over the large lower loops she favored for his name in her notebooks. She filled the margins first, then yielded and devoted whole pages, every line of every page given to his name over and over again in writing that made smooth reverse impressions on the backs of the sheets. Passion. That's what Elvira had taught her about writing that cut the page, and now she practiced it daily. In classes where she dared not write, Aspera lay the sheets on their faces and ran her fingers over their backs as though she were blind, depending on braille. At home, where she could write and destroy pages in safety, she wrote (again and again) riskier things: Wilson My Love, My Darling Will, Mrs. Wilson Hancock.

A succession of things she had been able to ignore as undergraduate stress: late nights and blind sleep in the mornings, a struggle to meet eight o'clocks she'd purposely signed up for, her early-morning rhythms oddly failing her. She went to bed early when she fell asleep over her studies anyhow and in the mornings meant to be firm with herself. Up and dressed and down the dormitory stairs by twenty of, and into the breakfast line. She forced herself, using Will's start-the-day strategy against weakness, illness. She made it down the stairs at five of, headed blearily for class. She had alternating eight o'clock sections of botany and zoology, and biology was never her strong point. Nor, of late, breakfast.

She had not thought of pregnancy and would not have thought of it when she did except that after lunch as she lay resting atop her yellow striped bedspread the girl down the hall came in to borrow a tampax. Aspera pointed to the closet, hung with a yellow striped curtain; she pointed to the heap of boxes that showed beneath the skirt hems and Levi cuffs, shoeboxes and fileboxes stacked on the dusty green asphalt tile. The girl could not locate the right box. Aspera lurched up and knelt on the cold floor, and as she stacked and restacked the wrong boxes she refused the thought, as though it would vanish if only she could find the unmarked blue one, the tampax box. When last? More than five weeks. She prayed for mononucleosis.

The senior girls upstairs in the dorm knew of a place; another senior girl had gone a few weeks ago. Delores-Nadine Delacroix, from Kansas, came shyly to her door the next evening at lights-out. Aspera had seen her, a grave slender girl with dull hair, had seen the name published on the dean's list. Delores-Nadine sat on the yellow bedspread and in a quiet twangy voice gave precise details. Aspera took down addresses, telephone numbers, airline schedules, dollar amounts in her red spiral assignment book; she left for New York eight days later.

Each step followed exactly as foretold: plane fare, cab fare, telephone contact, instructions, shabby building, clean table, doctor, the fee. Will had gone secretly to Bracken and withdrawn six hundred dollars from his college account.

Afterward the three spent evenings in Mankato studying together in a blur of shared misery. Life went on, they agreed, almost as before but hardly. Terrors of blood spots, cramping, flash-flood tears. Having Delores-Nadine to talk to made these things seem almost normal.

"Don't think *baby,*" she cautioned Aspera in their late-night talks. "Don't think *womb.* Stay with technical terms. *Zygote, uterus.*" It was good advice. Aspera cried less and less as her new friend helped her put words between what she felt and what she thought. When *uterus* didn't work anymore Aspera privately switched to a Greek word Elvira had favored: *calyx.*

"What is intelligence for," Delores-Nadine explained, "if not for avoiding pain?" Her fiancé from Des Moines was to come for a visit on a Friday night in October, and she and Aspera and Will sat waiting on the library steps until ten o'clock, checking hourly for phone messages. When the library clock struck the quarter-hour Delores-Nadine broke down sobbing with Aspera's arms around her. Then silence, all rationales for car trouble or confusion having been exhausted. The Friday night conversations that drifted past them from clots of couples, paired and quadrupled for gaiety, sounded piercingly young.

"Maybe he's just scared," Will offered. "When Aspera first

told me," he said significantly—and they knew what he meant, they were used to leaving words out—all I wanted to do was run away."

Aspera opened her eyes wide. "You never told me that!"

He shrugged. "I figured you knew. I felt so responsible, it's a scary thing."

"For everybody," Aspera returned bitterly.

Delores-Nadine rose with a deep sigh. "Well, I'm fresh out of a baby and a fiancé; what else can I part with?"

Will and Aspera looked up at this slight figure against the skydrop. They held on to one another.

"A shame to have all this come to nothing." Delores-Nadine's voice held a trembly tone that managed to sound both gay and determined.

The change was at first hard to remember, but after a time the effort came in recalling that this delicate self-transforming female had been called anything but Dena.

"Show me your hands," Elvira had demanded. She checked right palm against left, then on the right one she traced what she termed a sister lifeline.

"This is the hand that changes. See where the line becomes double from this crease to this star?" She tapped a honed and polished fingernail at an intersection low in the center of Aspera's palm, where a single curving crease feathered and then forked. The double track wound behind the thumb joint, reached toward the wrist. "This was not here before. Damage has been done. From the middle of your life until you die your life is not one with itself, it departs from itself. I advise against this marriage. Your hand shows a divided life."

She bent the wrist, twisted it back to show Aspera.

Every morning as the sun cleared the horizon, Elvira had begun to light candles. "I watch that which rises!" she hissed as she turned and pinched out each flaming wick with fingers she had moistened in her mouth. "An excess of elementals!"

The nearer the wedding approached, the stranger Elvira's pronouncements. Fending off her mother, Aspera had no time for her own fears. The summer night they'd bought their wedding rings, Will had run away. He had dropped her at home and disappeared from Bracken for two nights and a day without explanation. Other people whispered it as Aspera made her Saturday rounds of music rehearsal, bridal shower: Will had been seen rushing girls at a ballroom in Avon.

"We danced and I took them home," was what he finally said, pleading with her while she wiped her tears away in the tall wet grass in front of her house the morning of the wedding. "I wanted them to want me. All of a sudden I saw myself married and old before I had any fun. I don't *know* why. Someday you'll do something you can't explain."

She had clung to him, trying to merge her sickened heartbeat with his so they could have one heart between them, one shared net of circulation—the way it felt when they made love and she could swear she felt his pulse in her own veins. "Don't leave me, Will. I can't bear that, I'm so afraid of that. Tell me you won't leave me ever."

"I love you, Aspera."

Standing in her white gown in front of the double Gothic doors of the Lutheran church, Aspera whispered, "Wish us luck, Mama."

"Luck. You will need a charm more powerful than this one." Elvira pushed a finger at the white *peau de soie* that fell over her daughter's mound of Venus.

Aspera captured the strong hand. "Mama, it's time. Dalton will take you to a seat and then come back for me."

Dalton gently folded her mother's hand over his arm. "Great heat is the destroyer," Elvira told him. "We are all dangerous to one another, and your eyes"—she squinted at the wire-rimmed spectacles he wore—"are glassed with evil."

She turned to look at her daughter over a pink lace shoulder. Her mouth worked. "Love is just a grab in the dark. I expect you know that by now."

She came down the aisle trying not to cry. All hundred-and-odd of the great organ pipes in Bracken First Lutheran were jubilant. Mr. Peters plied the keys with his plump back toward her, and the racks and staggered rows of silvered bronze blew out Telemann's "Fanfare for Trumpets" in loud defiance of *Lohengrin.*

At the planning session the day before, Aspera had gone into the church carrying Will's absence like a great hollow stone.

She'd startled Mr. Peters by asking that he play for her the blowsy "Wedding March" of *Lohengrin.* Mr. Peters had thrown back his head on his short neck and laughed. And so she pretended to be joking, merely fey. She ought to get such a thing out of her system, didn't he think? With that he had fired up the great Baedeker and with the passion of arson roared through three dozen measures with—yes, exactly; with all the stops pulled out. The choir benches resonated with sound; the entire loft and then the church filled to bursting. Mr. Peters' small moist hands bobbed and flourished and tried to make of the music a caricature of a caricature.

And as the "Wedding March" forced open the mouths of the old pipes one more time, forced them to spew out once more through slotted valves "Here Comes the Bride," Aspera felt her heart open and contract to the music exactly as it had been programmed to do. Clichés sprang to mind, a pair of dolls formally mired in frosting. Did the truth remain buried in clichés because it's the last place you think to look?

She was to choose against the grain of expectation. Mr. Peters expected it of her. Reverend Dawes expected as much. But here Aspera put her foot down. No modern wedding ceremony. No blank verse, no exchange of personal testimonies. She knew beyond what she knew that romance would prove short-weight in a contractual act. In antiquity the bridal costume included a dagger at the waist. She might change her mind someday about Corso's "Marriage," repent of "The First Time Ever I Saw Your Face." The first time she saw Will's face in Bracken High School corridors she had been startled to notice the eyes shadowed under such a ruddy overhang of English brow. Blue they proved to be, a plain merry blue, no Heathcliff brooding there.

All right, not *Lohengrin* but something that had been settled for centuries. Telemann, the "Fanfare," yes, get on with it. But as for the marriage text, she would be married to the sound of the Old Testament. King James Version, the unfamiliar thees and thous, wouldsts and doths. The real thing with all the magic intact, the Latin or Greek or Babylonian if she could have got Reverend Dawes to pronounce it, for was she to sign her life away without suspicion of sorcery, a spell—promise these things against eternity? Eternity was what she and Will were up against.

Will. Wilson Carlisle Hancock—the full names, call out all of the incantation, every syllable's worth—do you take Sepharial Aspera Heimler . . . ?

Dena, engaged by now to Charles, stood smiling with her bouquet as Dalton formally presented Aspera to Will. The bride saw the wink of an engagement diamond underneath the flowers. Who giveth this woman? The scene shimmered in her eyes, tears, she thought, but her mother's whisper in the dark kitchen last night had been: Under a spell, my daughter, energy is burned to sustain illusion—watch, you will see it flicker and fail to hold, you will see what is real rise beneath. Aspera blinked; on the dais Will stood solid. She clutched his hand. For what I am about to do, Lord Christ have mercy upon my soul. And let me not please not while I set my seal to this litany of eternal promises please not let a scrim of blood nor dancing feet assail the labyrinth of my mind.

She lay on her back on one of their pairs of wedding sheets while above her Will pumped and pumped and pumped. She admired the muscular beauty of his naked body, tension rippling the flesh over his stony diaphragm, thigh muscles astride her like bands of iron. The upper surface of her body was sticky with sweat where his body descended to touch it, then peeled up again, like skin stripped from a grape. Grape skin was peeled and replaced, peeled and replaced. Will's breath was fast and labored now; is this how it is for men to get pleasure? Soon he would finish and she could get on with what she knew of it. He halted above her, jerked his head back so that his slender throat was exposed above her mouth. He plunged mightily, groaned and was done. He collapsed upon her, crushing the air from her lungs.

"You're wonderful," he panted. "Want me to move?"

"No," she whispered, smoothing his hair, stroking the moisture from his temple. "I want you just where you are." Indeed she did. In moments he was asleep. Now she could begin to feel something, now with him still joined to her and so still, she could feel the shape of him inside her, could take her time as her own body responded to that gentle pressure. The metal and stone had gone from his body; now it was flesh again. Underneath his weight she managed subtle swaying motions, a critical tilt of her pelvis to meet that tension where it wanted to be met, and O it was so easy so easy so easy.

"I love you," she breathed at his cheek when she too was finished, when her body had turned to slow liquid and she too fell tumbling into sleep.

Now Will lifted his head, said, "Love you too." Still asleep, he rolled to his other shoulder, pushed himself with the hand nearest Aspera. The hand soon relaxed. The waterbed settled and he slept on.

Suddenly frightened not to be connected with him, she seized the hand, laced it into both of hers. If she left the store, what would he do? What would *she* do? She shut her eyes and counted his square fingers with her own. Five, always five. She held them, traced their exact shapes.

As a girl she'd liked it that right answers could be had. She liked school because it offered a refuge from her mother's tutelage: the stars incline, they do not impel. As above, so below. But before long right answers satisfied no one; teachers wanted to see *steps*.

Steps: in fourth-grade arithmetic, having gone to sleep to the pounding of her father's hammer in one ear and her mother's turning of pages in the other, she could not think when she saw the columns of numbers. She moved her hand on the page and it seemed she got answers—but no steps. What if her mother was right? Fate had sealed everything; it was a matter of the envelope, please.

She'd ended up in South Minneapolis teaching Latin to high school students—because of Elvira, or in spite of her? Maybe there was no difference. The kids were of course more interested in counting on their fingers, in reading lips. She'd given up and pinned her hopes then on library science. Libraries housed all information without prejudice. Each item got a number and a place; neutral ground was so rare.

In college she'd been drawn to fixed studies like astronomy. But the whole subject matter resonated with star names and planetary habits. Astronomy had its own spook-parent in astrology, and each mathematical proof felt like a crack to break her mother's back.

She switched to classics. Texts already firmly made up, languages fixed in time—that part was solid and left room for the mythology. Stories and more stories, a fathomless confluence of explanations laid one over another. Here was something she knew. With no apologies, threads of cause and effect were skipped or fudged or shamelessly rewritten as propaganda. Or they vanished, since the past was famous for closing shop on any whim at all. Classical mythology had written the book on human behavior, was merely the large-print edition.

Nearly three in the morning. She hated the nights that her mind raced like this, she needed rest. She looked out the window again—pattern shift in the stars—and then sank back into her side of the waterbed. This hard-won uterine comfort. Her first week on the waterbed had been nightmarish, nights of startling awake dozens of times, feeling that the earth had shifted beneath her prone body and was not to be trusted. Someone should keep watch, her instincts told her, and dutifully refused her sleep.

She and Will had finally had no children, though they'd thought about it for years, thought: Next year we should really think about it. But all next-years were followed by others. The store was uncertainty enough. Did they really want a baby?

At one point Aspera thought she did. She and Will talked it over in the evenings, sitting on the living room floor with invoices and accounts receivables from the store spread about the rug. They were both thirty-six, reason enough to hesitate. More reasons: Will's brother, so severely retarded, all those years of trial and difficulty for the family, a nine-year babysitting job, and you could never be sure. Tears ran down Will's face as he told her, though Aspera marveled at how he gave no other sign. Face stiff, mouth regulated for words. She was silenced with awe. In the end Will had laid his head on her lap. She could swear she heard the words, "I'll be your baby."

By then there were no grandparents to appease. A few months after the wedding, Elvira had developed what was diagnosed as hypertension and diabetes. "Yes, they will say strange things," the doctors confirmed; "it's a kind of premature senility. Blood chemistry, too. Just give her these." But in February Elvira was dead; she was forty years old. Aspera sold the house and paid for the funeral. Elvira and Chester's line ended with her. From her father she had a necklace; from her mother, books and quilts. Ten years later Will's parents were gone, but their line had proved stronger, extending querulously through a mortgaged Hancock's Best. Not only that but a '68 Mercury, a house, items in the attic, diseased trees on the lawn.

The wind seemed to have picked up outside; Aspera listened to the lash of leaves against the dark pane across the room, listened to the creak and flap of shingles lifting on the dormer eaves. Above her head the narrow crawl space of the attic tapered; up there the antique high chair lay on its side.

She had stripped it, and the chair with its turned and carved natural oak had looked charming in the dining room after she redecorated Will's mother's house. Once used by Will and then for many years by his brother, the high chair had stayed as a convenience for other people's babies. But after a time it called attention to itself in some literal way that required explanation, and Aspera moved it to one of the small rooms upstairs. Then after those conversations on the rug with Will, she put it out of sight in the attic. Most everything in this life in Bracken was held in trust, anyway. She had thought of this house as a house for children. Calyx—the word, she had discovered, meant empty cup. Naming things, you told fortunes.

Empty cup. But, if the chair lay on its side as she did, maybe it passed down visions of a full hectic past lived out in the dining room, of a child at its father's right hand, of morning sun spilling across the hinged tray at a particular angle. Chair dreams, designs pressed into oak. House dreams.

Aspera flopped over on her stomach, which made her feel less vulnerable to what descended from the attic. Her mother's quilt went with the geometric pattern in the bedroom wallpaper, Will's mother's choice. The only room she hadn't changed. She'd talked about it with Will, and he told her of growing up in this house thinking the yellow diamonds were eyes watching. When she looked at the yellow diamonds, she thought of Will as a child. She left the paper for him.

The waterbed had been Dena's recommendation; it was the only way Dena could sleep on her stomach when she was pregnant. And Will, alert to weight distribution, had calculated, "That much water would be the same as having twenty people spaced out along your bedroom floor."

"I've never been that lucky," Dena laughed.

Will had gone out and brought home the waterbed the way he'd bought new sizes of pants. Structural accommodation. His parents' old sleigh bed had been hauled in pieces—curled headboard, footboard, box springs, brown button-dimpled mattress—to the attic.

Aspera turned again, craned her neck to stare at the ceiling above the bed. Her restless tossing woke Will. With a groan that was half-plea he reached for her. She slid into his arms, bringing her weight of loneliness.

After so many years in the dark, his was a functional knowledge: what worked, what did not. A certain persistent fondling worked, so long as he did not rub her nipples carelessly hard; this put her into her body and outside her mind. Mind or body was the choice, anger or pleasure. For a long time now, evidence of happiness had depended on what he did not know about what she thought. In the dark and without words, her body dependably yielded its protection.

The body does not lie? Ah, but the body can be persuaded. She could choose between body or mind, but persuasion was important; she didn't want to choose between going frigid or going crazy.

Will's body moved in strokes above her, a broad paintbrush. When Aspera was small she had painted a picture, a violent orange explosion on one half of the paper, her mother reading a book on the other. Between the two, a slash line that thickly divided these things, protecting her mother, containing the danger.

Afterward Will kissed her. She kissed him back, and he again relaxed into sleep. In the absence of information, belief.

"No margin," Will muttered.

Aspera put her fingers to the seven pearls linked on the chain at her throat. She thought of chairs and beds, protections. She had futures to reject as well as pasts, so Elvira said; did she say they changed places from one moment to another?

Magical thinking, superstition. Tools Elvira had used to web together the odd pieces of her life. Aspera had noticed in her own case how the fabric grew denser, began to take on the appearance of whole cloth. Was this the way middle-aged people acquired that look, of a life put together? O illusion was real stuff; palpable, binding. It affixed you marvelously well to all the things in your life that you feared to unravel.

Aspera blinked tears; blinked again. Again. The room, and Will beside her, stayed in place.

Back at college that fall, Aspera and Will had counted on Elvira to be more herself once the wedding was over. But months passed, and when Elvira spoke her thoughts, they seemed to come out of sequence, or sounded strangely speeded up. The last weekend Aspera had come from college, she'd taken her mother back to the doctor. The new pills were pink; Elvira seemed to be taking them.

This particular Sunday as Aspera helped fold the clean laundry on the kitchen table in the basement, Elvira was as serene as she'd been in over a year. Aspera's relief was physical, a tight band broken from around her rib cage. Elvira would be fine. No cause to worry: Will was right.

Together they folded the clothes, which as usual included several of Chester's ancient cotton twill work shirts. Aspera watched Elvira carefully folding long khaki sleeves behind the buttoned shirtfront. Folding, one of the labors Elvira did with such care—a benefit from years of compacted living in the Airstream.

"Why do you wash these, Ma?" Aspera tried to make her tone be tact itself.

For a time Elvira seemed not to have heard. Such a question was surely pushing things; the truth was that the daughter needed her mother's sanity in evidence.

"Nobody really wears these shirts, Mama, why do we wash them?"

"Such good shirts," Elvira replied, crimping the collar to lie flat. "Nothing good deserves neglect."

Aspera added it to the compendium of Elvira's regard for cloth. The pieced quilts they used, scrupulously inspected and repaired. Their clothing, washed exclusively in cool water though Aspera had found out that other Bracken mothers competed for laundry temperatures near boiling.

"Great heat is the destroyer," Elvira held. Dryers baked the life out of cloth. So did irons. In high school Aspera had kept an iron hidden away in her room, again for reasons of tact, though they both knew she used it mornings before school.

"Your clothes smell of burning," Elvira might say on a day when something else had already gone wrong. Aspera would duck out the door without answering, and in this way they never passed into particulars. The word iron had never come up between them.

Now Aspera folded the arm of another twill shirt, noticing the light-colored threads where her father's elbows had worn them pale. A light-colored patch showed on the pocket too, where he'd carried his Lucky Strikes. She sucked in a breath, recalled the night she and he had sat side by side on the foundation of the house to watch the sunset contend with rain clouds, his arm radiating heat over her shoulders.

"Honey, I guess your ma don't love me anymore," he had said. Lightly, as though he commented on the sky's progress now that the sheetrock had been secured under tarps. They watched the purple clouds lower and squeeze out the last of the orange light, both pretending he had not spoken. Silence was the only place things got a chance to rest, and this family understood silence.

She smoothed a cuff, then buttoned it as a quaver of fear passed over her stomach. She ought not leave Will for these weekends. He didn't want to visit his parents as often as she needed to see Elvira, but one time she'd come she hadn't been able to reach him on the phone. All day she called the number at their apartment in Mankato. Finally she worried enough to go back late Saturday night, and he had not come home till Sunday morning.

"Look, I thought nobody was expecting me," he said, reasonably enough. He held her and reassured her. Then in the bathroom where she'd followed him, he glanced at her face in the mirror and set down his razor. "I don't like it here without you. I go out and drink a little beer. You're not thinking anything else, are you?" He was incredulous, and gentle with her. "You're my true love. Think of history, remember?"

They ended by making a deal Will didn't like very well: he would drink at the apartment after midnight. Their Cinderella curfew, he called it. On the alternate weekends she was in Bracken, six-packs of beer entered and disappeared from their apartment refrigerator like magic. But no matter how much beer blinked through their refrigerator on those weekends, Will rose and shaved for his eight o'clock classes on Mondays. See, she had nothing to worry about; he was still the serious student of architecture by day.

Glancing above her mother's head to see the February morning that showed through the frost on the basement windows, Aspera noticed a scatter of clouds. They seemed to roll over the cold sky like dice. She finished the shirt she had been folding and laid it on its stack, thinking what Will might be doing, thinking of her father. Elvira reached over and in a quick motion undid the shirt and refolded the arms more crisply. Then she resettled it on the stack, finishing with a brisk pat to the breast pocket. Aspera was struck by this act of possessiveness. She understood it for the first time as love. Elvira kept these shirts and cared for them as a way of keeping Chester alive, because she loved him. No matter what was said or not said.

Elvira lifted her face and looked full into her daughter's eyes. Aspera blinked back tears that had gathered.

"What do you think of between the thoughts you are thinking?" Elvira asked this as she lifted the stack of shirts and turned to fit them into the cardboard boxes in the closet. Her broad back was turned, and the question was unexpected. Aspera looked with a stunned affection at the rounded shoulders that supported all that concentrated motion in her mother's arms. Suddenly Elvira's every gesture was part of a secret and fragile alphabet, whose combinations her daughter would never fathom.

"I don't know what that means, Ma." Aspera pinched the inside corners of her eyes. "What does that mean?"

"You need to pay attention." Elvira turned, her face alight, suffused with the healthy color that hypertension had lent her more usual pallor. "Between thoughts, that's when the future takes place."

Aspera drew a breath. She rolled a pair of Will's socks as she considered what she could say. "No, Mama, I don't think so," she began. Even more gently she said, "Not the future, that's not what I see."

"Ah." Elvira waved an impatient hand in front of her daughter's forehead. She would clear away cobwebs.

Aspera flinched. "Ma, I do know what you're talking about.

You mean the pictures—" She sorted words. "They get in between, these pictures, and not the thoughts you're really trying to think." She saw Elvira watch her with great alertness. She shrugged. "I see the pictures, Ma. But I see you, I see—Daddy." Saying this unfamiliar word, another she and her mother did not let fall between them, the tears broke from her eyes and started down her face. "I see Daddy sitting and waiting for rain ten years ago. That's not the future. I see Will in our apartment on a Sunday morning two months ago. That's what waits for me between thoughts. It's the past."

With an ecstatic motion Elvira lifted a clean unironed handkerchief from a neat stack on the table. She held it by a corner and it bloomed large and white in the air, one of Chester's. She pressed the soft linen into her daughter's hands. "Dry your eyes, the future is made of the past, dry your eyes." Elvira's face went still brighter as the color rose up into her thoughts. "The past comes undone, that's the way it is. That's the future. We live it backward, you see?"

Aspera wiped her face and tried a last time to follow the straying sparks of her mother's thinking. The memory of that conversation would stay clear. It would look after itself for years, the way last things do.

CHAPTER FIVE

"Want to get up and watch me take a shower?

"Want to get up and watch me shave?

"Want to watch me eat breakfast and read the newspaper?"

Aspera struggled to come awake after each pause in the questioning.

Will leaned over her, enjoying the struggle.

She groaned, pulled the sheet over her face. He kissed her through it.

"Lazy wench. Slugabed."

"Timesit?"

"Time for the industrious enterprising husband to be up and about. Time for the lazy wife to loll in bed."

"OK."

"I hope to God the kitchen is cleaned up. I'd hate to go downstairs and find a mess. Our friends are slobs. What time did you get to bed?"

"Late."

He had thought she would feel more playful. It was beginning to look as if she wasn't even going to open her eyes.

"Sure you don't want breakfast?"

"Sure."

"Sure you don't or sure you do?"

She squeezed open her eyes. Bright in the room. Yellow. She squinted in the direction of Will's face. "I want to sleep."

This was not working out right. What he had in mind was the two of them down having Sunday breakfast together. He'd go to the corner store and buy bakery rolls, the sticky kind.

"Hey!" he protested. "I'm supposed to be the one with the hangover."

She shut her eyes.

He felt disappointment go in sharply for just a second, only one second, but she liked to sleep in after they made love, OK, he'd let her sleep in. He tiptoed out of the room.

Next time she stirred awake the smell of coffee had made its way upstairs. The picture was an easy one for her: Will at the breakfast nook with coffee and rolls and Sunday papers. Or he'd have finished the rolls and taken his coffee to sit in the sun that by now spread over the sofa from the dining room windows. Coffee, rolls, two newspapers: this routine had been set in stone by Will's mother. Aspera knew he looked upon Sunday breakfast alone as a breach of contract.

She pulled a pillow over her face. They'd got up and done Sunday breakfasts for twenty years of marriage, and just this year she had found out: left to it, Sundays had a way of rolling out their own thread. What a brilliant rediscovery, staying in bed as she used to do in high school, lying—as she did this day—in the nomadic patches of light that swept into the room fresh from sunup, while outside shadows of treetops got pushed around on the grass. Fall. But not cold enough to think seriously about storm windows, not cold enough to face up to what lay ahead. This might be one of the last Sundays she could do this, lie here listening to the wind whip yellow leaves against the window screens.

She saw all these things without having to move because this year she had remembered how she hated waking up to curtained windows. All through the past spring and summer she hadn't closed them; now she meant to hold out on fall as long as she could. Curtains were for winter, for preserving warmth against temperatures that in Minnesota made the body radiate its heat to cold walls. All right, but winter wasn't here yet. She'd felt starved for light, and now she would have as much as she could. Maybe the body stored light; maybe she could make this supply last.

She pushed her limbs out, spread-eagled over the luxury of an entire bed to herself. Luxury, in which she included the beauty of the morning, caused her to smile. She shut her eyes. A passing shaft of sunlight made orange blinders of her eyelids. She dozed and dreamed.

Back to the earring counter again. Same single earring she'd seen before, same beautiful design: an enameled disc with the figure of a woman, lithe against a lilac ground, perhaps a lilac cloud. The woman's headdress and gown shot with emerald greens and rich blues. Aspera has been here many times admiring this figure. She simply will not buy one earring, no matter how beautiful. But this time another single earring is displayed, one quite as lovely as the first. Enamel, but squarish in shape, the background deep royal blue, the figure again contrasting—though she can't quite see this figure or design. Against her better judgment she argues with herself. How many pieces do I own already, things that don't go together? These two aren't a match, but, lilac and blue, wonder if I couldn't just—

Will shook her shoulder until she focused her eyes on him.

"I'm going now," he told her.

She took in the information, unwilling to be torn from the dream.

"Bye." The word went foggy.

He shook her. "Don't forget, I'll be in Tartarville, that new complex."

"Mmh."

"You really should look it over with me, but I know—" He watched her face for signs that she might change her mind. It was good last night; she might want to go with him. Seconds went by. With her eyes shut like that she looked lifeless, and that made him feel wild somehow, so alone. He needed her to open them and see him before he left.

"Well," he said loudly, "I'll go case the layout; maybe we'll go over together sometime if it's anything interesting. Want anything before I leave? Coffee? Juice? You ought to have something."

"Nmmmmmn." She shook her head once, as if a fly buzzed.

He sat beside her on the bed, and the mattress dipped and swayed. If she would just look at him. He'd carried on at the party, she'd forgiven him; hell, he hadn't done that much, but he didn't like this feeling of being disconnected this morning; he needed reassurance. He wanted to see it in her face, with her eyes open; was that so much to ask? He pushed her hip over and rearranged her leg to make room for himself. Like moving a rag doll, no resistance.

"If you think of it later, you could take a look at the new

stuff we ordered. Looks pretty good. Sunday paper has an article on New York interiors; maybe we can pick up some ideas. All right?"

She nodded against the pillows.

"You got to bed late, huh?"

"Extremely late." Surprised her tongue could move to make l's in the absence of saliva. She jumped a little as he brushed a strand of her hair off her eyelid. She rubbed her face. God, they'd had sex? She'd been so angry, that always scared her so much—if she got too angry he would leave her. Is that what she thought? Stupid! Now they'd never talk—and now she really did want him to leave. He couldn't leave fast enough.

"You rest then," Will conceded. He patted her shoulder and spoke softly, meaning to sound fatherly, to coddle her. She just wanted to sleep, was all; she was tired, he knew. But before he could help it, he'd shaken the shoulder and added in a rougher tone, "Give me a kiss, wife."

She kissed him back when his lips pressed hers, and then she turned over with a sigh that turned into a yawn. He thought it sounded faked. He stood up and the waterbed rocked her. When she heard the back door slam her eyes came open, stayed open.

Will got in the car and slammed the door. It sprang open from the force, and he slammed it harder. He hated the way she did that, floated away from him like he wasn't alive. Faking. Well, that was the last time he would make the move; he might as well be holding a bag of sand. They had just made love! What made her like that? The store was doing great; he was handling the whole thing now. A bad five years, granted, but he'd turned things around—no, she had turned things around, he knew that, how could he not know that? But she'd lost enthusiasm, didn't even want to do the books anymore. Well, she didn't have to do the books. He didn't need her help, didn't need her gratitude, either, that went without saying, but he wouldn't stick around while she floated around like some unavenged ghost. He'd leave her, go to fucking Tartarville alone, that's what she wanted, anyway. "You can go on your own, you know"—she'd said it to him again last night. In that smug voice. Well, no skin off him, let her sleep the whole damn day;

what did she do, walk around all night? Anytime *he'd* ever tried going off by himself there was hell to pay. Every damn time.

"Please don't leave me, Will"—high whiny voice this time—hell, she wasn't even there those weekends in Mankato, she was with her mother. "Drink in the apartment after midnight." That was when it started. He'd stuck around the place just in case she called. Hard to believe. He sat around by himself unless a couple guys felt sorry for him, brought in a six-pack. Will gunned the motor of the Pontiac, flung his arm over the seat back and backed out of the driveway fast. Did she tell him she'd be gone for half the night last night? What was he supposed to be feeling so sorry about anyway, what did he do that was so wrong? Had a good time and made a few people laugh. OK, some crude stuff—she could stand a sense of humor. He'd joked around with people, and that made him feel like he existed. Was that something he had to be forgiven for? She used to be with him all the time, when they were apart they both felt wrong, the way he did right now. He'd let her do that to him. Now by God she had changed, she wanted something else, and that didn't have to make sense to him either. He was supposed to leave her the hell alone. He would.

Aspera lay awake while the sun through the south window made a checkerboard of the bed. She thought of the dream, the mismatched earrings. No accidents, Elvira said, not in the mind or anywhere else.

Then with a start she recalled the other dream, the one with silk and cat fur. Her heart beat a hollow rhythm.

The dreams, both dreams were about her and Will. Their life together was supposed to flow like Chinese silk through the eye of a needle, ripple along without a hitch. But there *were* hitches, something always got in the way of that river of silk.

She massaged the bridge of her nose, looked down at the blocks of sunlight on the quilt, patterns on patterns. Pane at the Window, Elvira called this one, though that name had never surfaced in library books. Since Aspera was a child each repetition of the pattern had looked to her like eight fishes feeding on the same morsel, which was invisible. The fishes were drawn into a fitted circle, like wagon trains, except with melancholy fishtails fanning out. The quilt was heavy. Elvira had given it to her the year after Chester left for the Florida Keys; the new house had been so cold.

With her finger Aspera followed a train of stitches around a fishtail.

How had Will become this stranger she could hardly talk to? Since they'd come back to the store, there had been too much he didn't want to know. She'd had to screen life for him in case there were things he could feel hurt or rejected about. She'd learned what these were by the way he visibly sagged if she let one through. She learned very thoroughly during those first five years, back when they'd been so afraid of losing the store. When indeed the thing almost folded underneath them. Point by point he had taught her what it was she could not say.

"I have these invoices from the suppliers." A dozen pastel slips in her hands, thin tissues printed or hand-stamped with urgencies. "Second notice," "Warning—final notification," "Unless we receive your remittance by return mail . . ." It was February, time to reorder stock.

"Which ones do you think we ought to prefer?" she asked Will.

The look he gave her was blank. What she said had no meaning; had she used the wrong word?

"I mean, we can't pay them all. I called each one last month and made promises—" Before her eyes he shrank down, all the leavening gone out of his body. What held him up were constructs of bone and muscle, everything necessary to function but nothing to absorb shock. He stood where she had interrupted him, his hand grasping the hammer he'd been using to repair an entryway railing. He worried that a customer might lean on it, and it would give way under the pressure. The look on his face said he was doing everything he could, everything possible. And was she there to ask for more?

She folded the bunch of thin papers twice over. "Never mind," she said. "I can take care of it."

This became their pattern for the accounts and for the timing of sales and the seasonal selection of merchandise. For which employees to let go, for how they might arrange to make cost on certain shelf items. She learned to displace silence with safer references.

"That railing is looking better."

To such things he could turn voluble. He talked about the angle to the door, faulty construction, technical difficulties in making a sound repair; he said everything was just depressing, that was all. And when the bills came, and the colored versions followed with their stamps and legends, she took care of them. She went to the library and read books, discovered maneuvers and delaying tactics.

Six mornings a week Will hated getting up. He liked her to stay in bed with him and wanted to make love then, prolonging the safety. She lay with him afterward as long as she dared, and then getting up would still feel the pull of him lying there, not wanting her to leave him. Not that he ever said such a thing. Still there was pleading in his eyes, and accusation.

Here he was at last in Hancock's Best, where he was expected to do well, as a matter of course. His name was the one written over the door. If the family business was biting the hand too near the bone, who was going to make it better? A word burned in his brain, and she knew which word since it came out in his sleep. Incompetent. He ground his teeth to keep it in. In waking hours his face armored itself to prevent that word from burning through, branding his forehead. His whole pride was staked on the effort. Her part was not to disturb his concentration.

They worked it out that weekday mornings she got up and made a hasty breakfast; they drank coffee together and she left him in his plaid robe, a baleful eye on the newspaper. She opened the store, took care of mail and routine orders in the early part of the day. Will came midmorning when customers were more likely to be there, to do the things only he knew how to do. On slow or stormy days she called him at home before noon to say don't bother. Those days she came home to a house bristling with cleanliness, every room fiercely tidy. Will would be seated and ready for conversation when she let herself in the house at five. The kitchen: spotless but cold. While she got supper, she imagined he was offended by the clutter of food on his mother's counters, his mother's clean cutting board. These feelings were so unreasonable that she did not mention them, but locking up the store alone at night— that final sequence of turning the key and setting the alarm triggered a vision of the man at home, waiting for her in a clean house with a stubbornly cold kitchen. She shied away from thinking systematically about this; things waited for her that she was not prepared to face, and so she did not think them.

When the store turned around and started making money in their fifth spring, she stared at the account books as though sight had failed her. She was more astonished than exhausted, and certainly she was exhausted. But with money coming in, Will gained strength by the day. He rushed round the store, renewed his father's contacts with the downtown merchant coalitions, joined Rotary. He gave orders, and Aspera found herself running the register for him as though lobotomized. Afraid to breathe, afraid of a setback, she kept quiet and felt strangely guilty. When they'd stacked up enough credit to make the bank take notice, Will seized on the idea of expanding home improvements. He laid it out on paper, along with a finished plan for remodeling, and the bank went for it as though Bracken bankers knew of nothing else that could be done with money. A home store, complete with cabinetry, hardware, kitchenware, add-on plans for gardens and decking—a natural for a lumberyard. It was finally Will's success, and she wanted to let him have it, not think of the store anymore. She didn't want to think at all.

At quarter of eleven the phone rang. She reached for it on the bedside table before it could ring again and in her haste dropped the receiver as she spoke her hello. She retrieved it, but before she could speak again the voice in her ear said, "Aspera, I'm sorry, did I get you out of bed?"

Aspera cleared her throat. "Not yet."

Dena's laugh came back thin. She hesitated. "I'm still in Bracken. I can explain but—" The tremble in her voice sounded like an electrical problem, some fault in the connection. "I wondered if you'd have time to meet."

Through the front door Dena's face showed pale and chalky, her small sharp nose pink from friction; she clutched an exhausted Kleenex in her left hand. When the door was opened she attempted a smile that promptly quivered and folded the wrong way. The two embraced while Dena, failing at words, daubed again at her nose and eyes.

Aspera tried to gauge the crisis. Death or rape, kidnapping, Angie in an accident? Serious things had a wildness to them. That was missing.

Dena sucked in a trembly breath and withdrew from the embrace.

"Bad night?" Aspera guessed.

Dena nodded, her mouth crumpling again.

With some relief, Aspera took her arm and led her into the kitchen. "Let's start with coffee."

"I've been drinking motel coffee for hours."

"Motel coffee? Then how about juice?"

Dena sat on a bench in the breakfast nook and Aspera took a jug from the refrigerator. She also turned the flame on under the kettle. Turned it up high against the chill in the room, new these September mornings.

She asked Dena, "A rendezvous at the Holiday Inn?"

"Thrifty Scot. Poetic, isn't it?" And Dena popped into tears.

Aspera came to cradle Dena's head in her arms. Dena dug for tissues in the pocket of her coat, which she still wore. She extracted a packet, of the size that might be purchased from a motel vending machine. She plucked out the last one and blotted her nose, expelled a deep sigh. Then resolutely she brought her head upright to talk.

"I'm sorry," she squeaked, shaking her head. "I thought I was all done."

"No hurry," Aspera said. She set a box of tissues in front of Dena. "We've got plenty of time."

"Nothing but time," Dena said.

Aspera turned from the glasses cupboard to take in the bitter blue of eyes. She selected crystal goblets, mindful of the effect elegance can have on grief.

"Hang on," she told Dena, setting them brimming full on the table. From her angle the juice glowed orange, backlit from the windows. "Will also left us some pecan caramel rolls from the bakery."

She took the package from the breadbox and unwrapped cellophane, set the sticky aggregation on a plate in front of Dena. Then she went to the cupboard for tea. Among the stock she located a small bag of raspberry leaves. They were recommended in her mother's old herbals for pregnancy and uterine cramping, hysterectomies. The connection to hysteria was at least worth trying. Words had roots for something.

She warmed the china pot and put the leaves in, then leaned on the handle of the kettle, sensing the shimmer of boiling about to begin.

"Why is it so wonderful to enjoy something sweet when the weather turns cool?" Dena asked. She plucked out a pecan with her fingernails, leaving a filament of caramel to fall through the air. "My mother used to make fresh cardamom rolls for Sunday breakfast," she recalled, rolling her eyes up. "How I enjoyed them! Almonds, raisins, butter—now there's what I call an addiction."

Something in the tone. Dena's eyes again filled, and she tried to put off the moment when the drop would gather and spill down her cheek. Dena felt she cried too easily and too often. She feared she would cry continually unless effort were expended to prevent it.

"Can you feature anything so trendy," Dena's watery voice demanded, "as to be told that you have become an addiction and are to be given up?"

With caution Aspera nodded. "Imaginative," she said. "That means he's married?"

"Roman Catholic and married."

"Somebody from Minneapolis?"

"There are no somebodies in Minneapolis." The sigh sharp.

"In Bracken?"

Dena laughed. "Don't be so shocked."

"Well—I thought that's why you moved."

Dena's smile was patient. "Remember I used to work with the arts council to arrange the annual auction, the home tour and so forth. Quentin Howath."

"Quentin Howath? Of the political wife and five children? I've met him. You never even mentioned the man."

"I haven't needed to mention him; we've had a very comfortable relationship for about seven years. It's not been intense at any point, only comfortable. Only—" Dena shrugged—"sexual. He's nice in bed, a very nice man, and every two weeks or so for about seven years, we enjoyed one another. Not a relationship I would stay for, and not one I would leave because of. You understand."

"Not at all." Aspera folded her arms. "I didn't know you

had comfortable sexual relationships. I only heard about the other ones."

Dena gave her a sidelong look. Aspera's surprise was genuine; also the irritation. Dena's affairs often featured deceit, misunderstanding, crossed timing, bad surprises. One long and serious relationship had ended with her lover's marriage to somebody else. Another when a beau shyly persuaded her to wear black stockings and black three-inch heels for him and then phoned her after the date while she took them off. The full expression of his sexual nature turned out to be this secret nightly phone call from his mother's house.

Dena's pain still resonated in Aspera's memory. But comfortably sexual with Quentin Howath for seven years? And not ever mention him?

"Don't look at me like that," Dena sighed. "I enjoyed Quentin! Oh, Aspera, my mother raised me to be sweet all the time, and I just can't do it. Never could." She blew her nose carefully. "So I'm conniving and devious, and I always have been. You have to be sneaky about getting the things you really want if you have to look sweet the whole time you're doing it."

"That part I understand."

"Did I ever tell you about Sunday afternoons when I was a child? I've had a lot of time to think since I saw you last night. The whole family had to take a nap on Sunday afternoons. My mother and father would go into their bedroom, and my sister and I would have to go lie down in ours. Mother would make us leave the door to our room open, so she could hear if we were whispering, she said. But she and my dad didn't listen much. What they did was quietly copulate." Dena gave value to each of the word's hard consonants.

"And there we were, me and my little sister on Sunday afternoons, stuck lying there in bed in our nylon slips. We did the listening," she said, her voice a kind of warning. "Seems like every time I've felt hemmed in, I find somebody and take him quietly to bed. When Charles and I were first married, if I took the kids to visit my parents in Kansas City, I'd go to bed with the family dentist or the family lawyer. If I couldn't find a candidate there, I'd surely find one when I got back. The nice man in the IRS office. The nice man in the arts council."

"Quentin."

"Does that bring us up to date?"

Aspera felt peevish. She tossed her head. "What about the one you were engaged to in college?"

"Toby?" Dena smiled. "What sensitive hands he had! I was utterly faithful to him, of course." She peered at Aspera. "Maybe that's the only way marriages hold up, if both partners cut their teeth together."

"A nice infantile image."

"Otherwise you lose what it takes to stay with one person. Men are famous for fearing comparison. They have every right to be." Dena's smile went a degree crooked. She lifted a didactic finger. "Do you know Charles never failed to take it personally if one of his patients wanted a second opinion on a diagnosis? He couldn't stand it. Came home and had a tantrum every time. Here's a notion dear to my heart: imagine how it would change marriage if every woman claimed the right to a second opinion—not only on her salad dressing, but paddling a canoe or navigating the bedroom. Revolutionary! Makes perfect sense to have marriage be infantile as long as men get to be toddlers. It's certainly your trouble with Will; you won't accept your proper relation to the toddler in him."

"Is that a joke?" Aspera set her cup down.

Dena smiled. "Will's mother was always in the store, wasn't she? And that's where he expects you to be."

Against the blade in her stomach, Aspera said nothing.

Dena dipped a fingernail at a shred of raspberry leaf floating in her tea.

"A toddler is an intelligent being with supreme willpower. A toddler will not be denied. You do not ever tell him no. You can distract him, you can get him to trade you one thing for another, but you do not ever simply take something out of his hands. Doesn't Will want a new store? Give him a new store."

"I'd have to run the old one."

"Then give him a dog, for heaven's sake. A cat, or fishies in a bowl. You've got to keep little hands busy if you want them slipped off your coattail."

Aspera waited for words that would cushion what she felt. Dena looked like a stranger across the table, with those swollen red eyes. "I'd rather be married to an adult," Aspera said.

Dena laughed nervously and rubbed her hands together. "It seems to me that men get to a certain age and they just insist: either you let them be two years old, or they find somebody who will. And you know, there is so much untrained female talent in the world."

As Dena's wistfulness came through, Aspera sat back. "Why don't you tell me what happened last night?" she said.

Dena looked out the window. "Let's go on chatting awhile first. I'm just getting my bearings this morning." She put another piece of roll in her mouth and chewed for a moment. From the holder on the table she drew a napkin and meticulously cleaned each of her nails. They gleamed their pearly iridescence. "Do you know, at our age it doesn't make any sense at all to be heterosexual. Have you thought of that?"

Surprised once again, Aspera answered, "Who hasn't?"

"Right. Men are bottomless pits; they're at the very least going to die on you—I'm sick of men. I wish I could switch teams."

"What's stopping you?"

Dena sighed, one of the deep hopeless ones. "I need male validation. I have to have it. If I had a female lover I'd probably try and impress some man with the fact."

At that the two women laughed.

More at ease, Aspera poured tea. "There ought to be old boyfriends one could look up." She glanced up. "Just for a second opinion, of course."

Dena nodded. "What's stopping you?"

"Me? Before Will was Dewy Thorson. I used to have trouble recognizing Dewy on the phone because his voice was changing."

"The last child bride. Too bad, because I do recommend old boyfriends."

"You've done that?"

Dena pursed her lips. "Systematically. Everybody should do it. I thought everybody had."

"How does everybody manage?"

"Well, you can't tell people of course; you do it out of town. If you can't do it out of town, you have to borrow somebody else's car. You have to take precautions, because it does occur to everybody at some time or other. And it does pass. You don't want to burn any bridges if they still bear traffic."

Aspera thought a moment, then asked, "Toby too?"

Dena glanced up. "His hands felt almost coarse. I'm sure he had no idea. It was very satisfying, seeing the road not taken." She had slipped out of her coat; a rose cashmere sweater smoothed the rough look emotion had given her complexion.

Dena always dressed carefully, seductively, fabrics chosen to bring out or correct contours of her body, shades chosen to harmonize precisely with skin tones. She had this seen to professionally, had an analyst determine which fabric swatches ought to be pasted on the little card she carried in her handbag for shopping. Colored swatches represented the right bluish pinks (color of the inside of her lip), the right ivory-salmon (color of skin just behind the earlobe), the right violet prussians and tans (variegations in iris color), the right grayed yellows (whites of eyes and teeth). Thus forty-seven shades and textures had been derived, to which Dena matched cosmetics and clothing, providing that the clothing was of suitable line. For which other analysts had been consulted.

Yet for her pains, this elegant woman exuded not rippling magical appeal but a carefulness that alarmed. And like most crucial secrets friends keep from one another, this one might be thought obvious.

"Can you imagine," Dena said, pushing up the sleeves of her soft sweater, "I've had this on since three this morning." She brushed a few crumbs from her bosom.

"You look lovely," Aspera said.

It was true. It was always true, and the effect was that most women were terrorized by Dena. In her presence they could feel they'd been unaccountably turned out in frog costumes and camouflage makeup. As for men, other things came into play. Theory, for one. Theory had it that large breasts were free passes into masculine attention. Dena had them, and still all that energy left for the joys of entrapment, the pleasurable ways of turning the knife.

Four years ago Dena had divorced Charles, seeing that professionalism like hers was wasted on the same man. She'd left Bracken and moved to Minneapolis, intent on seducing others. But these other men, soul and purpose of her exactitude, men who could in theory be expected to queue up like touring Englishmen at the shrine of a sensuous woman, instead seemed to scatter and flee like wildebeests.

All this was complicated. Aspera, in her rust Shetland crewneck and jeans, in her pattern-book Simplicity marriage, tried to keep from feeling noticeably froglike. "You make me feel I'm halfway into the grave," she told Dena.

Dena put up a slim hand for a shield. "The problem is, what to do about being sexy after thirty-five?"

Aspera stared into Dena's eyes, hoping to outface the flush of embarrassment that crept up her neck.

"I believe something is built into the female mechanism," Dena said. "Whatever it is comes to a screeching halt at thirty-five and says: Hmmmm. Last chance to get what I want."

"It didn't happen to me."

"Well," Dena allowed, "I have another friend it didn't happen to. She had a baby. I have felt perhaps you did a version of that—by expanding the store with Will."

Aspera's whole being sagged. "What happens at forty?"

"I don't think you'll like it. At forty I think everybody has shot the old boyfriends' list and begins to get appropriately—" she chose a word—"frightened." She glanced up at Aspera, who didn't respond, who might not have heard. "Eyesight fails, the uterus flags. If we can, we go home and dust off what's left of the nesting urge."

Coldly Aspera asked, "Tend to the toddler?"

Dena reached out and patted her arm. "Don't take it so hard. This is what you do: reinforce him for good behavior; see to it that he doesn't take up all your life; give him something else to eat."

Under Dena's touch Aspera felt her body nicked and nibbled.

"And let's find him some playmates—other than Bunny, of course—what about Dalton?"

Aspera looked into Dena's eyes, now dry and sparkling with an entrepreneurial interest. She respected Dena's quick wit in defining problems, managing solutions. And yet there was in her head a muffled tone, things Vicky had said.

"Dalton's a good friend." Without quite realizing, she had whispered it.

"I'm sure he is," Dena whispered back. "Are you aware of the way he watches you?"

All thought flew from Aspera's mind. The window over the sink seemed to let in too much brightness. "No."

"His eyes follow you in the way of a small boy in love with his teacher."

Aspera shook her head. "We've been friends forever."

"He graduated before I knew you and Will, of course. But I noticed the threesome. I always wondered."

"I don't think there's a mystery." Aspera strove to sound offhand. Outside the window, the ragged molting of birches. "Are you ever going to tell me what happened with Quentin?"

Dena looked at her a long moment, then sighed.

"I met him last night after I left here—we were to have two entire evenings together, last night and tonight, while his wife and children visited grandparents. We went to bed, it was very nice, we *enjoy* one another. Afterward he likes to shower alone. I waited in bed, I carry those little scented feminine wipes, in packets? Quentin came out of the bathroom and buttoned his shirt and pants and said, 'You are an addiction, and I have decided I must give you up.' "

Dena's blue eyes had gone purplish with hurt.

Aspera found that her level of sympathy had somehow receded; she could not get to it. She rubbed her eyes. "Quentin said this *after* you had been to bed."

"Yes."

"So he was only theorizing." As she made the joke, Aspera understood Will better. Joking makes trouble unreal, sympathy beside the point. Diversion was good protection.

"But Quentin said this *before* the second night," Dena persisted. "The weekend was only half over."

"Maybe he was only half serious."

They smiled then, but soon another deep sigh rushed from Dena, as though her spirit escaped. "I'm so tired of being in this position. Do I simply look vulnerable? I think men use me!" Her voice caught, the tears began to stream. "I'm supposed to know better." She struck her small fist on the table. "You're so lucky to have Will," she said. "You do know that?"

"Lucky," Aspera repeated. Here it was, her tab. Having been spared the unkindnesses of a series of strangers, she had incurred a debt. She straightened on the bench, tried to keep her chin from lifting the way it wanted to. "Dena, how is it that we end up with you boosting my marriage? The fact is, it's not so easy right now."

Dena leaned back against the kitchen wallpaper. Her hair blended with the yellows and golds of the chrysanthemums in the pattern. She changed the angle of her face and looked sorrowfully at Aspera. "I wish you could think of Will as a child, and then remember that if you struggle with a child in public, you look—unfeminine." Dena said the word soothingly. "Why did you think I made it a point to let Charles divorce me? People didn't see the tantrums that ended with every shelf in the bathroom raked onto the ceramic tile, glass bottles spilled and broken; they didn't see who got to clean it up."

Aspera nodded.

"Nor did people see the connoisseur squaring up his napkin after a meal to announce, 'I don't care if I ever have veal prepared quite that way again.' "

Aspera nodded again. But the conditioned reflex of long marriage made her begin putting weights carefully on each side, to find some balance point for blame. Without it the seesaw slammed down; you could get stuck on one end of the plank and nothing left but to walk it.

"Charles could be awful, but he was good with Angie," Aspera said. "I always tried to like him for that."

Dena took another piece of roll. "Charles tried to like you too."

At some note carried in the tone, Aspera sat back.

"Oh, Charles was critical of everyone, of course. But after we'd visit with you and Will for an evening, he'd say—" Dena stopped.

"What?"

"Oh, I can't recall. It's been so long."

"Dena."

"Well, you have to allow for Charles. He'd say something like, 'Aspera has bad legs and bad teeth, and yet you come away thinking she's lovely.' "

A moment's pause before Aspera could laugh. "Bad legs and bad teeth are unbeatable," she allowed.

Dena flushed pink. "Charles could be cruel."

"I guess I asked." She felt attacked, but also guilty of provoking it. "Tell you what. I take back what I said about liking

Charles. Maybe neither of us can stand having our husbands defended today."

"Charles is my *ex*-husband," Dena returned. Then she smiled a little. "I didn't know it was bad to boost an incumbent."

"It shouldn't be."

"I shouldn't have repeated Charles's remark," Dena said. "You really are lovely, you have that quality of listening that makes everybody feel so important and comforted. And I think of your legs as dainty. Naturally you'd want to avoid dark hose, the opaques."

"Yes." For several moments Aspera could think of nothing else to say. *Sweet, and devious.* Under the table she crossed and recrossed her dainty legs. "Why does Quentin's wife go away on weekends?" she asked at last.

Dena sighed and settled back on the bench. "You know, I had to give up asking about wives. Since men love to talk and most have simply no idea how to get information—*they* don't know how to ask questions, have you noticed? Have you ever known a man who knew more about you than you knew about him?"

Aspera had a hard time getting her thoughts to clear. She shook her head no. Though in some part of her mind she now wondered: Dalton?

Dena tossed her head. "I don't ask anymore. If they start to tell me about their wives, I change the subject."

"You don't want to know?"

"I already know. Wives spring out of the dark side of the moon." She opened her hands as though a globe rested upon her pale palms. "People usually look all right by themselves; it's just in pairs that the pathology leaps out. And I do mean pathology. Anyway, the wife is always something you don't expect, a choice made from some unlit side of the personality."

"Husbands must spring out of the dark side of the moon too."

"Yes, but wives are so pitiful." Dena let a hand fold and drop. "I've been one, I know there's no cure. I don't want to hear about all the other incurables. I spent the major portion of my life trying to figure out how to get loved, and then how to get loved more. Wives hang around trying to get validation, keep on needing it, because it's never given. Men drop pieces of information for wives like unmatched socks. They keep on dropping them when they're with me, too, but I don't pick up anybody's unmatched socks anymore."

Aspera found that her heart was racing. She searched Dena's face, which was calm. "What must it be like for you, watching Will and me?" she asked. "Like consorting with dinosaurs?"

"Now, don't make me feel mean. You and Will are special."

"What makes us the least bit special?" Aspera shut her eyes against the blur of chrysanthemum wallpaper. She was convinced about the dinosaurs. She felt her heart age and compress, go heavy as wet sphagnum. She gave a start when Dena reached across the table and placed cool hands on her shoulders.

Dena smiled. "My dear, the truth is, you have what we all want."

Aspera rubbed her forehead, left her fingers there to bracket her astonishment. "Dena." The stiffening again in her thighs, her arms. "How can you tell me that? You don't want what I have, you don't want to be married. One man, one opinion? I haven't got what you want."

Dena withdrew her hands, clasped them together. "I think you have more than most people can hope for. *Enjoy* it! Perhaps it's true that I don't want a husband right now, but I do need human warmth. I *enjoy* men. I'd give anything to be pursued. I need and enjoy"—here her voice began to wobble—"the little daily pleasures of a man's companionship, you know?"

Aspera was surprised at the tears reappearing in her friend's eyes. She was further surprised at her own emotion, which was anger—at the intimate doubletalk that left her standing upright in the rubble of her luck. She was to offer comfort here, but she was all drained.

Dena foraged for words through her tears, foraged for Kleenex too. Her hands plucked blindly about the table. "I can take care of sexual needs by my own hand so to speak, but it's the daily human warmth I can't get along without, human warmth I need."

Aspera thrust a tissue into Dena's hand. She had begun substituting words as Dena spoke them: for *human warmth,* she pretended to hear *human blood.* When Dena said *enjoy*—"and truly I always *enjoyed* Quentin so much"—Aspera saw carnivore pictures in her mind, Dena with jaws dripping, claws newly sheathed. Madame Vampira.

The vast separation pulled things apart somewhere inside

her throat; tears rose to Aspera's eyes. When they fell Dena drank them up for sympathy.

How was it that all the people in this tangled circuit claimed to love one another? All these kinds of love, and not enough to go round?

Somebody was lying. Somebody in addition to herself.

CHAPTER SIX

"The leaves are going," Aspera said as she and Will got into the car for an early movie. Fifty feet above their heads the oak leaves had turned leathery and sparse, letting the rich blue of evening dominate them from beyond. She had put one foot into the Mercury, then leaned both elbows on its paint-patchy roof to look straight up. "It'll be dark by seven-thirty."

"I don't want to hear about it." Will said this with exaggerated heat, and she smiled. October meant storm windows and gutters, leaves to rake, a burning permit. He turned the key in the ignition, and the Mercury started with a roar. "Concentrate on getting into the car, OK?"

Pushing off her elbows, she snaked down into the passenger seat and pulled the heavy door closed by its curved chrome handle, which was loose. As Will drove she idly fitted the circular mount into the depression it had left, like a faerie ring, in the light-blue vinyl.

He glanced at her hand, then rattled his own door handle, testing. "Tell me why I'm driving such a heap," he said.

"I'd be happy to drive." She thought Will followed too closely in traffic. She had given up saying so but took the wheel whenever she got into the car first.

"No matter who drives it," Will said, "this is a heap."

Will was keen for innovation, for style. Aspera liked him for this, liked this glimpse of the architect in him showing through. "Think we ought to get a new car?" she asked.

He looked at her as though she'd lost her mind. Like figures on a Swiss clock, the architect swung on a pivot, and the businessman reappeared to explain how the Mercury was working fine, how small-town merchants couldn't afford to look too prosperous, how small-town customers were finicky about taking their trade where it didn't appear to be needed.

Will shook his head impatiently. "This is perfectly adequate transportation for us," he said.

He turned to see her broadly smiling and squinted his eyes. "What?"

"You don't even need me for this discussion," she laughed. "You're so ambivalent about this car, you could argue with yourself for hours."

"Take that back. I do so need you, it's not the same if you don't say your lines. Come on, give me one."

"Tell me why we're driving such a heap," she teased.

He put his arm over the seat to maneuver the car into a street slot directly in front of the Orpheum Theater. He glared at her. "This is not just an old car, this happens to be a classic automobile, you peasant."

Aspera was very attached to the Mercury. Its outdatedness was evidence, like the house, of her thrift and willingness to compromise. Years ago she'd promised herself she'd be out of the store before they bought a new car. The fact that the Mercury was still around was a kind of victory; at least she hadn't slipped by her own marker. Now that they had the money, it was time she made her move and talked to Will. But not tonight, not while they were getting along. She had a sense of thrift about that, too.

Outside on the sidewalk Will paused to admire the grille and nosepiece of the '68 Mercury. He savored these details, so baroquely overdone. By owning this relic, he considered he had earned the right to despise it.

"Happy?" she asked.

"It takes so little," he said, putting an arm around her and guiding her toward the ticket window. "You're so lucky to be married to me."

This joke of Will's always got a laugh, since it never failed to strike her as surprising. How would it feel to be so invulnerable? Tonight she began to laugh one more time, but Will had his back to her buying tickets, and laughing just for herself didn't seem worth the effort. She stood by the concession stand and watched her husband scoop his change from the mousehole in the glass ticket booth, watched him make his joke to the girl about the price of tickets.

He turned and caught up with her, looked at her empty hands. "Where's the popcorn?" he demanded, still in his brash mode. "Look, you've got to do your part."

"I don't want popcorn tonight."

He gaped. "Makes no difference, this is a movie, we have to have popcorn." He took her elbow, and she turned and accompanied him to the concessions counter.

"Give this woman a large butter corn," Will said to the high school boy who stood waiting. To Aspera he said with mock concern, "Will one be enough, honey?"

Aspera rolled her eyes at the boy and relaxed into Will's bullying. All the stations of ritual, so much easier.

They located seats midway down the near aisle, selecting two that had upholstery and hinges intact. The Orpheum was old. But it was large, and its casual state of repair was a small-town fact of life; the theater was rarely filled to the point that people didn't have a choice of seats.

Before the local ads started, Will spotted a bat darting between the ironwork grilles set into the ceiling and the furls of plaster over the red velvet curtain. He pointed, and together they watched the bat's erratic patterns.

"That kid at the concession counter," she said. "I think he works part-time at the library."

"Want his job?"

In the gloom Aspera peered at her husband's uptilted profile. "Yes. I sort of do."

"Think you'd be any good at selling popcorn?"

"That's not funny."

"Come on, you only *sort of* want his job," Will said. "Talk about *my* ambivalence."

She straightened in her seat, causing a creaking of old springs. "I'm not ambivalent at all. If you really want to know, I think it's time—"

"You're going to hurt my feelings," he warned. "Don't tell me you'd give up that beautiful store I created for you."

"Will." She pleaded for his sober nature. "The store is beautiful. It's truly wonderful, and I don't want to hurt your feelings."

"Tell me how much you adore every lucite bin, every suspended wall divider."

"Please don't make it so I can't say what I need to say."

"I was only joking," Will said. "We're at the movies, you know."

"I want to go back to library work," she said, feeling her face suffuse with heat.

"Have I missed something? Are there library jobs in Bracken?"

"I want to start looking around in the area," she whispered.

The ads had started rolling. Bracken Jewelers, Marney's Trailer Homes, Hancock's Best Lumber and the new Best Interiors Boutique.

"We need a new spot," Will said.

"Will."

He offered her the popcorn box. She started to put her hand in, but he put his in first. She tried it again with the same result.

"Damn you, Will!"

"Here. I was just trying to lighten things up."

She folded her arms and stared resolutely at the curtain.

"OK. It's not news to me that you'd want out someday." His whisper was sympathetic. "I'm a hundred percent behind you, and in a couple of years we'll have the second store in solid shape—"

"A couple of years!" she cried. She turned and glanced around to see if anyone sat within earshot, but the Tuesday night moviegoers were scattered through the seats like shot.

Previews were running. *Terms of Endearment, The Big Chill,* coming this Christmas. "I don't want a second store," she whispered. "The one we've got is thriving, Bobbie could take over the Boutique and anything else I do and probably do it better—"

"Bobbie?" Will said sharply. "If you don't want to stick around, I can do my own managing."

The sudden division of powers brought her up short. "I agree." She paused. "It's just that, if I left tomorrow, you could put Bobbie in charge and not have to worry about training anybody. She could handle the Boutique *and* break in her replacement."

"Bobbie is great, OK? Bobbie is wonderful. Most aggressive hardware clerk the world has ever seen, she could sure lend Best Boutique some local color." He did an imitation of Bobbie's intent nervous glare. " 'Say, let me ring that up for you once.' "

"I didn't think—"

" 'Your hairs look nice, where did you get them cut? And who is it you doctor with?' "

On the screen a beautiful, comical baby soared through the air.

"All right, she doesn't belong in your uptown Boutique. I don't either. You'll hire somebody, then?"

"Yes, boss," Will said, his hands up with a backward feint of terror. "Now can we watch the movie?" He nodded toward the titles now filling the screen. "Now can we start having a good time?" He offered her his hand.

From the time they had been fourteen, they'd held hands through every feature the Orpheum Theater had. She looked at Will's face, at the eyebrows lifted in invitation. She drew a breath and slipped her hand into her husband's.

She is on her back, a little apart from him. She can see the tousle of his dark hair, now backlighted with an orange-apricot sky darkening beyond the window, can see part of the squarish hand that cushions his forehead. His breathing is peaceful, natural as the way his eyelids stay over the eyes in sleep. Unconscious. Perfect. She relaxes, lets her eyes drift upward past the window's square of uninterrupted color, up to where the ceiling reflects a chalky blush. The air still clings to what it touches, heavy but cool, as though it too has been refreshed by the few hours' passage. Below, the traffic sends up its choppy startings and stoppings, gasps of air-pressure valves on buses, the synchronized roar of cars at the lights.

The air is the only thing moving in the room, ponderous with light waves and sound waves and reports of outside change and motion. Everything else is still. Even her thoughts have been still, for when he moves, when his hand finds its sure way to the ridge of her hipbone, only then does the waking current flare through her brain. She shuts her eyes, takes and holds her breath against the force. This current does not begin and end in her head but bursts into her body, bypassing nerve channel intersections by the million and going for the specific singing vibration of her sex. She opens her eyes, astonished, to look at him. A man, merely. Folds of skin puffed around the eyes from sleep, dark creases forced into the cheek where the hand has lain. Eyes that squint fine lines toward smiling. She turns, seizes, clings to him like the air itself. Not deciding to—O, the body played a part!—not deciding, but wanting. Wanting.

On the way home they talked about the movie, about the way Garp had blamed his wife for homebreaking and child-murder without confessing that the first domino in that horrible sequence had fallen with his own betrayal of her. Aspera focused on this with some heat, because at the point in the film when the wife had begun her affair with a young man, Aspera's hand, clasped securely in Will's, had begun to sweat.

Indeed, she had watched all the dominoes fall with a clutching horror on behalf of the film wife, and on behalf of her own moist hand. What would Will think? What if she removed the hand? In the end she had made herself sit very still, though every muscle of her body fought to squirm. Do not move. Think of history now.

In the car she attacked the filmmakers. "They just glossed it over. He wanted to kill her!"

Will looked over at her. "It was both their faults," he said simply. "All you have to do to make things happen is leave holes in your life, and sure enough . . ."

Will had said these words to her before. They came up in his most serious moments, and here they were again.

"What does that mean?" she demanded. "I've never really understood what that means to you, leave holes in your life."

Will drew back slightly, put the turn signal on and busied himself with negotiating a left turn. A stirring of memory so faint, so far back in the logs of what he knew. The image of his brother floated forward, a mere baby. And then the familiar needle of pain, as his brain clenched like a frog under the touch of electrodes.

A great deal escaped the net of Will's memory. He joked about this: "As far back as I can remember. I was twenty-two." But this clenching feeling was older than that. The baby. His mother tacking up leftover strips of wallpaper behind the rocking chair—this had to be the cellar room of the store where she tended him, and then later the baby, between customers. His mother rocking the baby, their combined form making a moving shape across the yellow diamonds in the pattern, forward and back, forward and back.

In the car, Will gave a jumpy shrug of his shoulders. "I don't know," he said impatiently. "Doesn't mean anything."

Silence reigned in the car for several minutes. They passed into the darkened center of town, the store, the library, the grocery.

They went by the grocer's window and she thought of the sealed vegetables. Winter was the season of buying things you couldn't touch. Bracken stores didn't carry fresh produce in the summer because so many people grew their own; come winter, battered lettuce and pale tomatoes were imported in plastic wrap from elsewhere. Meager carrots in bags, turnips and rutabagas embalmed in whitish wax.

Will reached over and patted her hand. "I didn't mean to snap like that. It's just so obvious, you leave room and something gets between you and whatever you're next to, that's all. Look at that wagon in front of us."

Aspera looked, instinctively pushing her shoulders against her seat-back. Sure enough, too close.

"If I dropped back, we'd have three tractors in between us in two minutes."

She pressed her foot on the floor of the passenger side, on imaginary brakes. She said, "Not true."

Will took his foot off the accelerator. The Mercury slowed, and soon they were several car-lengths behind the station wagon. Aspera felt her body ease. But as they reached the bridge, a motorcycle careened into their lane from a sidestreet. With a roar and a flash of lights and reflectors it was between the two cars.

Will lifted both hands from the steering wheel in the gesture that said, See?

They were both subdued getting out of the car and into the house. Because his voluble cheer was missing, Will actually seemed the quieter of the two. Aspera felt extremely uneasy. Had he noticed her sweating hand?

In bed Will lay quietly beside his wife. He wasn't thinking of her at all, wasn't aware of her back so tentatively curved into his side. He floated in and out of sleep, he saw babies rising and falling, rocking, swaying. He saw large feet, black shoes, saw whirls of darkness, heavy cloth furling, babies falling, saw diamonds appear and disappear like eyes watching.

At midnight Aspera sighed and changed position in the waterbed.

"Mine," Will said. "My baby."

CHAPTER SEVEN

In the St. Paul Science Museum bookstore, with Bunny at the next table examining bird feeders, Dalton and Will outside the door joking about stuffed mountain goats in their glass cases, Aspera spun rangy models of the solar system, models of the crag-bed moon, see-through models of star systems impressed in lucite shells around a solid globular earth.

Here they were, proofs for gravity and centrifugal force. Proofs of insularity, and ways to see beyond it into our rolling splash-print of night sky. The models failed at it too; not being infinite themselves, they offered just so many thicknesses of lucite. A brochure was careful to note a phrase, a humbling joke passed on by applied science: the earth-apparent sky.

It was point of view every time: Earth-apparent.

"Look at those two." Bunny spoke abruptly behind Aspera's left shoulder, nudging her with some urgency toward a handsome silver-haired couple looking through the book section a few yards away. Both were dressed in charcoal slacks and contrasting though harmonious pullover sweaters with neat collars showing at the necks.

"When I was attending my crisis-intervention clinic in Rochester, they were there. He wants to free-lance at grant writing. She'll handle books and appointments, that stuff. They're both sixty-three, and his firm in St. Paul let him go."

"Sad," Aspera whispered.

Bunny elbowed her. "I haven't told you the sad part. The last night of the conference we all went out to find a dance band. And here's this dear couple. Aren't they both cute? The whole bunch of us hung out together awhile, and one by one the women were all asking this sweet man to dance. He couldn't smile hard enough. Then you noticed she wasn't dancing. She was getting polite conversation—women can only do so much for one another—while the men in the group got the younger women to dance with. I did the two-step while this nice lady sat on a stool all night, like she was made for it."

Bunny's voice had a softness that could change instantly, like a saturated solution precipitating crystals. It changed then. "Let me tell you, I'd rather be the one dancing."

Aspera observed the woman, whose hips were trim and shapely in the wool slacks, whose well-cut hair showed as much blond as gray. She held herself with an air of certainty, the bearing of a habitually attractive woman.

"Maybe there's no choice," Aspera whispered.

"Then I'd be capable of breaking Dalton's ankles."

Aspera turned to see Bunny's face, but was pulled about by the arm and led toward the door of the shop.

"You don't want to say hello?" Aspera asked.

"No."

"It's contagious, this wallflower business?"

The look Bunny flung her made Aspera straighten her face.

"You're the one fresh off a birthday," Bunny snapped. She stopped abruptly short of the door, having spotted Will and Dalton in the children's section of the bookstore. The two men leaned over a glass display cube arranging small transparent building blocks.

"Isn't it touching," Bunny said. "Let's go mess up their little game."

Aspera put out her hand. "No. Those blocks are the shopping center at Tartarville. I don't want to go near it."

Bunny tossed her head and marched over. In her baby voice she said, "You boys put away Tartarville now."

Will colored and looked at Aspera.

Was it possible for all one's friends to go dangerous at the same time? Possible that misunderstandings operated on an orbital cycle like Halley's comet, coming around in one big ball every so often, and *this was it*?

Aspera dragged her feet over to the group.

"I'm ready for this movie we signed up for," Bunny said.

Her small voice carried. "This volcano thing, I'm ready."

"If we get in line now," Will said, his finger shifting a blue oblong, fitting it with a snap beside another, "it's just hurry up and wait."

"So what else is new?" Bunny neglected to take the edge off her voice. What was so effective was not just the raw tone, but the leap from harmless to imperious. Aspera felt herself go into a startle-reaction. The mood of any group would veer to make up that much lost ground.

Dalton gave Will a nervous smile and turned to his wife to urge quietly, "We'll just be a minute here."

"We're going to spend the day together, that was the agreement," Bunny said. "I don't want to stand around while you and Will play with blocks."

Dalton wore his pained smile. He looked from Will to Bunny and back again. From a display counter Aspera picked up a book on stargazing, one with luminescent charts printed on black paper in the centerfold.

Will swelled up his chest and thumped his breastbone. "Big he-men talk business talk. Little dumb squaws chitchat outside"—he gestured stiffly toward the white stuffed mountain goats rearing in their glass cases outside the door—"with livestock."

Aspera heard Bunny's giggle. Bullies shared a language, kept one another in trim. She gave Dalton a furtive look and saw Bunny put her hand on his arm.

"I'll be waiting outside," Bunny told him in her small voice. Then she turned and tapped Aspera on the shoulder. The two women left through the glass doors.

Conscious of Bunny's anger, Aspera walked beside her wondering at that voice. Like the hand on the arm, a gesture Bunny wouldn't waste, and if this was friendship it was frightening.

"We could push buttons," Aspera risked as they headed for the display area, walking across the main traffic patterns of the museum lobby. Streams of children and parents fed through the main doors and up the stairs, their footsteps muffled on great squares of rubber flooring.

"Wait till I get Dalton," Bunny promised. "He can keep his nose stuck in a book all week long, but this is my time."

Aspera shrugged. "They're happy playing blocks."

"I'm the one he's supposed to make happy. He's not playing with me." Bunny walked over to a series of display panels. She punched four buttons in succession, setting educational machineries to work in their inset glass cases. A lens moved forward and back, showing the effects of distance on magnification. Sand flowed through an hourglass, minutes demarcated on the glass. Mechanical male-scientist voices whirred, explained.

"You expect him to make you happy?"

Bunny eyed her dangerously. "I expect that when I'm not, he'd better try."

Aspera was fascinated, in the old sense of horror and compulsion. If other people thought like Bunny, they didn't say so out loud. All the same, the women Aspera knew kept secrets from men they loved.

She heaved a sigh, and an air of truce fell between them. Theirs was after all a kind of recipe exchange, the sole condition of which was that she suspend her loyalties to Dalton. Bunny's notion of survival in relationship meant keeping one's husband in the dark about motives and intentions.

"You have the right to make him unhappy if he doesn't meet your needs?" Aspera asked. "I don't understand that."

Bunny laughed, a dry sound. "Otherwise it isn't fair."

"What do you mean, not fair?"

"He'll be dancing without me in twenty years if I don't watch it. He has all the power."

Aspera pushed a button herself. A computer under yellow glass began a series of binary operations requiring her participation. She hit a random assortment of answers. The machine wrote its responses in sequence.

What was so disturbing was that Bunny was never totally off base. "You can justify anything," Aspera finally said, "if you assign the other person more power than you've got."

"He uses me," Bunny hissed. "He depends on me for comfort and shelter, and by God there's a price. That kind of comfort can be withheld."

Aspera fiddled with knobs. "I thought that kind of comfort was a given."

"Not in my book. How long have you been married to Will?"

"Twenty years next autumn. God."

"Twenty years, and you haven't figured out that comfort is

a bargaining tool? Read the newspapers! This culture kills women. You'd see it maybe if your mother had married again like mine did. I'm no special case; I know the statistics on sexual abuse by now. My stepfather didn't let us starve or get rained on, but don't try and tell me there's no price tag. Marriage is a contract." Bunny made the word flat, final. "The question is, how do you live with a privileged person without being continually ripped off? And the answer is, you do it first. If you love him, if you want the marriage, you get leverage and you keep it."

"You do this for love?"

"You want to love him from a stool on the sidelines?" Bunny snapped. "I'm there for Dalton *all the time.* If all else fails I want him to know *he owes me.*"

The notion drew Aspera like a tractor beam. Maybe this alone was revolutionary: to keep track of the bargains you struck. Bunny would never have got caught in Hancock's Best. Self-defense was needed for the married state, dagger at the waist.

She tried to think Bunny's way. "What if Dalton figures it all out someday and—"

Bunny cast her eyes to the ceiling. "Dalton. Oh, he complains. He even threatens sometimes. But I don't see him following up with action." The gray eyes strayed down to meet Aspera's. "So I don't pay any attention to what he *says.*"

The screen flashed yellow beside Aspera's hand. A message repeated: Response required.

"Besides," Bunny smiled, "I know exactly where my power lies with Dalton, or any other man. I know how much I have and approximately how long it's going to last. Marriage is the only extra leverage I've got, and I don't waste it."

Aspera tried to meet her eyes, but Bunny closed hers while she lifted her long hair off her neck, freeing it from her coat collar with a sweeping motion.

"I don't understand that," Aspera said.

"I know."

At last she blurted, "Are men that stupid?"

Aspera herself felt stupid. She knew by now how the affinities worked in this group: Bunny and Will were alike, and she and Dalton. Bunny and Will believed in preventive action; she and Dalton—just complained?

"The world is regulated by sex, my dear. It ought to be in

the encyclopedia, right after gravity. Since it isn't, take my word for it."

When Dalton and Will came swinging round the corner, they stopped short in front of their wives and saluted.

"Reporting for duty *sir!*" Will said.

They all watched Bunny, who stood still and looked up at Dalton reproachfully, all eyes. She clasped her hands like a girl and said in her small voice, "Where were you?"

The projection of vulnerability was staggering.

Dalton turned sheepish, tried reassurance. "We were in the neighborhood—"

"I missed you," Bunny said, tucking her chin.

"We missed you too," Will said. "We had a good time. Now let's go stand in line." He wheeled about.

But on Dalton's face tenderness amplified to radiance. As the four of them walked toward the stairs he put an arm around Bunny and hugged her to his side. Bunny smiled fleetingly up at him, then slipped free of his arm and righted herself.

The message was so explicit that even Aspera could have explained it to him: his proper place was beside his wife, forgiveness was to be earned.

Dalton didn't need anything explained. His mouth shifted to neutral. His eyebrows rose to examine the future for opportunities.

Bunny caught Aspera's eye for the merest fraction of a second, to see the lesson home.

Catechism: Displays of dependency can be alternated with demands. You can surely catch more flies with honey, but it works better if they've had a taste of the swatter first.

The omnitheater screen was a section of the roof dome that curved above their heads. Blue and purple upholstered seats gave back so that the audience could lean and gaze up and around the projection that would become their total environment. Aspera and Will had watched a film in this theater several years ago, an astonishing siege of cloud formations and whirling thunderstorms; today the scheduled film was a documentary on the eruptions of Mount Saint Helens in Washington State. Aspera did not wholly look forward to this. She respected the scarifying power of illusion: the next best thing to being there.

She reached for Will's hand on the cushioned armrest.

"I'm hot," he said, pulling free.

The theater was bathed in dim blue-violet light before show time. She gazed up and tried to lose herself in the surround of almost-convincing evening sky—almost, because under steady scrutiny, the seams of concrete-block construction showed their pattern of oblongs.

"I'm thirsty." Bunny's voice, in complaint.

Dalton craned his neck about to look for a fountain.

Aspera sighed. Dalton was a chump, and so, inevitably, was she. But Dena said women changed; something built into the mechanism. At thirty-five, however, Aspera's only mechanism had been vicarious. She and Will had been setting up an office in the store. She was upstairs at the old counter, the wooden stairs just behind her, Will below in the cellar they'd outfitted with government surplus. Style would have to wait. On all these things her memory was clear: gray government cubicle, gray metal desk, hand-cranked adding machine. At the counter where she stood, buzz of sound, telephone light blinking, Dena's voice, back from winter vacation.

"How about going out to dinner tonight?"

"You're not tired?"

"Listen, Charles has been alone for four days and he is ready. And I certainly can't sit still"—even in memory Aspera couldn't get over the elation that came purling into her ear—"I feel *wonderful*!"

Even Dena's laugh carried a strained note. Aspera listened hard; also she tuned some other part of her mind for the clatter of Will's adding machine.

"Dena, what is it?"

"I don't know if I can tell you over the telephone. Well, I suppose I'm going to have to. Listen: I met a *wonderful man* on the airplane."

"Oh, no."

"Oh, *nice.* That's a long connecting flight, Oklahoma City to Denver to Minneapolis. This man seemed to know about everything—fashion, interest rates, *est,* raising teenagers. I absolutely fell in love, and I'm never going to see him again! I don't even know his name! What a turn-on! We really had"—she sighed, a languorous one—"a lovely time."

Aspera was charmed and relieved. "Let's see. You're turned on, you don't know his name, you're never going to see him again," she teased. "That's lovely?"

"Well—we did what we could."

"You what?"

"After about an hour we got a blanket down. You can do a lot on a night flight under a blanket."

Aspera's mouth opened, but no words arrived. Dena's silence represented something else, a kind of purring or the slotted beacon of a Cheshire smile.

"Are you telling me you"—Aspera could not drag the incriminating phrase out. She protected the mouthpiece with her hand. When Dena giggled, Aspera drew a breath. "Well, how do you feel?"

"I feel wonderful!" The same floating wallow to the tone.

"You don't feel guilty at all?" Aspera still whispered, though from down the stairs Will's adding machine chittered out curtains of occluding noise.

"Guilty?" Dena fairly shrieked the word, changing the whole character of the conversation, changing with it Aspera's grasp of the predictable universe. The heavens had cranked open by mistake and let through a shaft of rainbow-spangled light. Where Aspera crouched over the phone, the store's trial attempt at carrying weather gear for outdoor laborers—orange and yellow rubberized rain jackets and pants hung in racks by size and sex—grew brilliant around her as Dena screeched in mock outrage: "How can I feel guilty about a forty-five-minute orgasm?"

Above her head the volcanic action was disappointing. Only vestiges of the Mount Saint Helens eruptions had been caught live on film; the rest was a montage of still shots explored with a moving camera. Simulation, and not in the least scarifying. Aspera regretted building up the experience to Bunny and Dalton. The scale was impressive, of course; the mountain's ash-drifted inclines studded with Douglas fir, smoking skies spread in color and black and white over the concrete dome of the theater. But scale alone couldn't redeem the show, so plainly static, so lacking in the sweeping effects of engulfment she'd remembered.

* * *

They sat at dinner high above the Mississippi. In their view from the slowly revolving restaurant, the tones of sunset made urban Minneapolis a more spectacular presentation than anything they'd seen in the omnitheater.

"Stop apologizing, Aspera!" Dalton told her, not for the first time. "We enjoyed it."

"Aspera knows what's not worth enjoying," Will said. "Probably your taste was impaired all those years out in California drinking recycled urine from the Colorado River."

"Will!" Bunny objected, dimples showing.

"You people had to say your prayers every night that the population of Denver would keep pace."

Dalton winked at Aspera. "Aren't you glad you didn't have children?" he asked her. "They could have been like him."

"We'd just send them away," Will said. "It worked for you, right?"

Dalton glanced at Bunny.

"Speaking of children," Bunny said, "how old was that cute little guy with your friend Vicky last weekend?"

"Cute?" Will asked. "I can see little, but cute? Twin dachshunds are little and cute."

Again Aspera had the sense of the conversation moving too fast.

"Kevin's twenty-six," she said.

"Baby Kevin, we call him," Will confided.

Aspera shot him a look.

Bunny laughed. "Think he's looking for a mother?"

"Kinky," Will leered. "I've heard they do that in California. We never see it here."

"Well, to me it seems—" here Bunny gave a wriggle of her shoulders—"incestuous, I guess."

Aspera took in all that had been communicated in that liquid gesture—discomfort, recoil, mammary intrusion. She glanced at Dalton, but he remained silent, cutting his square of Port Salut into uniform cubes.

"That's unkind and unfair." Aspera spoke to her plate.

"OK, let's be fair," Will said, waving his fork. He tipped the last of the wine into Bunny's glass, brandished the empty bottle at Dalton and grinned. "Vicky and Baby Kevin *must* have more in common than age difference."

Bunny burst out laughing.

"I'm thinking about incest taboos," Dalton said quietly. "In and of itself incest cannot be considered morally wrong. If the parties are consenting adults, if coercion is not a factor, if there's no question of offspring—" He shrugged. He took a cheese cube into his mouth and added a green grape.

"Laws deal with probabilities of abuse," Bunny came back, her eyes narrowed. "With incest the odds are incredibly bad. That's one of your ivory-tower arguments."

"Taboos can be largely functional, historically necessary," Dalton replied evenly. "You might say the same of certain customs, like marriage."

Will drank from his glass. Bunny's face was tense. Dalton ran the last crumbs around his plate with his fork. "Hume observed that custom is the great guide of life," he said. He glanced at Aspera, added, "But it can also become the enemy of vitality. Civilization is said to advance through the defeat of inadequate custom by insight."

Aspera leaned forward, trying to bring Dalton's words closer. He seemed to be offering something just outside her reach. "The defeat of inadequate custom . . ." she repeated.

"By insight."

Bunny put down her fork. "What he neglects to add," she said, "is that major advances in civilization wreck the societies where they happen."

"Historically, yes."

With her little-girl voice Bunny effected a transition. "I was trying to drum up a little gossip about Vicky and her boyfriend." She dimpled and spoke with her chin pushed in softly against the skin of her neck. She leaned toward Will. "Men never take the right things seriously."

Will cleared his throat. "Well, it's hard to take little cute guys seriously. We never did, even as college men, did we, Dalt?"

Dalton raised his eyebrows, considered. "We favored tall men, presidential material, generally."

"Let's order champagne and celebrate the fraternity service pledge!" Will pounded his fist on the table.

"Hurrah!" Bunny cheered. "What was your service pledge?"

Will burst out laughing, and after a moment Dalton broke

into an embarrassed grin. "I think you don't want to hear it," he said.

"I want to hear it," Bunny pouted. "You people and your college secrets make me feel left out."

Will glanced at the ceiling. "My recollection is, it went—" here he cupped his hands round his mouth for a megaphone "*—fuck, suck, gobble-nibble-chew! fuck, suck, gobble-nibble-chew!*"

He colored as Bunny ducked her head, covered her face.

Aspera looked at him, and he shrugged. Well. Wasn't this what she used to love him for? Being funny meant you risked making connections nobody else was willing to make. People would put up with a good deal for the sake of one good connection. Fuck suck gobblenibblechew.

After a moment Bunny peered out of her hands.

"Repeated like a mantra through four years of college," Aspera told her. "And you're worried about Kevin?"

"Now, now," Will warned. "These are fraternal secrets we touch upon."

Below them the city of Minneapolis glimmered along its strings of lights just coming on in the dusk. Aspera looked out from the high glass walls through stories of air and smoke colored by sunset, down to the river made unclean by civilization but which showed a brazen face, smooth and crimson.

Fuck suck gobblenibblechew.

"Thank God for rock music," Bunny said, her voice precipitating its hard crystals once again. "At least you can dance while you're being brainwashed."

Aspera flooded with kinship. Maybe they were on the same dance floor after all.

"Never mind brainwashing," Will said, "you outlive us."

Aspera tried to think of something, to add her voice to Bunny's.

That voice now came back soft as a girl's. "If you fellows can just hold out long enough, when you get to the nursing home the ratio will be twenty-five to one. You can hobble around with four sprightly old ladies supporting each limb. In the dining room you can sit and drool into your plates, and two dozen more will stand around for their turn to croon and wipe your chin."

"I can hardly wait," Will said. "Think I'll go home and start practicing my drooling and slobbering."

Aspera watched him resist Bunny's shaming. Connections rerouted, consequence derailed. But the connections these days were such a force-fit; was Will in his way as desperate as she?

"Maybe I'll merchandise a whole new line for old men," he went on. "Fruit of the Loom bibs and wipes. Exploding pacifiers."

At this they finally laughed a little.

"Ah, Will," Dalton sighed. "The Midas touch."

A spasm of unease shot down Aspera's arms and thighs at the renewal of laughter.

She crossed her legs and bumped a knee under the table; Dalton looked sharply around and with both hands lifted the white linen cloth to see what the problem was.

"My fault," Aspera told him.

But he did not meet her eyes, smiling instead at the tablecloth which he again let fall. He shifted his knees well out of range.

It was this awkwardness, which seemed almost a kind of tenderness, that made her think: good old Dalt. One man who never wished to be the cause of anything. His nature was to accommodate, and he had a knack of slipping into significance and then as easily free. In college he'd been available to shelter Will and Aspera, freshmen in love, because his old roommate had graduated early, his girl friend was studying abroad. Distance and separation seemed natural, since with Dalton each relationship was entertained with kindness, none seized. This temperament made it so easy to count on him, as they had in the years after college in South Minneapolis, when Will and she often had less margin to spare one another than Dalton did. Will, Aspera, Dalton: again a threesome. In threes the dividend could be awkward, and for some of those years Aspera believed Dalton loved her. As quickly, she also disbelieved, time and again. But what was his kindness if not love? And where were divisions made?

She saw a pattern to it, the way a strong energy between two people could pull in a third, a loosely configured single. She thought of herself trying to balance Chester and Elvira, Dalton doing the same for Will and herself. Two atoms may combine incompletely. This unstable molecule will angle for a little something from the nearest neighbor or passerby.

Physics had laid out nomenclature. Balance was always zero—no stigma attached to how a completing particle was acquired. But human affairs used a loaded geometry. Triangle, people said, plane and solid. Three people might sit at a dinner table presided over in peace, pure zero, all surely in order although not the order most apparent. Rivers of current might whirl under the tabletop, and above the surface invisible bands might connect heart to heart while faces and hands moved at their narrow business.

Dalton came for dinner. Available at a moment's notice, available for the meagerest sharing: come on over, Dalt, help us clean out the refrigerator. We have about eighty kinds of leftovers, all in good standing to this point, nothing risky. Come and we'll pretend it's a mandarin dinner, *riistaftel,* the merest taste of this or that. And that and that and that.

Equitable and fair: Dalt would come. He began to grow sleek at her table, losing first chin line and neck line; she remembered those first dress collars he would twist open for his comfort. When he rose she saw that the lines of his waist had smoothed outward. Dalton was given to formality; he wore white tab collars, and a lick of his fine blond hair was flipped back and held with a dressing. The shaggy flowing look of boys' hair was in those years spreading up the ranks into business; men of fifty wore their hair for Christopher Robin. His earnest unstylishness made Dalton seem the more delicate, and Aspera's heart swam toward the increasing moon of his face.

"What are you doing, trying for extinction?" Will demanded one night when Dalt was forking himself another helping of salad. "Don't historians know what happened to the giant herbivores?"

Dalton laughed, appeared unruffled. Aspera was the one who minded. She minded for Will, whose jealousy robbed him of essential grace. She minded for Dalton, who seemed to need someone's protection. Feeling things for two men who owned no such feelings did her no good at all.

Dalton would bring a girl to dinner when one happened past his life, but most often he came alone. He allowed himself to be drawn where he was needed, joking with Will, going out for a beer with him, ragging him while Will polished and polished and polished their old car behind the apartments. And when Aspera wanted somebody to listen to her, Dalt would be found perching on a kitchen stool with a beer in his hand, grinning and serious by turns. That was the way it occurred, the shift in the gravitational pattern; perhaps it was that Aspera needed Dalton in the kitchen more than Will needed him in the garage, and Dalton became hers. Not on the surface, never on the surface, just Dalton dropping in during the afternoon, Aspera depending on him to hear out her kitchen tales. Telling of the years in the basement, Elvira's eloquence on the evil that was Bracken's nuclear plant. Leakage, Elvira said; leukemia in central Minnesota, birth defects, altered weather under that billowing stack, a suspiciously extended growing season.

"She was right about localized climate," Dalton said. "I read somewhere, vapor exhaust trapped by the atmosphere."

"She wasn't crazy," Aspera said. "Though I thought so at the time. It was her arteries, her chemistry, a kind of premature senility—" She took a breath, lifted her eyebrows. "The chimney stack is a transforming station!" she parroted. Then began a run-on speech modeled after Elvira's. "Spell-walls expend energy and must be renewed, this affects the names and natures of things surrounding the transformed thing." Aspera let her brain spin free into memory, narrowed her eyes as the feeling of speaking from Elvira's face grew more real. "You ask, but the things they tell you go round and round they are so earnest, they insist on telling you their talking and so you find out the talking part keeps you busy while they do magic to make you forget to pay attention. This is how you tell: The less sense the talking makes the more they spend energy to do magic and less and less to offer you talking that fits, an insult. Don't listen, but watch how the weather changes, see what I'm saying?"

Dalton laughed with a shake of his head.

Telling him of sleeping in the basement under the piles of crazy quilts Elvira collected, the velvet, silk embroidery, all that weight. Telling of summer nights lying in bed with the kitchen light burning, the soft slap of cards on the table.

"She died when I was twenty-one. Maybe that was best, we didn't get to the blaming that women do with their mothers later on," Aspera said lightly. "I have no one to pin anything on."

"What about your father?" Dalton asked. "Tell me about him."

She sighed. "I'll tell you my favorite memory. When he first left and was driving truck all over the Southeast, he came back a couple of times. I was never so glad to see anybody in my life. Little kids—I think parents can't know how hugely they count in kids' lives, or they'd be too scared to have them. I used to dream about Chester every night, that first year he was gone. Each time he came home he had a bag of my favorite candies in his pockets for me. Butterscotch kisses. That meant so much—"

Smiling, but a band of pain curling over the bone from temple to temple. Stopping in the middle of that smile to sob and grab at a drying towel for her face, getting instead Dalton's quick soft shoulder, kisses on her face and eyes and mouth. Afternoon sun poured in the windows, and they stood shocked at the current jumping between them. Each stared into frightened eyes, arms locked into the position that said: this far and no farther.

When Dalton turned and left he did not ever come again in the afternoon, she did not so easily phone him for the casual dinners, and from then on when she saw him it was principally from the kitchen window where he stood outside in the sun with Will, pointing out gravel nicks in the chrome. Or with dates he punctiliously brought when they got together for the movies.

Bunny was one of those dates, merely one of them; a fix-up from Will's office. But it was Bunny who from the start approached Aspera in the kitchen to ask of her, as one does of an ally, an old friend of the family, "How should I act? He's so sweet and then so distant—I can't figure him out. Is there some reason he doesn't want to get married?"

Bunny worried that neither in Dalton's approaches nor his reserves was he wholly hers. She set about keeping herself at the point where the two intersected, which cost her in vigilance. It was a price she faithfully paid.

The questions in the kitchen went on short of half a year. Then she surprised Aspera by stating, "Anyone who really set her mind on it could get him. I think it should be me." Aspera pitied Bunny her labors. As though tricks could ever satisfy! But soon Bunny was pregnant.

Will heard the news at the office. His information had come directly from Bunny. He called Aspera at the high school, and at lunch she listened to his tense voice over the phone in the teacher's lounge. "I don't know why she told me," he whispered, "but I feel like part of a conspiracy."

After school, Aspera took a bus to the University of Minnesota. She stopped at the history department and was directed. The spring winds blew hard across the university campus, so much statelier than Mankato had been, so many more bodies bustling along the brick walkways. This was a larger world Dalton inhabited. Inside a broad granite building with heavy arches she found the class he taught that afternoon. Early Roman history.

She stood before the oak door facing which had been varnished brown but now peeled in patches like a sycamore. A slip of paper was tacked to the wood, and the day's date had been penciled in Dalton's precise hand. The printed message below specified that two soft-lead pencils might be brought into the examination room. Aspera intended to retreat and comb her hair in the ladies' room she had passed, but as she turned, the classroom door rattled and was pulled open from the inside, releasing a straggled series of freshly examined students, pale with effort.

"Aspera!" Dalton came through the door, holding it open as a last student passed through. Dalton's eyes were wide, inquiring.

"I was in the neighborhood," she lied.

"You should have come last week, you could have straightened me out on Roman religion."

"My dad liked the Romans," she said, relieved to find a topic so readily. "He once beat my mother in a high school Latin contest. Maybe that's why Elvira held for the Greeks. I used to get two versions of everything as a kid. Did I tell you that?"

He shook his head, directing her down a hall that was packed with students on the move.

"You had to remember Persephone if my mother was doing the telling, Proserpine if it was my father."

How early she'd accepted the idea that heroes performed deeds under more than one name, learned that one parent's truth was the other's apostasy, learned that variation was a fact of life and still a secret she must strive to keep.

"I never got it straight until college. Before that I thought I might have dreamed that stuff." Which was entirely possible: Chester's voice or Elvira's, droning into her childish sleep, voice-over from the bedtime stories. "I used to dream about heroes with two heads, and so on."

"What were you doing in the neighborhood?"

Aspera colored. "Seeing about becoming a librarian." She fetched up corroboration, a shred of truth to dress the lie: "I sent off a graduate application the other day."

Dalton turned to appraise her. "Now why wasn't that the first thing you said when you got here?"

She looked down the hall. She had come to save him? "Because I'm a lot like you." She turned to him. "And since when do you lay all your cards on the table?"

He juggled laughter inside his throat. "Did I ever tell you that my family used to play bridge?"

Like myth-of-the-month, family stories had become their medium of exchange. How hungry she was to hear a story.

"My father always used to say to me"—Dalton deepened his voice—"the point of the game is to get to know your opponent."

"Did it work?"

"I don't know. I'd start getting to know my opponent and forget the bidding sequence. Then my father would say"—the change in Dalton's voice came sudden and intense—"*There're only fifty-two cards in the deck, how can you make a mistake?*"

Aspera felt a sudden wave of fright, giddiness.

Dalton made a barricade of his body against the flow of students as she bent to drink water from a fountain. "To this day if I play bridge I feel like my hand is full of more cards than I can hang on to."

Aspera looked up, wiped her mouth.

"If I appear to have them up my sleeve," he said, "it's because I've already stuffed some in my back pocket, in the top of my socks. Is it possible the cards multiply in my hands? How's that for a Midas touch?"

Nervously she parried. "With talent like that," she said, "you should specialize in things people want more of. Oil wells. Fertility clinics."

They both flinched.

"I'm sorry," she whispered. She braved the look he gave her.

In those days when Dalton looked at her, a soft glow rose within his brown hawk's eyes. Once she'd noticed it, or noticed she'd imagined it, she kept wanting one more proof. Just now the warm light seemed to burn up through his eyes all the way from the heel bones.

"If I touch you," he said quietly, "will there be even one more of you? There's a need. One for Will, one for me. You think? What would happen if I touched you?"

They stood in the hall, students veering round them to the left and right, heading upstream, heading down, bodies brushing in passing, the muffled sorrys calibrated just below the level where sources could be distinguished. Aspera and Dalton stood out like siren rocks in the sea of bodies. Each saw the other's eyes go glassy with regret. He laid a single cool finger on the skin of her neck. Gooseflesh rose.

One of her, after all.

Seventeen years later Aspera could rarely locate in Dalton the tender friend she had known. The years insulated him. Tonight that brief glimpse, what was it? Custom versus insight! Do people change?

Such a good archaeologist she was, poking among the ruins, trying to restore from fragments all that had been lost. Men didn't do this; they dropped socks. Territory mattered, not history. Dalton himself told her once, break the conventions of territory and you break male loyalty. Well, how little these things had to do with tenderness. Dalton had loved her, she had loved Will, Will had loved her—past tense, all of it? Elvira, Chester—was a *d* forever lurking in the vicinity of *love*? With Will she had hoped love was the horizon, was what sustained. What would become of them now, living without an earnest love?

Love with a *d.* A bounded territory that Bunny knew up and down. And something Aspera had forgotten since second grade: you could get to the end.

Across the table Will was absorbed in the wine list. Could she still touch him, restore the two of them from the wide distance they inhabited? Taking care not to disturb Bunny's feet she sank low in her chair and eased her stockinged foot between table legs over to nudge what she knew would be

Will's knee. She and he used to do things like this, back when touch between them had been simple. She extended her leg as far as she comfortably could reach, then slid her toes in one sweep down his pantleg, stroking shin and instep. She watched for his eyes to come to hers.

Will gave a slight start and in a disguised motion glanced up at Bunny. Then smiling he ducked his head once again into the menu he held in his hands.

The shock Aspera felt—quick liquid dash to the belly—seeing Will's surreptitious glance go to Bunny and not herself: she tried to think it should not matter, but thinking didn't hold up against the scald of feeling. Somewhere between heart and stomach a wall had given way. She would reason it through later; that's what later was for. She folded her hands and listened to the blur of conversation concerning labels, good years for grapes. Asked for her opinion, she gave the one she was trying to hang on to: it doesn't matter.

When the champagne was poured she did not lift a glass, since neither stomach nor hand cooperated. She remembered this old mutiny from the dinner table in the Airstream, in the weeks after Chester had left them.

"We are vessels," Elvira had muttered, draining both their glasses. "We hold elixir and gall."

"Aspera's abstaining," Will remarked as he touched up the other three glasses.

She moved a shoulder, an arm, to dispel the sense of being frozen. "No champagne," she said. Wishing also to dispel the attention focused on her, she brushed crumbs from the table. "It's a long drive home."

Will reached over and with a flourish lifted her glass to her. "To the long drive home," he said, and drank it down.

"We are overdoing it," Dalton cautioned. He set his glass down as though he meant to leave it in just that spot, as an example. "I lecture tomorrow morning at nine myself. Aspera's the only one here using any intelligence."

Dena's words floated forward out of Aspera's mouth. "Intelligence is for avoiding pain."

Dalton looked at her.

"So is champagne," Will countered.

Bunny gave him her pout-smile, and he refilled her glass to brimming.

Dalton began elaborating on his lecture preparations. Like herself, Aspera recognized again, Dalton liked to disappear from where pain was real, slipping straight up into the mind.

To get away using the body would make an incredible scene, yet how easily the mind found an exit. Up and away from the real estate of pain—and who wouldn't wish to be high-minded about love, but love kept coming down, like a government satellite, to real estate. Public property isn't held in esteem, it's somebody else's pop bottle or spent napkin under the picnic table.

Aspera spun her empty glass. Love can be lost. Merely remembering that it once existed is not enough. People remember Dresden before the bombing, but what is there to return to?

Elvira taught her: love is energy. Energy! During last year's energy crisis, Bracken radio stations had urged citizens not to burn porch lights, not to use electrified Christmas displays. Energy-saving tips: line-dry washing in the basement, chop wood. One woman called in. "The electricity is wired into the walls," she shrilled. "If we don't use it, it just goes to waste."

The same generous notion of resource women's magazines drew on: "Put romance back into your marriage." Shrewder literature warned, "Expect him to remain faithful for twenty years, and you're asking to be lied to."

But in Bracken people expected, people asked. With everybody on the same circuit, it mattered which plugs the neighbors were using. Advice came from books and magazines, published in other places: "The successful affair is brief and disposable." "Try a weekend away."

In central Minnesota such romantic notions were aired; they were then taken in again, returned to domesticity like worn feather beds to be dressed with pads and clean fitted sheets. The fourth corner had to be forced, everybody knew that. They also knew the divorce statistics by heart, since one way to dramatize a dull life was to recall how the odds were against it.

White bread chafes again.

Aspera drove slowly so that Dalton and Bunny in the car behind could follow her lead through the intersections to the turnoff.

Will, reluctant passenger, turned the rearview mirror his way to have a look. "See if you can lose him," he challenged.

"Dalton doesn't know the city anymore."

She raised her hand to put the mirror right. She was more than half ready for him, ready for the hand that came to slap down the switch to the headlights, ready for the foot that pressed her own foot down over the accelerator. The Mercury spurted ahead, weaving out of its lane on the empty sidestreet, before she regained control of the car.

"That was suicidal!" she hissed, flicking her eyes from the street to Will's smiling face. She was too frightened to say more.

"Just livening things up," Will said.

He reached over and honked the horn as their car passed over the freeway interchange to head west, while Bunny and Dalton's signaled east. He laid on the horn until they'd made their segment of the cloverleaf and shot straight again.

"Good-bye to the Big D!" he sang. "And good-bye to the big B's!" His hand slid off the wheel.

She was ready too for the silence from the passenger seat as his head lolled asleep. Livening things up. So he felt it too, the deadness. She drove five miles above the speed limit, cruising easily over the empty freeway that lay across miles of farmland. The beginning of the great plains, the land at night entirely overmastered by skies. She had Cassiopeia and Orion for company; from their depth of space they forgave the landscape its plainness. The moon was westerly, tonight an incised crescent against clear midnight blue.

Midnight, indeed; the car clock glowed its unhealthy green. Bunny and Dalton would be home already, switching lights out. Goodnight to the big B's.

If it were energy rather than property she was to be concerned with, what then? How did energy move? It flowed from pole to dipole, moving from one place to another the way anything moves, as a function of difference.

Sameness, stability, the known: these were arguments for marriage. Two people wear down, weary of finding nothing surprising. Contact points corroded with matter, no juice flowed.

For relief they could turn, not to a god or to some universal energy, but to another person—some other mortal translation who had at least a few different chinks in the occluding armor.

Seeing the light come through in patterns not expected, they discovered desire. Teach me how to move that piece. Let me near, let me see how you let the light through in that place, I want to shine like you. We will generate new light and heat, a fibrillation of surprise: let us begin between us a flow of particles.

He laces his fingers underneath his head, leans on them. "Tell me a story. Myth of the month."

Her intake of breath is ragged. She lets her thoughts range. "Prometheus was a god, ashamed of how gods kept fire to themselves while mortals grubbed about in the cold dark. He brought down to earth the gift of fire, quite a gift."

"Risky?"

"Zeus had him chained to a rock and then sent eagles to devour his liver. Every night it grew back. Since the liver regenerates itself, the Greeks saw it as the seat of desire. So. Prometheus' liver grew back every night, and every day the eagles returned."

"What a mean story."

"He challenged the law for good cause, and he's honored for that. Eve should be, too, but that's another book of stories." With him her laugh is a warmth that begins low, then rises of its own lightness. "It's the same theme, you're in paradise and you blow it just once."

She worries suddenly that she is chattering away, taking their precious time. "I'm talking your ear off. Sorry."

He gets up on an elbow. "You have anybody else to tell stories to?"

She presses the backs of her hands to her own temples, once, twice. "Not anymore."

"I want you to tell me your favorite story. From when you were a kid."

The bubbling warmth again, beginning, rising. "There were so many."

"Come on." He shifts his position until he is sitting up against the headboard. He reaches for her head with both hands, places his fingers where her hands have been and presses gently.

She leans against his chest and sinks into the pressure spotted round her skull. A memory blooms: a pitcher of milk, two tall trees.

He keeps his hands in place. "Tell me. I want to know everything."

"Once upon a time," she begins, smiling under the warmth radiating from his hands, "an old man and an old woman lived beside a road. On the day they married, many years before, they'd planted two trees where the path to their door met the road. An elm tree for her, an oak

tree for him. So many years had passed that the trees shaded their hut from the afternoon sun, and when the old couple sat down to their supper of milk and bread they gave thanks for the trees that sheltered them." She looks at him, embarrassed.

"Go on," he says.

She takes a breath. "After their work was done every day, the old couple carried water from their well for the trees. One day a stranger stood underneath them—I can't remember this part—but he was traveling the road and they were kind to him. They were poor and had nothing to offer except what they had on the table, a pitcher of milk from their bony cow and a loaf of bread the old woman had baked, from the rye field the old man sweated in. But they shared their meal with him. Then it turned out the stranger had special powers; he was a wizard or maybe an angel."

"Ah, the stranger with special powers," he whispers into her ear.

"He asked what wish he could grant them, and they looked at one another a long time because they wanted nothing. Then finally they thought of something important. The one thing they worried about was how someday one of them would die, and the other would have the pain of being alone. So what would be a great solace to them both, they said, was if they could be spared that. If they could know they'd die together." She halts.

He lets his hands slip from her head and massages the cords of her neck, her shoulders where they have gone rigid. Then he draws her down so that her head rests against his chest. "Is that all?" he asks. "Your muscles are like fists."

"I didn't remember what a sad story it was." She draws a breath. "This stranger. He was moved. He promised to grant their wish along with another gift: the pitcher of milk on their table would never be empty." She swallows, rubs her eyes. "And so the pitcher was miraculously never empty, even after the cow died, and one day it did happen that the old couple themselves died and were buried by their neighbors on the same day. Long after their hovel had fallen to ruin, the two trees stood beside the road offering their shade, reminding travelers of the old couple's kindness, and of their steadfast love."

He slips a hand beneath her chin and turns her face up toward his, smoothing her cheeks with his hand. "Why does this story make you cry?"

She cannot answer. Then after a while she knows. "There's a birch clump in front of my house."

He waits.

"It's been diseased for years, between black ants and windstorms—every year I think it's going to go, but somehow—there are two trunks left of the four. One is caulked with tree cement at the base, and farther up there's a length of chain—I don't know how long it's been there, but long enough so the bark has wrinkled around where the chain was stuck in each trunk."

"What does the chain do?"

"It's stretched between the two, I guess against the wind, so one helps stabilize the other."

"So when they go, they go together?"

Suddenly racked with sobbing, she clings to him, and he holds her.

Aspera got the car safely into the garage, the two of them to bed. Will lay heavily beside her, earth-apparent mass plummeting toward sleep.

"We are getting worse," she whispered. She spoke to the ceiling, her voice sounded scared. She meant his drinking, she meant the way they turned hard surfaces toward one another. She was not expecting an answer.

"Worse than suicidal?" Will mumbled. "Nope."

Surprised, she put her fingers to the inner corners of her eyes, squeezed. "Yep."

He yawned, turned his back. "Suicide's top of the line, 'less you like homicide."

"Nope."

"Yep or nope? Make up your mind."

She thought about it a long moment. "You want me to make up my mind?"

But he was asleep.

Outside the bedroom window the tops of the birches glowed yellow and pale. This would be the reflection of the floodlights she had failed to turn off. The switch was downstairs; too far. Too late.

Taken by starlight, by moonlight, objects had a chance of retaining some private dimension. By daylight they were blasted from the realm of magic, strong light of any kind could render them pitiable. Exact. By moonlight, by starlight, possibility thrived. But not, she decided, by any other. The house she lived in was full of electricity; the very trees burned all night.

CHAPTER EIGHT

Mondays in the store had the character of crowd scenes in movies. "Pull some streamers down over that display," Will told one of the clerks, "and throw some confetti around. Make this look like a party." He was convinced the store needed to look new each week, and merchandising studies backed him up. Customers like to feel there's a point in returning to a place they've been before, so give them something worth their attention. All morning Will had moved rapidly through the store, setting the tone and pace. The week's resumption of business tasks—inventory, sales items counted, stock rearranged, vending machines emptied and coins counted, special display trolleys placed.

All the downtown stores stayed open till nine Monday and Friday nights. Monday night turned out to be prime time at Hancock's Best—people trafficking through all three departments, lumber, hardware and interiors, with this amazing grim intent to buy. He figured they brought in dissatisfactions stacked up from over the weekend and tried to make them good on merchandise. OK by him. Mondays were worth extra effort.

This particular Monday was also Moonlight Madness. Will looked forward to that, actually. Remembered it from when he was a kid, the one time a year when all the stores stayed open late at night—what a thrill, the lights, he and his buddies loose from their parents with pocket money. Now he saw the other side, saw how a merchant could unload odd bits of stock at a price. No junk brought in just to palm off on people; just the good stuff that hadn't moved. Customers know the difference, or they figure it out. Moonlight Madness Tonite, 8 till 11 P.M. He'd hung the old banner outside the store over the show window, where it had hung every year he could remember. Too bad they didn't have snow this year; the main streets of Bracken could look like something out of Brueghel.

He'd had Bobbie order in special giant sale tags, black with silver lettering. He started down the stairs to the storeroom to make sure they were in. Turning, Will scanned the store over his shoulder; all clerks and no customers. The rush would start later. Turning around again, he almost stumbled and—hell of a steep pitch, these old stairs. And rickety. Christ, he'd fixed everything else, where was his head? Why hadn't he taken care of these? This whole fucking cellar was wasted space—

Some fragment of memory hit him at the base of the stairs: woman nursing an infant. Jesus. His mother, his brother.

Will was used to thinking of Devon, when he thought of him, as a bigger kid, older. He had to be watched all the time, and the last year Devon lived, all those whispered discussions, the state facility at Cambridge. At age nine Will had flown raging out of any room at the very mention—leaving rooms was the only answer he'd hit upon; it got him away from what stayed in those rooms and ground into his insides. In the cellar, his mother giving the baby in the white blanket her breast. She had taken a strip of wallpaper and tacked it to a plywood panel to make it like home. Yellow diamonds. Nothing else came to mind, no other pictures. But one thought stood forward with a finished hardness like a carapace: Because I left them alone this happened. He was three years old when the baby was born, and at three found he couldn't govern his mother's quick comings and goings, her wedged heels clacking on the wooden floor between the store register and the cellar room—hadn't she hurt her arm when he was away helping his father upstairs? He'd come when she screamed and watched as the red streamed down her white arm. He couldn't bear it that his mother was so vulnerable; she was his whole world and so vulnerable. She stanched the blood with a handkerchief, and then, for what seemed forever, wore a strip of white adhesive tape over the site of the wound. Will grew angry with her each time he saw the piece of tape, angry as he felt his stomach go to water. He ducked her hand as it came to pat his hair; he would not leave her alone again, he would stay close to her, close. But then Devon was born, and they told him he must stay away. His father took him into the lumber warehouse and gave him a box of carpenter's pencils to count, a mixed tray of odd-sized nails to sort. He hurried, he hurried, then with the last pencils rattling in the deep pasteboard box, the last few nails rolling in the tray, the crushing in his chest would not stop until he flung the last few into a carton of folding rulers on the work shelf and ran down the stairs to the small room to see what had become of his mother. He pounded down the wooden stairs and breathless came upon her singing to the baby, holding this baby close and fondling the fat cheek. Blood pounded in his ears, he tore away, up the stairs and out the street door. The first time his mother ran after him, he was surprised—tears on her own face, she clutched him to her chest so wildly, picking him up as she ran and his legs dangling in their short pants. Then he grew to know it was something he could command from her, he could run away and she would come after him, her skirts flinging the wind about her ankles. He felt easier after that, decided to go back to those last pencils, those last few nails if his father had not discovered the ones thrown loose into the folding rulers, if his father were not indeed already waiting at the street door for his wife and elder son, the toe of his polished black shoe making its tap tap tap.

By five o'clock Aspera wore two smudged lines of black marker on her cheek and chin. Legs like stumps; she concentrated to stay on top of them. She finished entering her stack of tickets, watched Will come and go with boxes of glassware, with display modules. He was so sure about this, "making the store look new." Thanks to Moonlight Madness, this week would have two Mondays to outfit with newness, one today and one tomorrow.

Aspera stayed behind the boutique counter, out of his way. Change for the sake of change made her feel lost in pointlessness. Why did other people respond to it? How she'd hated it, trying to outguess these people when she had charge of the store; it took up every circuit of her brain, she felt her head was a beehive full of furry winged creatures that crawled and buzzed and made wax and filled and capped its hollows.

The house was such a relief, perfect counterpoint. Everything stayed put; she'd refused to change anything since the second bedroom was wallpapered and she had filled it with her books. All she wanted from the house was a fixed point of reference, she told Will. It was peace she was after. Will said he'd see she was buried in the basement.

"Let's unload those quilted throw pillows," he said now as he passed her. He motioned with his forehead toward the pillow bin while he wrestled a crate of ironstone dinnerware into a corner. He set it at an angle, looked up and called, "No, not on the front table. I want them back close to the register. Use the wagon, and dump those pasta forks into the sale barrel."

Aspera moved to do it. Will's energy increased at the end of the day, whereas she steadily lost clarity, heart, purpose. She stacked the pillows in the Red Flyer wagon, methodically crossing red X's over the manufacturers' labels.

"Aspera Hancock, I presume," said a voice behind her. "Or do I have the Stepford wife?"

She turned, and Vicky stood smiling. Aspera felt she had to blink away fathoms of water to see her clearly.

"If it's Monday, it must be the Stepford wife." She finished the stack of pillows.

Vicky walked around the wagon with a clean tissue in her hands. She handed it over and touched her own face in two places. "Ready for a break?"

Aspera wiped where Vicky had indicated. "Let me check."

Will walked back in carrying a stack of giant sale tags under one arm and knee-bumping a carton of foam toys along the floor.

"I've come to liberate the workers," Vicky called to him.

Will glanced over but didn't pause in the action that sent the carton jolting on its path. "You can have that one," he said, with a nod at Aspera.

"He always this friendly?" Vicky asked.

"No."

"Come on, Will," Vicky teased him, "I want you to show me your cash-register-side manner. Pretend I'm a customer. Be polite."

"Can't do it."

"Maybe you'd be more cheerful if you stopped to have dinner."

"Food is for mortals."

"My," Vicky said. "I hope widowhood isn't catching?"

Will forcibly restrained a smile. "I'm buying a dog to taste my food, just to be on the safe side." He glanced at Aspera. "That's what you can get me for my birthday, dear. I know you've been racking your brain."

"What's that?"

"A dog."

"How about a cat?" Vicky asked.

"Cats are persnickety. They only want you to touch them the way they want to be touched. They're not grateful."

"There's a theory," Vicky said, "that what people say about cats reveals how they feel about women."

"Get me a dog," Will said. "Attack-trained."

Aspera retrieved her purse from beneath the counter. "Want us to bring you a sub from the shop?"

"Nah."

"We could have them staple the bag shut," Vicky offered.

"You keep interrupting this conversation, a conversation of some delicacy between married people who are trying to talk man to man," Will said.

Vicky grinned at him, lifting her chin. "Just because somebody else talks doesn't mean you've been interrupted. How about if we bring a stapled bag and a live dog?"

Will waved them away.

Aspera got into her coat. "I'll be back by six," she called. He did not look around but nodded from where he stood, intently surveying the racks of coated-wire shelving.

"What's he so ornery about?" Vicky said as they strode down the street. They were moving briskly against the chill air.

"Will at work. You know what he's like."

"Like Walter Matthau with a bad script?"

"Right." Aspera laughed. Above the bank building the sky had that feathery gray look; rain or snow, depending.

"Ever notice how every jerk in the movie gets stuck with the job of assuming he's human? The audience loves it. They think they're Matthau."

Aspera sniffed. "In real life you don't get to be."

"I've noticed Will only gets muscley with me when he's pissed at you."

Aspera shook her head. "Best to stand back on Mondays."

Vicky tucked a hand under the elbow of Aspera's coat. "I'm waiting for you to say, that's just Will."

They reached the door of the café. Irene's thick homemade fries, juicy burgers, scooped ice cream malts and deli sandwiches. Soups that changed with the days; Monday was tomato dumpling, loaded with garlic. Aspera pushed at the door, its brass tongue of a latch long since frozen into the open position. Moist cooking odors—soup and hot oil and the active sizzle of onion and hamburg and garlic—rolled forward to meet them in a cloud of welcome.

They found a blue-checkered table away from the door and sat down. Vicky caught Irene's eye and held up two fingers, meaning two bowls of soup. Irene acted as though she hadn't noticed anything.

"I have plans to behave unreasonably," Vicky said, "so I can hear you say, that's just Vicky."

"OK, OK," Aspera said when they'd pushed their coats off on the chairbacks. "I have a story for you."

She told then about the under-the-table adventures with Dalton and Will and Bunny the night before. In the telling, Aspera made use of the blue and white tablecloth to exaggerate Dalton's shock at encountering her knee. She flipped the cloth as a cancan dancer might flip her skirts. Where did energy come from to make light of hurt? Maybe from the other half of the truth, where heaviness is ridiculous. Aspera sank completely under the table to show how she'd reached out for Will, when suddenly her throat closed. She couldn't make the rest sound funny.

When she trailed off, there was Vicky's gaze on her to bear, that singular criticism.

Vicky kept it up a full minute, and then with a quick glance sideward, she brought a hand down flat on the table with a loud smack. "We're all in the wrong places! Will jumps me because he's mad at you, he makes passes at Bunny for the same reason, Bunny flirts with Will to keep you and Dalton off balance, I yell at you when I'm mad at myself, Dena's fucking everybody because she knows *somebody* screwed her—"

"Wait a minute—"

"And now I'm going to Florida to take care of my father

because my mother's dead and can't make it. Now repeat after me: That's just Vicky."

Aspera looked into Vicky's calm round face. Too calm. "Back up and tell me what's going on," she said.

"I've been on the phone all week. My father has to go out of the care facility for sixty days before he can be readmitted and covered under Medicare. I either pay a nurse or go myself. And I thought, here I am with a perfectly portable occupation, I can review curriculum packages on the beach as easily as under a snowdrift. The average temperature in Florida through the winter months is sixty-five degrees, did you know that?"

"Your father's had two strokes."

"He needs a nurse."

"You can't stand him."

"It's the last frontier: see if you can accept the parent who used to beat the shit out of you, who taught you such nice tricks to use on your own kids. I'm doing this for me."

"Doing what?"

"Something hard. Seeing if I'm as solid as I think I am. Look, you haven't known me forever. Fifteen years ago I was a different person; I drank a quart of vodka a day, but I was clever about it, I used to hide it in my steam iron. I lied, I lumped my kids while they were in fucking *diapers,* I stole from my friends' purses; how's that? From their *houses.*"

"I didn't know you then," Aspera said. "I know you now, and you're the most solid person I know."

"Yeah? Let's see if I can keep from going apeshit over a weak old man who can't talk. Who can barely make it to the can on his walker."

Aspera shook her head. "There's so much history there."

"Precisely. This is now."

"Is it?"

Vicky grinned. "Most days."

Aspera found herself staring at Vicky's purse, expecting to see airline tickets stuck into the outside flap. "Florida is full of old people," she said. "The average age is probably the same as the average temperature."

Vicky smirked.

"What about Kevin?"

"You know *he's* in the wrong place. Are you so surprised I know it?"

"I don't know that. And what's this *tone* about? You've been yelling at me since we got here."

Vicky pursed her lips. She tapped the table for four beats and said, "Good question."

Two bowls of soup arrived, the hot liquid streaming over the edge of the thick bowls and onto the soup plates.

Vicky said, "Thanks, Irene."

Irene departed as though no one had spoken.

"Someday I'm going to haul off and give the old girl a big hug," Vicky whispered. "She's like some kind of stray cat that likes to be around people but doesn't want to be petted."

"It's a lot of work, trying not to notice her all the time."

"Like trying not to notice Will when he's hungover?"

"I didn't say—"

"Look, I've been there. He drinks too much, and you pretend not to notice anything."

Irene washed five sugar dispensers, separating glass jars and metal tops, and lined all of them up along the counter to dry. Five overturned wide-mouth jars. Five steel cones, each set on its apex, each hinged flap hanging over the edge of the counter like a tongue.

Aspera returned her gaze to Vicky's face.

Vicky laughed. "What mean little eyes you have."

Aspera bit her lip. "I'm tired." She let her shoulders drop. "OK, I'm listening."

"You think I'm a nut on drunks."

Aspera fidgeted under the steady gaze. "I think Will behaves badly when he drinks. He's also angry because I want out of the store."

"Will can take care of himself!"

Aspera felt a cold anger uncoil. "He hasn't seemed to in the past."

Vicky gave a short laugh. "Yeah. Why should he? He doesn't even have to ask."

"Will would die," Aspera said, giving each word its leaden weight, "before he'd *ask* for anything."

Vicky shrugged.

"Come on, Vick, you know how he is!"

"I know you have some choices." Vicky put her fingers up to tick them off in sequence. "One, you can quit concentrating on his vulnerability instead of your own. Two, you can be more honest, and three you could expect some relief." She sat back and folded her arms. "You know, Will isn't the only one with bad habits. I started figuring this out the other night, and it made the inside of my head look like the hall of mirrors. What we're all doing to one another: caretaking. Also called, in better circles, enabling."

Aspera recognized the AA jargon, rolled her eyes.

"The enabler makes destructive behavior pay off," Vicky recited. "That's you."

Aspera folded her arms. "Always wanted a job with a title."

Vicky looked suddenly lost. "Don't you see how everything repeats and repeats?"

Briefly Irene leaned between them, her yellow starched top riding high over black polyester pants. The material fell slack over her thin rear. She dropped a basket of garlic bread on the table and darted away while Vicky and Aspera stared at one another.

The soup had cooled enough to taste. Tomato broth thick and buttery, dumplings floating, white edges ruffled. "It's odd," Aspera said, giving in, "the things that connect. Last week Dena was talking about addiction."

"Right." Vicky waved her soupspoon. "Very trendy, addiction."

Suddenly Aspera felt heat rise to her face, "What is going on with you?"

Irene brought coffee and with a thump left them the pot.

"OK, I'm mad at Dena," Vicky sighed. "How long have we been giving Dena a shoulder to cry on, and how long has she been blowing her dainty nose on it?" She pointed her spoon at Aspera. "Dena is a world-class enabler, and she may flirt with the trendy words but she will always walk out, or burst into tears if she has to, just at the point she might have to face something. Let me tell you who she is." Vicky bit her lip and looked shrewd. "Ashley Wilkes."

Aspera had to smile.

"Don't you wish Scarlett had married Ashley and then caught him out at the barn making cow-eyes at somebody else—" Vicky rolled her eyes upward, savoring the thought—"*just once?*"

Aspera promptly saw the scene in her head, whistled under her breath. "Ugly."

"Milquetoast tartare!"

Aspera wiped the corners of her mouth and told Vicky about men as toddlers.

Vicky finished chewing and looked around the café. "I've got to hand it to Dena. Everything she says sounds brilliant, if you want to be the only nurse on the ward."

Aspera sat back and folded her arms, surprised to be so near tears.

"Why don't you get a clean fight out of Will?"

"Is that what you did with Kevin Stowe?"

Vicky looked up and met her friend's eyes. "I'm not married to Kevin." She laid her spoon on the rim of her soup plate. "And there's such a thing as working too hard."

"Sounds like marriage to me."

Vicky threw up her hands. "I don't know the answers! I just think if you confronted Will he'd have to stop being Walter Matthau." She leaned forward across the table. "You'd have to quit feeling sorry for yourself, too, and you're not done yet, right?"

Under Vicky's scrutiny Aspera blinked and blinked.

Vicky broke a piece of toast. "The trouble with keeping the lid on is that the stuff comes out sideways." Her shrug was dismissal.

"I don't have the energy," Aspera said. "You know what that feels like, or you wouldn't walk away from Kevin."

Vicky brushed toast crumbs from the table. "Here's what it feels like: I'm on a passenger train, and I thought I knew where I was going. Lately I've sort of come to and looked around, and there's nothing I recognize. No landmarks. I figure I have missed my stop—gone past it two stations already. I'm going to get off, see where the hell I am."

"By yourself."

Vicky rested her fist on her mouth a long moment, let it drop. "Let's say Kevin and I are friends. What can friends do for one another, finally? We can help each other get off at the right stop." She smiled. "I like closure. That's my idea of what grownups do, but—" She tapped her finger on the table, then leaned forward again. "Dena says, if a guy acts like a toddler half the time, why not treat him like one? To my mind that's settling for the wrong half. Treat anybody like a kid who isn't responsible, and they'll run your ass. You must have noticed how Will can summon up his adulthood when it's to his advantage."

Aspera glanced at her watch. Quarter of six.

They left a tip on the table and got up to split the bill at the register.

"That was terrific, Irene," Vicky said as she took her change and zipped up her coat.

Irene turned away, shutting the cash drawer. She pushed through the swinging door to the kitchen.

To the blank door Vicky explained, "You're a great cook and I love coming here, it reminds me of having a mean grandmother." To Aspera she whispered, "Irene's a pushover compared to my dad."

"I should have ordered Will a sandwich." Aspera frowned, hesitating at the counter.

"He said not to."

She scanned the list chalked on the takeout board. "He'll be impossible if I don't bring him something."

"Oh, my." Vicky backed toward the door. "I think this is your stop."

"Wait for me."

"I know it's mine."

When the door swung shut behind Vicky, Aspera clutched her coat together and followed, catching up at the crossing.

Their heels beat hard on the exposed bricks of the main street. They turned the last corner on the way back to the shop and found that the wind had picked up, whipping dirt from the street into their faces. They turned and walked backward for half a block, holding on to their hoods. A recessed doorway offered shelter, and they ducked in. The old tailor shop, the date 1896 pegged out in green hexagonal tiles on the threshhold. All these old buildings along Bracken's main street looked funereal, with their curved symmetrical tops, names and dates incised in blocks of local granite.

Leaning against the chiseled stone facing of the entry, out of breath, Aspera recalled how tired she was, remembered her legs. They again felt artificial. She blew out a cloud of breath and nudged Vicky's elbow. "When you first mentioned Florida tonight I thought you had the tickets in your purse."

"I have the car keys. I leave Thursday."

"This week? Do you have a place already?"

"Not yet. I'm going right away so I can take my time driving, then have a couple of weeks to find a place, see some friends, ease into this. I don't have much lined up. I want to rent a place on the Gulf side, near the nursing home in Sarasota. Cottage on the beach, sixty days, couldn't be too bad. How about looking after my place?"

"Of course." She looked at Vicky's face, lighted by street-lights, and now the red traffic signal at the corner.

"Let Dena know she's welcome to stay there; just tell her not to fuck anybody with the windows open." In a hard tone she added, "And Kevin may get in touch."

"Vick. Are you and he finished?"

For the first time Vicky looked scared. This came as a surprise to Aspera, to think Vicky's executive dispatch with emotion might spring from something besides courage.

"God," Vicky moaned. "There's something about him that makes me feel like I'm drinking again. I get—"she bared her teeth, resisting the words—"so weird and paranoid."

"About what?"

"Everything." She looked at Aspera, looked down at her feet. "The other night, did you think he was coming on to you?"

Aspera felt her shoulders go rigid under the cloth of her coat. "I thought he was sweet." She shook her head. "Maybe I've been married too long."

"Crazy!" Vicky said through her teeth. "I've been running into this too often, *sweet* boys who know too much about women. Used up by their moms." She sighed. "All that know-how and they can't help using it. They're sore, and they can't help that either—you think I'm not making any sense at all." She laughed, and said, "Hell, it must be my turn."

Aspera took Vicky's gloved hand in her own, a twice-muffled grip. "Anything I can do?"

"Tell me I'm not insane."

"You're not insane."

They hugged one another, more muffled contact.

"Maybe it's why I'm so hard on you. Also Dena. *I'm* not facing things."

"Are you sure you want to leave?"

"That's the only thing I'm sure of."

"What about Christmas? Will you be back?"

Vicky rubbed her arms. "If I'm not being arraigned for murder—you know how I feel about caretaking. Don't know if I can turn it off for a real invalid."

"Leaving Thursday!" Aspera complained, already sensing her loss. "Pretty short notice."

"Yeah," Vicky admitted. "I'm hardly used to the idea myself. The Gulf of Mexico? I don't even swim, you know. I'd say come visit me, but I don't believe in double drownings."

Moonlight Madness at the store. She was late getting back, customers everywhere. No eye contact from Will as she passed through hardware. Easy to go wrong here: try to apologize, try to tough it out? Which way meant caretaking?

In the Boutique she glanced around, tried to evaluate the place with Will's eye. What was needed was a fresh display. She gathered up items from sale tables already depleted and arranged them on the counter on a tray. She got the inventory list from the slot beside the cash register, ran her finger down merchandise in overstock and made her choice. A stockboy brought her the box she wanted—framed pictures she'd never liked. She lifted them out of the box one by one and stacked them on a standing chopping block. She put up the large black and silver tags.

A quarter of an hour later Will came in, silent on his rubber soles, and took a pad of order slips from the storage cabinet beneath her register. "You're back," he said with irony. "You love this place, am I right? Couldn't stay away."

She looked at him, feeling several years had passed since the long conversation with Vicky. She felt older, age settling behind her eyes, pulling at the corners of her mouth.

"Me, I can't imagine anything more fulfilling than working in a lumber store," he persisted. "Listen, tonight after the sale we'll do the town, go to the all-night Amoco and stock up on the antifreeze of our choice."

She folded her arms on the counter and leaned on them. He had turned and was standing poised at attention. She followed his gaze. "I thought we'd get rid of those things," she explained.

He walked over to the chopping block that appeared, from a distance, to be stacked with silver bricks.

"You can't stack pictures framed in glass!"

With a sigh she came and stood beside him. She looked down with distaste at the faces of these pictures, at the geometric shapes achieved by hundreds of colored strings wrapped around pegs and held under tension. All straining together, they made crystal or snowflake shapes describing a perfectly empty space, a center defined and not occupied. Just looking at them made her feel sick. She had been glad to stack them so she could see only the metal frame edges showing.

A woman in a blue slippery coat leaned over the counter and asked whether they still had the quilted pillows. Aspera saw to her surprise that the Red Flyer was empty, its tongue laid down where people might trip.

"Sorry," she told the woman. She bent to flip the wagon tongue back over its empty carriage. "We had some earlier this evening."

As the woman left, Will raised his arms and undid the big black and silver sale tag he had hung over the wagon. He creased it in his hands. With his face gathered in restraint, he pointed back toward the register. "What is that big ragtag book you've got out on the counter?"

She flushed red. "It's a book of wallpaper samples." The most incidental information had to be passed between them as though they handled knives! Grasp the blade yourself, extend the handle for the other's safety—all that deliberate effort was exhausting. "When people are in here picking out a sofa," she explained wearily, "they need to see it against some kind of pattern, a background. Nobody lives in a furniture store. They need some sense of surroundings."

He looked at her in consternation. "Why didn't you tell me before? We could tack wallboard on the back of those display shelves. It's been done." Sheet of plywood, yellow diamonds. He grew more agitated. "We could put free-standing partitions up and wallpaper them with anything you chose. But we have to do these things right! How am I supposed to know what you need if you don't tell me?" They had edged their way back to the counter, and now Will picked up the book of samples as though it were covered with slime. He flopped it open on the counter and riffled through the patterns. "How can people tell anything from samples this small?"

As the pages went by Aspera saw the wavery lines of russet and blue, soft blended swirls of cream, rust, coral. She knew exactly why she had allowed the supplier to leave this battered collection: the patterns looked like Italian endpapers, the watermarked kind used in old well-bound books. She ran her finger down a page, following a ripple of azure.

Will looked at her face, saw something there. Some silent pleasure, and he felt a stab of heat to his head: she was doing it deliberately, making this gap between them. How he hated the feeling he got, panic expanding like a balloon between his ribs, that whatever she kept from him might be what would cause her to leave him.

He flipped the cover shut. "This bothers me." With the heel of his hand he gave the thick volume a push. He avoided looking at her face, not wishing to see its closed expression. "It just looks like hell," he said angrily. He turned on his heel and left the room quickly to keep his emotions from catching up.

Aspera watched him walk briskly away. He always panicked at anything out of order; what she hated was the way he tuned her out of existence, refusing to meet her eyes as though she had failed him in some way too terrible to mention.

A woman with a bandaged wrist asked about the pillows they'd advertised.

"I can check to see if we'll be reordering," she told the woman sharply. "Did you have a color in mind?"

The woman backed away, dismayed to be taken for a serious customer. "I'll probably come back sometime," she hedged.

Aspera regretted the way she'd spoken; she'd virtually forced this woman to lie to her, and for nothing! She wanted to call her back, inquire about her injured hand. Then they could talk about politics, about how they had learned to lie in childhood, the first time they figured out that what was true was less important than who knew about it.

"It's a madhouse over in hardware, I haven't stopped ringing all night." An hour later, Will's voice in her ear. "And I'm starving. Got change in your register?"

While she rang the cash drawer and took out rolls of quarters, dimes and pennies for him, he complained, "I never got a chance to eat. I didn't have lunch today either. Lucky if I make it till eleven."

She kept her eyes on the heavyweight tubes of paper she handed him. He was gone as quietly as he had arrived on his feet-saving rubber soles.

The sight of Will's feet moving away from her again—as he pounded them on the hard tile floor without mercy—gave her a terrible sense of his vulnerability, the feeling that exceptions should be made for him. She should have assumed he was human, played the jerk in his movie, brought the sandwich. Poor stomach, poor feet. But—she had offered food. She herself had feet.

Men as toddlers, men as rapists, men as equals.

Aspera bit the insides of her cheeks. She began resorting the bins of small kitchen implements: lemon parers, garlic presses, egg shears with scissorlike handles. Metal teeth extended and retracted around the round opening.

Men are the same beings we are. They have the same feet and stomachs, the same cores, too—sensitive, emotional. But if they carry theirs like purses stashed away and won't dip into capital, won't operate from the core?

She stacked scallop shells for coquilles Saint Jacques, wanting suddenly to be swimming in the Gulf of Mexico. She gathered up meat-probe attachments for microwave ovens, placed them in a heavy earthen jar.

A red-faced woman with windblown hair walked in with a baby strapped to her back. She pivoted with care, then headed for the odds-and-ends shelf. Two jacketed children lagged behind her, an older one perhaps nine who flapped his feet down in useless resistance, a little quick one who turned the row of display blocks into a slalom course.

Aspera judged the displays unbreakable. Placemat sets, oven mitts, folded cotton drying towels. Despite the hazards, she preferred the lively younger children. The sullen adolescents, who'd lost their childish gloss and found nothing better, deserved cocoons until they were more fit. Armor. No wonder mythology was strong on props. Magic swords, helmets to make you invisible, disguises that really worked.

The woman smoothed her hair with one hand and with the other turned each item on the clearance shelf to see its price.

Gift shopping, looking for the right number. Or killing time, something Aspera could understand.

The elder child tugged at his mother's coat sleeve and pointed to a crystal bell with an angel molded on top. Twenty dollars plus. The mother shrugged the hand away from her coat and turned to collar the smaller boy who just then raced by.

"Sammy!" the mother hissed.

Threats, whispered promises. Whimpering. The baby on the woman's back began to cry. The woman bounced on her heels to gain time.

The most dangerous people operate from the core part-time. There's cause to fear the ones who can know your insides and ignore them for their own purposes.

Minutes till closing. Aspera opened the stock cupboard under the counter, neatened its contents. Put it together: a grown-up boy operating from the center only part-time—that is to say, a man—is dangerous.

The closer she got to Bunny's reasoning, the more desolate she felt.

"Don't touch anything, I said." The harried woman removed a set of plastic clothespins from Sammy's fingers. Her patience spent, she gave each ambulatory child a shove in the direction of the door. The nine-year-old sighed, placed one large foot before the other. Dropping behind his mother's line of vision, Sammy raced once more up the stairs and around the small loft Will had built to display dried-flower arrangements. He dropped into line behind his brother and skimmed ten fingers along the glass tabletops beside the door, walling his eyes cagily at Aspera as he traveled. When she smiled at him he turned shy, looked down at his shoelaces.

Best she and Will never had children. Who could abide being hemmed in from both sides by people who outranked you in vulnerability?

All right, no toddlers in the family. No caretaking in any guise. Hadn't Vicky just told her the steps?

Aspera used her fingers as Vicky had. One. Set no one's vulnerabilities above your own. Two. Be honest.

She gave the next customer, a solitary man looking for cheap wineglasses, brisk and efficient service. She pointed out the selection, left him to make his choice.

Three. Expect relief.

He brought her two four-packs of packaged stemware, placed his gloves on the counter and took out a wallet from his jacket pocket. As she worked the corrugated cartons into a carrying bag for him, he stared openly at her breasts.

Four. Take politics into account.

Her shoulders hunched together of their own accord. Her hand accepted the card he handed her, punched appropriate codes into her register.

After Kev died, Vicky had received a rash of obscene phone calls.

One anonymous male voice had bragged, "I've got the biggest dick in four counties."

"Which four?" Vicky had demanded, and heard the phone slammed down.

Disturbances in the power structure are routinely punished with a disconnect.

The customer signed the slips and she separated them, dropped one into the sack before she handed it over to him with a smile. Secrets must be borne in secret, else male anger, male vulnerability come forward.

His eyes swept downward again as he turned to leave. She stared at his back. Set nobody's vulnerabilities above your own.

How rapidly she had gone the whole circle. Her stomach felt tight; the rest of her body reported in tired. She leaned against the register and shut her eyes.

"My God, Aspera, it's five after. We could have been closed up and out by now."

She startled at Will's voice, stacked up receipts, opened the cash drawer.

"Never mind, I'll do it," he said.

"Sorry."

He swept the pieces of paper from her hands. She stood and watched his crisp motions. Rubbed her eyes.

"Vicky's going to Florida," she said. "Temporarily. Leaving in three days. God, I'll miss her."

"Florida," he said, stacking slips. "Life insurance must be great."

She blinked. "Did—"

"Ten more minutes and you can cash mine." He wound rubber bands around two order pads, stretching, twisting, doubling them with automatic speed. The bands sang like Jew's harps.

"Did I say? She's taking care of her father."

"Maybe you could start taking care of things around here," he said. "We could use you through the holidays."

She dropped her hands to her sides and stepped back. "Are you asking me to stay?"

"Two months, is that so bad? Training in new help now—"

"You said you'd hire someone. We talked about this, and you said—"

He kept his eyes on his hands, which expressed choppy motions, packets made, strings on drop envelopes wound and tied and snipped free. "I guess how I feel doesn't matter to you. You're already half gone."

She listened as the meaning settled at its sharp angle. A clean fight was the object. She searched for the proper arena, the locus of pain. "How you feel matters very much. I want to leave the store without causing hardship. I can't make out what you're feeling."

"Try tired." He turned and left her standing at the register.

She jerked the cupboard open and snatched her coat, hurried after him to the door. "You feel something besides tired, and so do I, Will."

He eyed her. He stood next to the main door and kept his hand on the light switch until she got the message—her exit stood entirely unopposed—and stepped out into the night. "Maybe that makes us even," he said.

The fluorescent lights behind diffusion panels flickered their once before going dead out. Stepping outside, Will pushed the door to, then bent and turned his key in both locks. Each of the heavy bolts slid true, with an end-stopped sound like *clock.* Aspera hunched her shoulders. She moved away as Will stepped backward to insert the smaller key into the alarm system.

"We have something to eat at home?" he asked.

"Cold cuts."

"Better than nothing."

The car was cold, would stay cold over the few minutes it took to get over the bridge and home. It didn't make sense to run the heater, and Will didn't. In the passenger seat Aspera looked out the window. Eight yellow-orange lights were mounted on poles high along the bridge rails, so the darkness seemed to expand and contract like some alternate means of propulsion.

Be honest.

How honest? Nobody can afford it unless others will absorb a share of pain, keep on loving.

Be honest. Take politics into account.

CHAPTER NINE

Beside the garage the garbage cans were tumbled, their contents spread about the driveway and alley. Will stopped the car short of the driveway. He yanked the parking brake up, a noise like clock chains pulled taut.

He jumped out of the car, and on her side Aspera got out to help. Toilet-paper cores, beer cans, Kleenex, stacks of torn envelopes, wet garbage in ripped plastic sacks. One yellow bag full of cooked rice; slashed with canine teeth, the mess brought to mind something she'd read in second grade: that in China a delicacy is roast dog, the stomach of which has been stuffed with rice. The rice swells up during cooking, the taut pouch of stomach removed and slit open for presentation.

Will slammed the lids on the cans, kicked them back into line.

Aspera walked through the leaf-strewn yard to the house, wiping her hands on a salvaged napkin. She unlocked the back door as Will pulled the car into the garage with a roar. Percussions of car door, garage door.

Wake the neighbors up, get even. She hung her coat carefully in the back closet, noticing how Will's anger displaced hers, sent it underground. The trembling about her stomach felt more like fear.

He came in the door, pushed it shut against the storm door. Air pressure quaked in the hall. He unbuttoned his coat and she took it from him, hung it beside hers.

He brushed past her. "I'm hungry," he muttered.

In the kitchen she got out liverwurst and rye bread and

cheese, and he opened a beer. He dispatched this cold supper in silence, and she went upstairs.

When he came at last to bed, his face had not changed. He undressed and got in beside her without a glance.

"Are you mad at me," she said when he turned off his light. "Or mad at the dog, or did you just have too much to drink last night?"

"Christ. I was starving."

"You've eaten."

Will sighed. "I'm worried about enough help. *And* I had too much to drink last night, *and* I think the neighbor's dog loves me about like you do."

Her eyes jerked to his.

"And I'm tired of being looked at like that. Can we turn off the other light now?"

She switched off her light. "Looked at like what?"

In the dark Will said, "Like you watch every move I make, just waiting to be disappointed one more time."

She was amazed. "Will, you wouldn't let me hire someone! That's all I'm—"

"Two months is not your whole life."

"You want a second store, Will, you want another five years!"

"Yeah, yeah, I know: you never wanted to move back here, you never wanted the store at all. Well, listen, it happens to be our life now, that's the point."

"It didn't look like *our* life two years ago."

He brought both palms down hard on his thighs, blows muffled by a thermal blanket, his choice, and a quilt, hers. Pane at the Window. In the dark his voice came strangled with fury. "And I'll never live that one down, right? I have finally made something out of that place, you aren't in there slaving in a dingy old lumber office, are you? But you won't give me credit, you want to keep the old picture in front of my eyes, Will the bum."

"I give you credit! I'd like credit, too, I ran the place for three years—what a relief it would be if we just acknowledged that."

"Come on, Aspera, you want me to feel guilty, you want me to feel like a royal fuckup and you want me to be grateful. Well, I don't feel grateful to you. Half the time you were being so noble and trooping off at six-fucking-A.M. I wanted to kill you. What was going on? The place was killing me, and there you were, Florence Nightingale nursing it along. I knew you were going to land me with it sooner or later, I knew I was going to have this sick albatross slung around my neck."

"I thought you needed me to—" Her throat closed around the words. "I thought I was doing it because I loved you. I thought I didn't have a choice."

"Well, you didn't do it for me." His voice had not lost its edge, but he spoke more quietly. "If you ever once would have asked me, I could have told you that. So yes, I finally got off my ass and took over. I made it better, I made it my store, not my parents' two-bit yard, but mine. I did things they never dreamed of, I could have central Minnesota sewed up in two years with a second store, but fuck it, right?" Will closed his mouth hard and took several fast breaths through his nostrils. "I'll tell you what, if you want to do something for me you can go in with me on the second store. That's something I actually could use, how about that?"

Her eyes flicked from side to side as though she'd somehow take sightings in the dark. Nothing new came to her.

"You're not in charge anymore so you won't play. OK. OK! But don't hand me the be-grateful stuff. If you want somebody to blame for you and me being stuck in a lumber store in Bracken, you're looking at her. You did it, and you didn't do it for me. I just picked up the pieces, made it something I could live with."

He turned over, and the waterbed swushed and settled. The room was silent otherwise. He craned his neck back toward her to say, "I just wish you'd told me then that you were going to drop it all in my lap. That information I could have used."

She lay in the darkness his anger had thinned. A slow tingling of nerves crept over her body, but no words came, and the tears that had gathered did not fall but sank back in. As her eyes adjusted to the dark, yellow diamonds in the wallpaper glowed forth. Will's head came clear on the pillow next to hers.

"I didn't know that's how you felt," she whispered.

He might not have heard. "Give me two weeks," he said in the direction of the opposite wall. "I'll hire somebody."

"Will—" She put her hand out to touch the side of his neck below the ear.

He drew the sheet sharply between her fingers and his skin.

They take turns, and now this other man is above her, coring her body with his, repeating patterns. She remembers a movie, messages drawn again and again on the palms of the blind. Something she is supposed to do here, something she is failing at. She arches her back higher and presses at the small of his back.

"Let's rest," she whispers.

He stops, his body bowed slightly into hers for anchorage. He slides his jaw along her neck, kisses the center of her throat. Then his breath labors beside her cheek while thumb and forefinger draw up her nipple.

Mistake? She should be about her business, producing orgasm. She reviews the inventory of fantasies that work, testing for a fit: a baby at her breast, a young boy entrapped by his schoolteacher, that short man on the rush-hour bus in South Minneapolis who'd crushed into her, setting his genitals into hers through her new silk dress.

She tries but the feeling is wrong, she lets them go.

This bed, this man. She returns to him, moves her mind by moving her fingers along the seam of their join, testing the sweat gathered along breasts and stomach, the slide of his skin, the topiary fit of her pubic bone into the dark thatch of hair below which he is thrust into her. She feels her own tissues give to the shape of his, senses the moist interior shift of those tissues as the rippling begins first as a small quaver. Then a steep gain in amplitude, jolt of connection. She arches again, turns. They move together, limbs accommodating limbs like a principle of movement, each receiving the other. She pushes her fingertips into the flesh of his smooth shoulders, digs in with fingernails and says to him as though she needed to and she did need and did say I want you O I want you I do. Words like these get lost in atmosphere on their way toward planets that whirl on anyway but he pauses in his motion, matches her words with his own, I love it when you open your legs for me when you show me you want me.

Tones struck through her body. Heart, lungs, breastbone jangling, same tune round and down and up again, flank, instep, shoulderblades. Then she notices the top of her head, the very cap of her cranium, lift and float away. Images rush in, trains, caverns opening red and burning into black, electric blue. Astonished, afraid to move, she lies still. He fears his body might crush her but no no your weight is perfect perfectper-

fect. At last he moves, rolls over. They hold to one another, clutching at what remains as they lie staring into the black that meant the ceiling of a motel room.

"I love you," he says. The words burst new into a jaded web. She feels breakage, shards falling.

He shakes his head. "I think that's as close as I can come."

They got through the next week in a kind of stupor. Neither mentioned their revelations of grudges, nobody brought up the two-week deadline. Aspera did not see that Will interviewed anyone, and she did not ask. She moved each day from house to store as though the earth had cracked, proved unstable as earthquake movies had always promised. Now it was a question of walking quietly, no shock or footfall that would cause the parts to split wide, crumble into planetary debris.

She avoided speaking to Will, afraid some tissue that held them together would finally tear. The end of love: in her ears a constant alarm rang, so that when Will did speak to her she had to ask him what he had said. It was always something she had left undone, some piece of business to harass her with. His voice was harsh; she tried not to hear the edge it carried. She moved through tasks as though proofs of duty and fidelity could be wrung from the numbness she felt, and numbness was the best of it, better than the sudden stabs of fear. In bed at night when their limbs brushed, he recoiled. She grew steadily colder in the bed a little apart from him, and her feet and hands and thighs actually began to register cold to the touch.

This cooling of her body she remembered from the trailer after Chester had gone for good. That spring she had shivered and her teeth had chattered in uncontrollable spasms, and the quilts Elvira piled on her had not helped. Still she felt more secure, all that weight pinning her down. Since she hadn't felt real or substantial with her father gone, the weight was reassurance that she would not fly up, float away in her sleep.

She had been glad, too, to gather Elvira's old crazy quilt up around her face at night, feel the familiar slink of velvet, rasp of gold thread. The old sensations would see her into sleep, and then there was only the fear of coming awake in the night in the recoil of some evil dream. The ringing in her ears, her very heartbeat struck her awake like the knock on a tomb.

The crazy quilt was long gone, chafed into strands of twisted thread. Aspera lay in bed with a knot of nausea in her stomach, a headache like a photographic plate slid permanently behind her eyes. She was head and stomach, head and stomach. In bed so distant from Will, she steadily lost heat, steadily lost sleep itself. She came into consciousness each day feeling sharply exposed, some protective presence having been stripped from her world.

That was the feeling that had surprised her after Elvira died. Coming off those basement years, Aspera had thought of herself as the protector, and of her mother's death as a burden lifted. She had actually agreed when people said: a blessing. Now she recalled waves and thrusts of feeling that had come on her much later in strange places: riding the rush-hour bus in South Minneapolis, the endless shoving and slipping of limbs in the crowd. Elvira's presence seemed close then, and Aspera had gone with it as she clung to her strap. She was not alone. This reverie allowed her to feel among strangers as pressed and pushed and darkly sustained as she had always felt in Elvira's love, and as much at home.

Now Will floated on the waterbed out of reach, discrete as the Statue of Liberty.

And as it happened, as sleepless.

Walls were what bothered Will. He had been able to focus on nothing but walls since Moonlight Madness. Two years ago, he would have sworn he'd thought of everything. Now it turned out walls were a problem: no room for furniture groupings, no areas large enough to erect partitions, no wall space to display the goddamned wallpaper patterns. What had they done over at Tartarville? Go look that over again. He knew what was needed. It struck him that he'd been on the right track downstairs the night of the sale—that whole cellar! They didn't need the storage, hell, they had the warehouse for storage, he could put dividers upstairs for an office enclosure, glass, all he'd need was a corner, two laminated panes that would carry the Plexi and lucite look like the rest of the store. Nice teak desk and fittings, everything built in. Use the whole cellar for Interiors, break out the walls around those crummy stairs—

those stairs always made him feel sick to his stomach anyway. Two days it would take him. He saw himself taking a sledge, one swing into those walls, satisfying shatter of old plaster.

When he remembered her sleeping curled away from him in the dark, a seizure of anger made his limbs jerk. She could care whatever he did, whatever he felt—he had spilled his guts and then what? Nothing. He felt as though he were bleeding from the inside and she turned away.

At the store he hovered as near to her as he dared. He saw himself as hovering, looking foolish for being forever so near at hand, with nothing whatever to say. He found things, details that needed her attention; each time he discovered these reasons to speak she looked at him with a blank look that pierced his hopes. She forced him to repeat every single word he spoke. He felt humiliated, yet could not seem to stop looking for things to say.

He tossed, determined to stay on his side of the bed. He let his mind play over the new plan for the cellar, he mumbled figures as though they came from a dream. Furniture and drapes—no, hell no, not drapes, what were those canvas things she showed him called, window treatments? Libraries weren't called libraries anymore either. Maybe at the landing he should slot in a couple of long windows, very impressive, on the street side. He'd reinforce the foundation and make a wide graduated-slope entry to the lower level, terraced. He'd seen that done with textured concrete and quarry tile, very classy, neutral taupes and blended grays. Those long windows over the terracing, all that light and space? She'd be knocked out, he knew it would work.

CHAPTER TEN

Sunday morning and she tried not to hear it: dresser drawers shuffled through, runners slid shut again, the pulls whacking wood. Closet door unlatched, wire hangers going *scree scree* along the metal rod. She buried both ears between the pillows, curled her body into a ball.

Not warm enough. They'd started to make love last night, however that had happened. Some accident of finding one another in the dark, a quick scrambling for the last safety they had known, and then losing it first to silence, then uneasiness.

"Are you falling asleep, or what?" he asked. She finally said yes, that's what it was. They disentangled, and she lay beside him half thinking she should get up and put her nightgown back on. But that would make the whole thing so formal a failure.

Dropping into sleep warm and forgetful was the blessing of sex. They hadn't been blessed, and she dreamed of being in the car at night with Will driving when there arose a matter of desperate urgency, she had to get out of the car. She told him. He began to sullenly spread and bloat over the steering wheel, and instead of slowing, the car gained speed. She had to get out; she pushed open the door, leapt, and her body had slammed into the mud of the shoulder, so hard! Breath knocked from her, ragged tin-can cuts of pain shooting up knees and elbows buried in mud, she had raised her head to see the Mercury speeding away.

Waking, she believed this dream. She still felt its hard impact physically. Lying tense on her stomach with her neck muscles straining—she was under the covers naked, alone. *Scree, scree, scree* from the closet. She shivered. That driver was the man she had shared this cold bed with. She curled into a tighter ball, fingers crimped between the lukewarm flesh of her thighs.

Now Will bent over her, lifting the covers. A rush of cool air chased down her face, neck, spine. His hand, warm from the shower, shook the naked shoulder he'd exposed.

"Hey," he said, "did you pick up the cleaning? I can't find my tan slacks."

Her arms twitched convulsively. She held her eyes shut, groped with one hand for the covers. "In the closet."

"I looked."

"In the closet." She scrunched her shoulders together and pulled the quilt back over her head.

Scree, scree, scree, scree. Two-inch increments along the metal rod. Will was methodical. *Scree, scree, scree, scree.*

Covers down, wave of cold air.

"I can't find them. The last golf of the season, dammit, and I'm late. Dalton'll have a fit."

"Honest to God," she croaked. "Maybe they're hanging under a shirt. Go look."

Scree, scree, screee, screee. Scree, scree, screee.

The next time his hand lifted the covers, she flung them back with her arm and jumped out of bed, her entire musculature clenched against the morning cool.

"You can't find your tan slacks, Will!" She bit through the words as though they blocked her path to him. "So what do you think you should do?"

A flicker of amusement crossed his face, and she yelled, "*What should you do?*"

Will hunched his shoulders and slunk theatrically from the room. He showed a mocking face through the last crack of the opening and shut the door firmly. Nothing in her life had infuriated her so greatly as that face, that closed door. In three strides she had yanked it open. It whammed against the doorstop, sending up a noise like African hunters in the bush.

"What about Plan B, Will?" she screeched, starting down the hall the way he had gone. She pumped down the stairs, breasts jerking, nipples spearpointed in the cold air. The flesh of her naked thighs and buttocks rippled with each heel thump.

"You can't find the goddamn tan slacks!" She forced her voice, her hands into rhythm. "You're a businessman, what about Plan B? Why don't you fucking *go to Plan B*?"

She made the corner into the living room with her arms outthrust. On the downstroke of *Plan B,* she saw that on the sofa, beyond where Will stood grinning and gaping in his junior boxer shorts, sat Dalton.

The feeling was of being emptied, as though insides had been turned out for display instead of skin. Skin reported nothing beyond a predictable shivering; all real sensation concentrated on the infinite hollowing in the pit of the stomach.

No one had laughed. No sound at all dropped into those first few shell-shocked moments of stillness. Aspera had turned from the eyes in the room, ascended the stairs slowly—she had no illusions of majestically—in silence. The body was nothing, a housing for humiliation. Surely Dalton had found his own feet more than worthy of his gaze.

A moment of terror back in the bedroom, door shut—where to hide? Her ears rang a continuous alarm. She dropped on her knees and crouched on the floor, ground her fists into her eyes. Yellow-rimmed blotches exploded against the cornea. Will's voice at the door. "Aspera?"

She crawled toward the foot of the bed, thinking of the sleigh bed, thinking to crawl under it. A waterbed cannot be crawled under. She shoved her head underneath the overhanging lip of the bed, fitted her body into the narrow slot created by bed and wall, shot hunched into it, compressed her breath.

Creak and spring and rake of door latch. Will's feet. "Aspera?" Foot thumps shaking floorboards into the hall, back again. Hesitation. Scream of metal hangers, cloth flapped down, waist snaps. Floor shocks, Will's voice down to Dalton from the landing: "Let's just go."

Long minutes, low voices downstairs. Slam of back door. A convulsive shivering took her body, knocked her head against the overhang of bed. She yanked the free edge of the quilt down into the space she occupied and tried to wrap herself in the muffle of cloth, but there was not room enough for both quilt and body. Half covered, she let go, let her face push into the tufts of shag carpet, rubbed her face between the worms of yarn to breathe dust and jute and cold safety. She could simply stay here. She need never move at all, not even as far as the basement.

A hot shower cured her of chattering teeth. She trapped the shower water in the tub and when it reached her shins sank into it, turning the hot water full on at the faucet until no sense memory remained of what cold meant. As the water rose to her chin a wave of intense sleepiness stole over her. Sheer fancy, these thoughts of an easy death. An easy life, for that matter. She hadn't the gift. The body will struggle on its own behalf without dignity—hadn't it wriggled out of the bed slot, knowing exposure would be a long time killing, starvation not worth the wait?

Vicky, hot sun, hot beach in Florida. Dear Vick, showed Dalton a little skin today. Showed the naked harridan Will keeps in the attic, firebrand who leaped and screamed and hid under the bed.

The rest of the day to get through. Continuity was the killer. No desire to see Will or Dalton ever again in her life, and yet it would be done. The way Vicky felt after Kev died, one day laid unwanted on another. You learn. You play hearts with your friends; that was the continuity they had offered Vicky, supper and a game of hearts on Wednesday nights to mark the weeks, making days connect. Which also opened their own constricted world one more stop—store, scrap of weekend, suppers at Irene's Café, hearts with Vicky. And then in the end, Vicky taking care of them. Caretaking. A job she didn't want; who would?

Aspera rose out of the water so fast that silver curtains fell from both arms and water sloshed over the tub rim. Dark splotches on the carpet turned black, expanded. She caught herself on the towel rack and did not faint, did not fall. The bathroom regained its rigid proportions.

Spoor of Will in a hurry: water splashed all over the sink and counter, reddish whisker ends in the bowl, towels on the floor and crammed into the racks. She flung towels and brushes in greater confusion than he had left, looked about for other things to throw or break. Flipped the medicine cabinet open on its whiny hinge and thought of Charles, of what pleasure he must have had raking all Dena's bottles and glass jars into the sink, how beautifully they must have bounced and splintered on the hard floor. But Charles was smart enough not to have witnesses, and Charles didn't have to clean up.

Aspera lifted and folded the towels, dropped them neatly onto the racks. In the bedroom she picked up her nightgown from the floor and pushed it down the laundry chute. Dena had to pick up her own nightgowns, too: the time Charles found her stash of sexy Hollywood numbers in a suitcase, stuff he'd never laid eyes on himself? He went through the house dumping the contents of every cupboard and drawer—kitchen, bathrooms, bedrooms, linen closets. All of it spilled and tumbled on the floor, Charles kicking through pillowcases, dish towels, lacy handkerchiefs in frustrated rage.

Aspera leaned against the closet door and laughed. It was funny now, maybe even to Charles. Everything got to be funny sooner or later, that much continuity you could count on.

Out of doors she felt better. Not less murderous, but less likely to leave damage where it would show. She took no chances, wore sturdy shoes, headed for the river. She walked in long scissor strides, discovered she felt better with her hands stuck in her pockets, elbows pointed wide, chin jutted forward into the brisk air.

People she'd like to run into in such a mood: the guy in the store with the wineglasses, the high school kid who jogged through the yard when he thought no one was home. She could hire herself out: Rent-an-Explosion, all occasions.

She almost didn't see the kid in the red and black wool plaid overshirt, though she was in a way staring through him. He came to a halt a couple of paces in front of her, and when she focused a deliberately savage stare on him he was looking intently into her face, a sort of smile on his lips. Her gaze wavered between eyes and lips as if this were a two-column addition problem and she'd forgotten to carry.

"Aspera?" The smile got broader as he supplied his own name. "Kevin Stowe."

"Hi." She looked at her feet, stamped at the damp leaves that clung to the thick rubber soles. "Sorry, I was off somewhere." She rubbed a hand over her face. "How are you?"

"Great," he said. "You know, I thought it wasn't you there for a second."

She looked out over the Mississippi, where the wind lifted the surface in short gray chops. "People tell me that lately." She added, "I'm getting real sick of it."

It surprised both of them, that remark, so that they both laughed aloud.

He nodded his head and said, "You sure do look pissed off at somebody."

In the face of the truth, Aspera felt her shoulders relax. She'd been carrying them folded up for such a long time, it was something of a surprise that she could relax them, that her head would stay on top of her neck without her having to hold it there.

"You headed anyplace special?" he asked.

"No." She said it flatly and realized a half-second later that one normally added more syllables, just to round things off. "No, I'm not."

When she looked up at him to see what effect this had, he grinned. "Um," he stammered, shoving his hands in his pants pockets, "I'm going to ask if it's OK for me to turn around and walk with you. I'm pretty sure you'll tell me if it isn't, so I'm asking."

It took a second for her face to unfreeze again; perhaps she didn't have to hold her face on, either. "Starting now?"

He laughed, turning his face a little away. It was this averted motion that she came to associate with him, the feeling that even at close range he would not press too close.

"Starting now was the idea," he said.

"OK." She strode forward and he turned and fell in step. They walked rapidly, saying nothing at all for perhaps two hundred yards. At which point continuity asserted itself, and the whole scene seemed funny to Aspera. She grinned and turned to look at him, and the look he returned with eyes and eyebrows said, "What?"

She said, "I like being treated like a dangerous person."

He gave a nod, his hands still thrust into his pockets.

She went on, "I feel dangerous. I want that respected."

"Absolutely."

They walked on past the row of red brick houses that looked like angry little square furnaces.

"What do you do when you're dangerous?" he inquired, looking out over the river as the path swerved away from the bank.

"Not too much," she admitted. "Take walks. Neaten up the bathroom." She laughed again, spread her arms up toward the treetops and shook her fists.

"Sometimes it helps to punch something out," he said. He punched one fist into the other palm. "I don't have a dog so I kick the wastebasket when I'm home; sometimes I punch out the back of the couch or kick the door."

"Does it help?"

"Yeah." He stopped suddenly on the path, and a half-step later she stopped, too.

"Here," he said. He crouched and offered her his two palms held up at shoulder level. "You try."

She stood looking at him. "You're kidding."

"Come on."

"Really?"

He shifted his weight with a dancing step and balanced his palms. "Come on."

She stepped toward him as she swung her right fist into his open palm. It landed with a satisfying whack.

"Again."

She swung first one fist and then the other into his hands, pulled back and swung again, and again. She swung as hard as she could; he accepted the blows and brought his palms back to cushion the impact. But he was right: it felt good to hit something. It felt wonderful to hit something as solid as flesh.

Flushed and breathing hard, she dropped her arms to her sides. She looked at him, trying to grasp what it was they were doing and how it had come about.

"All done?"

"For today," she puffed.

"One day at a time," he replied, looking off. He broke his stance, straightened and rubbed his palms briefly together. Looking at her, he nodded as though he were evaluating or perhaps even appreciating the force of the blows.

"Thanks," she told him.

He made a half-turn to resume their forward progress. She mirrored his motion.

He was looking over her shoulder toward the naked elms

behind them as she caught his glance, saw his eyes clear of any notion that something extraordinary had taken place.

The hospital was four blocks off the river. Streets lined with houses that were just beginning to turn living room and kitchen lights on in the dusk. The lowering sun promoted a suggestion of orange along the western horizon, and above it the sky was that crystalline blue that in fall turns deep cerulean before it goes to black.

Houses nearer the hospital were large and well manicured, feeding the town's belief that the whole area had been bought up by doctors. With a nod Kevin suggested they turn, and within two blocks the character of the houses changed, became part of the early-settled part of Bracken. Upright brick boxes with windows too narrow and too few, giving a mean look that went beyond the bland common-brick façades. The look was conceived with violent winters in mind. Dark inside, with high ceilings and small rooms that barely acknowledged changes of season. Life is hard, they said. The houses themselves stood for winter; the little afterthought-porches tacked on one side or another were brusque gestures remembering summer, perhaps pleasure. Here is the measure of Minnesota: hippies never thrived here. The definition of a hippie is: anybody who doesn't survive the winter.

"I grew up in that house," Kevin said. With his hands still in his pockets he nodded with his forehead toward a boxy brick house that someone, in the grip of defiance, had painted lavender. Shutters had been added to make the windows appear larger.

In Minnesota, innovation is certain death. Nothing personal. But there is to be nothing foolish or fancy, nothing that would not endure. The great plains express it all: keep a low profile, wear overalls. In the central prairie, grasslands and a water table that laps at every surface. In the north, a spread of woodland. Here birch forests do not give ease, since they are a known waystation for what must follow: scrub oak, blighted elegance of elm, spruce and scraggle pine.

"That house?" Aspera wouldn't have credited him with such an achievement, of emerging still youthful from one of Bracken's brick houses.

"Well, not that particular house," he confessed. His eyes

held hers, clear green, the green of wet sea glass. "And not this particular town. But a house just like it, in a town just like this one, northwest of here."

As they crossed the bridge over the Mississippi the wind took away all occasion for words. Weekdays these last two years she'd walked home this way at four, leaving Will to close up the store while she started supper. She walked willingly on all but the worst days of December and January, when the wind was a gale and temperature and wind chill promised defeat even for snowmobile suits. Today the promise was merely for winter: a low-lying cloud layer filming the western horizon, a decided whistle to the breeze.

Below them the merest skim of ice tarnished the river's finish, a dulling mail of flexible linked crystals. Winter claimed the year from November through March, sliding a week here or there, the time would be made up this season or next, one year or another. Early gardens were routinely snuffed, late ones frazzled to a tangle of scorched cellulose—witness the tomato vines last week.

The ritual blast of summer was all that bound life to this land, and it was brief. Minnesotans grew corn and listened with its ears for tornado howl; grew sunflowers, watched the clock-faces go round and down. Spring and fall could be skipped altogether on a whim or sudden cartel between the two major powers—October nervous as a storm warning; on occasional April mornings snow flew horizontal. The radio spoke then of record insult, hiding congratulations among the decimals.

Winter was religion, the northern lights confronting the landscape with splendor, the finality of ice.

"This was maybe a mistake, crossing the bridge," she said to Kevin.

He nodded rueful assent.

They said nothing more till they got to the Townsend Café, the only one of Bracken's cafés that stayed open on Sunday, and so the old man who ran it was reputed an atheist. Aspera thought his name was Townsend until Will discovered this, only last year, and set her straight. "Town's end," he said, repeating the separate words till Aspera got the emphasis. "Town's End Café. Nobody has ever known what that old guy's name is."

Now Kevin gestured at the trapezoidal entry cove, floored in grimy red ceramic tiles. The same red was painted halfway up the plate glass window on either side of the inset door.

"Are you as cold as I am?" he asked her. When he pulled the door open, country music wailed out at them. A cord connected over the door made a ship's bell clang, alerting the old man who now seemed a stranger without the name Aspera had assigned him.

"Wait."

Aspera pushed the door shut again with her shoulder. She shook her head at Kevin. The old man came up to the window in his white apron and peered out, holding a hand over his bald head against the reflection of the interior lights. On shared impulse, Aspera and Kevin both ducked and fled past the window and then down the street.

A block later they leaned panting against the office-supply building, in the hilarious flush of conspiracy.

"I don't know what that was!" she laughed, knowing she didn't want to face explaining Kevin to anybody. "I'd say come and warm up at the house, but the truth is I'm in the middle of a scene with Will—"

The green eyes peered at her. "Ah," he said.

"We could have coffee at Vicky's place. That's where I was headed when we met; I have keys. Think we can make it back there?"

"Maybe." He frowned, looked at her. "In fact I was headed for your place to ask if I could stay at Vicky's tonight. I have meetings in Bracken tomorrow."

She shrugged. She hadn't wanted details fixing either of them in real life, but here they were. She remembered he worked for the state. "Fine." She stopped, faced him with her hands tucked into the back pockets of her jeans. She brought out Vicky's keys, stared at them. "Look, I don't know if you want company at all—" She stopped, searched for the word, the concept.

He listened with his forehead tilted toward her, chin tucked. His eyes rested on the ground, or just past her shoulder, which appeared to offer her some margin for error. She thought of Will's chin thrust habitually forward, eyes trained and sharp. "I mean, for coffee." She reddened.

Kevin nodded. "I'd like your company."

She returned the keys to her pocket. Back across the bridge, they dropped down the stairs to the park for shelter from the wind. When they took the turn that led to Vicky's building, Aspera detoured through a dry ditch piled with brown oak leaves, yellow curls of elm leaves. She walked through it kicking up dust and papery clouds of fragments. They gave off a composty odor of must, of chemical heat.

Kevin walked ahead and waited for her to complete her course. When she got to the end and looked up at him, he had a merry look about the eyes.

"You could tell me about this scene you're in the middle of," he said.

"No thanks." Her voice came out flat. "I'd rather be here than there."

Bravura failed as she fit the keys into the locks of Vicky's building. At the apartment door with Kevin waiting behind her, a picture of his body without clothes flashed through her mind. She was shocked by her mind, not by his body. Inside the apartment, she balanced on one foot with one hand braced against the wall. She unlaced her walking shoes and left them beside the front closet; he slipped out of his loafers. The very coordination of their activities was embarrassing.

"Why does it seem so bare in here?" she demanded. It was that no books or papers were set out, no transient clutter on the mail table, no lists or reminders magneted to the refrigerator door.

Ease was fragile. Indoors she had lost the physical certainty of it. This empty apartment raised questions of intent. What was she doing here with him? Stop thinking *in relation to.* Better to proceed as though the world were populated with objects, she herself the only one capable of feeling and decision.

She'd shut the hall door with unnecessary force, and now she rifled through kitchen cupboards setting up tympanic rhythms of bouncing doors. Learning Vicky's methods: violence and noise were forms of magic. All else fell in their path. Physical violence forces intimacy, there is no denying: contact.

No coffee at all? But there it sat, a folded bag alone on the freezer shelf. Prospectors looked out for one another that way, left behind canned goods, other necessities.

"I miss Vicky," she said loudly. Here was something that needed saying, more magic to ward off misunderstanding. "With her gone I'm short of somebody sensible to talk to."

"Same here," he said, leaning in the doorway. "I think I'm ticked off about that."

As a joke, she held her two palms up for him, offering.

He smiled, politely kept distance. "Another time."

Still clattering things, she set up the coffeemaker, wearing her jacket. Kevin watched without comment. She did not see so much as sense that he'd left the doorway and turned to see him in the hall, resetting the thermostat.

When she'd wiped her hands she walked into the living room He had opened the heavy drapes as well as the backup of sheers along the west wall of sliding glass doors. He stood looking at the first concentrated orange light of sunset.

"Sometimes I wish I were in the navy," he said. "I'd want to be the color guard, you know those guys who dress sharp and carry flags and fire cannon at sunset? Sunset tends to make me feel like shooting somebody."

She laughed.

"Is that weird?"

She shook her head gravely: no. He returned to looking at the sinking sun, striations of hyacinth and slatey blue.

"In fact I know I'd like it. All that noise. And you could count on it every night, it would be your job." He shook his head in wistful admiration. "Maybe I should own a cannon."

"Then there'd be the problem of waiting till sunset every day," she teased. "Some mornings you might want to start in first thing."

He turned from the window and sat down on a leather hassock. Facing her, he spread his knees wide and dropped his folded hands between them. "Days like this one?"

She hesitated. "Let's make it so we can both watch the sunset."

She pulled a chair from the dining table over to a spot near where he waited on the hassock.

"Did Vicky tell you that we met over a game of hearts?" she asked him.

"Yeah." He unbuttoned his red plaid overshirt. "She said you hit it off inside of two minutes."

Aspera smiled. A neighbor had invited the two couples, Hancocks and Varneys, for an evening of cards shortly after Will and Aspera moved back to town. Vicky had admired Will's scarf, a soft alpaca wool that Aspera had knitted.

"You did all this for him?" Vicky had queried her, laying the soft brown stuff its full six feet on a divan.

"Back when I used to love him," Aspera replied. The people shocked were the neighbor and Aspera herself, while Vicky had laughed out loud.

"She was the only sensible person I found in this town," Aspera told Kevin now. "Even though all she ever did in hearts was shoot the moon."

Kevin grinned. "Sounds about right."

Aspera squinted at the sky. The sun was sinking toward an opaque layer of milky blue clouds that lined the horizon just above Bracken's patchy skyline.

"I'm pretty sensible," Kevin said. "Why don't you try me on what happened with you this morning?"

When she looked down, half Kevin's face was pumpkin-colored in the rich light.

"This has been a very strange day," she began, then was caught by the green eyes. She shook her head, addressing his request, after all. "It would take more time than we've got."

At seven o'clock Aspera walked home in the dark, quite talked out. And relaxed—when was the last time she'd just spilled over like that? About nothing, about everything: high school teaching, library science at the U., moving back to Bracken, the game of hearts. She lay down on top of the waterbed with her clothes still on. Not tired, just thinking. The first lead of hearts must be presaged by one heart dropped as though innocently upon an unprotected hand. Hearts are broken. This first drop—malicious, determinant—ends a certain awkwardness bred of not knowing who the enemy might be this time. Smiling, she fell into a devouring sleep. She woke at eight when Will shut the car off inside the garage, that chuffing way the Mercury struggled with its last swallows of gasoline after the ignition was cut.

She got to her feet and combed her hair quickly. She could hardly keep the day in its correct frame. Too much had happened from beginning to end, and how different the morning's mad scene had sounded, told to a stranger! Embarrassment had evaporated. Now she was able to think of everyone, even Will, even herself, as essentially harmless. *Nice!* Kevin so free of opinions and advice, maybe his youth, but she could see the ridiculous side of the melodrama as she told it to him. Well—think of the whole comedy, twenty years of Aspera and Will, all the connecting links turned amusing! She should find someone to tell that to.

The phone rang. She and Will both answered, upstairs and down. Dalton.

"I'll talk to the lady of the house first," he said, and Will hung up.

Alone on the line, at first the two of them did a side step of bested apologies—sorry to surprise you like that, sorry to surprise *you!*—and then ordinary exchange.

"You guys have fun today?"

Will came into the bedroom and she nodded cheerfully to him as Dalton answered, "Let's see: we played eighteen holes, had a couple of beers and found a place that would serve us walleye for dinner. The answer is yes. What did you do?"

"Took a bath, took a walk. *Got dressed,*" she emphasized, and Dalton chuckled. Then she laughed, too. "Where are you calling from?" she asked. "Will just walked in the door, you can't be home already?"

"Yep, I am. Will stayed on for a few at the Townsend. Let me talk to him if he's handy," Dalton said. "Something I forgot to tell him."

She handed the phone over to Will, still smiling. Then lay back down on the bed. One point scored against you for every heart accumulated in the course of the game, plus thirteen for the queen of spades. Unless, of course, you took them all. Take a chance, all right or all wrong, shoot the moon. Not her style, shooting the moon, today's display to the contrary. She smiled, thought of Kevin and fisticuffs, cannon fire, of all she'd write to Vicky.

"What's all the grinning about?" Will asked, hanging up the phone.

"Thinking about the day," Aspera said, straightening her face. "How's Dalt?"

"I believe you spoke to him. I believe he's recovered from the sights you visited on him."

She glanced at him, raised herself on her elbow. "So he said."

"Also the sounds."

She swung her legs to the side of the bed and sat up. "You're angry with me. There are two sides to everything, I guess."

He reached in his pockets, put fistfuls of change on the dresser. "As I recall, all yours were on display."

She looked at him in disbelief. The casual note in his voice was in no way well intended. He meant to have this fight, whether she was willing or not. Now she was willing.

"You could have told me Dalton was coming to the house."

"You could have asked."

Her voice rose. "I was trying to sleep!"

"Are you sleepy now?" All mildness. "I notice your voice gets real loud when you want to sleep."

She pressed her fists to the sides of her head, all of the day's lightness gone. The slicing headache of last week found its place. "Do you mean to be heartless?"

He was silent as he kicked off his shoes, pulled off one sock by tugging at the toe; then the other. He rolled them in his hands as he looked over at her. His eyes seemed rounder, the face more the one she could, if she tried, remember loving. He dropped the dark ball of socks into the laundry piled in his closet.

"Sorry. I don't know what the hell to say. All day I felt bad, I don't like being caught out. What I did was so idiotic, I was standing next to Dalton grinning like a dope before I realized." He shook his head. "I tried to come in and apologize—where in God's name did you hide?"

Shame returned and she flushed hot. Her eyes traveled to the space between the bed and the wall. She didn't say anything.

"I meant to come in tonight and apologize right off the bat." He turned his head, looked at a new spot on the carpet. "Then I got mad again."

"I wasn't mad at all by the time you got here, I had a pretty good day, in fact—"

"Well, I wasted a lot of time worrying, then!" Eyes small again. "I didn't *have* such a hot day, I thought *both* of us were feeling bad, and then I come in and you're laughing it up with Dalton!"

She set aside all thoughts of telling Will about her afternoon with Kevin. "If you were so worried, why did you leave?"

"I couldn't find you—and what is this?" His voice climbed high. "You make it sound like I went away for ten years! You must have me mixed up with your old man! I didn't leave you forever, I went golfing, I'm Will, I'm the guy that always sticks around!"

"Not always!"

"Oh, right, not always. The night before the wedding, OK? It's only been twenty years. Some guys do it on purpose; they call it a bachelor party. Aspera, I'm sorry I did the polka with somebody in Avon twenty years ago. And I'm sorry I stayed out all night, once—" he rolled his eyes upward mocking the calculations—"nineteen and three-quarter years ago. You didn't deserve it, God knows."

"Will you stop?"

"I'd like to know if you have any new business to discuss, because I don't think you like me. You'd rather spend time with anybody else—Christ, you talk to Vicky, you talk to Dena, you giggle with Dalton—"

"Dalton was trying to make things easy!"

"You go for that, don't you?"

"You bet I do!"

"I can't even get the time of day, it's not like you even bother talking to me."

"I talk to people who care at least one single goddamn about what I think and how I feel. Why *should* I talk to you?"

"Why don't you just leave, it's what you want to do, right? The store is just the first step, tip of the old icepick. Go ahead!" He threw his arms outward, exposing his chest. "Stick it in!"

She drew back, took a breath. "I want to leave the store. I'm not trying to leave you."

"You *say!*" He fired the words at her one syllable at a time. "I don't believe a thing you say."

She folded her arms into a brace. She would be as hard as he was. "I admit it doesn't make sense," she said coolly. "Why would I stay with somebody that makes my life this hard? We don't have any fun at all—certainly we don't have fun at the same time. I can remember when we did, but it's been so long—are we sick? Are we just stuck, like flies in wallpaper?"

His face had a peculiar rigid cast that, at that moment, made the right word fly out of her head.

"Flypaper," she said. That look—she remembered it from

how many years ago?—meant he was fighting tears.

Rather than lose that fight, Will walked out of the room.

Monday morning two weeks later Aspera got one leg into her pantyhose, when Will walked into the bedroom toweling his hair. "First day of vacation, right?" he said.

She gathered the spare leg in her hand and looked up.

He blotted the back of his neck, where the wet rust-colored tendrils sprang out.

"Does that mean you've hired someone?" she asked.

"Yep."

"Who? And when?"

"Bobbie's daughter. She starts this morning."

"Bobbie's daughter goes to college in Kansas."

"Not this term. She's on a work-study program."

The furnace clicked downstairs, and a rush of hot air pushed past Aspera's face.

"Well, that should be perfect," she said, "for a couple of months."

"Right."

She pulled the hose off, got up and poked them back into the drawer, pulled out knee socks. She tried to order a flutter of thoughts. "Then I guess I can get started on a resumé today, and then come help you at six."

"No need," he said. "But come if you want."

"Will, why didn't you tell me before this morning?"

He looked up and smiled from doing the buttons on his shirt. "Surprise," he said.

She sighed, feeling tears rise. "I've been worried," she said. "I had no idea you'd done anything at all. I'm not even really prepared to start looking for a job, I—"

"Look, I thought this was what you wanted." With his back to her he shoved his wallet into his pants pocket.

"Yes," she said, a tear escaping down one cheek. She wiped it away. "It's just, I'm surprised. I hadn't counted on you helping me."

"Don't make me into a hero," he said. "I don't like this, you know I don't."

She sighed again. She wanted—she sought Vicky's word, lost it. She wanted comfort, somehow, for both of them. Else the fear lurked—she would not say so, it was childish—that he would leave her. She wanted to draw upon Will's feelings for her as Elvira might have drawn a cross in the air, for protection.

She watched him sort his change. He took quarters and dimes for the machines, leaving every day a scatter of pennies that she took from the dressertop and dropped into a jar. "You used to be the one wanting out," she said to him. "Things have changed for you. You've changed them, I mean, it's plain you love the place—really love it, in a way I can't feel for myself. I think it's really your home."

"Look. Don't analyze me because you're feeling guilty."

The justice in this remark fell on her like a stone.

After a moment Will shifted his weight and expelled a breath. "You want things balanced out, is that it? OK, here's what I'd like. Say you take a couple months to scout around, see what you can find in the way of a job you want. Say three months. If you don't have a job by January one, we forget the second store, but we do some more remodeling. I've been thinking, we can get the space we need if we move the office upstairs, then move your whole Interiors operation into the cellar—"

The pit of her stomach rolled. "Into the basement?" She saw gray walls, a ring of fluorescent light. "You want me to be down there?"

"We take out all the existing structures. We can have furniture groupings and partitions, with any kind of wall coverings we want, we can do window treatments—"

"What are you asking?" Her voice rose, a wail of betrayal. "Will, I can't do that."

His face closed. "Forget it then. Forget I said anything."

He turned and was gone. Closure. It was closure she wanted.

"Will!" She went to the top of the stairs and called after him. "I'll see you at six."

Ahead of the slam of the back door came, "Don't bother."

She spent the hours after breakfast at the kitchen table with Sunday's want ads, then canvassed the Bracken public library for books on job hunting and résumé writing. How to stretch forty credits in library science and a part-time library job in college into "qualifications"? The two hours of library supervision she put in daily as a high school Latin teacher, did that count? Pretty thin. And if *she* knew it, whom could she fool?

Lunch at Irene's, conscious of her jeans and loafers, thinking she might see Will. She dreaded seeing him, yet his steady anger would tell her who she was. She would remember why she wanted to do this. At one o'clock she reminded herself to feel free instead of abandoned. She gathered herself up, went home and skimmed two books on job skills, dug through files for the last résumé she'd written. Fifteen years ago.

Dinnertime she gave in and phoned the store. Will was out. She looked at the clean kitchen and ate two slices of salami over the sink. She phoned Dena at home, stared out at the blue light of evening while the phone rang and rang. Monday night; Will would be home by nine-fifteen. She'd build a fire, read. She'd picked up novels at the library this morning, surprising both the librarian and herself. Well, maybe some new stories had cropped up in the last few centuries.

Sitting on the sofa with one of the recommended volumes—they all were slender, all had heroines younger than she was—she feared fragility. In her chest, a bubble of glass. She defended against it: blazing fire, heavy sherry in a glass that fit to her hand, Mahler playing softly on tape.

Elvira had died alone in a basement nineteen years ago. The tears rose and Aspera comforted herself: a good solid reason to cry.

A noise that sounded like the Mercury gasping, then the slam of the back door.

Will came into the living room in his jacket. "Nice life you have here. Where's dinner?"

"Will," she said. "I called," she said then, unsure whether or not he was teasing about dinner. "Bobbie said you'd gone out."

"I'm doing errands. I decided to stop by and pick up that shelf unit I was working on." As he spoke he slipped the jacket off and laid it on the stairs. "It'll take me five minutes to finish the dowel ends and I can take it back to the store with me."

Seconds later she heard the thump-thump-thump of his feet on the basement stairs.

When he came back up he still wore his work apron. He brought the wooden organizer he'd built, a display model for a kit they sold in the store, also meant for her to use behind the register in the Best Boutique. Will cherished organization, thought ready-made compartments the supreme expression. He had taken such care with the sanding and staining, and the look on his face—how long it had been since she'd seen love there.

"A beauty, eh? Bobbie can put it to use." At the doorway he held it for her to see.

Aspera got up, feeling awkward to stand so near him. She admired the design and his handiwork. The wood looked so satiny that she put out a finger to touch—and then, relinquishing any claim, went back to her couch.

"I did some research today, not much else," she told him as he turned the shelf so that he could hold it under one arm.

He stood in the light fingering a hole in the pocket of his apron, a hole gone unrepaired in the two years since he'd first wiggled a finger through it to bring the matter to her attention. Now he again poked the finger through the hole.

"Right," she admitted. "I'll have time to do that now."

Will spread the apron and curtsied. "What a homebody you are, Aspera. Isn't it amazing? Here we are, your basic homebody and your basic laborer."

"My husband the laborer," she offered lamely.

"Except you don't look like a laborer's wife," he smiled, setting the shelf down to lean against the newel post and wiping his hands on the apron.

She saw herself with his eyes, reclining in the lamplight with a book before the fire, sherry at her elbow.

"I'd have to have you as a mistress," he told her.

Supposed to pass as a joke. A dull knife, but the edge had been pressed down often and the threat came not from sharpness but from repeated applications of pressure. What words should she use? Not to thrust back but the other thing, parry. "Laborers don't have mistresses, Will. They have wives, maybe drudges."

"We wouldn't know what to make of one of those, would we?"

She wedged her sherry glass between the cushions of the sofa. "Why do you say such things to me?"

He shrugged his apron off, laid it over the banister. "I didn't have to come by at all, you know. Hope I didn't interrupt anything important."

She raised her arms and folded them over her head. The pose could pass for confidence if she fought back a sense of her chest undefended.

"Watch your sherry," he mumbled, gesturing. He turned and zipped his jacket. "I didn't come to make you feel bad."

"No?"

He sighed. "I think you look glamourous and elegant on your divan," he said, sweeping a hand at her props. "A lady of leisure whose favor—" He moved round the sofa, behind her head, as though he would take her hand. She bent her head back to see him come. He put a finger on the cuff of her sweater, stopped to pick at a white something that clung.

"What is that?" he asked.

She lowered her wrists and examined the shred in question. "A piece of price sticker."

"Looked like a Band-Aid." Will had changed direction, was picking up the shelf. "I've got to get back," he said. "Don't forget about that sherry glass."

The Mercury roared, and Aspera considered the empty channel driven down her chest through the top of her head as she sat rooted in glamorous elegance upon her divan, sherry glass spitefully drained.

Comfort can be withheld! Stop wanting things that can be withheld.

Oh, a sound plan. Perfect in truth and logic. She would generate comfort so that she might have, of her own making, enough. Comfort was what you wanted anyway, because as soon as you got angry somebody else got angrier.

How free she had felt, flinging out anger and tromping around like a troll in the woods with Kevin. She had shown herself violent and peremptory and whole, and with that much comfort—mere conversation, mere company—had come home believing: I can get on with it.

Which lasted long enough to get through not quite two weeks, not quite one more full Monday and then, O Christ just let me read this book pretend to read it don't make me feel let me be alone with this book this sherry this fire.

CHAPTER ELEVEN

The following Sunday morning Will decided not to get up and go downstairs for breakfast without Aspera. He lay in bed beside her pretending to sleep. He waited for her to open her eyes. He had waited a long time, he could hold out till nine-thirty. If they could just make contact before everything started up—

She tossed. She thought she must have lost her sense of time. Why hadn't Will gone downstairs yet? She wanted to lift her head and look over his body to see what the clock said, but if she woke him—she clenched her hands. Where was the sun? Gradually, she turned her head. Through the window a brightness diffused through gray haze.

"It's quarter after nine," Will said.

She jumped.

"Sorry," he said. "It's after nine, I thought you'd be awake. How about a late breakfast?"

She could see them silent in the kitchen nook, two people watching the trickle of white sand for soft-boiled eggs. "I was thinking I'd go out for a walk," she said.

He turned and looked out the window. "Doesn't look *too* cold," he decided. "We'll work up an appetite that way."

Insulated in wool and goosedown, they picked their way along the path beside the Mississippi. The river shallows had frozen and thawed and frozen again, and the trunks of trees bore jagged shelves of ice just above the river surface. Aspera felt perspiration begin to trickle under her clothes. Too many layers. She unzipped her jacket at the throat. Will unwrapped his muffler. Their words loosened, too, and before she thought it possible, they had gone through it all again, everything they had already said and disagreed over. They said it louder, and discovered in the other no improvement.

Will went stony; he couldn't get the picture across. "You won't see!" he accused her.

She broke into tears; she couldn't get through to him. "Nothing I can say makes you hear me!"

He stopped replying to anything she said because pointless arguing had to stop somewhere. First law of the jungle: don't let them get your scent and most of the danger will pass right by.

"Will, say something to me!" She knew she was screeching at him. She could not help it.

"Say what, exactly?"

"I don't know, but it's your turn!"

What could he say, anyway? If he answered her they argued, he lost his cool. He saw no way he could win.

She recognized the threat in his silence. If she didn't give over, she'd be alone. Well, she already was alone. Nobody could be more alone than she was with Will.

They walked with their hands in their pockets down the lower path beside the water to the pilings of the bridge. There they stopped, seemingly of one mind, to listen to the loud grinding of traffic overhead. The criss-crossed metal pieces in the bridge support vibrated in the cold air, making a secondary hum that relieved silence.

Will's face was rigid. He bit his lip and squinted up at the shadows of cars passing above them. Two thousand pounds per vehicle, an average of four thousand crossings daily, load coefficient of . . .

Aspera wiped tears, and in the cold her eyelids felt acid-burned. She saw where Will put his attention. She could stand beside him forever at ground level while he thought everything of importance in the world happened two stories up. She turned from the wind and idly placed her boot on the nearest of the boulders that lay exposed, when the river was this low, in rough sequence from the shore to the foot of the first piling in the river. The boulder wore a thin shell of ice on its north face, but the scaly rough granite on top—she shifted her weight and sprang up—was dry and secure. The next rock was an easy foot and a half away. The next no problem either; in late summer she'd jumped the whole series without even thinking. She liked the feeling of strength in her legs; she took the next gap easily. The water rippling below her feet had to be wildly cold. She grinned to think of it, felt suddenly bold, took the next step.

Twelve steps later she placed a mittened palm on the cold steel of the bridge piling and turned around on the generous sloping skirt of concrete that anchored it. She glanced to shore, where Will stood still. He shifted his eyes and looked past her, upriver. She started back.

She leaped the gap between the last two granite boulders, and he turned away at last from watching her. Under the thick jacket his heart pounded, his lower lip had gone numb to the edges of his teeth. She hopped smiling from the last boulder to the shore and spread her arms in triumph. He regarded her steely-eyed. She shrugged at him, then dropped her arms and stuck her hands deep into her jacket pockets. She pointed herself toward home and took one brisk step that direction. On the glaze of shore ice her foot flew up, she tumbled easily backward with her hands still in her pockets. One thing that broke her fall was a small jutting rock, where she struck her jaw.

Will turned white. He didn't move. Do not panic. If he got near her he might jerk her up by the shoulders and shake her.

Aspera pulled off her mitten and touched her jaw with her fingers. Her tongue found the places where she had cracked the enamel of her tooth, found where the tooth had punched and shredded the lining of her cheek. She tasted blood in her mouth, looked up at Will. Who just stood there. Nothing moved him; she would show him nothing. She swallowed the blood, got to her feet, kept swallowing.

When she stood up he went weak with relief. His chest, his legs—he could fall down that way himself. Then a slender tensor beam of fury shot through his brain: that she could pull such a stunt, just scare the shit out of him like that. She did fall, though, got the blow to her pride that she deserved.

They trudged home some wide distance from one another on the path, Will in the lead. Inside the back door, he kicked off his boots, hung up his coat and went into the kitchen. He turned the gas on and with cold fingers removed eggs from a carton. She came in and went upstairs with her coat and boots still on, and in the bathroom with the water running cried as though he had struck her.

II

Dividedness

Whenever I have to choose between two evils, I always like to try the one I haven't tried before.

—Mae West

CHAPTER TWELVE

Aspera felt divided as she sat in the dentist chair. Dentists were the terrorists of physical intimacy, dentists and gynecologists. Vulnerability can't miss where furniture is designed for opening the body.

The dentist's assistant settled a rubber cone over the patient's nose to supply the gas. She also adjusted the volume of Jackson Browne in the earphones.

With rock music funneled to her brain and nitrous oxide to her lungs, the patient grew suddenly aware of every flexible place of her body, aware of that running slope from shin to ankle, heels resting on the padded chaise, aware of tight muscles in her right thigh that set first one knee and then one ankle over its counterpart to form the extension of her leg. Aware of the double French seam of her jeans sliced in against her vulva, aware of the semicircle of breast that rested on the skin of her rib cage, of the slight weight of upper lip on lower, of the insertions of hair along the crown of her scalp and the layer of insulation they created. She drew air over the rims of her nostrils and felt a light shiver begin at the hipbones and slurry down the skin of her thighs to her kneecaps.

She began the roster that she kept these days, men she had noticed or wondered about. Kevin, Dalton, two muscular joggers she'd seen in the park. The teenager next door. The dentist. But he was married, of course, good Catholic with framed photographs on the walls, five clean dependents including a smallish wife. Married and Catholic, just like Quentin Howath.

She shifted about in the cupping vinyl upholstery and shook

her shoulders, rotated her neck till it made cracking sounds, briskly rubbed the fabric of her jeans.

On Dena's behalf she had become an expert on situations that were sexually and personally pointless—she could spot one for Dena coming four counties away. Married was not inexperienced. It was just that apart from married, you were supposed to be inexperienced. To be thinking what she was now thinking, she ought to have been divorced at least once.

The dentist entered the room. Perhaps he'd close the door and simply remove his unsullied smock, an act as simple as it was unlikely. In real life she watched while he approached in full attire, smiling like a mind reader. He reached for the syringe the assistant had left dripping on a porcelain tray. He placed fingers on her mouth; she opened; he drove in a needle.

"Just a pinprick," he murmured.

His skin temperature was distinctly cooler than his assistant's had been. Looking carefully into his face as he bent over her now, she noted the size of his pores, the clipped transparent hair in his nostrils. Spic and span, worthy sire of all those wombfruit. Chemicals swam the channels of her face to her brain. When she was a child in Indiana—this was before the Airstream—she'd had a fatherly dentist who rested her head against his comfortable belly and drilled her teeth without anesthetic. Black hair had sprouted from his nostrils, also his eyebrows and ears. He'd drawn her attention to it, told her he was part elf. She'd screamed anyway. First the elfin scream of the drill, then her trolling harmony.

This dentist was hygienic and handsome. So German: tawny khaki hair, tawny khaki eyes. Repeated four times in miniature in the photos on the wall, plus the dark-eyed wife on whose shoulder he'd placed a well-washed hand. Visible gold ring.

How serious was marriage? This was a question still asked in the Midwest. The heart of the country, heartland, or in some versions, breadbasket. Say it with compound words: Heartland, breadbasket, motherlove. Motherland, breadlove, heartbasket. Bracken was a German town, which fact could be deduced by noting that the number of restaurants exceeded the population. Also the number of dentists.

Mother is connected to bread, heart to land, unconditional love to sex. Opening the body: remember the goose who laid the golden eggs. Was the whole point the escalation of greed? Once you possessed a living thing, the temptation to kill was strong. Did that explain the estate of women in marriage?

As a child in Indiana, she had a dog that Chester said must stay behind with the house they'd sold, in the country. "Butter is too old to make a new home."

Elvira had sighed with the effort of convincing herself along with the child. "She'll have a new family to love her, that's all."

"She's got new owners now," Chester told his daughter, who had failed to understand how Butter could be owned the same way the house was. She'd thought the dog was part of the family.

If you are owned you can be abandoned.

If you are possessed, of course, it's much worse.

With his drill-finger the dentist mimed a one-moment to her. Aspera mimed back a smile, lips curving over the nozzle as he left the room. She nodded to his assembled family as she removed it.

How serious was marriage? The Catholic Church spelled out terms for breach of contract. Divorce was violent, the sundering of a bond. Annulment, more spiritual, recognized that nothing like a bond existed. Sex made a mess of things since the Church could annul marriages but not children—something did not come of nothing, and children were clearly something.

Spirit was always running into matter in these schemes. Matter and its litter of flesh. Solomon staked his reputation for wisdom on the indivisibility of a child, and that was still one of the scariest stories Aspera had ever heard.

The dentist was back, making faces at her. Her heart raced; the chemicals? Animal, vegetable, mineral. Personably, this dentist seated himself on a stool behind her right shoulder, reached past her and placed the suction nozzle in her mouth. Animal.

She removed the nozzle. "Exactly what is the gas supposed to do for me?" She tipped one earcup away to hear his answer. Her voice sounded like someone else's voice, her hand moved slowly to its task. She turned and found her face unexpectedly close to his. Flirting?

His eyes were truly the exact color of his hair. Dena would be amazed.

He grinned at her with his clean teeth. "The clinical effects are lightheadedness, followed by death."

Together they laughed. This was flirting all right.

"Too bad," she heard herself say, while Jackson Browne sang in a tiny voice next to her ear. "I thought somewhere in between there might be heightened sexual response."

He chuckled. "Oh, that," he said. He leaned close, a metal pick poised above her nose. He replaced the suction nozzle. "True, but the problem is keeping all the hoses out of the way."

He winked at the assistant, who had entered the room while he spoke, and who ignored the wink. Aspera felt transparent as a glass bead, the sort you could put to your eye and read within it the entire text of the conversation she'd just had with this man.

Jackson Browne accompanied the drill.

When he'd polished the filling in Aspera's flawed bicuspid, the dentist bowed out. He smiled genially and patted the patient's knee. He left the assistant to clean the patient's mouth and use the hose to seek out particles of metal compound that had strayed along the crevices of the relaxed jaw and tongue. The patient fancied that the woman's hands were cooler now, that she intentionally raked the nozzle and mirror along tooth enamel.

How serious was adultery? Solomon wasn't so clear. But anything was serious, if it had to be kept secret. The only thing nature abhorred worse than a vacuum was a secret. Pitted against the wall-dissolving tendencies of the universe, odds were terrible. What with small towns and small children and broad daylight and coincidence, what with telepathy and intuition and the need to borrow someone else's car.

The assistant's use of dental floss was markedly savage. Aspera looked at the wall, at the homemade display of dental instruments sprayed bronze and arranged upon a bronzed bed of surgical gauze. Beside her handiwork, the dark-eyed woman in the photo smiled as the patient spat blood into a suction nozzle.

This flirtation business was not one for amateurs. Aspera

walked out of the dentist's office with her body still liquid, her mind and mouth hard and contracted.

Dividedness was where innocence was lost.

The first time she called Kevin she thought it was plausible enough. He, a state job-training supervisor based in Saint Paul who traveled to small towns like Princeton and Bracken to do what is called outreach. She, a former library-science part-time graduate student looking for a position.

She wanted to work in a medical library; she had questions she wanted answered about the body. She asked Kevin: which local hospitals have libraries? Do social-service agencies require special training for archives personnel?

He had answers: I really don't know. I'll check for you.

It could have been done over the telephone, but there they were in a roadhouse in Little Falls, with a river outside and a bridge that begged to be crossed over.

After lunch, they went on foot while the wind whipped their hair friable. No snow had fallen, though November wore on and made gestures: this dull gray sky, a wind with teeth. Soon something would fall from the sky, justify all this. Where the bridge railing made a small bay over the water, Aspera and Kevin lingered as though something of portent might be seen from there. But the river merely slid below, a disturbed brown-gray. The jacket she'd carried was not warm enough; the winds blew with authority down this track of river, channeled by borders of willow and birch. Their limbs and twigs clamored. Kevin's nose turned red along with his cheeks, and her lips she was quite sure were white. They both sniffled, and she thought they would be quite safe after all.

The park on the other side was deserted but small. The low fulcrums of seesaws were bare, bereft of function; children's swings gone, chains and all, from their hooks. The undersides of park benches were edged with frost. After twenty minutes of courage, they retraced their path over the bridge. Any words they exchanged had been forced out against the high cautionary sound of wind among bare sticks. She would remember the dull ringing of their footsteps on the steel mesh of the walkway over the river. No pauses now; if there were falls to look at in Little Falls it wasn't from here. They hustled back single file along the railing, hands in pockets.

They reached her car first. She'd left it in the lot of the River Inn unlocked, small-town habit. Just now she felt small in most every sense. She opened the driver's door with fumbling haste and turned to offer a grim smile along with her thanks, her hand. Kevin hunched his back and, looking over her shoulder, captured the hand. His own had no warmth to offer, but he leaned close and said near her ear, "I want to run away with you."

Certain things affected the speech centers. Flowers—in high school she had orchids cool and odorless on her wrist—could crush her into silence, and now it was these words he had said.

Her first cogent thought was of how conspicuous they were. The two of them in this unguarded stance a mere two blocks from the main highway to Bracken. And she knew clearly why she feared the main highway, and what it was could be deduced from a distance.

"I don't know how to do these things," she whispered. She guarded against a wish to fall against his chest and say this where her face could be hidden. "I didn't mean to make you take the lead."

"As long as I'm leading someplace you want to go."

There was no place that day, no time left either. Perhaps they were both relieved. Still he kept his hand on the door handle and leaned on it beside her.

"I'm not sure what this is," he was saying. How easily they assumed they were talking about the same thing. She divined that he meant the strong band of current that she felt running between them, that solid horizontal spike of energy—"but maybe we need to be in the same place at the same time to find out."

So easy. So free of the sleaziness she expected as the aura of an affair, the way migraines are said to have auras. Her body thrummed, a kind of pain began high in her chest, and they talked a few more minutes in this shorthand of assumptions. Standing in the wind, they made statements.

Hers (for he had been her friend's lover, and he was a single young man, living in the Cities): "You don't have to tell me the truth all the time, but I don't want to be lied to."

His (for she put things oddly): "You're very complex."

She laughed, assuming this was irony on his part, and felt understood. They established another time, another place. One of the things he said somewhere in the middle rang in her head for weeks: "Half the world runs on secrets."

She came home to an unlighted house. Cold days like this, she liked to set great pots of soup boiling just for the warmth. More than she and Will needed, but she took comfort from the clouds of steam that filled the kitchen. She could always freeze what was left over. She took out an iron kettle and seasoned it with olive oil, then set it in the warm oven. Leaning against the stove, she read paragraphs in one of Elvira's books on prophecy.

It did not escape her, as she thumbed through the pages, that fire was repeatedly conjoined with wind, with the whirlwind in particular. A trinity: fire, wind, madness. Whirlwinds of the mind.

She worked in the kitchen with more purpose toward dinnertime, moving without hurry but perhaps more absently than usual. Clam chowder, the easy way, and a salad would do it. She took down a can of Crosse and Blackwell's, a can of minced clams, cream from the refrigerator. She opened the cans and drained liquid into the heavy kettle, added sherry, black pepper, bay leaf. Turned the dial to high to reduce the stock. Reduction meant you heated things up, evaporated the liquid, made the solid pieces move faster—they bounced off the walls and one another and became laughable.

She turned down the gas flame in time, poured a thick belt of cream from the pint bottle. From Bracken Dairy she still bought heavy cream this way. Old joke about elephants: what's gray and comes in pints? She chopped leftover boiled potatoes, diced an onion. Neither heart nor mind was with the knife—she added the jumble of odd-sized pieces to the pot anyway—nor on the crease she ran down two paper napkins with a thumbnail. Kevin. She couldn't take him seriously, of course. She was married, and *that* was serious. But the secret thoughts were so sweet, so thrilling; it was hard to see the harm. Of course she valued honesty. Still she didn't see how she could be expected to be honest with an onion.

Terrible things went on in the world: ears hacked off prisoners, brides burned for cash, old women locked in cellars living on Ken-L-Ration. What she was thinking in her kitchen in Bracken wasn't so bad. She was harming no one, cutting no one into giblet soup.

She extracted a whole bay leaf from the bottle, ran her finger along the serrations. Transformation stories always were hard to buy, and innocence no excuse for anything—look at Eurydice, dead on her wedding day from a serpent bite. Dead more than once, since the bridegroom bungled his instructions underground. Don't turn until you reach the light, Orpheus was told, but he couldn't help himself—looking for his tan pants?—and his wife drifted back to the shades.

Heroes got to make mistakes and live. Cut to pieces, Orpheus still sang. Prometheus got a replacement. Working over the pot, Aspera grated in the Parmesan Will liked, then put a spoonful of chowder to her lips. The hot liquid burned. She dropped the spoon. Playing with fire. All right, sacred flame; but nobody thought to call it that till some got stolen.

"I could show you on paper that it would work," Will said at dinner, pushing his empty soup bowl toward her. "I sat and looked at some numbers before I came home. We could get back the money we put into remodeling in under two years. The figures are all there."

She looked at Will's bowl on the edge of her placemat. Milky drops clung to its sides. "Are you finished, or do you want more?"

"You don't care about the figures, do you?"

"I'm asking if you want more chowder. Did you put your bowl here for me to fill?"

He shook his head, as if seeing the dish for the first time.

She thought about onions. Had she put in the chopped onions?

"So what did you find in Little Falls," he asked, "something nice and quiet, a job in a mausoleum?"

She felt her face color. "Nothing definite." She hurried to swallow a spoonful of chowder, was surprised to find the single bayleaf fitted perfectly to the roof of her mouth. Her tongue tried the leathery surface; she pulled out the entire leaf by its stem. Embarrassed while Will watched, she put the leaf on her napkin, then stacked their two bowls and set them aside. "I'll have to set up more appointments."

He forked the last bits of lettuce and carrot from the salad bowl. "Basically I don't think you understand risk. Taking a risk is the only fun in business."

"I remember when one store was a risk."

"Yeah." He rubbed his chin in the speculative way he had, his expression growing crafty. "But that was years ago. What have you done for me *lately*?"

She looked at him. Half the world runs on secrets.

He smiled. "I ran into Charles today. He came into the store with his new Mrs. Doctor."

"How is Charles?"

"Fine. He asked to be remembered to you. But not, as I recall, to Dena."

"What's his new wife like?"

"Quiet type. I said, 'And where do you keep *your* suitcase full of fancy underdainties?' But she acted as if she hadn't heard."

Will made it sound convincing enough so that Aspera covered her ears and shut her eyes.

"Some people, you know?" He made his voice go steep with concern. "They're afraid of intimacy. Once you really have a feeling for it, you keep a suitcase packed like Dena so you can be ready in a flash."

Her heart lurched. "You're so liberal, Will. You and Dena."

"We are. We're what you might call pro-intimate. For instance we wouldn't give it a thought if you wanted to have an affair."

Aspera opened her eyes wide. She looked down, pulled a spoon out from between the soupbowls she'd stacked.

"As long as one of us was dead," Will finished.

She looked at him.

"If *you* were dead," he went on, "of course there would be no problem. You have some right to privacy; what could I say? Now if I were dead—likewise. I'd have no objection" —he frowned— "as long as you followed the codicil in my will, the one you've already agreed to."

She rose and took dishes to the sink. "What codicil?"

"The one where you mix my ashes with luminescent paint, and cover the bedroom ceiling with it."

She turned and looked at the back of his head.

"Right after where it says you fill the waterbed with formaldehyde."

She stood behind him. A sick feeling spread along the floor of her stomach.

Ashes, formaldehyde. She recognized the language of love. She could translate: Be mine. She could make out: Don't leave me. She was tired of the extra effort. Love was butterscotch kisses, love was a pink satin ribbon; she had teethed on symbols. Love was two pearls a year, was ashes and formaldehyde.

Will stood up, picked up his own bowl and silverware. He put them in the sink, moving so that she had to step aside. When his hands were empty he placed them on her shoulders. "Just don't drip the paint on my mother's good wallpaper," he said.

She shrugged free. "I have real feelings about what you're saying—maybe you don't want to hear about those?"

Will leaned against the counter. "Of course not. People who are sensitive enough to share their real feelings are usually sensitive enough to be divorced."

This ring of spikes he threw between them—maybe he was right. Maybe it kept them from coming together in some kind of death grip. She expected too much from him, too much from marriage. Well, then, be realistic.

"What would happen if one of us were attracted to someone else?" The question scared her before she got it out, so she rushed on. "Has it ever happened to you?"

Will looked at her. "Of course it's happened to me. But you're not the one I want to talk to about it."

"But time passes. There's a before and after, like everything else."

"There's a Before and After"—he took up the words sing-song—"but they don't Connect. That's why people call it a Breakup."

Aspera wiped the sink with a sponge. "People don't always break up."

"People pretend to be very sophisticated. For sophisticated, I give you Dena and Charles."

She drew a breath. "I keep thinking they could settle things if they wanted to. I don't mean get remarried, but—people do get over things. After a few years, don't you think?"

"How long since we were in high school?"

"More than twenty years."

"Twenty years since I heard you were getting letters from some guy in Fridley?"

"Dewy Thorson! One letter, out of the absolute blue."

"Dewy Thorson. You know, twenty years later and I still hate that guy?"

Aspera smiled while her stomach poured acid.

For centuries people have kept a stakeout on the genital area, knowing they'd see action. A great clemency must attend sexual matters—here was sophistication. But clemency was old-fashioned, as old-fashioned as charity and as scarce. Mercy falling like rain in the heart of the country would this time of year come down as sleet.

Will lifted the lid on the pot of chowder. Condensation ran around the rim, dripped into the pot. "What happens to the rest of this?"

She shrugged. "It freezes well."

"Let's just dump it, shall we? It lacks something, just doesn't do it for me."

Talk about real feelings? They couldn't talk about leftovers without emotion.

CHAPTER THIRTEEN

She came breathless up the stairs and turned the wrong way, the numbers on the rooms diminishing—507, 503. She spun about and in forty paces had it, 525. She put up her knuckles to knock, then saw that the door had been left ajar. She wouldn't have thought of that, probably less awkward. She pushed it open, saw him poised to hook a hanging bag over the clothes rod that served for a closet. Kevin glanced over his shoulder at her, grinned.

"Welcome, what do you think of this place?"

She looked around. The double bed, so blatantly centered in the room. A hired room with a bed, a hired bed with a room. Bedspread made of thick blue plush, electric blue. Curtains of the same stuff; he'd closed them. The effect was not bordello, red plush was bordello. She set her purse on the bed to take off her coat. The knot of the camel wool belt seemed large, untying it unbearably intimate. Electric blue plush. What did it make her?

She met his eyes. Kevin had hooked fingers into his waistband, waiting for her coat, pretend host. He stood on the matted yellow industrial-strength shag and smiled at her. They hadn't fallen into one another's arms, and she didn't know what to do next, somehow get to the bathroom. Best to do that now. She smiled back at him and then pushed past in the small corridor between bed and cinderblock wall, saying, "I'll just go in here first."

First. Second, third? Her stomach churned. She closed the door, ran cold water in the sink. She hadn't been able to bring her diaphragm case, it didn't seem like hers alone; what did people do? She'd stopped in the drugstore of this town, had to ask the man at the counter to see "the selection." In flaming embarrassment she'd made a choice and paid him, dropped the small bag into her purse.

Which was on the bed in the next room. She whacked her forehead with the heel of her palm.

She came out of the bathroom and closed the door on the flushing noise. Kevin was slipping his briefcase under the clothes bag. He smiled at her again and then sat on the bed to remove his shoes, brown Hush Puppies with brown laces; she looked at her own shoes, sat on the bed and kicked them off. The synchronized postures felt very odd. They looked at one another for an uncertain moment.

"I'll just turn the TV on," Kevin said. He rose from the bed, clumsily pushing off with his hands. He bent and switched the set on, changed channels while she gaped. Her identity was returning; she could recognize herself in the instant dislike she took to his turning on the television and in the way she was simultaneously won by his efforts against the endless awkwardness.

"You've got to be kidding," she heard herself say.

He sat back down on the bed without turning his face from the active screen. "I love this show," he protested.

She couldn't tell if he was kidding or not.

After one thirty-second spot on dog food and one on instant cameras he stood and turned the thing off. He eased back down on the bed, now regarding her as though her mind's printout read across her eyes. "Not very smooth, I guess. And you don't really want to make love."

She pushed her hair out of her eyes, then forgot the hand and left it clutched to the back of her head. The bent arm hid her face from him while she said, "I don't guess so."

Gently he moved the arm aside. She let it drop between them and looked at the blue plush beneath the knot of her fingers. With his hand he brushed the hair out of her eyes again. "Then we won't," he said.

Expectation ground swiftly to a halt. Did she or did she not want to; what had she come for?

"Will you lie down with me and let me hold you?"

Sheepishly she brought her arms up around his neck and pressed the side of her head to his, as though they were old friends, ancient friends. After a while he loosened her arms and pushed himself back so that his head rested on the pillows. He stretched his arms to her.

She didn't move. "Really?" she begged.

He smiled. "Really."

She got up and repositioned her body on the bed so that she lay alongside him. He slipped an arm under her and held her firmly against his rib cage. Amazing, how solid he felt. How warm.

"Don't you believe in gravity?" He pointed to the way her hand rose stiffly off the bedspread, unsupported, a stop-gesture waiting for a context. She looked at it, recognized the hand as her own, let it drop with a great outrush of breath.

A long pattering of leaves blowing against brick and glass outside the building. A long sweet time of breathing his trace of lilac scent while she lay with her face nestled into his neck.

"I can't believe this," she whispered.

"Mmmmh?"

She didn't know herself what it was she couldn't believe. She wanted to fall asleep in the incredible ease of her body, this absence of resistance. "You mean," she finally asked, "this is for free?"

He clasped her two hands in his, the slow pressure melting her bones like fluid. "I'd rather be your lover than your friend," he said, "but that's not your problem. Do you believe that?"

Probably it was the gentleness of his voice that made the tears start, made her cling to the places where she could touch the skin of his neck.

"Can I ask you one thing?" he whispered when she was calm again. "If you ever do want me to make love to you, will you tell me?"

Her eyes stayed wide. She held in check the information offered up freely by her body, and with her head she nodded yes against his chest. Between the two of them it was the first lie she knew about.

She ran this meeting over and over through her head to make it last. It made her heart speed feathery-fast every time.

She floated through four days of helping out at the store, flitted right past Will's determined focusing of his charms on Bobbie's daughter. Aspera held to her perpetual afterglow. That way, things she'd thought would be hard—time and place—seemed easy. She interviewed for jobs. On Sunday she circled advertisements in three newspapers, and during the week she followed up. And things she'd thought impossible—taking a lover, betraying her husband—turned out to be natural as taking breath. Nomenclature again: the old phrases terrified, but put functional words in their place and see the difference—respond to Kevin, avoid Will. Nothing but good sense here.

"Wilderness! Christ. What did your mother have against you?"

She closed her eyes. "My mother was the best high school Latin scholar that Union City, Indiana, ever saw. She was the teacher's pride—one teacher, you know, for everything, and he thought Elvira was tops. He held a Latin contest for the county, ran it like a spell-down, he was so sure the other schools couldn't measure up." She smiled, took her time. "Sure enough, it got down to the last two pupils standing, and the teacher gave my mother—you're ready?—*aspera.* Elvira didn't hesitate. 'Hope,' she said. 'Wrong.' "

Aspera opened her eyes.

Kevin's were shining. "She named you for her mistake? Your own mother?"

"She fell in love with the boy who won. She hadn't even looked at him before she lost that contest, but she married him. My father. So, according to her, she named me for the most important moment of her life."

Kevin lay down on his back again, resumed his butterfly pose among the pillows. Soon the bed began to shake with his laughter.

She waited.

"I think it's great," he said.

She waited. "My father had green eyes," she told him. "Like yours."

These hours with Kevin, sparse as they were, flashed through her life like blanks in a slide carousel—blinding, utterly outside continuity, and they conditioned every scene of everyday life. This everyday life she floated through while she waited for another stunning glimpse of the secret behind the machine.

What do you think of between the thoughts you are thinking?

In this motel room the bed was placed beside a window. Aspera drew a blanket over her shoulder and up to his chest. A thought arrested her hand.

She decided not to ask, then asked. "Do you think about Vicky?"

"Do you?"

"Yes."

He shrugged. "She's an amazing woman. I hope she's happy."

"That's all?"

"Should there be more?"

Jagged webs of frost etched across the storm window beyond the nearer pane, brambles of interconnection. Like something a spider had dreamed.

He saw where she'd fixed her stare. "Complicated, isn't it?"

"How many women have you slept with?"

He gazed at her, mouth pursed.

"Is it bad manners, asking?"

"I'll tell you. You want me to count up? My whole life? OK, a hundred. A hundred and, I don't know!" He waved a hand at a number—"Thirty."

Aspera swallowed her amazement. He watched her face.

"That includes college," he said. "You know how that is."

She did, for her. White sheets, red. "Tell me about the last five years."

His eyes rolled as he calculated. "Maybe twenty."

"Slowing down," she mused. "And this year?"

"This year?"

"This is fall."

The window beside them argued winter.

He sighed. Pressed his mouth into a line. "Four."

She nodded slowly.

"You getting all the information you need?"

Aspera sat up in the bed beside him. She held up one finger for him to see, moving it solemnly to his lips. He let it rest there while they looked at one another.

"One." Under her fingertip his lips moved softly.

Deliberately then she put up the second finger. He kissed both fingers, took them into his mouth and bit down, still looking into her eyes. He moved his hand, fitted it to her hipbone. She was astonished at the blaze of desire.

She pulled her fingers free. "I need to make a point." She hoped to avoid the names, did not want to say *Will,* did not want to say again *Vicky.* "The point is, this is going to mean a lot more to me than it does to you."

He tilted his head back to look into her eyes from that new distance. A slow smile began in his eyes and spread down his face. He pressed his lips together then, looked away from her and toward the window, as though the source of his amusement might lie in that direction.

"I guess we'll see," Kevin said.

Centaurs, maidens bearing wheat sheaves or scales, goats with fishtails looped like a mermaid's—for Aspera the world seemed open to mythology again, to beast-monsters and legend. Astrology was not to be dismissed, nothing that might account for new music among spheres she had presumed dead. Maybe it was just a fact that the finished adult personality was not much use in times of deep change or crisis. Those last few layers of veneer had been stripped back in her own case, and when she found what had been covered over, it was a patchwork with seams showing bold as stitches on Frankenstein's forehead. None of the finishwork she had applied in the name of maturity—a talent for compromise, taking the long view—offered enough grit to support a spark. And it was the spark that interested her.

Now she saw all men as repositories of sex. She looked over those she walked past on the street, thought, and was amazed to find that she thought: You? Do you understand what I have just learned, do you all know and I have just tumbled to it?

At nineteen sex had not opened her world but narrowed its focus. Now the universe seemed to be expanding the way scientists had always advertised. That Kevin could replace Will was impossible to consider, and indeed at the beginning she thought only of Prometheus, of how fire may be borrowed from one realm to brighten another. But illumination spread, and

Will in their neutral zone of marital embraces became not only Will but everyone else, too: Kevin, the men in the park, Dalton, the dentist—Vicky and Dena if she chose. She understood everything about sex. Understood desire and compulsion; understood pornography, molestation, giving and receiving pain.

All these years she'd discounted Elvira's science, the vocabulary of stars and planets in a calculus of destiny: as above, so below. But since below was behaving most uncharacteristically, she would look above. Back to the mysteries. Back to her mother's text.

She dug out crates of Elvira's books, became a student again. She would not sit and scrawl upon her notebooks and pieces of paper *Kevin Stowe, Kevin Stowe, Kevin Kevin Kevin Mrs. Kevin Stowe,* but she could look up transits and progressions, angles and orbs. She could learn the queer symbols, read notes in the margins in her mother's hard pencil about Venus as it was visited by dour Saturn, by erratic Uranus.

Will saw her crouched on the rug in the small upstairs bedroom when he'd walk past the door, the room he'd shared with his brother. She didn't look guilty. She was applying for jobs in libraries. She wrote things down in code, he saw note pads full of picturelike symbols. He didn't recognize them and he didn't ask; they were living their lives in the dark, weren't they? Both wearing miners' helmets with their own single beams pointed parallel. She could lead her own life, he never said otherwise, he didn't interfere with her, did he? He had nothing really to complain of, he guessed it was working. Still: that look of embarrassment when she glanced up to see him standing in the doorway. He returned to a joke from years ago when he'd seen the puddles of books around her change from ancient culture to library science, from bookkeeping and business management to fertility references to marital adjustment. Shelf-help, he called it.

When she cleared the table at night and disappeared up the stairs to job-hunting books, Elvira's astrology books, mythology books, even modern novels—that was a new category—he said in a flat voice, "More shelf-help?"

She squared her shoulders, went up anyway.

Reading the novels, Aspera discovered that this century's storytellers still followed heroes down paths that she herself would avoid. She had more sense than people in novels. Sensible people pulled back when crisis presented itself too threateningly. Her own sense of danger was well developed. She wished to preserve her life, spotty and time-shattered as it was. Leave it to fictitious people to go the extra and fatal mile; what good were they to her otherwise? Characters were to address issues and push through. If they failed in this, she could merely toss the book aside, try another. The whole point was to feel that something just the other side of her courage or luck had been tried, the consequences laid out. From her own life she knew how character dissolved plot—she herself daily smudged over any clean story lines within reach.

The truth was, she never thought of leaving Will, but these days she would have obliterated him if she could, in the blameless way it was brought off in novels. How they cheated, sending husbands away for archaeological missions or photographic jaunts, putting them in comas or sales meetings on another continent, giving them batty dispositions or beastly ones that fairly begged for desertion.

In real life it was her own attention that wandered, not the inconvenient mate. Domestic details slipped as the mind traveled twilight zones of fantasy. Out of body indeed. It was necessary to keep the illusion suspended, all the plates spinning, energies devoted to the look of a seamless web of normalcy. As in all magic acts, one could not falter and let the props clatter to the floor; the lady being sawed must not scream or bleed. The balloons, not the human target, may burst for approval.

All the while Will showed himself impressively corporeal, unforgivably legitimate. Romance hinged on sabbatical thinking, elsewhere again. Not simple when one lived day to day with the person one wished sabbaticalized. But possible.

Spirit and matter were not very securely joined; if Elvira was right about a silver cord linking the two, it would have to be a very flexible material indeed to take the abuse Aspera now gave it. Nominally at Will's side in the house, at table, in bed, she roamed other levels where Kevin's voice and touch framed existence. Will, though physically near, was for all that hardly present; she could make him disappear in mid-sentence, mid-kiss. She was elated, horrified, but finally adept.

The corporeal Will countered with sly protests aimed at her absence in the store; that much he could certify. He complained with newspapers or laundry dropped on the kitchen table, at the sofa's edge, beside the bed. At last, foretold by Dena, socks appeared singly on the bedroom floor.

None of their words together touched anything that still had pulse. She turned to shelf-help, and once she was up the stairs each night she plunged into questions of utmost consequence. By principle of energy, by house and sign position, what took place when the love principle of Venus was activated by the deceiver-dissolver Neptune? Venus, refugee from Jupiter, goddess of love in her element again, at home with the ruler of the sea.

Cross-checking the myths with their planetary equivalents, Aspera again fell in with the whole lurching pantheon of Greek heroes, whose exploits were too marked by arrogance to be mortal. Diagnostic: if you survived arrogance, it was a sure sign of divinity.

Mortals tended toward prying into forbidden knowledge, like children rifling their mothers' dresser drawers, and that was good for a one-way ticket underground. Eve, Eurydice—castaways associated with serpents and state secrets and the underworld. Like sacred fire, what was forbidden usually proved to be lines of protection for the gods—and did gods need protection?

Psyche was told that her husband and secret lover was a serpent, so she lit a candle and tried to see for herself. For which error she was sent underground for a box she was not to open. Secrets withheld from women. What were they not supposed to see?

Frustrated, Aspera turned to handwritten notes in the margins, the thin twisted lower loops denoting Elvira's hand. Slanted across the bottom of a page she read, "Serpent did not mean snake but any crawling creature, including dragon—ancient beast of unspeakable wisdom." Of course: Eve tempted to the tree of knowledge not by a snake but a beautiful dragon.

On the top of the next page, more of Elvira's crimped hand. "Pre-Hellenic cultures worshiped the all-powerful goddess. Her sacred animal the serpent."

Eurydice? The story had haunted Aspera since her own wedding, this bride consigned to the shades for serpent bite. Aspera looked up Eurydice in the index of one book, tried another. Eventually she found entries under Orpheus, the hero-bridegroom who meant to redeem his wife from the underworld except *he turned.* Elvira had underlined the phrase. Orpheus went on to found a religion for men that spurned female sexuality. Raging women tore the musician-poet to pieces, and the text writers failed to make sense of it.

The scent of politics was very strong. Elvira had underlined again where the text told how Orpheus, even dismembered, *went on singing his verses.*

Eurydice betrayed underground, and it was Orpheus' voice we listened to?

Aspera turned pages in a kind of frenzy. No more handwritten notes. In another book she found passages checked and underlined; they concerned the management of illusion, the garbled version of which had been Elvira's warning to her at her marriage. Aspera read through them all. Then tumbling through the rest of the books, she shook out three folded onionskin slips. Invoices, thirty years old and more. She had seen them before, often used them for place markers, but now reverently she examined these pieces of her mother's life.

What had Elvira ordered from San Francisco? Item 12747, ten dollars plus tax and shipping. The same thing three times, Decembers and Septembers. That meant Christmases and birthdays—quickly Aspera calculated the years—when she was twelve and thirteen.

Without quite allowing the idea to form, she brought her fingers to touch the seven pearls at her neck.

Her fingertips went numb. The cold white nodules felt utterly unfamiliar—this necklace was anything, a reliquary for baby teeth. She blinked hard and focused hard on the slips of paper. She thought of running downstairs to tell Will, but then she pictured his face.

Shelf-help. Aspera sat back and slowly dug her fingernails into the skin of her neck. She began to think she might catch up with what she needed to know.

That night, still traveling in the dream, she comes to herself on a steep precipice walking a pavement that suddenly drops.

She can't see the cause, but gravity pulls her flat-footed and resisting to the edge. She throws herself down on the crumbled sandy ledge, which gives way. She falls down and down through colored space until she again grips sand under her hands. She gets to her feet, the pull begins again. When she falls this time, the sand in her hand is wet. She looks up, sees she is on a wide, pale ocean beach strewn with bits of green; green ocean glass. She picks it up as the tide comes in and laps, warm, at her fingers. So many pieces of glass, smooth in her palm. She can find them under the churning water even when night descends; she does not need to see to keep finding pieces. When she lifts them up, they are in ropes; necklaces strung with chunks of green ocean glass. Embedded in each piece, a secret. In the dream she sees in zooming closeup, like Superman's X-ray vision, a single pearl.

She stretched skin to skin the length of Kevin's body, her own body racing. How she desired this man! He sensed it, and after a time of teasing entered her with a rough and absolute authority, saying just before the bank and dive of orgasm, "This is as good as love gets." And she, certain that she had displaced the others, all the others in his mind and hers, gave herself over to the pleasure of her body with his, this particular body, this particular man. Chester and Elvira had lost this first, lost one another and then—fear flashed through her and she clung to him, burst into tears.

"Where were you?" he whispered afterward.

"With you," she lied. She clutched him along his shoulder and thigh, where her hands lay; she set her nails into his flesh with a shudder, afterbirth of ferocity.

He looked away from her, gazed up at the ceiling for some time. He relaxed then, folded his arms under his head, having removed them from her grasp.

"Sometimes," he mused, still with his eyes focused high, "I think you and I need to kill something together. I mean, kill something alive, some animal—and eat it raw with our hands." He didn't look at her. "That idea appeal to you?" He spoke to the air that hovered between them, above them.

She answered to the same stretch of ceiling that had come to seem a part of their communication, the essential third party.

"With you I could do that. How dreadful. Is that being in love?"
"More like being possessed," he said.

Oppression fostered romance, that much politics she knew. But secrecy was oppressive, too. Cars weren't the only difficulty; a division fell across all lines of communication. It fell between those who had legitimate use of the telephone, and those who did not. She belonged in the latter group, unable to place calls to Kevin from home, unable to explain toll charges that would appear in such detail on the telephone bill: number called, time of day, time connected.

She learned how public public telephones were. Why would she walk down to Irene's or the Townsend to place calls when she could use the phone at home? Why would she linger over a phone booth in the library when the librarian knew the store was two minutes down the street? How often could her car be seen parked in front of the Shell station's drive-up phone without exciting comment? Would she kill something alive?

Calls received at home had to be timed with precision. If a man answers was a very old joke, still not funny for the same reasons.

What rights of privacy did one retain in the married state? A few; all that secrecy and cunning allow. Some that boldness can seize.

What did marital trust include? Things that cannot be guessed.

"I may chase you around the bed tonight," Will said to her as they climbed into bed.

She glanced at him. Think of history now. As she clambered over the quilted coverlet to her side of the bed, her toenail caught on a thread. She stopped to unhook it, and to examine the ragged nail.

"Here I am talking about making love, and you stop to pick your toes like a damn monkey."

She got off the bed, her anger subsumed in seeing to the nail. As she left the bedroom Will demanded, as one who has been wronged, "Come back here. I was kidding. Come back here, Aspera."

She felt the power of leaving the room. If you couldn't have power inside the relationship, you got it by stepping outside. Clearer and clearer. She trimmed her toenail in the bathroom and returned to the bedroom doorway, where she paused.

Will sat propped on the pillows. He stretched out his arm to her. "Come here, I want to tell you something I saw today." He made room next to his side, but she sat warily beside his feet.

"Wait," she said. "I don't like your jokes when you use them to cover up being mad."

"You're making a big deal out of it. I wasn't angry."

"Sex is a big deal."

"Since when? Anyway, I didn't have any real expectations for sex."

She folded her arms.

"Look, I apologize, OK? Now please come here."

She went stiffly to crawl into bed beside him. He put an arm around her, said amiably, "I saw the damnedest thing today, a picture in the paper of monkeys with a two-year-old kid looking at them. But the two-year-old looked exactly like a monkey. Monkeys can look so human, but this kid—you couldn't tell them apart, he looked exactly like a damn flea-picking monkey."

Aspera sat up from the headboard, from his arm.

"What now?" he said.

"What are you trying to do?"

Will's face closed. "You forced me to apologize, but I really don't think what I said was so bad."

They stared at one another.

She said, "Do you have any other stories before I go to sleep?"

"None. How about you?"

At such times the thought flashed through her mind to tell him about Kevin, but she crossed the thought out. A clean breast—the very words pointed vulnerability. What could come of truth? Will enraged, Will crushed. Either way she could not leave him, her loyalty wearing to the surface like an eroded fossil. She and Kevin would have to stop. Then what would she have? None of her heart, all of a damaged trust.

In the morning she got up when Will did, made a point of being dressed and sitting over her materials—letters, ads, résumés, telephone notes, job files spread over the dining room table—before he came down to breakfast.

"Sometime I'd like to have a meal in the dining room again," he said when she emerged from the passage for a second glass of juice.

Glaring at him hunched over his cereal, she stepped on a pile of clothing near the kitchen door. "What's all this?"

"Some cleaning," he said, napkin corner to his mouth. "I thought I'd put it there so you wouldn't miss it."

She freed her foot from a shirt-sleeve. "The cleaner is two blocks from the store. You can take it with you and drop it, the way we always have."

He shrugged, getting up and setting his coffee cup on the counter. "I'm a little rushed this morning, I thought since you're just here around the house today—"

"I'm leaving for the VA Hospital in Saint Cloud in exactly eleven minutes. I have an appointment at personnel in one hour."

"Never mind then." He bent to pick up the shirts and sweaters. "Some of your things are in here, too, you know. I didn't know we were quite so inflexible these days."

"Then leave my things. You don't—"

"I'll take care of it. You worry about your January deadline."

"What deadline?"

He straightened. "If you don't have a job by January, we expand the store and you come back to work full-time."

"I never agreed to that."

He looked at her, his face puffy, sore-looking. Technicalities, terms. They both knew about business contracts, that they worked when there was good faith and didn't work when there wasn't.

"I'm late," he muttered. He dropped the clothes to the floor, kicked the mass aside. "I'll have to get these tomorrow. You don't mind stepping over them for another day, do you?"

She followed him to the coat closet, ducked as the ends of his alpaca muffler overshot the shoulders of his down jacket.

"I do mind. I mind the cups and cereal bowls you've started leaving unrinsed on the counter. I mind the newspapers you drop. I mind all these ways you have of telling me—whatever it is you're telling me."

"Have a nice day," Will said.

When the back door shut, she gave the pile of clothes in the kitchen a kick that scattered them. It took several more kicks to get them into one pile again.

"You don't know the way, do you? You dumb fuck, you don't know." The whispered voice sneering, intense. Then the man who had leaned toward her to deliver this message, pea green shirt, gray rumpled slacks, raced away. She wheeled about, alone in the long corridor.

Not a dream. The corner of the man's shirttail tucked wrong way up into the waistband of his slacks. Detail, detail. A patient surely, merely a patient in this hospital, not an oracle. Jumpy. No cause: this was the government, Veterans Administration Hospital; fish would be fried in orderly procession. Civil-service exam, point scores, top three candidates. Disabled veterans preferred, bonus points, five points per phantom limb. Reasonable effort to contact. Weeks and weeks of orderly procession. Procession of the equinoxes, reliable forecasting. Reliable as any. Months would pass.

As soon as she had stepped into the corridor from the sidewalk, brilliant chill November outside, dim pungent sweat and stale cigarettes inside, she'd lost her bearings. First the oracle, now scuffle noises. Patients in paper slippers rounded a corner, bathrobes hung crookedly as they would on wire hangers, these old men not much different, sick old wires. Bathrobes with belts yanked askew. Hands stiffly trailing cigarettes, long negligent ash, tarry filters smoldering in wall-mounted aluminum urns. Three haggard men passed her without any sign. She tried not to breathe. Schizophrenia someday may be chemically defined; a characteristic odor. Meanwhile instant mythology, old men who speak in riddles and rhymes.

She wanted the job. Doctors, not patients, would come to the medical library. Libraries smelled like books. Maybe in this case like Thorazine. Don't be so jumpy.

She found her way to the cafeteria by following odors of overcooked eggs, got directions. Woman wearing a sanitary hair net pointed with fingers she wiped on her apron front. A mile of gray corridor away, two floors up; personnel office, man with creamy gray hair in swirls like frosting. Mr. Engel, officious and adenoidal in brown-tinted glasses, furtive. Tinted glasses in this dim building, grudging windows set high up in brickwork? Library remodeled, the Learning Resource Center of the Saint Cloud VA Hospital announces an opening for qualified person. Courtesy interview now, blanks filled in a form handed her, woman with sparkling rings. Availability. Previous government service. Phone. Box for official use only.

This was the world at the other end of the telephone calls she made, the letters of application sent out. If she got lucky, a job interview down the road.

She handed in the form, took a breath, walked down the corridor again. A vacant-faced old man rode slumped in a wheelchair, pushed by an orderly. Who was young, but otherwise the faces matched. Family resemblance?

As far as she knew, Will's father had never said to his son, "You will follow me in the lumber business." This expectation he had no need to voice. Good children had table manners, did they not? Well-brought-up sons knew where their duty lay; they kept bargains in good faith.

Wilson Hancock, Sr., had not approved of the architect nonsense. He chose to believe that his son was garnering a couple of years' experience before entering the family business. He saw the parabola of decision returning, Will's independence a bouquet gathered in his honor. This vision he confided to his wife, who dropped confident hints to her daughter-in-law. "Soon you children will want to get settled," she would whisper.

After "the children" had been in Minneapolis four years—had Will run away from home without ever having to say so?—a snappish look had come to the old man's eyes when his son mentioned long-term projects on drawing boards. Never a talkative parent, the father, with his firm straight mouth, kept silences that grew burnished. Seven years in Minneapolis, and the change in his pocket was heard from. His feet in their polished black shoes scraped wood or carpet in somatic protest.

"When did you and Will mean to settle down?" was how Mrs. Hancock began to put the matter. Settling down, Aspera had thought at first, meant children. She and Will "hoped to someday." To which Mrs. Hancock replied by excitedly pointing up small-town wholesomeness, urban squalor. The linkage was tight in her mind: settling down meant Bracken.

"My Willie is so good with little ones. Your children will have a wonderful father, experienced, you know. All those years he took care of his brother. Couldn't bear to be parted from him, you know—'Ma, I'll give Devvie his bottle,' he would say, 'I can get him to sleep.' He saved Devvie from tumbling down those cellar stairs at the store one time—I'll never forget. I heard the screaming and came on the run—high heels, you know, ladies didn't wear pants in those days—and there was Willie, holding Devon by the scruff of his collar. Those stairs! I saw to it that Wilson put up a gate after that."

The year Mr. Hancock died, Will began commuting from Minneapolis to Bracken every day in the Mercury to help his mother. This without any discussion. When had it been settled? As an adult Will had never been alone with his parents, never visited them except in Aspera's company. She had sensed she was his guarantor against them, against what they wanted from him: his life.

Clearly this secret compact between them had been made long ago, but now she saw what her part had been. All those discussions of "settling down" had been the line of communication between father and son! Mrs. Hancock and Aspera, acting as seconds. The question the father refused to ask, and which the son, seeing freedom glimmer between the bricks of expectation, neglected to address. *When are you coming into the business, son?*

Will's mother died a few months after her husband. With both his parents gone, Will had returned "home" to the store. Meeting its demands, he had been overwhelmed like a child, and Aspera had become, once again, his guarantor.

Don't analyze me just because you're feeling guilty.

Medical Learning Resources Center. Letters grooved into layers of plastic. She turned the handle, pushed open the door: yes. Odor of books. Checkout desk, magazine racks. Cartoon tacked to card-dating machine: librarian, beside a child bound and gagged, speaking into a telephone, "We're serious, Mr. Hooper. You have our books, we have your son." Copy machine. New carpet. Back in the stacks, between racks of books shelved on gray metal, one person moved. Quietly, calmly. Not waiting to sell something, be sold. A job in this place, her days apart from Will. A tremor captured her stomach. Leave him alone to manage? Yes, dammit. Would he actually force her hand, keep her in the store by taking on too much? He could try.

Back in the hospital corridor she found the door to the outside, pushed hard. Light spilled in, she breathed cold clean air. It was the authority of the voice that stayed with her, the tuneless contempt. "You dumb fuck, *you don't know.*"

Imagine: a man she couldn't seem to displease.

In the motel in Elk River, Kevin got back into bed. He wrapped cold feet and legs around Aspera's warm ones and murmured, "Tell me about wanting. Tell me how anybody forgets how."

She drew a breath. "Every time you lose something important," she said, "you pretend you exchanged it for something else." She looked at him, saw he was listening. "It's not passive, the way you say. It's active. It takes effort."

He said, "Is there a story goes with this?"

She smiled, let herself relax against the white-sheeted mattress. "After my father had been away from home for months driving a truck, he came in to the trailer and picked me up. His jacket pockets rattled. Two big cellophane bags of butterscotch kisses. The thing was, I'd found the candy the day before in my mother's dresser drawer."

Kevin looked at her, lifted an eyebrow.

"So I pretended. I wanted so much to be surprised at what he had brought, just for me, that after twenty-five years I've almost forgotten for real."

"Does it matter?"

She shut her eyes. The strength of feeling drained her of words. "Well, you keep trading off one thing for another and pretty soon"—the words that tumbled out were not her own—"everybody is in the wrong place."

Vicky's words. Vicky had told her that. Aspera pleated the sheet with her hands, folding, pressing.

Kevin cocked his head. "Will all right?" he asked.

The question startled her. The boundaries of their floating world, which already seemed to her too fragile, achieved with great concentration, were dissolving.

"You cannot infiltrate everything," she said angrily. "I need to keep things separate." She put her hands over her ears. "But I can't even remember straight anymore."

With his fingers he shaped the hair that dovetailed at the nape of her neck.

"You get in between the steps of what happened—maybe it shifts around," she moaned. What she saw as she spoke were layers of rock shifting; packed down like that, the earth would always have to crack so that rivers could find beds. The muscles in her arms and legs clenched hard. "I should never have got so I would need this so much."

He smoothed her hair, and time took its pulse from his stroke. After an eternity he said, "You mean us."

So simple. Yes, that's what she meant. She felt like crying.

"Things happen one after another," he said mildly. "Going back to what you should-never"—he paused, let her catch up—"puts a loop in the string."

Aspera tried to imagine it: world without loops.

"When I'm with you," she said, "I can't think why anything could ever be complicated, when the truth is I don't know anything that isn't." She felt the warm pathways his fingers made on her neck and back, like streaks of sunlight. "If I could do one thing after another in a simple string," she whispered, "I'd go home from here with you and crawl into your bed and wake up next to you tomorrow morning. I wonder how long we could stay with that string. One week? Fifteen years?"

He had taken his hands away. He sat up and tossed her a towel from the motel table. "You're going to have to rush today. You don't want to be late."

She took the towel and shifted out of the white motel sheets. She had done this, had tried to lean on a shaft of light and produced these shadows. There were things Kevin didn't want to hear. She was learning what they were. Just outside the radiance of pleasure, a ring of spikes.

When he got back from showering she was dressed and sitting on the bed she had made and patted smooth. He stood hipshot in front of a battered bureau. Above it was a carved mirror, probably oak but painted over; at its apex an eagle clutched a bundle of sticks.

"How come you made the bed?" he asked.

This small-town motel room had become unbearably real

in the short time he had been showering. These particular walls had begun to lose the floating quality that had made all the others shimmer in space and time. These seemed earthen. The old woman she'd glimpsed through the office window of this motel—Aspera could see her cleaning up after them, inspecting the mends on the upholstered chair in the corner. That world had broken through the dream entirely, and Aspera knew that when she left today she wouldn't be able to pull this hour around herself like a cloud. She would be back in time with no protection. She needed to see him again soon, more often now to make it last, to make this world keep filling the cracks and fissures in the other one.

Ask for what you want, just go for it. She addressed Kevin's wavery reflection. "Do you think of us together sometimes?"

He looked up, met her eyes in the mottled glass. "Sometimes." He sorted through his tumbled clothes. "I have this plan," he said. "That we could be lifetime lovers."

Thrilled, she made herself listen for nomenclature. "Lifetime lovers?"

He pulled on his jockey shorts, flannel slacks, a pinstriped shirt. He draped the tie around his neck and held one sock aloft. She pointed to the other one on the floor. He picked it up and came to sit beside her on the bed.

"The thing about you," he said, "you like sex. I wasn't sure at first, but you really do." He kissed her forehead. "I don't expect I'll be your last lover."

The green eyes glancing past hers. Her throat caught.

"I'm supposed to have others?" Her laugh came pinched, more breath than sound. She watched his face.

He smiled. "You can have it all," he assured her.

CHAPTER FOURTEEN

"The weekend? The whole weekend?" Will's tone dipped into the store of outrage he kept handy these days.

"I need to get out of here." Aspera's tone never far from breaking.

His hands in his pockets. "Maybe I'd like to do that, too."

She knotted her hands. "I want to spend some time in the city. Shopping with Dena, for God sake."

He paced the kitchen in short quick steps, stopped abruptly. "Why don't you go with Bunny? At least that way I could make plans with Dalton."

Reluctantly she considered, juggling in her mind: afternoon, evening, overnight. Couples without children weren't supposed to have trouble like this, trouble getting time. Modern myth. "All right, I'll call Bunny."

Will left for the store.

Aspera hadn't any plans for the weekend at all. She was making things up out of whole cloth, wholly desperate. She wanted to see Kevin. Maybe it would all fall into place. When Bunny didn't answer at home, Aspera rang Dalton's department at the University.

"Count us in," he enthused. "Bunny would love to see you and Dena, and I'd love to make Will take me ice fishing, this great macho event he talks about. Isn't there some lake near Bracken that rents ice houses?"

"Saint Anthony Lake. It's primitive, though, not the kind of place that comes with rented female services," Aspera teased him. "For that you have to go to Mille Lacs."

"First time out we'll just go after the fish."

"You're sure Bunny will go along with all this?"

"Sure I'm sure. She doesn't want me to go all the way to Mille Lacs either."

It was working. When Aspera reached Dena at the Harkness Gallery she arranged the afternoon of shopping, then said, "I need to include Bunny in our dinner plans. You don't have to cook, we'll go out."

Dena hesitated. "Actually I'd be pleased to entertain."

"Since when?"

"Let's say I've reconsidered. Perhaps you were right, Bunny could introduce me to some people."

"Oh, dear. Quentin still hasn't—"

"He has not."

"Oh, Dena, I'm sorry."

"Life goes on." Dena gave a deep sigh. "Bring on the panderers and go-betweens."

Aspera hesitated. "Can you be polite to Bunny?"

"Being polite is my specialty. I'll put Bunny at ease and make her feel less conspicuous by wearing a long black velvet skirt, topless with just some glitter sprinkled on my nipples."

Aspera's laugh was nervous. "Promise you won't."

"I promise."

"Now promise to wear a bra."

"Tell you what. I'll just leave a few extra ones in a bowl by the door with a little sign, the way restaurants do. 'For our matchless friends?' "

Aspera hung up smiling and dialed Kevin's office. She leaned against the bedpost and wedged the receiver against one ear. With her hand she kneaded the skin of her stomach, kneaded the hollow bubble that bloomed there.

"Aspera?" On the line Kevin's voice changed to a husky office-intimate. "I meant to call you Monday, or Tuesday morning at the latest. But then I thought, nah, I've been bugging her too much."

This had a wrong sound, came from the wrong place; even for office cover she could feel the words coming from the wrong place. She hadn't seen him for a week, hadn't heard from him.

She stood upright, both feet.

"Yes." He filled the silence. "Thank you."

Colleagues within earshot. One of those phone calls when

his voice would alter from one moment to another: warmth within the confines of business, then a whisper of something intimate, everything cross purpose.

"Kevin. Please call me back when you can."

He chuckled, his voice softly insinuating. "Come on. I've been missing you."

She shut her eyes against the ease in his tone. She didn't mean to do this today, get so jumpy. "I'm feeling a little crazed," she said.

"Aspera." His voice muffled against the receiver. "Think a minute. Can you feel how much I love you in the way I touch you?"

She felt her mind go numb. His voice, conjoined with the memory of his touch.

"I'm going to be in the city Saturday. Overnight."

"MMmmmm," he said. "Good news."

"I'll be out with Dena that afternoon, and then there's dinner with Bunny at Dena's place. I can meet you afterward."

"Not till after?"

She felt a rush of joy. He was free.

"I want to see you," he said. "Can't we make it earlier?"

"You could call Dena and see if you can't get yourself invited."

"Seriously?"

She hadn't been, but now she said, "Why not?" She gave him the number. "You're on your own."

"If I manage this feat," he said, "will you stay with me all night?"

Her heart thudded in her ears. "Yes."

"You want that?"

"Yes."

"Good."

The tone held something of the teacher well answered. She was learning the aphrodisiac powers of recklessness.

"Do you want me to sit next to you?" he asked.

"No." She sat down on the bed holding the telephone, stared at the diamonds watching in the wallpaper. "But sometime I might need to know that I'm not crazy, and I'll need a look from you that tells me."

"You mean the kind of look we're supposed to be careful not to exchange."

"Exactly."

"I'll have to chat up the others, you know."

She hesitated.

"I'll be doing that for us, you know."

"Smoke screen," she said. He had done this before.

Kevin said, "Do you want me to sit next to you at dinner?"

"Yes."

"Good."

She hung up knowing something was at stake. Some part of herself that she could lose if she needed him like this, if she learned to settle for lines drawn where she couldn't see them.

When the phone rang in her lap it was like being electrocuted. She seized the receiver: Will.

"You've been on the phone," he accused. "What's the story?"

A sound like the slippage of bicycle gears in her head. The story, what story? "Oh," she faltered. "You're to rent an ice house on Saint Anthony Lake for you and Dalt Saturday night."

"Oh. Fine."

In the moment's pause she heard, on his end of the line, a door open and close, cash-register sounds.

"I was trying to reach you because one of the contractors was in picking up an order. I wanted to let him get an idea of what we might do in the cellar. He'll come back to do a formal estimate."

"Fine." Her voice came clipped.

"That sound all right to you?"

"Will, we have more than enough margin to do what you want to do in the cellar. Is that what you're asking me?"

His voice rose. "I'm just trying to make sure you're in on the planning if you want to be."

She let go a breath. "Will, I'll be glad to help you plan the thing if you like."

"I didn't ask you to do that," he said quickly. A pause. Then, "What's for dinner tonight?"

She couldn't seem to change gears. The phone in her hand felt like a plastic toy, one you had to pretend into.

"You're a woman," he went on, "you have to think of these things."

"Let's go to Irene's," she said.

After good-bye, she let the phone fall to the floor. When

the alarm trill of disconnect sounded, she got down off the bed, knelt in a blind haste to put the parts together. She joggled the receiver so it wouldn't slide off the cradle again, then stretched out facedown on the carpet beside the telephone.

At the store Will sat on the cellar stairs. He could hear Bobbie's kid behind him, chirping to an old lady with a shopping bag at the register. With the heel of his hand he struck the bare wood of the old door facing where it was worn free of paint. Solid. He blew out a breath and rubbed his hand. He tried not to listen to the conversation behind him. This kid Marlys was an airhead, but here he sat, the original. Supposed to know his business, babbling to a contractor like a jerk. Just rip this old hulk out in two seconds, it'll practically fall out by itself. Hell, the man said, built like Gibraltar. Absolutely right. How had he got it fixed in his mind that this structure was rickety, unsafe? Solid as rock. Be twice the work getting it out than he'd been thinking, what a total incompetent.

And then he had to call her up, didn't he, put the pressure on. He slammed the door facing again with his hand. Give him that, he was subtle.

He took a folding knife out of his pocket and opened it, scraped away at the shale of paint layers where an edge jutted. Blue, cocoa, yellow, white. She said he loved this place, was it true? In architecture school he loved the patterns, lines arcing through clean space, loved the materials things were made of—even the names. Waterstruck brick. Spalted maple. Amaranth. Will slipped the knife blade under the layers, and, trapping them with this thumb, he peeled back skins of oil-base enamel. Underneath were obvious patches of wood filler—places where the old gate hinges had been screwed in. Toddler gate, for his brother, for the stairs. He dug the point of his knife in, worked it back and forth. The filler shattered. Getting mad always does this to him, he feels so cut off, getting this mad is dangerous. You can't control her coming and going, that's hopeless, no way you can control anything. He dropped his head into his arms, and a picture floats to mind: baby playing near the stairs. His mother weighs sacks of nails for a customer. He is supposed to watch the baby. He watches all right, watches Devon hold to the door facing, teeter over the drop to the first stair. No gate. Devon teeters, pulls back. Teeters again.

This baby crowds everything else out of his world; when the baby is there he can't smell the sawdust or burned smell of sawed wood from the shop; everything smells like milk or diapers. The nails his mother chunks down into the bag don't make their music sounds, he can't hear anything but babble-noise; the baby has changed everything and it would just take a little push, it would almost be an accident. He rivets his stare on the top-heavy flounderings of his brother, so clumsy, he could just fall by himself but he never does. He doesn't know anything. All the tending in the world won't make him right, Dad says. He scoots over on the floor next to Devon and the baby turns to smile, round eyes, drool shining on its chin. Doesn't know anything. Will hands him a Tinkertoy to make him let go the hand that holds on to the facing. Devon drops his rattle from his other hand and reaches and takes the solid disc. Will hands him another. Devon blinks and the hand on the wall quavers, lets go. Will turns away not to watch, hears the bang of the cash drawer, click of his mother's step. He flings himself forward, arms around his brother. Devon lets out a screech and the clicks speed fast as his heart. His mother screams. He has Devon round the neck, holding him struggling on the first step, so heavy! In a rush of skirts and scent his mother scoops the baby up and she is crying and that frightens him more. She gets down on the floor and hugs both of them together tight, he can feel the damp squirm of the baby's face next to his on his mother's soft shirt, he hears the crooning pigeon sounds that come from deep in the baby's chest. "Wilson! Wilson!" His mother shrieks loudly for his father. He is wildly afraid. When his father finds out they will take him away, the way they said about Devon.

Saturday morning Aspera found a rock station on the car radio and played it loudly, moving her shoulders and head and even her hips to the beat. She sang with the lyrics, her jaw slung forward for the sensual delivery. She squinted her eyes against the lowered gray skies, not wanting to see the bleak ponds saddled with their coats of ice, fields with their litter of frozen stubble. Music would swallow it all.

By the time she passed the stacks of the Bracken power plant, snow beat suddenly down the air. The prairie she left behind her disappeared into whiteness, into music.

Just before the Minneapolis bypass, this obliteration was pierced by some finger lettering on the dirt-sprayed back of a semi. She drove up close, intending to pass, and read "BOOBY INSPECTOR." A long arrow was drawn to point to the left, where she would pass the driver. "*Ladies show me your boobies,*" read the subscript.

She floored the accelerator as she passed. The driver honked. Stroke of genius, employing the word *ladies.* Safety counts.

When she drove up to Dena's building it was already eleven. She turned the music down to concentrate on traffic and, finding a parking place, discovered herself hungry and slightly sick-feeling. The effects of eyestrain, all those individual asterisks of snow to account for. In the small air lock of an entry she stood in front of the rows of names and black buttons, thinking where they'd go to get quick service for lunch. She pressed the button beside Dena's nameplate with her other hand on the inside door, ready to be buzzed in.

But Dena was some time replying, and then it was her voice over the intercom.

"Aspera, I'll be just a sec. Sorry."

Two floors up, she rang the door chime. Dena opened the door almost too suddenly, and then Aspera was surprised to find her friend still in her lounging robe.

Flushed and her face shining with embarrassment, Dena leaned against the door, propping it open with her body so that Aspera stood in the hall.

"You don't look ready for lunch."

"I've had the loveliest sleeping-in," Dena sighed, arching, stretching, pulling her fingers through tousled hair. "I was up all night. I'm sorry, I should have called you before you left."

Aspera had forgotten this about Dena, the vague regretful disorganization that could come over her when she hadn't prepared a public face.

"Dena, I'm absolutely starved. I don't think I can wait for you to get dressed."

Dena did not move from the door. "That's my other problem," she said. "I have no food in the house, not the first scrap! I can't even make lunch for us. And I'm utterly unprepared for a dinner party."

"Why don't we go out this evening? Bunny won't care."

"Oh, no, no, I mean to do dinner here. In fact I've added to our party. But I'll need the afternoon—" Dena's blue eyes skittered back toward the depths of the apartment. "I'm sorry. Do you mind terribly, shopping alone?"

Added to the party. Aspera pressed down her reaction and felt a miserable guilt, involving Dena in this way.

"I meant to take you to lunch, Dena, so look, I'll take us all out for cocktails before dinner. Let me do that much."

"Well—" Dena bit her lip. "We could meet at L'Encantada just round the corner at five-thirty; are you sure?"

"Very sure. I really insist."

Dena gave her a beatific smile. "I'll phone Bunny. You don't hate me for being so incompetent? For sending you out into the big city alone?"

Aspera thought of Kevin, of surprising him with this gift of the afternoon. A riff of elation, then another wave of guilt. She twisted her mouth to smile, and Dena beamed happily back. Aspera noticed her then as though for the first time. Something shiny and silky about her look, face pink, eyes bright, something just right in the way the hair framed the face.

Aspera squinted at her smile, at some wisp trapped just between Dena's small front teeth.

"You've got a hair caught there," she told her, tapping her own tooth.

Dena blanched, plucked at the crevice with her polished fingernails without success. She ran her tongue over the place and in a nervous gesture pulled at her hair. "Just some of this stuff, I suppose?"

It was Dena's unease that made Aspera look more closely. Dena pressed her lips tight and covered them with a hand, but Aspera had seen the kink of hair. She felt herself flood with merriment.

Shaking her head, she backed away from Dena's door. She made her voice as low and musical as she could make it, sang: "Looks pubic to me!"

On a last sight of Dena's prussian-violet eyes set off in a brilliant pink face, Aspera wheeled about and strode down the hall. She thought of the telephone in the downstairs lobby. "See you at five-thirty!" she called over her shoulder.

* * *

By five she and Bunny sat drinking in the Hilton lounge. At the sight of the bank of telephones beyond the entry, Aspera grimaced for the ninetieth time that afternoon. Didn't passion guarantee some minimum degree of telepathy?

"Well, what did you buy?" Bunny was asking. She sat across the table wearing a crimson V-neck silk shirt. Aspera felt pale in her white nubby sweater, wished she'd worn something softer, warmer.

"Not a bloody thing."

Last thing she'd come to Minneapolis for—an afternoon alone. Worse—alone in every telephone booth on Nicollet Mall. She could still feel the ridged impress of coin edges on her index finger, quarters inserted and returned.

"I hate shopping," Aspera said.

"I thought that's what you came to do. Wasn't this whole girls' night out your idea?"

Aspera flushed to match Bunny's blouse. "Didn't see anything. I've spent too much time in a store to enjoy looking." She sipped her oversize margarita. "How come you're early?"

Bunny lifted a shoulder. "I finished my shift at the crisis clinic and didn't have anything else on. You arranged for my husband to make plans without me."

Surprised, Aspera sat back while Bunny gave her the baby tones of innocence.

"Since shopping was the agenda, I amused myself by ordering a new sofa. In case Dalton gets to thinking this was a good idea."

"My God, you keep the screws in tight!"

"Yes, I thought you understood that. I hold you responsible for this episode, and I'd like to make it clear that I don't care for you calling my husband at his office."

"What are you getting at?" Aspera drew herself up. "This whole plan was Will's—"

Bunny held up a hand. Stop. Then she lifted her head and said in a clear small voice, "Couples in this society make social plans through the wife. There are good reasons for that. It's one of the few conventions that work in my favor, and I'd like you to observe the convention."

Aspera fought down anger. "Dalton and I have been friends for two centuries." Just now this seemed to her an utterly final explanation.

Bunny answered it with one syllable, cool and impenetrable. "Yes?"

"If we carried on like you and Will do, I could see how you'd be upset."

"We've all known from day one which two of us needed watching."

"You don't give anybody credit. Dalton is devoted to you. He'd never think of—"

"Don't tell me what he wouldn't think. He's male; he's forty-three years old. I don't want him thinking, actually. I want him reacting below the threshold, I want him used to having me with him the way he's used to his arms attached to his shoulders. Do you understand?"

Did she? And was the world as desperate a place as Bunny made it out? Maybe. Under the glare of Bunny's eyes some urgent sense of Elvira danced forward from the recesses of Aspera's thinking. We can see evil if we stick to simple definitions, if we don't scare ourselves past recognizing common forms. Causing fear constitutes evil; so does withholding information when it is justly sought. Be godly in your dealings!

Aspera ran her hand over her face. Somewhere between Elvira's world and Bunny's she hoped for a favorable thumb on the scale.

Bunny's gray eyes were still augered on hers. *Natural the way that the lamprey is the natural companion of alewives, we can still hope not to feed it with ourselves.*

Aspera said, "You talk about Dalton like you would a rat or a pigeon in a box."

"As you like." Dimples bracketed the straight line Bunny's mouth made. "But he's my husband, and if we are friends, I expect you to cooperate with what I need to maintain my marriage."

If we are friends sang in the air. Aspera drained her drink.

"Otherwise I would certainly be uncomfortable, and I don't like discomfort when my marriage is at stake. We'd be inclined to avoid the situation, Dalton and I."

Aspera concentrated on setting the stemmed glass down with care, the flat disc of base meeting tabletop flush. "You don't care how this makes me feel. Or how Dalton would feel."

"I'm very conservative where it counts, and my marriage counts for a lot."

Aspera looked into the eyes, tried to learn from the gaze that did not waver. Nothing at all made sense, and then something clicked into place. She said, "At fourteen your daughter got more of Dalton's attention than you were comfortable with?"

Tears filmed Bunny's eyes and she lifted her chin. "You didn't grow up like I did, you don't have a teenage daughter; you don't know anything about it."

Aspera gazed across the room at people taking small meatballs skewered on toothpicks into their mouths, extracting the toothpicks. Cellophane frills lay discarded on small plates.

"Dalton goes along with this?"

"Oh, you know Dalton, he's very softhearted. If I have to cry and fall apart to make him hear me, I'll cry and fall apart. If it's important, I don't have the kind of pride that can't bend that far."

Slippage. Aspera pressed her spine against the chairback.

Bunny leaned over the table. "I don't think you're in a position to judge my life or my choices. You think you know Dalton, you think he's a saint. I know better. I know he's a normal male, and that means I can't count on him. I intend to stay married to Dalton, and for that I need time with him." Her gray eyes narrowed. "I'm already going to be away on business Sunday through Tuesday—I didn't need my husband taken away from me tonight, too. You've had things by the book, Aspera—virgin bride, child-free marriage, a family business—it's different for me. I want that respected."

Aspera unclenched her jaw. "I couldn't stand to be married on your terms."

Bunny's eyes slid slowly away, slowly back. "You and Will tell each other everything, is that it?"

Flushed with hypocrisy, Aspera was taking up her fresh drink when Dena arrived in a rush of lemony blossom scent.

"Hello!" she greeted them, settling with a flurry into a chair.

"Hello," Bunny replied with a smile. "Are you alone?"

Dena smiled. "Alone. But we'll be four for dinner. Kevin Stowe will be joining us, did I tell you that before?"

"No." Aspera's heart missed its rhythm.

"You told me," Bunny said.

"He called, out of the blue," Dena told Aspera, her eyes

bright. She added to Bunny, "He'll be joining us for dinner at my apartment. Let's be back by seven." She beamed at them. "Now I see you've started without me; what have I missed?"

"Two margaritas and an ultimatum," Aspera volunteered. She signaled for a waiter, ignored the look Bunny gave her. Not knowing herself how far she meant to go.

"Oooohh," Dena cooed, looking from face to face. "I'll order a triple if you let me in on it."

"Done. Now the deal is"—Aspera glanced from Dena's expectant face to Bunny's hard one—"we can't call Dalton." A wave of hysteria caught her; she began to laugh. "Also, nobody gets to call Bunny. On anything."

After a hesitation Dena and Bunny laughed a little. A tray arrived with colored cellophane frills sticking up out of meatballs. Aspera pictured twenty-five tiny one-legged capons playing dead on the plate; this began to seem very funny indeed. Little chickens, cowardice everywhere.

"You two have been here longer than I thought," Dena said. "I might have known it was a joke."

Bunny took over, recognizing a failure of nerve when she saw one. "It's not really very interesting," she told Dena smoothly. "My real name is Marijka, and I've asked people at the crisis center to call me that."

"It's more professional," Dena assured her.

"It's a safety measure; I'd like to be anonymous with our clientele, not to mention the homicidal maniacs that call up."

"Names are so difficult," Dena sighed. She touched the tip of her tongue to the rock salt crusted on the rim of her glass.

"What did they call *you* in grade school?" Bunny directed the question to Aspera. "Aspirin? Or The Pill?"

"Right."

"But in college," Dena said with mischief, "after she and Will were married, she was known as Her Does."

Aspera's turn to sigh.

"From a joke that went around. How did it go, Aspera? A boy invited a little girl to play, and his mother took him aside and said, 'I don't want you to play with that girl, her neck's dirty.' The little boy looked simply delighted and said, 'Her does?' "

"Her does!" Bunny discovered, and she and Dena laughed.

Aspera folded her arms. "Her didn't," she muttered. "Not much."

"Well," Dena said. "Viergier was my married name; my maiden name was Deveraux. When I got divorced I decided it didn't matter which one I kept because people couldn't spell either one."

Bunny bared her teeth. "Where did we get these fucking names?"

"That's exactly what they are," Aspera said. "Fucking-names." She was surprised when the other two started into laughter.

"Oh, I can hardly wait!" Dena cried. "The next time somebody asks me if I used to be Dena Viergier, I'm going to say, 'Yes, that was my fucking-name.' "

The three women joined together laughing.

"That's what they're for, isn't it?" Dena squeaked. "To make it OK for women to screw."

"Like a fishing license," Bunny said. "Penalties if you're caught doing it without one."

"Well, mine needs renewing," Dena said. "And of course Vicky's has expired."

All three of them shrank their heads lower on their shoulders in order to laugh at what they weren't supposed to find funny.

"Mine's still good," Aspera told them. "Well, it's not exactly good, but it's legal."

And again they shook with laughter.

On the walk to Dena's apartment it was plain the temperature had dropped. A dusting of snow lay over the sidewalk and outlined tufts of brown grass along the curb, and more was on its way. Ice-block puddles in the street threatened their footing. The three of them linked arms, and in the cold air Aspera decided it was pointless to be godly in your dealings when clearly God was One Who'd have real trouble in an equal relationship.

The cold air caused her to claim first bathroom rights, but once they were inside the apartment Dena slipped in and so it was during Aspera's turn that the buzzer and then the door chime sounded, announcing Kevin's arrival. Before she left the bathroom she borrowed a drop of Dena's perfume, admired the bloom of excitement, maybe liquor, on her cheeks.

Atop the deep plush of the hall carpet her high heels rose and fell like movie Arabs fighting among dunes. Her short hair felt lifted from her scalp—lacquered in place, something she had not done. Her smile, too, felt lacquered, stalemate of excitement and determination. Half the world ran on secrets.

In Dena's living room, furnished in pale apricot and deep burnt orange, the shades were borne out in satins and velvets down to the silk flowers on the coffee table with coral velvet throats and caterpillar tongues. Dena's fourth guest sat on the apricot sectional sofa with an oversized coffee table book in his hands. He held the book awkwardly, as though he had been pretending to read.

As Aspera stepped down into the living room, Dena and Bunny followed her, each bearing a tray from the kitchen. Kevin had known enough about Dena to wear a tie—Aspera marveled at this perspicacity. Yet he still looked out of place in Dena's parlor. Hair too emphatically brown, combed too straight, too boyish. Skin too ruddy, hands too squarish to have serious intentions toward the glossy impressionist art. He glanced up, green eyes, and Aspera felt a piercing pity for them both. This useless dare.

"Hello," he said, pushing the book onto the table. He rose and nodded circumspectly to Aspera, and then again to Bunny and to Dena. They had moved ahead of her to place their trays bearing wine and wineglasses, fruit and cheese on the table. He dropped his eyes, did not return them to Aspera or leave them overlong on her, as she was free to do to him.

"Now these are *not* hors d'oeuvres," Dena declared. She was flushed and bright with her responsibilities, and Aspera noticed for the first time the long cream satin hostess affair she now wore. The bodice was tailored to overlap and tie at the waist, secured with a thick corded rope. The smooth skirt fell slashed to the floor.

"These are merely things to keep you all busy while I perform last rites over dinner. Kevin missed cocktails, so he shouldn't expect to linger over these."

The tray contained several cut clusters of green grapes, a pot of pâté, an assortment of crackers. A small silver-and-pearl knife curved beside the pâté.

Dena's teasing tone was merely part of the aggregate of surprises Aspera couldn't make out among things she should, of course, have known. For one, that this meal would become a state occasion.

"We will keep this young man surrounded," Bunny assured her, lowering herself to the pastel velvet of the sofa beside Kevin. She leaned and nudged him on the shoulder. "He's a bit of a national resource, protected species."

Kevin looked at Bunny with something like gratitude. "I need protection," he grinned.

"Kevin, if you'll just pour the wine—" Dena instructed. "Then when I melodiously call you all, you may bring glasses with you."

"Do you need help?" Aspera asked.

"Not yet." Smiling demurely at each of them, Dena turned and strode from the room. With each step a length of leg flashed out like a pink stamen.

Aspera sat on the harmonizing rose settee opposite the sofa.

"What a surprise finding you here in Minneapolis," Bunny told Kevin, biting her full lower lip. "You know how you associate people with the places you meet them, and somehow I just assumed you lived in Bracken."

"No," Kevin told her, "you've got me mixed up with Aspera. I *am* mixed up with Aspera. If you want the truth—" he stopped, allowing Aspera's heart to leap to her throat—"actually I'm thinking of moving to Bracken."

"You are?" Bunny squeaked.

"Or maybe it's Aspera, thinking of moving to Minneapolis. Which way is it?" This question he directed, the power of his eyes on her, to Aspera.

Aspera flushed and shook her head. "I'm not following this," she stammered.

Bunny wagged a finger at him. "You're too mixed up to go anywhere alone after dark. I knew someone like you once."

"What happened to him?"

Bunny laughed, glancing over at Aspera before making a pout face at Kevin. In her small voice she said, "He got lost."

She rolled her eyes in sorrow, and Kevin put an arm around her. "There, there," he said.

Bunny looked slyly at Aspera and pointed to the arm. "This boy's lonely," she announced.

Pulling his arm tighter, Kevin looked full at Aspera. "You don't know," he said.

These crossfires of intent made Aspera go shaky. Most of the time she knew herself sane, a grown-up female who would bear what she knew. Now her certainty dissolved like new putty rained on, the glazing again at risk.

Dena came to the threshold, paused. "I was going to ask Aspera to come help me," she said in a thin tone. Aspera had to look to see that the smile was in place. "But I think Bunny's the one I want."

Bunny giggled and got up. "Your turn, Aspera," she said. "Aren't we awful?"

Turning to leave, Dena smiled at Kevin and said, "You'll find cigarettes in that small case on the table." Aspera was astonished to see him reach for it.

When she and Kevin were alone he said, "Come and sit next to me."

She shook her head. "I didn't know you smoked," she said.

He tossed the unlit cigarette on the table, where it rolled a few inches. "If I'm nervous enough," he said. Then he spread his knees and sat forward on the sofa.

Her face went soft with feeling for him. But she said, "This is a mistake. I'm shaking inside. I hate not being connected with you, I feel crazy."

"The connection is there, didn't you see Bunny get caught in it?"

"I don't like it."

He brushed her hand and she jerked it away. "Kevin, Dena's got her hopes up. I should have known."

His face went taut. "Dena can take care of herself."

"No, she can't. She's very vulnerable."

"She gets what she wants. Helpless ladies always do." He did not smile. "There's something you don't know."

She looked into the green eyes.

"I spent the night here last night." He paused as if in courtesy, to wait for something to happen, but nothing did; no word or motion or breath found its way into the space he left. He himself picked up the thread. "In some ways that's none of your business. But it happened. And I've been a wreck all day, walking and walking, I have been so afraid of losing you."

The world inside Aspera's head spun and spun and finally locked on Dena that morning. Leaning tousled against the door, a single hair curled between her teeth. Pubic, I assume. Aspera shut her eyes and began to laugh.

"Jesus, this is funny to you?"

"You don't know. I said something to Dena this morning— at the time I thought—"

"Stop laughing."

"Oh, dear. You were right to tell me." Aspera stood up. The room swung.

"I'm crazy about you," he whispered fiercely.

Dena appeared briefly in the hall, inclined her head toward the dining room. A summons. Aspera acknowledged it, smiled. Through the smile she replied to Kevin, "That does not compute," and walked toward the hall where Bunny now stood waiting for them. The three made their way down the passage into the dining room, following the way Dena had gone.

"Don't you love these classy old buildings?" Bunny whispered. "Reminds me of church, or at least the theater."

Dena stood glowing beside the table as she leaned to light the last candle. It seemed not to catch but then as she took the match away, the smoldering wick held, produced its own small flame. First the table surface set with silver candlesticks on persimmon lace grew visible, and then it appeared in three dimensions—folds of cloth draped to the floor—as the small room around it took form, grew brighter.

Dena sighed expressively toward Kevin and then turned to Aspera. "Ah, my friend, Prometheus lives. Wouldn't you say?"

"No." To the look of surprise in Dena's eyes, she added hastily, "I think of Psyche's lamp." She grasped the back of a chrome chair, glad of its cool solidity in her hands. "Is this me?"

"Tell the story," Kevin said.

"Yes!" Dena urged.

"It's too depressing—it's candlefire and spilled wax, wounds that don't heal." She held to her chair. "Can I sit here?"

"Of course. We're the four points of the compass this evening, so you may choose. Kevin?"

"South. I favor warmth." His green eyes glittered at her.

Aspera shifted one chair over, sat down heavily at North. In the transit her elbow grazed something on the sideboard. A silvered bowl spun, then dropped to the carpet, spilling wrapped hard candies to the carpet. Aspera got off her chair in a flood of apology. She bent and tried to scoop the candies back into the dish, but they seemed to leap about on the thick plush carpet, wrappers crinkling. Her stomach pulled as Kevin knelt beside her. He picked up candies, and they landed in the dish with a rattling and a metal tone. His arm brushed hers. She did not look at him; her vision had blurred into four spikes of candle flame and he seemed far away indeed, as far away as Vicky, as far as the Florida Keys.

Bunny and Dena smiled at one another over the awkwardness, then moved to take their places. "East and West!" Dena exclaimed. "It just looks like you and I shall never meet."

At which Bunny inclined her head toward Kevin. "Unless, of course, we both move South."

They looked to him. With a wry gesture of accommodation Kevin spread his arms. But in the bowed head and in the eyes he raised to Aspera was depicted the lamb of sacrifice.

CHAPTER FIFTEEN

Oh, she was a beginner. Drawn in on the oldest scam, something for nothing. Thrills and chills and no piper to pay. No pay involved at all, because as it happened she was not a citizen of Hamlin but one of the charmed rats.

Aspera knocked hard on Kevin's door. She brushed snow from her hair and from her coat, but in seconds she was covered again. One more rat drawn out into the weather in pursuit of a compelling music, and where had Pan cut his pipes? From a bed of reeds. Transformed into vegetation, a maid still had her uses. *Do you know how passive you are?*

Aspera knocked again, and Kevin answered so promptly that she was startled.

He seemed to stagger holding to the door. "I am so relieved," he began, but Aspera was not seeing this man but her path through him. Wasn't that his way? Didn't he see his own path in other people's faces? He stood back, and she walked through the apartment.

"Have you been out in this weather two hours?" he exclaimed, shutting the door. "I've been calling your house, you said you were driving home—"

"I drove around the city." Her voice was strong enough, but it shook with anger, with the very force. "The ring roads go round and round. Are you alone?"

At the sarcasm he stopped. "Yes."

Sliding doors to a balcony caught her eye. Feeling compelled, she strode to them and opened the catch, stepped outside. In the fresh air resolve and calm returned. Grownups. She took two deep breaths of night-charged air. Anger wound the armature of the machine, did not favor release. Vicky's word? Closure. Grownups liked it.

She came back into the room full of a clean purpose, the rumbling doors shut behind her.

"You are amazing," he said.

She saw he was still dressed from the evening, tie loosened, blue oxford shirt now crumpled.

"You look happy," he said.

She took off her coat, dropped it on a chair. As he moved to take it for her, she put her hand up—stop gesture.

He ran a hand through his fine dark hair, then jammed the hand into his pants pockets. "This is the good-bye scene, I guess."

"Is that what you want?"

"No!" His eyes flashed a fierce green. "I told you what I want, I was perfectly honest—"

"Lifetime lovers," she said drily. She let go the breath she seemed to have been saving.

Kevin rubbed his face with his hands, still standing in the center of the room.

Aspera turned from him. She had not been in his apartment before. She hardly felt at home, and somehow she meant to see that he didn't. She sat down on one arm of the sofa.

He stood still and said in a low voice, "Tell me where you want me."

She had not been prepared for the yielding that made her feel old, that made him seem so young. She hesitated, then lifted two fingers toward the other end of the sofa. "We don't have to start out shouting," she said.

He slouched into the place she'd indicated, his legs stretched out stiff along the shag carpet. "I wouldn't blame you if you shouted."

For a long moment they regarded one another. She saw his face wearing shifting gradations of fear, of daring.

When she could no longer look at him and still couldn't speak, she looked at her hands and at his, four hands so separately placed on cushion, lap, sofa back, mouth. Both of them squinted into the space of his living room, too harshly lit by the antique overhead fixture. Its six shaded bulbs glared over the oak table where Kevin's sheaf of case notes lay. She could see partitioned forms. Six hundred watts made good light for making small clear marks between lines; not much to do with peacemaking. He didn't move, and neither did she have enough courage to rise and attend to lighting. One or the other might bolt or throw a paperweight or begin the cry of battle.

Under the strain, certainty bloomed for Aspera that she was correctly placed in time for once. Correct in choosing not to shear off the filaments that linked them, not to escape and turn knowledge out cold into the dark.

Kevin inclined his head sideways. His eyes slid to hers and locked. A fleeting image—Aspera saw herself leaning sideways, reaching to touch his hair—yet she stayed utterly still, leaving it to the expression of her eyes to convey a strange and almost maternal confluence of feeling, expressing permanence, expressing permanent loss.

She closed her eyes. She said, "You and Dena?"

More of the thrumming silence.

"She doesn't know anything about us."

"I know that."

He clasped his hands, sat up to face her squarely. "You've never gotten yourself into something you couldn't explain to people that mattered, have you?"

"I got involved with you."

The green eyes point-focused. "Listen, you are not just involved. You are in love. I think you ought to face that."

Something in her chest threatened to fold and break under the weight of his words. She drew breath to hold it intact. "Love keeps people alive. I think—I think you were trying to kill me."

He looked away toward the bright table under the lights. "I would have waited to tell you. That was brutal, I'm sorry, but Dena—God, she was dropping clues left and right!" he marveled. "And I panicked."

She let the weight compress again before she spoke. "Don't you know about women who are friends?"

"Right." He lifted both hands, opened them palms up. "This is your out," he announced. "You like things uncomplicated, and they aren't, so here's your out." He gestured toward the door. "You can still take it, you know."

She looked calmly at his hands. "I may still take it."

He put the hands down, tired policeman overcome by gravity. "Maybe I'm a whore," he said quietly. "Is that what you came all the way back to hear me say?"

She slid her hands over her eyes, pressed the lids with her fingers. What had she come back to hear? Driving the ring roads of Minneapolis, snow had traveled round the windshield of the Mercury in clumps. Wet snow winding in a slipstream—winter had forgotten its casual way with a snowstorm, meanwhile this dense stuff like spring snow. Each clump suddenly appeared to be of some weight and account, and a moment came when motion was suspended. It seized up and snowflakes came to a stop in midair, white dots set against black background of night. They rested a fraction of a second merely. Then by reverse action those heavy dots, their precise number counting for something, had swum patiently toward her. She moved through them the way cinema starships moved through stars, the bright blotches growing large, coming forward: they had information she might need. She was convinced, ready, but they slipped sidewise; the current moved round her and she kept driving round, kept learning nothing except the cells of the body will expand and try to come apart to follow the example before them.

Aspera rubbed her eyes. Try to fix upon the instant the world began grinding slow on its axis—she let her eyes rest on her coat where spots of snow moisture pearled. To Kevin she said, "Coming here took courage, I thought. Maybe not." She sighed. "Maybe I just haven't learned how to cut off clean. Do you care about any of us?"

Kevin said, "Do you know how much time you spend staring at things?"

She pulled her eyes over to meet his. "I was thinking that we have so little time, we have to be careful."

He gave a twisted smile. "You keep thinking you're going to make all this fit."

"I've known people who don't register anybody else's pain. Am I one of those people now? Is that who I am with you, and who you are?"

When he had formed the answer, his voice came hoarse. "Are you going to believe it when I say I fucked your friend because I felt sorry for her?"

Aspera looked at her coat. "No."

His head snapped backward, then he let the tension go out of his body. His head sank to rest on the sofa back. "I don't believe it either, and goddamn it's true. You and I think we have demons to deal with, and we do not rate demon one next to Dena. She looked at me—we're sitting there in her living room, we were having coffee because I called to say, 'What do you hear from anybody in Bracken and by the way I'm free for dinner Saturday night'—we're talking-distance on the couch and she turns to me with the trembly eyes and says, 'Please hold me. Hold me. Please.' "

Aspera flinched to recognize the degree of need. Would Dena let it show so nakedly? If a beautiful young man were beside her on her cream velvet sofa; if no woman were present as witness. Yes.

She shut her eyes. "I knew this about you. I *knew.*"

"At least I didn't let you down."

When she had nothing to say to that, he went on in the same mocking voice. "Here's what I know how to do. I can make women think that between me and them the boundaries have disappeared." His eyes narrowed. "They never do, of course. But I know how to do that, I had a lot of practice with my mom. My old man"—he shook his head, stopped. "What my mom wanted wasn't that tough—she used to tell me, you ask a question, you listen to the answer, so people don't feel so alone. She told me that was *politeness.*" The word rose and fell with its own lyrical hush. Kevin shrugged. "Well, politeness gets taken for something else. Poof"—he made the gesture, flicking out his gathered fingers—"there go the boundaries! Sometimes I even believe that myself." The fingers flicked. "Sometimes for two or three minutes."

The green eyes, the smile, bore down too hard. Her gaze fell to his throat instead, to the juncture of bone and hollow which, unlike smiles—*sweet boys, used up by*—unlike eyes, never seemed anything but human and vulnerable.

"This is *your* out," she said.

He stared at her, blinking.

One of her shoulders twitched, and on reflex she looked about the room as though somebody else might be present. The light threw harsh projections from every object. A lamp beside the sofa put half Kevin's face into shadow.

"The fact is," she said, her voice faint as if she spoke only to herself, "you are free."

"Free." In his throat the word died, guttered like a fuse. He took a deep breath and squinted past her into the lamplight. "Everytime I try to exercise one of my freedoms, I end up lying to somebody."

It was a plea for sympathy. She said, "Half the world runs on secrets."

"Fucking right."

"Especially the half working on seduction."

"People *like* to be seduced!" Kevin smiled and returned his eyes to hers. "All I do is give them what they want."

"No," she said, discovering the difference as she spoke, "you give something that looks like it."

Kevin blew out an angry breath. "*Women don't want to know anything.* You say you do, but what you really want is to *be known,* which is different. You can see how it might get boring for the other person." He let his shoulders drop. "People will bore the piss out of you if you let them." He tapped his chest. "I want to know what goes on *inside*."

Aspera sat in the room's quiet, hearing the scrape of a snow shovel somewhere outside. "Why do I get this picture," she asked, "of you with your ear pressed to a combination lock, listening for the clicks?"

His face rearranged into a smirk. "Safecracker." He savored the word. "Maybe it's the only thing I'm good at."

She looked at the way his eyes had gone alight. Those eyes, glittery and sharp, hearing her rusty locks tumble?

He leaned forward. "I wanted to be close to you," he told her, seeming once again able to tune to her thoughts. "But I would have settled for a lot less."

A flush of heat rose up her neck. "Less than bed, you mean? Was that my idea?"

"You needed to know you could."

She sat back, bit her lip. "I remember thinking: my body wants to do this. I hope we do this before I find out too much about him, things that would turn me off."

He frowned.

"Early on, I felt so dead. I thought you might be my last chance." She crossed her arms over her midriff, held on to each elbow. "And now I know too much."

"No." He shook his head. "You understand all this."

From beyond the walls came the muffled gritty push of the snow shovel against cinders.

"I can't live it," she said. "People always talk smarter than they can live."

They gazed at one another as though they were outcroppings of native granite.

"Women want too much," he said. He rubbed his cheek with the edge of his palm. "I have to do things to protect what I need for myself."

She felt suddenly tired of the effort it took to make sense. "Maybe you ought think it over," she said, "this thing of making boundaries seem to disappear." She held his eyes with hers. "Is Bunny next?"

He gave a short bark of laughter. "Some of the stuff I did tonight was for cover. I told you that."

"Is Bunny next?"

When he drew breath his stomach jumped. His eyes flicked sideways. "Piece of cake." Kevin's face tightened. He reached under the pleated lampshade beside the sofa, jerked the chain under the bulb. The lamp clicked alight and Aspera watched astonished as Kevin sprang up and, at the opposite wall near the door, slapped down the overhead switch. In this more forgiving light he folded his arms and leaned back against the wall, his weight falling heavily on one shoulder.

"You know me better than anyone ever has," he announced from across the room.

"Well," she said. "There was Vicky."

He pressed the back of his head, too, against the wall. "Oh, God, don't. I don't think I could take it."

Feeling ancient, removed, struggling to raise the stone she carried bundled in her rib cage, Aspera got to her feet. She had one arm pushed into a coatsleeve when he caught her, pulled her roughly around to face him. And then to her surprise the momentum carried; she brought round the arm and the fist it bore, round and swinging hard, hard, hard against his chest. Her fists beat down, again, again. Earnest monotonous force, no hope or suspense in these blows; he made no resistance. She did not strike at his face or throat or belly, did not aim for softness to injure but for solid places to hurt him, relieve what hurt her, hurt him.

Then she fell back and stumbled against the sofa, lacking stamina to go on lifting the fists. She wedged herself upright against the wall, panting. Sweating, jaws clenched. Not crying.

"Did you use all your strength?" he demanded.

"No!" She held her jaws tight. "I'm *afraid* to hit you as hard as I want to!"

"That's why you're tired. You waste so much force, holding back."

Sobbing wracked up from the floor of her lungs, and she lifted her arm, lifted the winter coat still partly hung there, and buried her face. She blanketed the spasms of her shoulders with the cloth, allowed her body to slide down the wall to the floor.

He came and sat beside her, lifted the wet hot wool that wrapped her face and head. The table lamp now burned above them, naked from this angle beneath its shade. In her pockets he located Kleenex and offered them to her. When she closed her eyes against the light he smoothed his hands over the wet crepe of her eyelids, rested the backs of his cool fingers against her cheek, her forehead. While she clutched her coat he allowed her to fall against him, held her head to his chest while he smoothed her hair as she had wanted to do for him earlier. The same feelings rose up: of permanence, permanent loss.

As his hands rubbed, her thoughts darted in and away, returned in schools like minnows. Her mind swung between the gentling weight of his hands on her head and the riot of pressure from the thoughts within. Sitting with her father she had first noticed how words changed everything. That night they'd waited on the new foundation for the rainstorm his words had made the skies seem so far away that the rain, when it came, couldn't possibly touch her, would not be wet when it met earth. "I guess your ma don't love me anymore," he had said. Silence was the only place things got a chance to rest; she understood silence, but that night her father went on talking, his arm laid around her shoulders—a weight she loved, but that night the weight was choking her. He had taken out one of his rare cigarettes: Lucky Strikes. She smelled the tobacco as it rested in his fingers unlit. He kept talking, her heart shriveling like a dead thing inside her. She wanted to stop her ears to bring back the silence, but his words tunneled all the way into her belly. "I reckon there's more than one way to leave. I just want you to know. I want you to think about it someday; your pa wasn't the first one to leave just because he's the one gone. You remember that. Someday if I'm not around." How she flew at him then, screaming, pounding him with her fists. "You can't leave, don't leave me Daddy please I love you, you can't leave!" She struck him and struck him, she would kill him for killing her this way inside her body. He let her fists fall on him for a little time, bent manfully under the puny blows. Then he straightened and let his cigarette drop to the ground. He seized her two fists in his hardened hands, and shook his head. "Wildcat," he said. He transferred both her wrists into one hand. He stood and released them with a throwing motion, the way she'd seen him throw a slug of excess putty to the ground. "You and your ma don't need a man," he said. He shook his head, then turned it at an angle where light caught dangerously in the green eyes: "Clean your face. Straighten it up, there's no telling either one of you."

And then he had sat down again, lowering himself to the cured concrete without touching her. She wiped her streaked face with her shirt and cautiously moved next to him. He sat stonelike and so she held her legs and arms like the vise he had showed her how to use, held tight so they would not strike or kick anymore and she promised him all the things she knew to promise: she never would lose her temper again, never shout, never hit; she would remember what he told her, she already remembered it, did he want her to say it back now because she would never forget, she promised him, please would he stay? Wanting, wanting so badly was a sharp ache she felt high in her chest. Her father had looked away from her, up at the purpling sky. His fisted hands he kept folded against his chest. The rain had not come while they watched, and during a brief turn when a single star braved the cauldron of cloud, she pinched the bridge of her nose hard to keep away the tears that did not belong on a face that was straight. She felt older that night with her weight of promises, but she had been young enough to fix on the single star and entrust it with her wish.

After that she had noticed, sitting out on the foundation alone that long rack of spring evenings that followed his going, how far away the stars were, and how they were set shallow in the sky like chips of rhinestone glass. Thoughts like these stopped her crying over Chester but made her feel smaller and colder, as remote as the stars themselves, and she had shivered under the quilts Elvira piled on her as she lay all those nights in her bed waiting for him to come back.

Years later she'd blurted this thing out loud: stars looked to her like cold shattered glass. Said it to interrupt one of Elvira's long recitations on stellar influence, and in the basement kitchen her mother had turned in a fury. "You are enchanted with distance!" she shrilled. "Stars are not cold, only distance is cold. I tell you, the stars roar like furnaces."

These were Kevin's hands. Consciousness glided into a ringing delirium. She sensed the edge of fall, a shattering as mind rose and shipped full of fragments and pieces, snow shovel on cinders, ocean wave in full toss gritted with glass and sand. Nothing to hold her, nothing preserved till morning could break in her place. She clung to the warmth of hands—she felt it like the sun—clung to warmth while waves beat at the shores of mind, regular as heartbeats; they would go on without her tending, she could rest. Let ocean tear and grind blending battered shell and wood and foam, she would concentrate on the warmth of fire, warmth of bright light, bright sun above the waves. She held fast on the warmth until it stung her eyes, produced in them gouts of tears pooled like hot wax over her eyelids, her eyelashes. When the wax dripped down into her hair she brought hands up and opened them like wings beside her head. Thought flew wide away. Her eyes came open; Psyche's lamp tipped to burn flesh.

Aspera tried to look up at the face above her. A bubbling of fatigue in her ears. Tears started again and she shut her eyes. Kevin shifted her weight from his lap and knelt straining to reach the light cord on the lamp, pulled once, twice. In the dark he returned and gathered her up.

"I don't know how to trust you." A child's complaint, as though this were a problem in arithmetic that he might sometime solve for her.

He put both of them into the same bed and lighted a candle,

then cradled her and smoothed her hair, and when he stopped, her ear stayed cupped to his heartbeat.

Can you feel how much I love you in the way I touch you?

She wanted to believe she could. She wanted this more than she wanted to know whether Dena believed in this touch or not, or whether Vicky had; she wanted to believe more than she wanted to solve any problem by arithmetic, more than she wanted to count how many stops she had gone past the place she meant to get off.

From the underworld, a box she must this time remember not to open, a journey of repentance ending with a debt of sleep. O, a debt of sleep.

For a time she is back in college struggling through a statistics examination, strings of statistical formulae knotting her brain. Things she ought not have forgotten; she is wearing her slip, her thin bowlegs bare in winter boots. She falls into bed in the Airstream, dreaming of numbers, strings and swirls of numbers. She wakes up to Will's hand rooting frantically under her pillow and his.

"Will, what is it? What have you lost?" She sits up and watches him shift between the pillows, then hold out his hand to her, squinting at the light.

"Here."

"What?"

"Take this." He fumbles at her hands, trying to place something small into her palm.

"What is it?" she cries, finding nothing in her hands and looking to see whether she has dropped the object back among the pillows. Her hand cups empty as he lies back and buries his face under the sheet.

"A pearl," he mumbles, and is asleep.

In the dream she throws her arms about him and weeps.

She struggled to wake from formlessness, a blank less like darkness than emptiness dazzlingly lit. She knew, as if she had only remembered it, a steady drawing sensation at her groin. Drawing, as water or blood is drawn. Sudden dream image: a well, a rope, cylindrical steel bucket. An echo of sound convinced her it was a dream; a voice? She couldn't stay with the waking except in slow cycles, the way the mind arrives at consciousness following deep fatigue, or the way a body is washed to shore by the unsteady lapped progress of wave motion. She focused. A slow, light, steady pressure drawing sexual response. Her eyes fell open on eyes watching her, Kevin's face as he touched her, deftly touched.

"Come for me," the echo urged again. "I want you to come for me."

Fog settled round her mind as the wave rhythm carried her adrift again. Her eyelids fell closed of their own weight.

The first spasm sent a needle of electricity to her brain, announcing connection. She opened her eyes to the small smile on Kevin's mouth, and her body convulsed with its independent conviction. She flung out her arms, which windmilled till they found the headboard behind her head. She held to the lipped wooden rail and pulled her body away from him, coiling her legs. Then, with leverage at the headboard, she kicked at him, kicked and pushed him off the bed. It took several violent tries; he protested, scrambled for a hold; she repositioned her hands, braced and thrust hard with her legs until he went over the side flailing.

His face appeared above the horizon of bed; in the dimness, that face showed pleasure. He stood naked and smiling at her, his hands on slim hips. He shook his head admiringly.

"You need to do more of that, don't you?"

Still astonished at her own fury, her jaws remained clenched.

He turned and opened the window behind him. No wind; a bloom of winter air entered the room. Slowly he lifted the sheet and blanket to climb in beside her. He propped his head on one elbow and looked into her eyes.

"It was supposed to be a gift."

"A gift."

His face turned incredulous. "You're really angry."

"What was I being given?"

"I was wrong. Sorry."

Gift of morning orgasm, theft of sleep. Gift of orgasm? Come for me. Giving, taking: words common as house dust. She sank limp into the pillows.

"You done with this fight?" he asked.

She moved her head miserably on the pillow, yes.

"Right." He stumbled out of bed and down the hall to the bathroom. Doorknob knocked against wallboard; she heard the stinging sound of water striking porcelain, striking water. She heard the whine of hot-water pipes as a shower went on. Immediately he reappeared in the doorway, a pink towel slung over a shoulder, the outline of his body framed clear.

"One thing," he said. He rubbed his eyes with his fists. "You won't like it, which is why I didn't want to tell you. When I called your house last night Will answered the phone."

"Will?" Her eyes froze wide. "*Was home?*"

Kevin opened his palms. "It was about twelve-thirty."

She came bolt upright. "Will answered the phone? Why didn't you tell me?"

"Listen to me. Just listen. I asked for you before I thought to hang up," Kevin said carefully. "But he doesn't know my voice, there's no damage done. You have a story."

Story. She tried to think but her mind stared back blank, a shield.

"Snowstorms are always good," he said.

She shook her head as a shudder traveled up her spine. "You called my house, you talked to Will and you didn't tell me?"

Kevin lifted his chin, said, "It was supposed to be you and me last night."

She let go the handfuls of blanket she'd clutched. "By whose count?" Her voice rose half a decibel. "Kevin, when it's my life, *you* get it straight about the boundary!"

Kevin blew breath into his cheeks, let it out.

"You can handle this," he said.

"Maybe I can't! Maybe I'm in enough trouble, maybe my marriage is already—"

In the quiet they heard the drill of the shower on the plastic curtain.

Kevin said softly, "Then what's the problem?"

CHAPTER SIXTEEN

She could only go home. She could only go home unworried. She slowed to fifty-five miles per hour, the Mercury's V–8 engine humming a halftone lower. She worked the hinge of her jaw. Will could be there with something as simple as a head cold.

Will at home. Under the seat belt her stomach contracted. Her story: car trouble, some freeway motel, battery dead this morning. She had left Dena's early last night, disturbed about Dena and Kevin. Her story: disturbed on Vicky's behalf.

She forced another breath, remembered to drop her shoulders.

Betraying Dena, betraying Kevin? *No damage, you have a story.*

How she'd like to call Dena, talk. Explain! Except she was in the wrong place. Caught on foreign soil behind enemy lines, she had to keep on speaking the language till she crossed the border again. Sweet, and devious.

Describe the enemy. Not Will, not Kevin. Herself? She couldn't see a self, no more than she could picture the shape of the Atlantic Ocean. North America, she could see that, eastern coastland ragged as loosely strung vertebrae. She could see Europe, hanging nipple of Gibraltar, tip of Normandy—Kevin was Europe, the *elsewhere*. Will was North America, all familiar anthems and irritations, deepest allegiances. Not seeing the Atlantic Ocean was a trick of vision, a habit. She would have to learn some other trick or habit.

"I want us to continue," Kevin had said after they had dug her car out. The line of cars parked along his street ahead and behind hers had been packed with snow, like white mortar, when the plow had come through during the night. When she turned the key, the only sound the Mercury made was the clicking of the solenoid. Her lights on! Kevin had laughed, pushed in the switch and got his Ford Escort from the apartment's underground garage. With cables he connected the two batteries pole to pole, and soon the Mercury's cold engine roared. Now she and he sat in the garage under Kevin's building. She was anxious to leave; she idled the engine to keep the cell charging.

"We're good for one another," he told her. He patted the dashboard. "You need me."

She wedged herself against her door. "I need a friend," she said. With a finger she made a clear, isolated dot on the steamed window. "I have got so cut off."

With his forearm Kevin rubbed the passenger window clear. Gray cement walls were revealed. They were underground, and around them loomed gray cement posts with apartment numbers stenciled in black.

Kevin took his gloves off, rubbed his hands together. "I'm the best friend you have," he said. "Who else would recognize the woman I know, the one with the fists and feet?"

She pressed her palms into her eye sockets to relieve a pressure there. "That was desperate behavior."

His whisper was dramatic. "What would happen if you got desperate more often?"

She suffered bodily then from a vision of herself, lying naked on the bedroom carpet between the bed and the wallpaper. "That's how we got started."

He shook his head. "We got started because we're both hooked on danger."

"No."

He tapped his finger on the steering wheel. "All these moves, right under people's noses? Come on."

"I'm not hooked on danger," she insisted. "Not on deception, either."

He smiled, his eyes rich and dark with pleasure. "We all like to play it two-handed," he said, "left and right unacquainted. Give things up on the tabletop, take the payoff underneath." He made motions with his two hands: back-to-back, high-low, gimme. "It's what you said yourself, one trade after another. Once you know," he reached over and clasped her knee, his palm and fingers warm, making his point, "you don't forget how to want things. And you can have it all."

The freeways were clear all the way to Bracken. Bright sun glared off drifted pastures, melting a top crust that would freeze a few hours later. On the shaded access roads two ruts had been worn through to the blacktop; inside city limits were clear signs that the town had already fallen out of love with new snow. Ice and slush were relegated to patches of gutter and sidewalk. Snow tilted over the eaves of houses in blanketfolds. Along the municipal buildings the snow peeled down walls where sidewalks had been shoveled.

No sign of Dalton's car on their street. No cars at all parked along the piled snowbanks halfway up the birches, nothing in the driveway. She reminded herself to park in the garage as usual. Get out and lift the door, drive in, pull the door down. She carried her overnight bag in one hand, handbag in the other. She made new prints in the snow.

Back door locked. She let herself in with a key, shifting both bags to her left arm. She closed the door with her foot, carried the bags through the kitchen, down the hall—dining room and living room empty—and up the stairs. No one, no sign. She walked past two doors standing ajar—bathroom, study—and into their bedroom. She started to put her things on a chair but sank down on it herself.

Back downstairs in the living room she turned up the thermostat. Called down the basement stairs, just to be sure. In the kitchen she threw away a piece of toast she had forgotten in the toaster Saturday morning. A habit of hers Will detested. He himself had a habit of leaving crumbs and smears of jam in the butter; in the refrigerator compartment the stick was clean.

He had not been here; there had been no phone call? Kevin wouldn't—? She didn't know what to believe. She stared at the clock as though it would tell something else for a change. Punished with time, having to watch it pass. She saw Elvira's folded arms, elbow skin pulled tight and yellow, bone-hard. Voice also bonelike, such a surprise issuing from the open throat of soft print housedresses. Punishment was sitting on the kitchen stool in front of the stove clock. For talking back, ten minutes watching the second hand grind round, watching the minute hand push past the dots between numbers. For saying, "I hate this trailer." For saying, "I want Daddy back, I wish you would die."

Punishment was assurance that cause and effect still worked. The first unpunished crime made a milestone of consciousness, just like the first undetected lie.

Not hooked on deception? But this would be the last round. Lying was functional behavior, since truth was a source of irritation to adults. Nothing quite so dangerous as irritation. Numbers of homicides on hot summer nights proved it, crime rates jumping up like prickly heat. Never underestimate weather, or the maddening effect of human contact. What else about homicide? That it's done in families. Things to watch out for: hot weather, too many people, blood relations.

In the mailbox was Saturday's newspaper, with Saturday's mail jammed between its folds. She slid the envelopes out: a bill, two pieces of metered mail from candidates in Washington, one letter addressed in a familiar hand.

Inside, typewritten pages. The date but no formal greeting, no paragraph breaks, Vicky's style all the way.

"I no longer understand the connection between winter and snow. Still I can't stay on the beach all day, or tend my father either. I walk at dawn and sunset, eyes glued to the sand ten inches in front of my toenails. Occasional glance to the horizon in case of dolphins, or the Armageddon, which is popular here, but not on my strip of beach. Outdoors we get to be subrational creatures, visual, auditory, tactile. Indoors we may think, since it's the privilege of the housebroken. Tell Will I don't really mean We. My father doesn't think indoors, he sits and stares, mind long gone. Not Mouth, however, and not Personal Hygiene, thank God for that. I make it back to the house by breakfast time, rouse wash dress feed and prop him in a chair by the open screen till lunch. Then I do think, and even work. The ocean sets a good example. I've got two big jobs. Dependency program for a Colorado rehab center and one in curriculum design, elementary level, in Maryland. In my head the two mix strangely. In the elementary stuff there's something called the Five-Finger Rule. When second-graders start reading a new book, they keep track on their fingers of words they don't know. When they get to five fingers they put the book down. Too hard. I'm adopting the Five-Finger Rule to use with the people in my life. When five things go by that make no sense, I mean to give up. By the time it gets to three, in fact, I'm looking for the exit. When I think about dependency, by the way, I turn my own chair toward the ocean—looking out on the beach you can't ignore the fact that people are naked except for one or two careful little patches, and we all know why that is. I ought to write a curriculum for love and sex and romance, I'm sure I have very peculiar views. Have developed a cantankerous style for the purpose which I get from old people who know just how much time there is to be wasted. Glossary follows.

"*Men:* penis-encumbered individuals who don't learn.
"*Women:* breast-encumbered individuals addicted to men.
"*Addiction:* the unnoticed evolution of a source of pleasure into a source of pain.
"*Withdrawal:* weird behaviors that crop up when you learn you're not fused to the source.
"*Learning:* the successful defeat of belief."

Aspera read the glossary part twice before taking on the rest.

"Thesis: Addiction becomes pain, and that includes addiction to a person. Mommy or daddy or hubby or baby or buddy. 'We'll eat you up, we love you so.' Users always turn possessive, this cuts off trade routes to and from the Supply. (Dogs bury bones and dig them up again—users are bedeviled by possession.) My papa, this *old* man who stares at the ocean all day, who talks only in his sleep—wild shouts of threat and injury—wanted my mother all to himself, hated us kids because we existed. Here's what I think: family bonds are such screamers because the outlet for abuse is also the intake for nurturance. This is sheer stupidity, and lethal stupidity—the body, clever survivor, is much better organized. It solved the intake-outlet problem eons ago, separating the systems, keeping waste and nourishment separate. It teaches us the appropriate behaviors:

do not foul the nest. Curriculum for newborns: develop your own air supply, find clean avenues for nourishment and waste disposal. Damn if us uptown mammals don't got the same homework in the psychic economy. *Do not foul the nest.* Well. Here I sit, typewriter keys bloodied with my passion for emotional hygiene. Doubt that Colorado will buy it, Maryland either. I miss talking with you. Nothing wrong here aside from sex deprivation; the fix is available but what of one's Five-Finger Rule?"

The letter was signed with the initial V, and the assurance of love.

When Aspera took out pen and stationery to reply, her hands were clammy on behalf of all she would not put in writing. She took the pen, wrote, "We court risk because we're afraid we're dying in the middle of our lives." Through the triple glazing of storm windows she heard the muffled four o'clock bells from the hospital chapel. She waited until no more sound penetrated glass, then decided to try to think like Vicky. "In music a pure tone may be struck, but then it decays, becomes disorganized. This is the action of harmonics, where a loss of purity is not necessarily sad."

In her hand the pen behaved like a blunt instrument. She studied the pits and jerks of her handwriting on the page. If this handwriting were a green salad, she would send it back for something fresher, less ragged or winter-killed at the edges. Round those o's; don't let them dig into the line like clams into ocean sand. Exert even pressure. Stretch this stuff out into the horizontal plane, pretend you're the one in Florida.

The page was a goner anyhow, nothing she'd ever send. Rapidly she wrote more: "Delivered by any instrument too blunt for the purpose, even the most delicate touch becomes a blow. Sex without love is no message, monkeys going in and jumping up and down on the telegraph key."

It took effort not to deal from the center; look at all that evidence of circumnavigation, which Vicky would be the first to spot. When we can't deal with the facts, we move, us uptown mammals do, into metaphor. Aspera crumpled the page in her fist and with greater care guided her thoughts, and her hand, on a fresh page.

"Thanks for your letter. I'm looking for a job, split in half in more ways than I can tell you. But here's something for your research: one of Elvira's books holds that sex is a low-energy form vibrationally, owing to all the *matter* associated. Concerning passion, the laws of matter apply, and possession becomes (as you suggest) nine-tenths. So this book says sweet old-fashioned love carries the most charge. Fancy that.

"Sorry about the handwriting," she put at the bottom.

To kill time, or perhaps the impulse to destroy what she had written, she got coat and boots on. Vicky was right, outdoors you didn't have to think. A relief to leave the empty house, and all the sidewalks had been shoveled clear. She walked to the village post office between knee-high banks of snow and met no one.

Like the rest of downtown Bracken, the post office was closed on Sundays, though there was access to the box area. On the plyboard partition that separated off the mail room, two hand-sawed slots offered themselves. Above them were hand-stenciled categories, *Local* and *Elsewhere.* Aspera dropped her letter through its proper slot and returned the way she had come.

When she got back and tried the back door she had to push it open against a straggling pile of gear. Rucksack, duffel bag, tackle box, weather suit.

In the kitchen doorway Will showed himself briefly, his mouth full of something.

"Hwmmmo," he said. Above the packed mouth the eyes were neutral.

She was glad to see him, and scared. When she had hung her coat in the back closet she came into the kitchen, rubbing her hands.

"How was the fishing?"

He stood with his back to the sink, chewing on the sandwich he held in one hand. He shrugged in answer and took another disabling bite.

Aspera felt nervousness in the walls of her stomach. Something was required of her.

"I think I'll put a kettle on for tea," she said. "Interested?"

He closed his eyes, shook his head to dismiss the possibility.

He moved aside for her and she filled the kettle at the tap.

Standing so close to him, she felt the conspicuous absence of touch. When the kettle was full she stretched up and placed a kiss on his jaw, which seemed to make the feeling worse. He kept chewing, and she turned and set the kettle on the stove, dialed the flame to high. There remained other things to do, and she did them: pry open the can of tea, fill the clay teapot with hot water, rummage in a drawer for the small strainer.

"So where did you go?" he asked her, his arms folded.

"You mean, just now?" She felt her face color. One story at a time. "The post office."

He bit an apple. "I saw the car."

She was confused. "What do you mean, you saw the car?"

"I saw the car in the garage."

"You mean, our garage?"

"Yes, I mean our garage. What's wrong with you?"

"I—had trouble with the car. I started to come home last night, but on the highway the storm—"

He stopped chewing and listened while she told about blowing snow, the motel, a guy with cables who started the car this morning. In the motel garage. To Aspera it seemed a very long story, one with too many moving parts.

"Last night," Will said, "did you try to call me?"

"Call you?" The kettle whistled and she panicked. She lifted it up and it came too fast, still screaming and bubbling at the spout.

She forced a laugh. "You weren't here, remember?" She turned off the gas jet.

"Hmmp," he said. He moved his tongue over his teeth and sucked at particles of sandwich. "The icehouse Dalt and I rented was fine till midnight, when our heater stopped functioning. Must have been twenty degrees below zero out on that ice. Rather than freeze to death we came back and slept here."

"You *were* here?"

"We had a phone call, in fact."

Aspera tried to govern the panic that raced through her body. "Who was it?"

"Don't know." Will shrugged. "Dalt answered, said it was a wrong number."

"I didn't—" She struggled for words that fit. "Didn't find a trace of you today."

"Dalton." Will shook his head. "What a nut. It wasn't macho to spend the night indoors with central heating, see, so we had coffee from the thermos and put our sleeping bags in front of the fireplace. Can you picture this? Then he got us up at dawn so we could go have breakfast in a truck stop." Will threw his head back and laughed. "I'll be damned if we didn't have to go back and fish some more."

She took pinches of tea leaves, poured water from here to there. "The car seemed fine this morning on the way home," she said, feeling she was chattering to fill a vacuum she sensed. She found she was still holding the kettle in her hands and set it down. "It seems fine, but I've been on pins and needles all day, waiting for the next whistle to blow."

"We should keep the car serviced, since we're putting more miles on it."

We. Miles. She tried to murmur agreement but swallowed instead.

"Is that why you walked downtown, you're nervous about using the car now?"

"No," she said, uncomfortable. "I just had to get out of the house."

Regretting the words sooner than she got them out.

Will dropped his arms. "When I saw the car in the garage I thought maybe you'd be in the kitchen cooking up an intimate dinner for two. But the place was empty." He picked up his sandwich crusts and wagged them at her.

"You and Dalt didn't have any luck ice fishing?" She did not look at the crusts. "Sounds like you had a great time, though."

Will let his face go slack. "Dalt and I talked about some stuff. I wouldn't mind doing more of that."

"I'm exhausted," Aspera said. "I'm going up."

"This early?"

"I feel like I'm getting a chill." Indeed her voice shook. "Maybe the exposure last night; it took a while to flag somebody down."

"Don't forget your tea," Will reminded her. He poured her a cup, watched to see that the leaves went to the bottom. Before he handed it to her he took several sips. "Maybe I will have some," he decided.

Aspera took a hot shower and crawled into bed. Uptown

mammals have to make certain breaks with stupidity. *You can have it all.* There was stupidity, start with that.

She got past Monday. All day Tuesday she prowled the house like a leopard, pacing and restless, trying this corner and that one, this sofa and that chair. Normally she let herself range, knew that sooner or later she would come upon the right thing. She and Will would go to a movie tonight, maybe a double feature, that would help. She found yesterday's paper and checked the times. Then she scanned Sunday's want ads, got the mail, tried reading one more novel. She wrote checks for bills not yet due, wrote dates in the squares where stamps would go. She picked up the soft alpaca yarn she'd been saving for Will's birthday present, a hat to go with his scarf. For two hours she knitted at the Icelandic pattern, counting stitches, alternating the muted grayish brown and cream yarns. Soft or not, the filaments rubbed over the joint of her index finger so that during the third hour she went to the mirror and tried on the hat herself, one needle dangling down beside her face. Too large, not her colors, Dena would—the needle fell jangling to the floor.

She took the ring of knitting down to the basement, stretched it over a styrofoam wig form she still kept. She pulled the unfinished hat down low over where eyes would have been, pinched the Styrofoam planes where cheeks were indicated.

She would not see Kevin again. As for dealing two-handed, she was too cowardly. She couldn't lie, she never wanted to lie again in her whole life. One story was hard enough to keep straight—who could bear the labor of two? Not her. So. Think about history now, think about Will's birthday, think about growing old with Will.

There was a list of calls she meant to make, there was the kitchen and a hundred thousand untried recipes. The notion was so overwhelming that she stayed in the kitchen only long enough to turn the radio up as loud as she could stand it, loud on the public radio station Will listened to over breakfast. She reached the stairs and hung on to the banister while she recognized that she could not bear it, not this miserably thin harpsichord and flute. She ran back and flipped the dial away, the edits of stations blatting by until she slid into the nearest jungle rhythm, the hard obliterating refuge of rock music. The kitchen sounded hollow around its pulse, echo chamber of Formica and tile. The answering vibration for her caged leopard; do not foul the nest.

The phone rang at four. "You'll have to go to that movie by yourself," Will said. "I forgot this was Rotary night. I'll walk over to Schiller's Sports and catch a ride with Tom Schiller at six-thirty. Don't wait up," he said. Meaning they would drink at Vet's Bar afterward.

"Wait," she said. "About your birthday. Have you changed your mind about a party? Decade birthday, pretty big deal."

"You're trying to make it into one."

"This is your last chance, we've got a bedpan to give away—" She stopped, gave up the effort for a cheeriness that wasn't carrying. "Will, if you want to celebrate I'd be glad to arrange it."

"That's beside the point."

"What point?"

"About a hundred times," he said, his voice rising, "I've said I don't want a lot of fuss."

"Well, how much is a lot?"

He exhaled into the receiver. "You could take me out for dinner, OK? You wouldn't even have to cook."

"You mean, the two of us?" she asked.

"The two of us, yeah, the two of us. Dinner out. Isn't that exciting enough?"

"It's enough for me," she said, confused. "Where would you like to go?"

"Christ! Do I have to spell everything out?" He shouted. His voice in her ear made a connection to her brain that produced panic. "You want me to tell you what I want to eat in advance, too?"

The answer was yes, but Aspera's mind filled with confusion. She was making a mistake. She could not decide which mistake it was.

Silence was the right answer. When he had secured it, Will hung up.

She looked at the clock. Four-ten. Ten-four, it was a birthday dinner for two. Take him out in the Cities? Special occasion, but Will hated driving that distance on a Friday night, with Saturday a business day. She thought about calling him back, making the celebration Saturday, but she didn't have the nerve. She took the Bracken directory from the kitchen drawer and looked up the new place at the edge of Cold Spring. She phoned for a reservation, spoke to the foreign-sounding hostess about the menu and hung up with what should have felt like relief, but which didn't.

Rotary dinner meeting, Tom Schiller. Drinks at the Vet's Bar, don't wait up.

She was on the road to Minneapolis by four-twenty.

CHAPTER SEVENTEEN

"Mmm-hmmm," Kevin agreed when he opened the door, "I wanted to see you, too." He held her tightly to him. When they sat down on the sofa together he tucked her hand under his upper arm, compressed it against his chest.

"Tell me your car lights are off this time," he said.

Aspera leaned her head against his shoulder. She thought she would shut her eyes, rest. But they stayed open. On the lamp table beside the sofa she noticed a clear glass Christmas ornament bearing three painted stripes, pale green, red, dark green. They circled the globe like a triple equator. The delicacy was catching; she felt she wore the thin bulb like a lining in her chest cavity.

She put out a finger and touched the satin bow tied to the top of the attachment wire.

Kevin leaned over and took the bulb from her hand, set it on the carpet under the end table. "Let's concentrate on each other." He tilted her face to his and smoothed her hair so that he could speak into her ear. "Let me tell you what I do," he whispered. "When I'm with you I push all sensation right out to my skin. I know exactly where you are, how far your body is from mine, I feel it on my skin. I'm one hundred percent perimeter. Have you ever noticed the way I'm always touching something when you're around? When we're not in bed I have to make my hands carry the load for the rest of me."

It was the longest speech she could remember from him. Somehow because of that, she could not concentrate on what he said.

"After you left here yesterday," he went on, "I nearly wore out everything in reach." Her eyes had returned to the Christmas ball which lay on its side on the carpet when he clenched his bicep, squeezing her hand. "Do you know what I mean? Is that the way it is for you?"

She closed her eyes against the hollowness she felt, tried to redirect feeling to her extremities. The car heater had not seemed to work properly; her feet ached. The hand that Kevin had not captured lay upon her own thigh, also cold, thumb tucked tightly inside a curl of fingers. Sitting like this she sincerely wished to be overwhelmed once again, as he wished her to be.

"I've lost it," she said.

"Lost what?"

She looked at him, looked away. Thought of how she had felt in those first days, those first afternoons, lying beside him. She tried again. "I want to say the inside of me, but I think I mean—the connection, inside to outside."

He shifted his shoulders, took her other hand. "We need to make love."

"Yes."

But the word fell and neither of them moved.

Kevin sat forward, looked into her eyes. "We'll make it right in bed," he said.

The bedroom seemed very far from where they sat. He stood up and took her hand; as she rose to her feet a small noise came from the carpet, a small pop and crush of thin glass.

He did not light the candle. They undressed in the dark. In bed, her body remembered him. Her mind remembered a book, a story about a young boy whose teacher grabbed him inside his pants, saying with severity, "Next time let me know *in time*."

They explored the bed as though one place would prove better than another, one configuration of bodies forge better than another the hieroglyph for what was missing. She cast through her mind for pictures, a man on a crowded bus, a boy hanging jack-o'-lanterns. In the moments before her body found its way to the classroom, Kevin seized her hips with both hands and rolled her astride him, arched his body.

"Fuck me," he commanded through his teeth. "Fuckme-fuckme."

He addressed her body, and her body complied. In her mind teacher and pupil joined together at last, one more time.

The sky looked frozen brilliant as she left the freeway at Osseo and crossed to the old highway, which would take her back to Bracken through fields and farm towns, a stop sign or two in Anoka and then Big Bend. She wanted interruptions, some destruction of endless continuity. The freeway connected Minneapolis and Bracken like two linked ends of a single inhospitable continuum, Will to Kevin, Kevin to Will. You must show steps.

At Anoka she waited for a left turn, her turn signal blinking steadily. Dalton might travel this way into the city every day. The old highway held more northerly than the freeway, might be more efficient to the university.

She made the turn. Dalton in her kitchen all those years ago: she'd cried, and did she fall? He'd caught her. She'd sat on a stool looking into his eyes. A sudden vertigo and then she held on to his arms. She remembered holding on hard—some things were so vivid. The rigidity she recalled clearly, and also that she'd looked while he extinguished a soft light in his eyes.

She shook her head. Where did these things come from? Black sky surrounded the old highway above the flat prairie; even in daytime the feeling was that you were somehow riding high on the world. Cloud formations appeared to be a very long way off; this gave plenty of warning, plenty of time to take steps. Weather could be violent, but there were always signs: sudden icy gusts on a warm afternoon, a swipe of cirrus formations over mackerel spots, the peculiar yellow of a tornado sky. You sat on the front porch with iced lemonade and a radio, listening, watching. Rainstorms were serious, too, but then all afternoon the sky would be gathering its purple, huge buffalo heads mulling and blowsing dark into the evenings. Leisurely preambles of sheet lightning at the horizon led to grumbles of thunder that went on so long as to seem paternal, halfhearted about the extreme measures to follow. The bargaining might continue until the slash and spatter of water sang at the windows and soaked into basements. Panes rattled and shook with full-artillery thunder, and bright spiderwebs splayed across the sky, electrified just long enough to show that the world and daytime colors might exist in the hereafter.

No violence tonight. Odd that she should even imagine it, so out of season and in the company of this wide calm sky. Extremes were spawned by the coasts but land mass contributed intensity, a characteristic lack of relief in temperature, humidity, velocity, volume. Staying power was the trademark of middle ground.

She leaned over the steering wheel to see more of the sky. Ghostly twists of clouds were strung way up high, arcing up and over the highway like fading contrails. Bunny away at a counselors' retreat? Aspera leaned over the dashboard, rested her breasts in the metal webbing of the steering wheel. The evening star was long gone, but Sirius trailed Orion in the south, glimmering blue and purple and orange from its triple source.

At the sign marked Trempeleau she followed the slant of the arrow off the highway. She thought she could find the house in the dark. Nothing at stake; no hurry. A brief grid of streets, a stop sign, the right cul de sac.

The town of Trempeleau was quiet, its day-old snow brushed up deep against curbsides as though in hiding. She stopped at the main intersection, saw on one of its corners a commemorative stone set inside an iron fence. Christians used to leave crosses at crossroads on behalf of the unconsecrated dead buried there. A block beyond the intersection, lights shone on the triangle of civic park beside an old railroad station. The rest of the town was dark. Energy conservation left no porch lights burning, and few living room lamps argued life within; not one house where television flickered blue and untended. What time? Not even nine-thirty. She'd be home long before Will; Bunny was away on business through Tuesday. Would Dalton be up, grading papers? She would drive by.

Through the town now, she slowed along the dotted blacktop to find the road. Freneau, Delaplane, Curtis, Imperial. She decided on Delaplane and executed a halting U-turn.

On Delaplane Court she crept from one house to the next,

large new bilevels set on spacious lots. Lights here and there, since these weren't town folk but some other category. Nomenclature for people living in a bedroom community: somnambulists.

Sure now of the street, she slowed. If the house showed light, she would knock on the door. Dalton could be watching a movie. She would demand popcorn.

Dalton could be having an affair. She smiled. Statistics in favor of probable; ask Bunny. When her headlights picked up the house, she switched to parking lights on guilty impulse. Look for a strange car—no, strange cars were kept in garages against mischance, neighbors taking a wrong turn down the cul de sac. Look for a light in the bedroom. Candle, red bulb, pulsating strobe? For some reason Aspera laughed out loud. She stopped the Mercury where the driveway met the long oval of turnaround. The house stood quite dark.

She opened the car door, got out and slammed it.

On the flagstone porch under the Mediterranean overhang, a bell and brass knocker awaited her touch. She slipped her hands into her coat pockets and took a deep breath before the fortress look of the door, its frames and elaborate casings, its bells and knockers and knobs. Her heart beat against her coat. In her pockets were wadded solids of Kleenex, two coins and a matchbook; she tried the shape of each as if to press out information or courage. To hell with Bunny.

She put her hand on the knob, tried it gently.

The mechanism clicked; the door swung open.

She stood pulling the heavy door back from opening further into the dark house. It felt weighted strongly enough to pull her in. She trembled; action had outstripped intention, and she could feel the pulse in her temples.

Behind her Dalton said, "I don't lock up—"

Aspera jumped and screamed.

He put his hands on her shoulders. "Shhhhhhhhhh!" he whispered, incredulous and laughing. "I'm sorry—I didn't mean—"

She recovered her breath, clutching her throat. He said, "I was about to say, I don't lock up when I go out for walks at night. Are you coming in?"

"Why is it dark?" she blurted. Everything was wrong; this

was the wrong thing to do, the wrong order of things.

"It's dark because I like to go stand under those trees over there in the corner"—he took her arm and swung her round so that she looked where he pointed—"I lean against that big cottonwood there, you can see where the trunk curves that it would be a good place to lean—and I look at the stars. Tonight I was watching the northern lights. Did you see them as you drove?"

"No, I—" But those twists of white light she had been following above the highway, she had taken them for clouds. "Well, yes. Mostly I was looking the other way."

He laughed gently. "Well, it's quite a surprise, but a nice one."

"I thought they only came out in the fall and spring," Aspera said of the northern lights. Dalton's hand had stayed on her arm, and she felt she'd lost her way somehow, one of those nightmares you walk into where intelligence is in the atmosphere and you cannot pick it up, cannot seem to find out what everybody else knows and thinks you know.

"Dalt, I'm walking in a nightmare."

"Maybe it's just somebody else's dream." He chuffed a breath of uneasy cloud laughter. He added solemnly, "Maybe that's what a nightmare is: walking in somebody else's dream."

She looked at him amazed. Did he understand everything? "Don't ask me what I'm doing here," she said at last. "I don't know what I'd tell you."

"I won't ask." He looked skyward. "Or maybe I know. I did answer the phone for you at your place the other night. Maybe I've been expecting you."

"Oh God." She turned and hid her eyes against his jacket.

"Are you all right?" Dalton asked, putting an arm around her shoulders. "Do you want to go in and turn on the lights and have daytime conversation?"

Beside her and against the snow brightness, he looked like a silhouette, a place holder for what light would show her. "No. I mean—I want to try your cottonwood tree, see the lights from there. Is that all right? Are you cold?"

"No, but I think you're still trembling." He pulled his arm tighter around her. "Come. The wonders of the universe will unfold." With his free arm Dalton was describing a great arc against the sky, which was glimmering in streaks and portions up to its center, where stars showed through. The wispy light that Aspera had taken for vapor above the highway winked and glowed and showed faint colors, changed and changed back like uncertain torchlight playing on a cracked globe of ice.

Even holding to the cottonwood trunk, standing firmly on frozen prairie grass in the middle of Minnesota, Aspera had the feeling she had with the grace of a somnambulist fallen away into starry isolate space.

"I ran across something the other day and thought about you," Dalton said, breaking a silence of several minutes. His eyes still followed patterns of light in the sky. "Is Ariadne still myth-of-the-month?"

"Maybe."

"Maybe? Listen, I'm still on Ariadne, so let me tell you what I read. Did you know spiders take balloon trips? They spin little bubbles with their webs and zip along on air currents—sometimes they're found raining down over the ocean five hundred miles from land. Doesn't that cheer you up?"

Aspera looked up at the millions of dots of light in the Milky Way. "Can they swim?"

"Ah. I see what you mean."

They smiled at one another.

"Now," Dalton resumed, "tell me what you saw in the southern sky that caused you to miss this display of aurora borealis?"

Aspera turned and pointed to Orion.

"Ah, the giant," Dalton said. "Or so the Babylonians thought. Also the Hebrews, who figured it was Nimrod, fellow who built the Tower of Babel. In Hebrew Orion is translated as *fool.* In any case, a giant, shackled for presumption against the gods."

Her body sagged. "Can't people think of any new endings?"

Dalton looked at her. "Historically speaking, giants make ideal enemies. Giants and talking snakes."

She laughed and looked up at Sirius. Eye of the dog. "Remember what you said the other night about civilization progressing on insight? But even my mother's lovely Greeks killed the messenger."

Dalton sighed. "Nobody likes a threat. First thing you know, people are stashing their favorite brand of tuna fish in queen-size crates. Next come the guns to protect the tuna fish. It's hard to sell insight to armed citizens with an investment in tuna fish under their beds."

Aspera smiled at this wry comfort. She felt comfort, not desire—a rush of peace just being here with someone who could find harmless things to say.

The side of her body next to Dalton was warm. Through the padded layers of coats and gloves, she leaned into the weight of his arm across her shoulders, felt the grip of his hand on her upper arm. The sky with its array of lights had absorbed proximity and its shoddier possibilities. Now wonder faded and attention fell to earth. *Fuckmefuckme.* Acids corroded her stomach wall. Why not? was a question that answered itself. That question appeared in her mind as the two of them stood together against the great impersonal backrest of cottonwood. She tilted her head to see the lights; her hood fell back and one ear was exposed to the sky. The ear grew sharply colder while the side of her face that rested on Dalton's jacket was pressed to warmth. Why not fuck all your friends? Why not just get on with it? Too late in all these exchanges to parse names, be picky about which wrong man it was.

Dalton placed his gloved hand over her cold ear.

"This won't do," he said. "Let's go in."

The house was set into a knoll so that its lower floor was exposed from the rear. They entered the dark house underground through sliding glass doors. Once they were inside and the night shut out, no constellations or northern lights to populate space, the darkness turned oppressive.

"Design flaw," Dalton said, taking Aspera's hand and leading her through the room, "all light switches are on the far wall."

"I don't want the lights on," she told the black room.

A slight ease in tension between their hands as he paused.

"There's a fire in my study," he said. Again he pulled her along, guiding her around the sharp turn that led to the basement room. He would touch her, kiss her; the rest would go like clockwork.

"Stand right here," he directed, stationing her beside the door.

On her face she could feel the shimmer of heat. Then with a rasping of metal and squeal of rough-cast hinges he had thrown open the twin doors of a freestanding fireplace. The room leaped with golden contours and the certainty of objects.

Kneeling before the open flames, Dalton once again appeared as a black shadow.

Aspera came forward and knelt beside him while he poked the coals and put on another chop of wood. She untied and unwrapped her coat and let it fall about her.

"I was working in here tonight," he said. "I even have tea on the warmer." He stood and took the pot from atop the stove and from the shadows over his desk produced a mug. "One cup, though. We'll have to share." He concentrated on the pouring, then handed her the heavy hot stoneware.

She sipped the tea, herbs blended with flowers and mint, she could not tell color. She offered him the mug.

He shook his head. "You," he said.

She was self-conscious as she drank; perhaps she would feel too human at anything, the way Dalton watched her.

"I wish you wouldn't do that," she said.

"What?"

"Watch."

"Why?"

"Because I—" She looked at the shapes around them, suggestions of solidity limned in firelight, concealed in shadow. "I want to be like the rest. Like the furniture."

He said nothing. After a moment he took a stick of wood and shifted the arrangement inside the stove. When he put down the stick he said, "So what's the latest in myth-of-the-month?"

Aspera sighed. The sound came out broken into parts. Dalton would know about the god of commerce, the one who served both shopkeepers and thieves, a god made happy by the mere fact that money changed hands over or under any number of tables. She set her jaw against the name.

"You're thinking too hard."

She sighed again. "Right. I guess—it's Eurydice that bothers me."

"Bad ending to that one. No second chances."

"Bad. So I've been reading novels." A flash of impatience. Aspera steeled herself. "I read one story, there's this couple who have been friends a long time, both married to other people, and one day she says to him, You think in another ten years we might have an affair?"

She didn't risk looking at Dalton. "It sounded so easy that

way, simply asking for an opinion. Nice because nobody was really forced to dive for the tuna fish."

Dalton smiled. "And in the story, what did he say?"

"He said, *Another ten years*?"

Dalton nodded. He kept looking into the fire. "It is nice. But you do want to think hard if you seem to be in a dream and it might be someone else's."

She let out a breath of relief. That was settled then. They would stay where they were, friends who regarded the world side by side. But fast behind the relief rode anger. *Couldn't seduce me if you tried*—was she trying?

"Dalt," she said, "what if that was a hint?"

He patted her arm, let his hand rest lightly on her elbow, let it drop.

She felt frozen into position, silly. She wanted to shake Dalton. If the root of violence was impotence—she groped about on the floor for her coat.

She struggled to find the armholes. She stood up. The coat could have been a thick blanket she turned in her hands.

"Do you want me to put on the light?" Dalton asked.

She looked down at the black shape in front of the stove, no face she could read. She remembered who he was.

"Dalton, I can't even begin to explain. It has nothing to do with you, believe me."

"I believe you." The dark head shook. "That's just it. We've been through this crossroads before."

She stopped. She sank to her knees beside him, careful not to come too near. "Yes. That's why I came here tonight—or it's why I thought I was coming. Do you remember that, too, that afternoon in the kitchen?"

He cupped his hand over his mouth. "I think so. We were young, Aspera."

"Dalt, where does the energy come from to care about things twenty years in the past? Isn't it from things cut off unfinished, like phantom limbs of feeling that still reach out? Or maybe"—she thought of the intersection in the little town—"we leave markers for our unblessed alternatives." Was that it? Alternatives left straggling at crossroads like orphans who would never grow up, like Peter Pan, till grownups returned for them?

"Maybe *what*?" Dalton asked.

She let out a long breath. Smiled at his confusion, and her own. "Elvira once asked me what I thought about *between thoughts.* You understand?"

Dalton nodded.

"I told her I saw the past. She told me it was the future, and I thought she was crazy. She was trying to tell me a shortcut. Dalt, you and I have always felt close, and what I think we did twenty years ago was try to hold on to some middle ground—some safe place between affection and—" She stopped short of the ugly word, the stripped-down hiss of *lust.*

"It was love," Dalton said. "But love between friends."

He offered his hand, and she seized it with both of hers.

"That was wise of us," she said, "wasn't it? And brave—maybe too smart and too brave to handle." She glanced at his face. She said, "I'm sorry you had to cover for me on the phone the other night. And I'm sorry about tonight. I needed your help finding middle ground again."

"Don't thank me," he said. "I'm a born coward."

"Well, I had a lapse of cowardice a few months ago, and as a result—" She stopped.

"You fell in love?"

She withdrew her hands from his. "Elvira used to talk about seven devils. How you cast one out and then into the space you made came seven more. I tried to get rid of a deadness"—she clutched the area over her heart—"and in swept this horde of small active evils. The earth didn't open up and swallow me, no lightning struck, but now instead of deadness"—she spread both hands over her breastbone—"I have this anthill."

Dalton made a sound between his teeth. "I don't think it really benefits anybody to look too hard at their personal life, or expect life at forty to measure up to dreams you had when you were younger. Now with history it's a discipline; you can separate the factors, you have some kind of record to go by when you start asking why did this happen, why didn't this happen instead. But in life—I don't think it pays off. I notice I just get depressed." He shrugged. "But I can be useful in my field; there's plenty to do; I don't have to let myself think about anything else."

She let his words sink in. How they tempted her, with their promise of peace. But something didn't fit, something she already knew. "Not letting myself think was one way I got in trouble," she whispered. "And then the things that made me feel alive—I tripped over them like land mines. Trying to get out of the store. Blam! Falling in love. Blam! Hitting somebody"—she looked at her hands, absorbed in her own surprise. Neither Dalton nor she seemed to be breathing. In the hush she said, "Now you look at those three things and it's a very practical decision to choose the most constructive one, which is—"

"Hitting someone?"

They had screwed up their faces at the unlikelihood. Then grinned.

"—which is trying to find a job doing something I love. But the other two things mattered, Dalt." She slapped her fist lightly into her other hand. The sound came feeble and flat. She pressed the enclosed fist to her mouth. "How do you make decisions without knowing what you want?"

"Are you going to tell me about the hitting?"

She felt her face grow hot. "Probably nothing that would make sense. I was finding out where a lot of energy has been tied up—since I was a kid. I hope I'm done with that. I hope coming here tonight was the end of the chain, my last act of violence."

"You're done with the love affair, too?"

She nodded yes.

"Doesn't sound like two of your three things were worth the trouble."

They watched a charred limb crack into glowing sections, and she made up her mind. "They were worth some. Will and I have been married twenty years, and I just thought the earth was flat, I thought it was possible to fall off. What I found out was, the earth is in fact so very pear-shaped that you can go all the way round and end up just where you started."

The pieces of limb blackened. "Which is?"

"Caught between something real dead, and something unreal but lively."

Dalton coughed. "I'm sorry to say I believe I know exactly what you mean. History always adds a dimension, doesn't it? We do have one, sort of an add-on history, like those pearls you used to get from your dad."

Pearls by mail from San Francisco.

"Elvira was the one who sent those." Saying this, Aspera sat up straight. "There were some old invoices—I never really paid attention."

Dalton lifted his head. "Elvira? But your dad—"

"He gave me the first four. Then maybe he just wrote us off, and she decided to protect me. I guess."

"I'll be damned." He turned the idea over. "I thought Elvira warned you off illusion?"

Slowly Aspera shook her head, looked down at the orange webs that were her hands on her thighs. "Maybe she thought it was all right for me to believe that somebody else loved me better than she could—sort of like Santa Claus. She used to stuff candy in my dad's pockets for me, and the pearls are the same thing. Kids need proofs."

"That could screw a kid up, though."

"It makes me happy. I keep thinking she knew I'd figure things out when I wanted to—one last secret between us. A love message." Aspera blinked back tears. She said, "It's a little like finding out I was adopted, except by my real mother."

"Santa Claus." Dalton was shaking his head. "I think if you don't get disabused of your notions while you're young, they just stick around and abuse you when you're old."

Aspera laughed. "Do you feel old and abused?"

"When I was medium-old," Dalton said, "I was disabused of the notion that I could share Will's room and Will's girl friend and Will's bride. Even though I did get the incriminating bedsheets."

She drew a sharp breath. "What sheets? Not—"

"Jesus." Dalton put his head in his hands. "I thought you knew. Will switched the sheets to my bed. Well, actually, he just moved the beds around." He put up both hands. "It was the best idea at the time. Remember those maids?"

Now her head was in her hands.

Dalton sighed. "If Will didn't tell you, he didn't want you to know. Shit. I can't ever remember being innocent. Can you?"

She kept her eyes covered.

"For Christ's sake don't let him know I told you. We're all—" He stopped. "You and I married very similar people, do you know that, Aspera?"

"Which means we have the same things wrong with us?"

He laughed. "I suppose."

"I seem to be the only one sneaking around."

Dalton gritted his teeth. "Here goes." He took a breath. "Bunny and I left California because I was falling in love with my graduate assistant. You want to know how my personal decisions are made? There it is."

She stared into the dark room. "Oh, God. I ought to feel relieved. The truth is, I'd rather think Bunny was just paranoid."

Dalton held up his hand. "There's more. I know what you mean by that, because Will has been thinking you and I were having an affair."

Aspera went rigid. "Will said that?"

"The night we were supposed to spend in the icehouse. The night your phone rang and I said it was a wrong number. 'Things haven't been right since about the time you moved back,' Will says. So the timing adds up, also the mileage—which he checks. I was flattered." Dalton watched her face. "But I can't cover for you."

With the ringing still going on in her head Aspera said, "He's never asked me anything, never acted as though there was anything he cared to know. I thought he was spinning himself into a cocoon with the store and all his new plans—you mean he's been snooping around like some—"

"He talked to me, and here I am talking to you. Where's the fairness? People sneak around because the open road is too damned scary."

"Tell me about it."

Dalton sighed. "You have to see the other side—maybe like the pearls turning out to be from your mother. Who knows what the coverups are all about? You just can't afford to look too closely. Bunny runs incredible numbers because she's dependent on me and can't stand for anybody to know it. Including me. And I think Will is like that."

"Bunny whips you around like you're some kind of hand tool! That's how vulnerable Bunny is."

He nodded. "About as vulnerable as Will."

Her anger climbed. "I keep thinking of you as Bunny's victim, but it's not true, is it?" She brought her hands down hard on her thighs. "Vicky just wrote me about this! What she didn't say was, *it takes two.*"

Dalton pursed his mouth. "Somebody has to be the voice of reason. I don't have room to do anything but stay calm, because Bunny gets absolutely hysterical. I can't push her. You're pushing Will, and *he's* hysterical—I don't know how you justify that. I don't know what makes you think it's worth it. You're taking big risks—really big ones when you step over the lines you're stepping over."

"I know things I didn't know before," she said stubbornly. "There's a way to feel alive with somebody and a way to feel dead with the same person. I know that, it's important and I'm not going to be talked out of knowing it!"

"You're going to get caught knowing it. Is that the same thing?"

She pulled a deep breath. "I don't know."

"You may have heard that the truth would set you free," Dalton said. He reached over and put his hand over one of hers. "But take it from me, the truth is what makes blackmail possible. Not to mention divorce."

She watched orange coals collapse and fall into the bed of other collapsing coals. "I have more hopes than you do."

"But the same results." Dalton picked up the poker and jabbed at the fire again. "Hell, what do I know? Maybe we should have both blown it off." He raked the coals back and forth, scattering sparks that snuffed themselves with small ticks of sound. "What was my line again? *Another ten years?*"

She turned to look at the man beside her. "You're my friend, Dalt, and Will's friend, and you're a good man with the cold water."

He shook his head. "Cowardice. I'd like us all to be close again, but it'll be difficult if you're in Minnesota and I'm with Bunny in a remote village in the Philippines."

For some minutes they sat watching the stove with its bellyful of hot light.

"We're not going to be close," Aspera told him. "Bunny's made that plain."

"She needs to be reassured."

Aspera looked at him. "Think you can do that?"

He smiled. "That's my job."

She took a breath. "I'm stepping way out of line with this, but is putting your daughter in boarding school part of reassuring Bunny?"

Dalton fumbled with the poker, dropped it. "The last year has been hard on us, the move from California"—he picked up the poker where it had rattled to a stop, glanced at Aspera—"and all. I think it's just temporary—I'm sure it is—till we get settled again. Till Bunny feels more herself."

Again he jabbed at the fire.

She watched his agitation. He didn't like to look at personal things too closely. Was this one more form of violence she was practicing, maybe Vicky's brand, making him look? "It's late," she said. "I'd better go home." She thought of Will and added bitterly, "Though I don't know what the point is. Mileage is mileage."

Dalton offered her his hand and she rose with him.

"Don't blame Will for being suspicious," he said quietly. "The fact is, there are clues and he's picking them up." He gave her a playful tap on the chin with his knuckles. "After that, it gets hard to sort out cause and effect, and who's behaving the worst."

Again she sought the armholes in her coat. "What floors me," she said, "is how I've completely lost the picture that Will is any kind of sensitive instrument. I expect nothing to register, nothing that matters to me. I expect to be tuned out. And when I'm not tuned out—" she slipped the coat on, tied the belt—"it feels like an invasion of privacy. My God. Don't you miss being in love, Dalt?"

"Will loves you, Aspera. You shouldn't have to take my word for it, but for the time being maybe you'd better. You and your hopes. You still want romance, don't you?" Taking her hand, he guided her to the dark stairs. Then his voice led the way up to the first floor. "I'll settle for less. Bunny needs me. She will go to elaborate and ultimately touching lengths to keep me because she can't trust being loved. And maybe she's right."

Aspera placed her hands on the invisible banister, pulling herself up one step at a time. "If you settle for less, then isn't that what you end up with? Less, and then less than that, and then less still?" In the darkness her eyes strained to see. Almost to herself, she murmured, "At the same time I almost wish I could settle for that."

At the front door Dalton whispered, "How many wishes do you have left?"

She took a moment. "None."

He made a sound like laughter, a sound of commiseration. Outside on the front porch without his jacket he shivered and asked, "Is Will having a birthday party?"

"He absolutely refuses." She drew her hood up. "God, I feel so edgy these days, I wish he would have a party. You could come, and then there'd be one person in the house on my wavelength. I really need a friend." She shook her head, began to laugh. "Aren't you relieved that we don't have to be lovers?"

Dalton groaned, put his arms around her. "You would never need me enough. You're too much like me, Aspera, you want somebody else to do the needing."

They pressed their faces, cheeks already cooling in the night air, close together. They were moving apart from this last gesture at sheltering one another when Bunny's headlights swept the cul de sac and caught them.

CHAPTER EIGHTEEN

Aspera and Dalton stood apart and faced Bunny, who brushed past them on the dark porch without granting a single human sign of recognition. From inside the house Bunny switched the porchlight and floodlights on, and slammed the front door.

Life was simpler with the world flat. That was the power of the old explanations, and Aspera had lapsed back into a world they explained. Go too far, and there's an end. She could look at the horizon and convince herself, maybe, that a round world accounted for it. If things burned, could she be certain that phlogiston was not the cause? If it happened that molecules were not equipped with small hooks that linked them one to another, as once was taught, then the new explanations—equal and opposite force, mutual attraction of particles—did little to change what she understood of matter.

"Go on home," Dalton said, hurrying a pat to her shoulder. His tone was final. His hurry was of one used to trying his hand along the edge of a flattened earth. Bunny might have her hand already poised over the telephone faceplate, dialing.

Aspera fled. She left Dalton to convince his wife how there was this time no need to move. To explain with delicacy this veteran affection of theirs which was always being turned back by finer feeling. Back on the highway, she wondered if delicacy might not enrage a hanging judge. Bunny's business was survival by sexual control. Touch was sexual, and Bunny had seen touch, would be in no mood for finer feeling.

Aspera floored the accelerator, hoping to talk to Will before

Bunny did. Her legs and feet felt too weak to keep the pedal pushed down while her hands shook on the wheel in a useless expenditure of energy.

At eleven-thirty she pulled into the garage. One light shone in their bedroom upstairs. She would tell Will the truth, all of it.

Once inside the house and upstairs, she found the lighted room empty. On the waterbed was her own letter, the one she'd written to Vicky and discarded, smoothed out and laid on the pillow like a farewell note. "Sex without love," she read. "Monkeys jumping up and down on a telegraph key."

She crushed the letter in her hands, her stomach responding as though it had the task of dissolving a similar soiled lump. When she began shivering, she got under the blankets in her clothes and watched the numerals in the bedside clock flip, flip.

With cold hands Will disarmed the alarm and with his keys let himself into the warehouse door of the lumberyard complex. Thank God he still had keys in his pockets. Midnight by his watch; it had taken fifteen minutes to make the walk. Bitter cold out—he took off his down jacket, kicked off his street shoes—he thought his feet would freeze on the way here, those thin little soles—the warehouse wasn't heated, the lumber office had wall heaters but—he thought about turning on a light, thought about the Bracken police on their patrols. Sheriff Unger himself might knock on the door, what difference would that make? Will took a swipe at the switchplate; all over the warehouse ceiling, fluorescent tubes began to blink. He fumbled to get all the switches off again. He wasn't eager for callers just now, was all. Christ, this cement floor! Feet must have got wet. Nothing like the cheap booze at the Vet's to keep your mind off your troubles, and walking fast in the snow he hadn't even noticed. This business of lights—he looked around, recalling suddenly that the store's cellar room had no windows. He remembered also the little space heater down there. Hell, that's where they stashed the sleeping bags Schiller couldn't unload at Moonlight Madness. A heater, sleeping bags—he could hole up a week, she'd never figure it, scare her good. Will felt his way in the dark to the rack where the warehouse foremen kept a flashlight. Some of those back bins were dark, guys used a light to read labels back there. Been doing it for forty years—he smacked the side of his face. Where was his brain? He ought to install a spot on an overhead track. Obvious.

By the unsteady beam of the flashlight he made his way across the slab floor of the warehouse to the hardware door. He searched for the right key on his key ring. Now they make novelty items, he'd seen a catalog, little plastic key envelopes with bulbs so you could see to unlock a door in the dark. Bobbie should order, tell her so. With the flashlight tucked under one arm he fumbled the keys, dropped them. He dropped the flashlight, which bounced on the concrete with an unhealthy sound. Nothing broken, no harm done, start over. He found the key again, tucked the flashlight, unlocked the door into hardware.

Didn't smell like it used to when he was a kid, remember that odor, sawdust and machine oil? God, he loved that odor. Now the place smelled like liquid plastic, exactly like a goddamn dry cleaner's, fumes that might do in your nasal membranes and every other membrane. In that case, best to knock off the brain cells first. How many had he hoisted with Tom? Hell, they were home early, wasn't even eleven when he got home. She was still at the movies, who cared where she was. He was emptying his pockets on the way upstairs and went into his old bedroom—wrong turn actually, he just needed to chuck some bar matches from the Vet's in the wastebasket. The whole room was hers now, she'd taken over—that, too, books all over the goddamn place, wastebasket already full; didn't she even keep the place picked up? And then it was the color that caught his eye, that piece of stationery all wadded up, just sitting on top; wasn't that the blue parchment stuff his mother had used? He'd picked it up and smoothed it out—

Will smashed the keys down on the counter where the register sat. They made the noise he longed to make with his hands; how he'd love to smash her, who did she think she was, anyhow? He wheeled about and with the flashlight beat beat beat on the door to the cellar; sound thundered through the building and then a vicious crack as the wood split—goddamn cheap hollow door, God, he was going to get rid of everything, every last bloody stick of cheap wood in the place. Wasn't going to sneak around in the dark like a scared kid, either—he reached over and turned on the lights, then whirled and heaved the flashlight at the shelf unit that hung above the register, missed—he fell to the floor. Didn't matter, didn't matter, he got up, slapped at his knees. He'd do the job right.

In hardware he found the mallet and the sledge he needed, a crowbar, hammer, pliers, chisel. He brought the tools back and dumped them in front of the shattered door. It was the sledge he really wanted. He got himself set, lifted it over his head and brought it smashing down on the door, which shot into splinters. Next he hit the plaster next to the door facing. The stuff exploded like pillow stuffing, crashed and spattered to the floor. What the hell, it all had to go. He smashed several more holes and exposed one entire lathe strip. He leaned his arm against the door facing and bent over, breathing hard. Use the crowbar, jam it in and rip this rotten stuff right off the foundation. His face was hot, sweat running down like tears God he hated those cellar stairs. Hated the way they were always in shadow—he wiped his whole face with his sleeve, his eyes stung—sometimes he could swear shadows were moving back and forth, back and forth. He stuck the crowbar into the crack and put his weight on it. She used to take the baby down there to rock it, nurse it, how he hated that, it made him sick to his stomach. A cracking of wood. He dropped to his knees on the floor, fingers tight on the crowbar, his stomach wrenching. Wet small intense heat baby smell sour milk between him and his mother not the same never the same again but I'm big I can do other things I'm still alive she is not lost to me though I lose her body to another every day I am not lost.

Aspera woke when the phone rang. Eight-thirty by the numerals. Gray light outside, early sun dulled by clouds. Dalton, calling from his office, whispering faintly he'd had a long talk with Bunny.

"Will was gone when I got home," Aspera said, clearing her throat. "Did Bunny call him?"

"Of course not," Dalton protested. "He'll be back, don't worry."

She worried. All night she'd dreamed of standing with feet astride the crack of a trapdoor, the way it went when serial heroes stood before the throne in the enemy stronghold. "What did Bunny say?" she asked Dalton, her voice hoarse.

"She was great," he said wonderingly. "I'm confident you'll straighten things out with Will, too. Bunny didn't get hysterical at all; she listened and asked questions."

Aspera hung up and heard the questions. When, where, how, how far, how many times, why?

She called the store and got Bobbie. No, the older woman hadn't seen Mr. Hancock yet—thirty years and nothing would move Bobbie from formal address for her employers—but she saw he'd begun his remodeling project. She'd have thought that could have waited till after Christmas. Marlys was having a time of it, those plastic sheets hanging there between the register and cellar storage. Did Mrs. Hancock know the cellar room was a heap of rubble?

Aspera put the phone down and squeezed her eyes till black circles widened inside her eyelids. Think of history now. Think of anything.

At the dining room table she took out the listing of telephone contacts she'd kept, format stipulated in one of the library's job-hunting books She started at the top of the list and spent the afternoon getting to the bottom. "Aspera Hancock speaking, just checking back with you—I spoke with you the other week and we discussed—wondered if any positions have opened—wondered if you have any leads—"

The deadness allowed her to do this efficiently, without the embarrassment that had hemmed her during previous rounds. She followed the formulas given in the book, penciled check marks beside calls completed, x's by those she'd have to try again, circles around anything promising. The left margin was decidedly short of circles by three o'clock. Still when January came she'd salvage a portion of honor, knowing she'd job-searched to the best of her shelf-help and goddammit would be content working in Hancock's Best Basement.

Marriage was serious. A ropy mixture of fear and bitterness surged in her stomach. She wouldn't make it till the store closed at six o'clock. She got on her coat and boots and headed downtown. Walking fast in the crusted snow gave her a chance to stamp down hard, breathe deep. "Only 16 more shopping days till Christmas!" shrilled the red script of the banner strung over the main door. Tomorrow the numeral would have to be replaced.

Will wasn't at the store. They thought he'd taken the lumber truck, somebody in the warehouse said, for supplies. Inside the store Aspera withstood Bobbie's sharp glances and, impassively as she could manage, looked at the wounded mouth of the cellar stairs. She looked for messages in the shattered wood and bashed-in plaster, notations left by Will in a language she'd been learning to read.

In the dusk she returned home by way of the river path. It had softened in the day's sun and frozen again. Her boot skidded briefly as she set each foot down. Two weeks now of temperatures held to single digits, and the Mississippi was a broad hard surface put to use. The snow was polished down in strips by cross-country skiers; a lumpy broad path that skirted the shore had been made by boots of walkers like herself. She took each step cautiously. Making herself notice everything with care seemed to make the world move more slowly, and this she transmitted as a message to Will: Go slow. She pictured him now with a sledge in his hands, rubble at his feet, arms upraised yet again: Go slow.

At places the path branched out over the ice toward the far bank, narrow cuts made by first-year nursing students looking for a quicker way up to the hospital. Across from here—though in this blue winter fog she could not see across—the banks of the Mississippi rose steeply. Stairs were set into the cliffside under the hospital, but these had filled with snow and formed a glossy ramp. No access from below; all shortcuts amounted to a longer way.

In the flattish cloud light the river was a sheet of ice, but a rumpled sheet. Dull snow-struck stuff, and under the top glazing was a drifted eight-inch mesoderm soft and porous as cork.

The base plate had formed in shards that had fractured and cracked aloud in the uncertainties of November. The beginning had been silent enough; branches and low-hanging roots of willow had sagged over the cold water, showing hard crystal tears poised in regular sequence. The teardrops stretched into combs, laced from one twig to another, while on the river skins of ice approached the shoreline, slid away the next day, came back again. Larger patches formed, at first lacking the size and reach to join up, but temperatures dropped steadily and the river body at last lay painted in whitish streaks. Days of thaw, days of freeze, and thickened ice floes broke over one another, jutted hard in contest. A groaning could be heard, a series of snaps. Buckles rose up along the seams like praying hands; shales of ice stacked and shuffled like cards. Then the snow fell, muffling and covering it all.

At one veering of the path Aspera turned and walked out over the river where no trail had yet been cut. With each step her weight rested briefly on the crusted snow. Then she felt it give way, felt herself plunge with a muffled crunch to the solid ice beneath. A matter of inches, half a yard, depending on how the wind had done its work. With each step and delayed crunch, an ankle might disappear, a knee. This after the lurch of her heart in her chest. The thrill of it: walking on water, testing the kind of breakage that would be tolerated, falling to safety. Underneath the thicknesses of ice, the river still ran. She could sense the current, cold friction carried between ice and rock. She recovered ankle or knee and soon plunged again. Surely nothing unnatural had ever occurred between water and rock, nothing so that she could not match them, story for story.

Outside the tinted driver's window, snowy fields rocked greenish and smooth up to the windbreaks. The swaying made Will feel slightly sick. Truck needed springs. He gripped the cold ridges of the steering wheel, hearing the creaking of his leather gloves.

The first time he touched her was at the freshman dance the year after Devon died, the year he discovered beer could be bought at the back door of the Townsend. That night he'd finished off one last can of Bud in the school parking lot, then made his way to the door with the others, grinning while he paid and got his hand stamped. In the gym the darkness, the loud rock beat seemed to affect his knees, though he grinned and winked in case somebody was looking his way. He had no idea of looking for her, new kid with the bird legs. But there she was, standing close to the door alone, ankles showing slim underneath a long felt skirt. Did she dance? He wasn't even sure she could stand up, he only saw her at a desk in civics class. Now he moved toward her, setting one surprising foot in front of the other. Couldn't hurt to bump her shoulder, say excuse me. Putting this plan in action, though, his shoulder planted itself squarely between her shoulder blades and she went flying into the wall. He put his hands out to help, and when she turned and saw it was him, she smiled. Waves of relief; next thing he knew the music had turned slow and they were dancing. It was strange, for dancing. Aspera Heimler. Aspera. She moved with him so easily, he had the weird feeling he was out on the floor floating all by himself. He pulled his arm tighter, to make things seem more real. Smoothness, a warmth, the two of them sinking. His heart pounded and a flash of heat shot down his thighs and a second later, up the back of his head. "I must be drunk," he said, in a voice he hardly recognized himself. After he got over that voice, he remembered his arm and relaxed it too fast. She pulled back to look at him and he looked away, gave her back a little pat as if that explained something. His head felt jammed full of cotton floss. When a fast record came on, they dropped hands, startled into separateness. Across the glare of gym floor he saw chairs at a cafeteria table, and inside the din of music they made their way together. Sitting beside her, his head still soft and packed, he could think of nothing to say. He pretended to watch the other dancers. What he wanted was more of that sinking thrill of touching her, already he could feel next to his bare arm the heat of hers. Taking her hand was too much risk. He let his arm drop between their folding chairs, slid his fingers under the tail of her skirt where it lay flat on the cold floor. The material, its cut edge spongy and stiff, rested lightly between his two fingers. This light touch had terrible importance. He shut his eyes and before he thought, he'd said it out loud again: "I must be drunk."

Twenty-five years ago. Will steadied the trembling of the old lumber truck's upright gear shift, which had begun to oscillate in rhythm with the seams in the Tartarville highway. Slow dancing. Not with anybody but her since that night, except for one time when he had to prove to himself—he'd held those girls at Avon as close as they'd let him, it was nice, no question about nice. But not magic; maybe like trying to dance with those rental units from hardware, those electric shampooers and buffers, things powered from some other source. Nobody made him feel like she did in his arms, should he have told her that? The thought of telling her now made him feel gut-sick. He worked at keeping things under control, it mattered too much and that made him feel—Will tightened his jaw, then dropped it open to suck air in against the surging in his stomach. He unlatched the vent windows on both sides of the cab and pushed them open. He didn't know what went on in her head anymore. If he ever did. Did she know he was holding on to her skirt that first time, how overwhelmed—? She'd never mentioned it. He certainly never had. *People sensitive enough to share their real feelings*—okay. Maybe he made a mistake that way, but hell, it was just one more. In a cast of thousands. The rattling started again, and he held the truck in gear as it clambered over a railroad crossing. Turns out he isn't the only one making mistakes these days. Let *her* explain. He flicked the knobs on the dashboard of the cab, let them spin on their screwshafts. Identical brown knobs for wipers, headlights, cigarette lighter, choke. Forty years old tomorrow, and he'd come awake this morning on a pile of sleeping bags in the cellar of the store. My God. Hunks of plaster under the pile: the princess and the peas. Hadn't felt a thing. He shook his head. Surprise, he was no princess. He'd raked the place out a little, hung some plastic sheeting and like it or not he was on his way now. He still had the figures logged in his head, square footage, unit price, sources. Had those numbers at the ready—how long? Revamping the place was the right move, he knew that before, even if he blundered into it now like—but at least it was his own goddamned china shop. *I must be drunk.* He squeezed his eyes to clear them. Quarry tile in Tartarville. Quarry tile in Tartarville. He was positive he had the rest in stock: plaster, cement, reinforcing mesh, grout sealer, two-by-fours, scaffolding, dry wall, the rest. He was the way he was, it wasn't as if he'd changed. He still wanted the same things, wouldn't mind dancing the way they used to but she didn't think about him that way, *sex without love,* and he—he had this sick feeling, and getting smashed was not the cure. Wasn't the cause, either. Will lifted his chin, breathed in, cracked the back of his neck. He was forty years old. His record wasn't that bad, if he *wanted* to celebrate it'd be a party with music and dancing; why not? He had a lot of friends, good friends. That was reason to celebrate. And he'd built up a solid business, don't forget that. It really was his own goddamned china shop, and right this minute, he had things to see about. Masonry, materials. Go back over the list, every item, get the feel of everything you need all the way down to water-struck brick, spalted maple, amaranth.

Standing in the front hall of the empty house Aspera tore the envelope with cold fingers. "My education has been taken up again by my father," began the letter from Vicky—a note, really. She was disheartened to see how soon it would end; one paragraph of Vicky's typing formed a block in the center of a folded half-page of bond. How like Vicky to know in advance how brief she meant to be. "He time-travels back to his youth," the letter went on, "plays out courting scenes, gives nightmare shouts from his dreams, remembers me variously as my mother, my aunt, his second wife. I believe he does know who I am since he calls every female name but my own from sheer cussedness. I am in his direct bloodline, however; no doubt he is pleased to find in me, one more time in his long career, a worthy opponent. Yesterday he spat a mouthful of food (hamburger, ground baby-fine) in my face. Before my left hand had its chance to put in a discouraging word, my right had smacked him. How shocked we both were—I at myself, an unpleasant return to the scene of the high chair. Here goes the hall of mirrors again, and I see once again the deadly impatience I had with my babies. So I time-travel too, sick at how quickly I'm brought back. The man pushes all my buttons, but the favor he does me is, now I know where they all are. Sometimes you have to wait years for a good education. Love."

It took Aspera minutes to find the number, and four rings till she heard Vicky's curt long-distance hello.

"I mailed that stupid note on impulse, of course," Vicky cut in when she recognized Aspera's voice, "Sorry."

"You sound so much like you, Vick." Aspera breathed relief. "Are you all right?"

"He doesn't spit any more food and I don't paste him one. So both of us are learning. I just wish I'd behave some way I could respect," she grumbled. "My brain's so much slower than the flat of my hand."

"You're only human, I guess."

"It still hurts. Such old stuff."

"I loved what you wrote me about emotional hygiene. I understand now why you're there with your dad—"

"Can't recommend it. It doesn't feel good." Vicky sighed. "But I guess it feels *right.* I'm not really with him, you know. The man that was my father is long gone, so I'm with me. Trying to clean up my act."

"Do not foul the nest," Aspera quoted. She sighed and looked about the empty kitchen. "Do not foul the nest."

"Yeah. Maybe I should say the thought isn't original. It started when I read about a man who kept a piece of chicken heart alive in a solution for twenty-five years. After which he tossed it out, because the principle was so simple: all you needed to sustain cellular life was fluid circulation to carry in nutrients and carry away waste. But"—Vicky's tone altered—"you didn't call to hear about a piece of chicken heart. What am I hearing in your voice?"

Aspera caught her breath; the pause was long.

"Aspera?"

"It sounds worse than it is, I think. Will didn't come home last night, we're—that's one thing." Her heart pounded. Chicken heart. She took a breath. "The rest is too hard to say."

"Aspera, don't fade out on me. I can barely hear you, but I hear enough to know you're scared. Now talk out loud."

Aspera mustered force. "Will hasn't come home," she said. "I think he'll be back, it's not—"

'I heard that. What was the rest?"

'Oh, Vicky!" The words rose in a wail. "It's all stuff I should have known. A good clean fight—you told me that months ago. Otherwise you do dumb things. Violent things."

"I hear you," Vicky said softly, then in the same cadence: ' I'm with you."

"No, not this time. You're going to be hurt by this, and I hate the whole thing. This mess! I thought I could keep secrets."

Vicky waited.

Aspera took a breath. She said the two words that connected to *mess,* connected to *secrets.* "Kevin Stowe," she whispered. "I've been involved with him."

"With Kevin!" The line carried a split second of silence. Then a kind of gasping.

"Don't laugh, Vick! God, I feel like such a—I don't know what. I've spent the last three months feeling things I didn't want to feel! I've been so sick—don't laugh."

"I'm sorry," Vicky sighed, smoothing down the sounds. "Well," she began again, "I guess you're alive. That's settled, anyway."

"I got in way over my head, Vicky. I'm sorry."

Vicky's tone went level. "I'm OK with it."

"You can't be. You weren't over him when you left, and I—"

"When I left, I was trying to take my own advice and stop trying to be in love with a toddler. I was trying to remember that a grown-up needs another one to be in love with. Running away is great for some things. But—does Will know? Is that why he left?"

"He knows things are wrong, he just doesn't know which ones."

"I suspect Will has been feeling cut off from his supply. Now he's cut *you* off. Not a bad move."

These brisk computations were several mental levels above where Aspera could operate. She held on to the phone.

"And what good is running away from home if nobody gets upset? That's your job if it's a job you want," Vicky said, her voice shading into exasperation. "How come you two want to take turns listening to the other one slam the back door?"

Aspera's voice stuck. "I have screwed up every single relationship I have with this."

"You and I are OK. Does that count?"

"God, yes! I just can't believe you aren't hurt or—furious. I have felt so isolated."

"Keeping secrets has that effect, cuts off the circulation." Vicky stopped. "I don't mean to sound so tough. I guess I'm shocked a little. I thought our circle was small, but—funny, the one I would have actually worried about, to tell you the truth, was Dena."

Aspera stared. She found her teeth clamped together.

"Oh, no," Vicky groaned.

Aspera covered her eyes with the hand that wasn't gripping the receiver.

"I get this vision," Vicky said, "Kevin watching us all roll out for him like little yellow ducks in a shooting gallery." She made a sound, air sucked through teeth. "Sportfucking, my mother used to call it. Well. I feel like I let the fox into the chicken coop. Should I have said, *Stay away from him, he'll only hurt you*—?" She paused. "A hundred women would want to find out just how, Dena first in line. Well, damn. Education courtesy of Kevin. Good traits in an educator, though—patient, perceptive, pitiless. He's very good at it, isn't he?"

Aspera's knuckles went white on the receiver. "At what?"

"At all of it," Vicky laughed. "But especially at enticement. You and Will must have looked ripe."

Aspera's thoughts slid back to the beginning, the unexpected meeting in the park, unlikely fists. "When I was first attracted to him," she murmured, "it seemed like the most important thing in my life, the only door that led anyplace."

"First attracted to Kevin, or Will?"

Aspera was startled. High school civics, the boy with shaggy cinnamon hair, splash of red on sheets.

"Either one," she realized. "Both."

Aspera looked around the kitchen. Empty, except—she wrinkled her nose. Garbage in the bag under the sink.

Bending to pull out the brown bag, the odor was overpowering. She saw the empty green tuna fish can, left from Will's sandwich two nights ago. Chicken of the Sea. Empty of everything except oily shreds and odor. She winced. The prospect of coat and boots again tempted her to shortcuts; she could just set it outside the back door, cold air was good for something. Household hint offered by Dena twenty years ago: when something smells bad in the refrigerator, turn the temperature down.

She pulled the stained paper bag out of the can and carried it to the back door. Elvira used to fold down a collar on garbage bags. The single lesson she'd offered on married life was a demonstration of the technique. "Here's how I do it." One catechism that didn't take.

Before she opened the storm door to set it on the back stoop Aspera understood this bag would have to go all the way out to the street. Tribute to Elvira, tribute to the guy with twenty-five years of well-circulated chicken heart. Before she got on her coat and boots she pulled out a new garbage bag, snapped it out full and, with much rattling and crinkling of brown paper, turned down a passable collar. Turn over a new leaf. Try a whole tree.

Opening the back door five minutes later, she heard the phone. Still in coat and gloves, she made a grab for it. The receiver flew out of her hands, clattered to the floor. She pulled off a glove and snatched it up, scattering apologies.

Bobbie's voice. Not Will's.

"Mrs. Hancock, I've been trying to reach you since you left this afternoon. Someone from the hospital called—"

Aspera flooded with panic while Bobbie shifted slips of paper. Will in the hospital. "Which hospital?"

"Well, he didn't say, exactly. Or Marlys didn't write it down. Anyhow, he said you should call back right away. Here's the number."

Aspera said thanks, hung up and pressed her head against the wall next to the cup rack. A blue Virgo mug wobbled on its peg. The number was Kevin's.

"Job Service," answered a switchboard voice.

"Mr. Stowe," Aspera said. She took a breath, gave her name.

Kevin came on the line, his business voice. "Aspera, this place is jumping and I've got one minute. Something's come up you might want to know about. The V.A. here is looking for a temporary appointee—"

"Kevin, I've applied at the V.A.; I'm on a list for the civil-service exam, it takes months."

"This is special. Their library service is appointing a vendor—that's governmentese for a temporary. Eight hundred hours of employment, which is like five months full-time. No guarantee it would go permanent—interested?"

She stopped and let it sink in.

"What do I do?"

His voice warmed. "As of tomorrow morning somebody on staff is going on emergency medical leave. They want to fill the spot fast—that way everybody sees the whole system might collapse otherwise. They sometimes hire the first live candidate who shows."

"All I have to do is show?"

"No, I set up an interview. It's a long shot, they may have a backlog of applicants waiting by the phone. It's past five now," he considered. "Too late to reach Arlene."

"Arlene?"

"Chief of Learning Resources." Kevin spoke rapidly now.

"I'll call her first thing tomorrow, seven-thirty. Then call you. Quarter of eight? If she's interviewing and you could be there in an hour—"

"Kevin, you're really going out of your way.'

"Not really. What you want to tell them is, you have experience and you can go to work that minute." He paused. "This vendor thing is sort of the one-night stand of employment. It's a foot in the door, but I wasn't sure you'd go for it."

She braced an arm against the wall. "It isn't what I'd choose. But if it's a door in the right wall, I've done that before."

"Aspera"—his voice low—"you have that dangerous sound again."

She straightened. "You have a good ear," she said. She thought about tomorrow: Will's birthday. "You'll have to call me at the store tomorrow morning," she decided, and gave him the number slowly.

Silence as he noted it. "Listen," he said, "you'll be in the city in time for lunch tomorrow. We could get together."

She turned quickly to the wall, then stopped the cup she'd nudged from swinging on its peg. "Kevin, this lead on the job means a lot. But anything else—that's over for me." Slowly she said, "So if that's the reason . . ."

He waited for her to finish, but she didn't.

"This isn't blackmail," he said at last. "You weren't thinking that, were you?"

"We left some big gaps somehow."

"Which leaves us where?" he asked.

She tried to think of the answer. "How do people do these things?"

"We need to talk."

"I need a job, I need sleep, I need one life." Her voice was thinning to a wail, but she couldn't help that. "I need to get things straight with Will if I can."

Kevin let the pause stretch out. "Maybe you can," he said, "straighten things out." And then, "He's always going to make you go the long way around, you know."

Aspera lowered her eyes, and when she raised them an anger rose up, too. "That's not your business."

"No." He spoke softly then as ever. "Still, I don't think walls that thick"—his voice a slow sinuous rhythm—"just tumble down like Jericho. We said quarter of eight. I'll call you."

That night she finished knitting the hat for Will, working past midnight. Ariadne, Penelope—but these women were chaste, women who waited, women and thread. She let out a breath. Knit and purl, efforts by turns, two-handed game with weapons. Thrust ana parry didn't cancel one another but over time provided the continuity of a fight.

You could go wrong two ways, too much together and too much apart. When they were young she'd never thought of leaving Will, couldn't have, they were so fused they had no border left undisputed. She could see him by looking between her own ribs, Garden of Eden. The weird behavior comes up when you discover you're not fused.

Weird behavior, and then the litany of denial: it doesn't matter wasn't important didn't hurt wasn't true didn't mean anything so forget about it don't even think. The long way around.

She knitted to within an inch of the end of the strand, tied it to the end of the next skein. The needles clicked. This hat the record of where two needles met and tangled with yarn.

She tied off the last stitch, tucked in the loose ends with a crochet hook, then stretched the garment over her hands. The hands collapsed, made fists, and she folded the hat noisily in tissue paper, put it in a box. She found ribbon, found in her desk the card she'd bought. She started to write, but the words jerked under her hand—he'd gone through her papers, must have seen the card. She tore it in half.

When she went to bed she lay under the pieced quilt and dreamed of the green glass necklace again, of the pearls centered inside each glass bead. This time as she pulled ropes of glass from the shallow water her hands came up streaming ribbons of blood.

She snapped awake, face wet with tears, remembering the story Elvira had read to her when she was a child. The story made her weep and so it had not been told often. A green glass necklace, gift from a dying queen to her young daughter. The daughter was cast out into the world, bearing from her mother the necklace and a single gold piece. A loaf of stale bread in the story—yes, the gold piece bitten and declared false, a storekeeper seized it and sent the hungry child into the street with a curse, the stale loaf flung at her. Here Aspera's childish tears had poured. But then came triumph: shoes the girl fashions for herself from swamp rushes. A job in a town and a true love—who holds the necklace to the light and discovers sealed within each bead a gold crown; he knows her for her mother's daughter.

Aspera gathered up her robe from the end of the bed and walked down the hall, turning lights on in the upstairs rooms. At the landing, halfway down the stairs, she called out, "Will?"

No answer, no one. For the first time it seemed odd she hadn't checked for suitcases he'd taken, clothing, money—don't have such thoughts, that alone could make them true. Charles finding Dena's suitcase, flinging drawers open through the house. No. The secrets in this house weren't in drawers or suitcases.

On the way back upstairs she stopped in the small bedroom. Will's old room, shared nine years. Two sons in this family, then only Will, with the burden of being perfect.

She found the book she was looking for in one of the stacks on the floor and went back to bed. She didn't turn the reading lamp on but crawled under the covers holding the book. It was small, the paper jacket cover tattered. It showed a girl wearing a necklace; her ragged skirt and bare feet dipped in the reedy waterline of a marsh.

Aspera imagined opening the book and finding pressed between the small square pages and smelling of cornmeal, the way this particular book always had, a pink satin ribbon. Language of love. She lifted the book and cracked it just enough to inhale the scent still held between the pages. Because there would be no ribbon if she opened it wide and ransacked this little volume, she left it closed on the pillow under her cheek and slept.

Spring is dangerous, yet she walks in the cold snap of April morning beside Will. In this dream snow is nearly gone in Bracken; rain has come and now in the freezing weather crusts of ice form over standing water. In the road that cuts into Birch Circle, slush and sludge are pushed to the curbs. Ruts where cars churn through have divided the gray masses of leftover winter matter into triangles, pointed shards of shapes. Each is pocked with a thin dome of brittle ice.

Oak and elm trees reach bare overhead. Birches show catkins

fisted but no green; even willows are cautious with their flush of orange this year. April is not to be trusted.

She walks beside Will; they wear puffy down jackets and wool mufflers and padded mittens, looking exactly as they might have looked a year ago, or twenty years ago.

Their breath precedes them in billows. Crystals cling to brows and lashes. She has put her arm through his, through his jacket sleeve anyway. Now she steps out over the curb and smashes beneath her boot the ice crust of a puddle. Ice that tinkles and sings. As Will forges ahead she slips her arm from his—a small cat scream of nylon.

In the small wells and pockets along the curb, hollows of frozen mud are capped like honeycomb. She taps them with her boot and they shatter, thin caps webbed over air. Of larger and deeper puddles she is more careful; their thick envelopes of ice still adhere to water. She presses a toe into the glazing where it shows concentric white. Further pressure, and the ice goes brown into muddy water with a groan; she takes her weight off.

Will stands in the middle of the intersection of streets. He has noticed through layers of nylon and feathers that she is missing from his side. He adjusts his alpaca hat and muffler and turns in this dream as a soft-sculptured monolith might turn, pivoting on his feet. He sees what she is about and stands waiting, almost floating. Then he calls to her from the center of the road.

"You're trying to kill me, aren't you?"

She looks up startled from an expanse of brown ice. Sees her husband wavering at this crossroad. He indicates by glancing left and right, side to side from where he stands, that he is in danger. Hypothetical danger from hypothetical traffic. He means, of course, it's time she came to him.

She smiles underneath her muffler; from this distance he can see the squint of it in her eyes. But she shakes her head.

"No?" he says. "No?" A split second, then he broadens his stance. Spreads his arms. Tilting his jacketed body so his eyes can appeal heavenward, he calls, "Help!"

She laughs, a sound so free it surprises them both. With a grin he turns again, walks back to her.

At quarter after seven she parked the car and tried the door of the warehouse, not surprised to find it open. In the lumber business you didn't lock early trade out. The boutique wouldn't open till ten-thirty, but the warehouse door stayed on the latch from the time Bobbie got there. When Aspera walked into the lumber office, making her way past unfamiliar paperbound stacks of flat gray quarry tile, Will said, "What are you doing here?"

She stopped. He was sitting on a corner of the desk, a clipboard and pen in his hands. "Happy birthday," she said, startled. This sounded silly and out of place, things she recognized as soon as he delivered his mocking thanks. She looked at him. Shaven and kempt; perhaps tired about the eyes; a new shirt.

"I like your shirt," she blurted. Then: "I'm glad to see you."

His eyes flicked down her clothes.

"I have an interview this morning," she explained. "At least, I'm expecting a phone call." When his eyes went blank, she asked, "Where did you go?"

He made a straight mouth. "Nowhere that would interest you."

She decided to avoid questions. "I'd like to talk things over."

"With me?" he said. "I'm just a guy that likes monkey stories."

Bobbie came into the office, and her hooded eyes grew large as she absorbed the nonnegotiable presence of tension. She turned and fiddled over the doorknob, fumbling to pull it closed behind her as she left. The glass panels shook.

"Will, there are things you don't know."

His eyes narrowed. "Maybe."

Frightened, she lifted a sheet of paper bearing her handwriting from the desk. One of her telephone lists. "I just came to see you, I mean, in case you were here. I came yesterday and saw where you'd"—she made herself talk over the catch in her voice—"started remodeling."

He folded his arms.

"I may have to leave within"—she looked at the clock—"very soon."

He said nothing to fill in the spaces.

She went on, feeling like a high-wire act. "If I'm lucky, there may be a library job for me at the V.A. in the Cities. Temporary, but I'm going to try for it."

He picked up an inventory clipboard from the desk.

She took a breath. "We have a date for dinner at seven. I made reservations—"

"What?" He turned sharply her way.

"—the two of us. If you're going to get around to talking to me, I'd still like to go."

The pencil slipped from his fingers and swung briefly on its chain from the clipboard.

He let his eyes travel to a point and stop, travel, stop—as though each object he found was rejected for being too near, too close to hand. "This is really it, the big decade celebration?"

She watched his face. His gaze seemed fastened on an invoice for asbestos-coated oven mitts.

"Will," she said, astonished. "I asked you—"

"Ask for what you want, ask for what you want," he mimicked. "If I hear that one more time—I don't want to have to ask for everything on my own birthday. Why should I have to? You can't be bothered to think about what I'd like, you push it off on me instead of going ahead and planning anything. If you gave one damn—"

"You wanted a party? You expected one?"

"I didn't expect anything. I just thought people who cared about me might want to wish me well on my birthday."

"Then why—"

"Some things," he rode over her, waving the invoice at her, "lose value if you have to spell them out."

She snatched the sheet of paper from the air. "Do they gain value when you don't get them?"

"I don't think you care about me at all, I keep looking for signs and I don't see any!"

"Signs." She pulled a breath that cut round her heart like a dull knife. No circulation, pipes and tubes bubbling their fluids. "Maybe you're right. Maybe there haven't been signs." In the quiet of the office she said, "Listen. It's late notice but a Wednesday night, people can probably make it—"

"Never mind," he said. "You were a little slow."

She looked at the clock. "For my birthday," she flared, turning back to him, "I called everybody and said, I'm having cake and candles, I'm forty years old and I want a party. I'd gladly do that for you, but it's unfair to expect me to read your mind!"

"Maybe you've had too many other things on yours."

"You're right," she said. "I have. And we need to talk about that."

The telephone rang on the desk; they both jumped.

His eyes pierced hers. "Then stay here today and talk to me," he said.

Fluids swept up to close her throat. Her eyes didn't leave his as she reached for the telephone. Will gave the clipboard a jerk and the pencil flew its short arc as he walked away.

CHAPTER NINETEEN

Aspera, when she arrived home that night, was late for the party. In the dining room a keg of beer rode astride the oak dining table. Two pressed Styrofoam platters of cheese and cold cuts from Hobrin's Market flanked the keg. Plastic cartons were piled with jumbo shrimp; the lids served for the shells. A heavy foil roasting pan caught beer keg drips that would have spattered the hardwood floor. In the living room rock music roared from the stereo speakers and a strobe light set into the ceiling fixture flicked its stilted pictures: six people seated round the coffee table, eight dancing on the rug, five ranged about the sofa floor. Three reaching for oversized paper cups, two for triangled slices of take-out pizza. Dark shapes of hands to mouths, hands upraised or pronated midair, faces revealed in profile and dead on, heads tilted toward food or drink or other heads. Flick, flick, flick. New pictures, new poses.

Aspera lifted a hand to greet two neighbors and an employee from the store's hardware section; the waves they returned stuttered in the light. She made her way toward Will, put a hand on his ribs as he reached for something on the table.

"Happy birthday," she shouted over the Grateful Dead.

"Welcome to the party!" Will yelped, jumping back as if in surprise. "Notice, completely disposable!" He swept a hand at the dining room, pushing his voice out. "How appropriate! Now—just ask for what you want." He made the t's flick as separate as the strobe pattern. "Want a beer? Want cold cuts?"

Flick: Someone at the table held aloft a large cardboard

square, a square which—flick: flapped open—flick: closed. Faces showed smiles, tilted and pivoted; lips formed words. Hands which lifted the weighty paper cups. Sound over sound.

"No mark left by civilized man!" Will's face loomed larger. "Whoever he was. Want some pizza?"

A slice appeared in one of Will's hands. Flick: she had it in hers. Opened her mouth, bit down, chewed the cold melt of cheese.

"Paper napkins!" Will daubed at the corners of her mouth, showed her the spots of sauce which flashed black in the light.

"I'm employed," she told him, using her hand as an ear trumpet for him.

"Good for you," he trumpeted back. "Great party, eh?"

"I'm impressed," she shouted. "All in one day! Is that Bunny?" She tried to make out the profile. Flick, flick.

"Something for everyone!" he shouted near her ear. "Fruit basket upset! There's you and Dalton, Bunny and me, and Dena brought her own lunch."

Aspera made herself look steadily at him. "What does that mean?"

"About Dena? She brought Baby Kevin!" Will informed her. "She asked me, and I said, great, we can always use one more mixed couple. Did I say the right thing?"

Aspera's words stayed at the bottom of her stomach.

Will put a cup under the keg spigot, and a froth of beer foamed out.

She took the cup he offered, though she didn't trust the trembling in her hands.

Do people change? No, they just practice.

Kevin found her sitting on the stair landing.

"I've been looking for you," he said, sitting down beside her.

She looked at her empty cup. "Why in hell did you come?"

In the living room below where they sat the strobe was winking out couples dancing in macabre grace. Will and Bunny flickered among the others. Kevin watched for a moment, then said, "Thought you might need me here."

"My secret pal."

"This is the part I hate, the part where you try to make me sound deceased."

Aspera smiled in spite of herself.

"Kevin, here's one more story," she said. "When I was a kid there was a lake close to my house. I loved swimming. But once I was out and dressed, I could never be talked back into a cold wet suit."

Kevin suppressed a smile. He admired her when she was difficult; this no longer moved her.

He said, "How warm and dry is the marriage?"

She pressed fingers to the bridge of her nose. "I'm not sure."

Kevin shook his head. "I saw you talking to him. He's not going to come through for you, Aspera."

"Neither are you." She surprised herself by smiling. "I know which of you wants to be part of a couple. I mean, only one couple. With me."

"There's other ways," he warned.

"Not to have what I want. I mean to stop courting things that divide my life." Meeting his eyes, she said, "You helped. You reminded me about the two-handed game, hands over and under the table. Now I'm going to do without the table."

"Then I take it back," he said.

She shook her head slowly. "Too late."

They looked at one another and smiled, as people do who have achieved perfect understanding.

He reached over and patted her hand. "Look how fucked we are," he whispered. "You think this is healthy, splitting up when we're the only two people here who know how to have a good time?" He sighed. Gave her a sidelong look. "Something weird happened to me this morning," he said. "I guess I want to tell you this. I woke up early, I had a woman in bed with me—"

"Do I want to hear this?" Her hands tried the lip of the stair.

Before she could rise, Kevin put a hand on her knee. "I'm trying to tell you something's changing. I woke up and there she was, and all I could think was, Christ, I hope she's not the avid type. I pretended to be asleep. Can you believe it?"

Aspera made her eyes follow the pairs of dancers below them. "Maybe you'll have to cut back," she said. "Only three to four major love affairs a year." She stood up. "In the meantime, you've got to find somebody else to tell these things to."

From beyond the music she heard the ring of a telephone. She signaled with her head to show she was going.

"You intend to tell Will about us?" he asked.

"If he doesn't already know."

"Dena too?" he asked.

"No prisoners."

"High stakes," he grinned. "I like it."

"That's not why I'm doing it."

By the time she got to the kitchen, the phone had stopped ringing. She lifted the receiver anyhow, heard the dial tone, hung up. Feeling a queer exhaustion, she leaned against the kitchen wall, felt the vibration of the music in the cool plaster. She shifted her weight and pressed her forehead hard against it, tried to make the resonance spread. Headbone connected to—behind her head the cup racks rattled; something struck her left shoulder and she jerked arms up to stop its fall. In that motion she managed to propel a spinning mug the more rapidly to the floor. It did not bounce against the quarry tiles but smashed on contact, leapt into white fragments. Aspera flinched from the corolla of spray and in a daze sank to her knees to pick up the pieces. Another mug tumbled and smashed to the floor in what seemed like the aftershock.

Footsteps rapid in the dining room passage behind her; the swinging door pushed inward with some speed. The door slammed solidly against her shoulder and hip. Dalton looked through the door as she put a hand down on the floor to keep her balance.

Instantly he was beside her, gathering her up off the floor. Words, words. He lifted her to her feet, seeing red dots on the heels of her hands. She allowed him to settle her on a chair. Because it was Dalton her tears streamed; odd how safety tilted the chemistry that way.

"I'm all right," she told him. She took the handkerchief he offered and blotted the tiny cuts on her hand, then wiped her cheeks, her nose. Dalton bent over her, a hand on her shoulder. She folded the handkerchief, pressed it to her eyes. When he removed the hand she opened them. The scene had changed. Now Bunny stood halfway into the room, arms held stiff between door and doorway. She didn't speak at first; Aspera couldn't know how long Bunny's eyes had held Dalton in their glare.

"I'll take care of this," Bunny said in her baby voice.

Dalton's guilt showed in his careful motion, his neutral face. "OK," he said. As his wife pushed the door wider he moved past her out of the kitchen. In the passage he gently turned away two more guests attuned to breakage.

With her toe Bunny scattered a few fragments at Aspera's feet. "Tell me where I'll find a broom."

"Let me do this," Aspera said.

"Don't be silly," Bunny said, the small voice gone.

Aspera pointed at the broom closet beside the back door. Broom, dustpan, whisk broom hung separately on white pegs Will had installed. While Bunny swept the debris away, Aspera dried her face and once more blew her nose. She wrung the handkerchief in her hands, feeling this time pinpricks of glass. She picked them out with her fingernails while Bunny focused on the task, the systematic and tedious brushing and brushing of broom, then whisk broom; the emptying of glass chips into the garbage sack—its neat collar glimpsed between Bunny's hands. Bunny rehung the brooms and pan, then returned to Aspera and held out a hand.

Aspera looked up amazed. After all this, a hand in friendship? She put out her own hand.

Bunny jerked hers an impatient six inches sideways. "Handkerchief," she said.

Responding to the tone of command, Aspera hurriedly folded the damp places to the inside. Then she closed her fingers over the handkerchief. "Bunny," she said, "I hope—"

"Don't waste breath," Bunny said. "You've made your choice."

Clutching her fingers tight, Aspera stood up. She said, "You're right." She brushed past Bunny out of the kitchen. In the passageway as the swinging door beat back and forth she heard a screech above the din of music, "Handkerchief!"

Aspera met Dalton on his way into the passage. "This belongs to you," she said. She put the refolded handkerchief in his hand and met his eyes, which showed uncertainty and then alarm. "Thanks, Dalton," she said. He hurried on toward the kitchen, stuffing the evidence in his pocket.

She was starting up the stairs with someone's coat when the phone rang again. She went on up and answered it in the bedroom.

"I wanted to wish Will happy birthday," Vicky said. "He did make it home?"

"Yes."

"Hmmmm. What do I hear?"

"There's a party downstairs, actually."

"Who's there?"

Aspera considered. "Everybody."

"Everybody?" Vicky gave it a few beats. "If Dena finds out about you and Kevin, she'll have your gizzard on a plate."

Aspera thought of Bunny. "There's a lot," she said, "that could go wrong. I'll write you and bring you up to date. Let me get Will."

"One thing. Let me try this out on you, my rewrite on the Garden of Eden. I decided innocence is what you get *after* you know something."

Aspera slowly shook her head, relaxing somehow at the very unreasonableness. "Except you've lost it by then."

"No, you've lost dependency, fusion—you knew there'd be a tie-in, right? Listen, I'm going to work this up: after the fall you get withdrawal, and then innocence without dependency! Doesn't that sound like the part they left out?"

"I wish."

"Listen, a just God would hate dependency as much as I do."

Aspera laughed. "Vicky, when are you coming home?"

"Good," Vicky said. "You sound human again. My dad goes back into the care facility next week. But I like it here and I'm working well—I may hang out another month."

"Is that the truth?"

Vicky sniffed. "Part of it. One of my dad's doctors, I've seen him a few times and I still have four or five fingers left—if you remember the rule."

Aspera gripped the phone. "Listen, I have a fear of people walking out of my life and disappearing."

"No chance. I'll see you in February. Promise to have your life straight by then?"

"Pretty short notice."

Vicky laughed. "That's more like it."

Aspera called down the stairs to Tom Schiller, who sent a shout across the music for Will. Seconds later Will came into the bedroom. He looked at her with accusation.

"Vicky's on the phone."

He took the receiver and said tersely, "The day is full of surprises."

Aspera sat on the bed.

"You're missing a great party," Will told Vicky after a few minutes. "In fact I'm missing a great party, standing here talking to you." He listened intently for a few seconds. "More birthday advice. I don't need it. Remember, I'm as smart as you were three years ago." A little more, and he hung up. When at last he looked over at Aspera, his eyes were small.

"You could have told me yourself," he said

She searched his eyes. The walls of the room shrank nearer on all four sides. The closet door handle seemed to jut into the notch where her rib cage divided.

"What are we talking about?" she asked him.

"I'm not supposed to know. I get my information secondhand."

She frowned. "From Vicky?"

"Hell, maybe I should have asked. *Bunny* tells me she doesn't know what you were doing in her house with her husband the other night, but I think she does. I think everybody does. Funny the way we all know, all of a sudden. Dalton didn't want me to believe it, my good buddy."

"You've got it wrong."

"I do? Nah. There's just me and my gut"—he slugged his fist into his abdomen—"and my gut says *fucking around.*"

Her stomach contracted as though she too had taken the blow.

"Not Dalton," she said. It surprised her, the way her voice trembled coming out of her throat. Will had it wrong; she had room enough and she saw how she could do it, skim by one more time. Cast out a long shimmering line, web a path skyscraper to skyscraper like Spiderman. Scuttle away. Things you can do when the open road looks too scary.

"This is what happened." She balled a fist, shoved it between her knees to steady them. "Not Dalton, I *talked* to Dalton. I was with Kevin Stowe."

Will's face looked immobile, frozen. He wheeled then; she thought he would leave the room. He put a foot down heavily, stopped. Her stomach jerked as though the last foot he placed had landed on it. "What the fuck," he said, directing his voice to the floor. "Whoever."

The look he flung at her slammed home. It would sweep her over the earth's flat edge. Still, the silence between them threw ropes and lines, binding her limbs, tying them to his.

"You went to Dalt," he said. "You didn't come to me."

"You were the one I was running from."

"Why?" he roared.

"I've got to have some margin between what you need from me and what I need—to survive! I can't make you understand how I need that."

"I have needs," Will told her. "And I don't think you care about me at all."

"Neither of us feels—" She stopped. "How did that get to be something we're not good at?"

"But I was here for you." His mouth twisted, as though left to itself it would make some other shape. "The whole time, I was here."

"No!"

"Where was I then?"

"Making noise. Making true things appear and disappear with jokes and interruptions."

"That's the way I am."

"That's what you show me. It's a wall you raise between us, and I can't love you through it. I send messages out and they bounce back, I can't feel you through this wall. I have to go around convincing myself you're there. Why don't you want me to *know*?"

"You should know," he accused. "But you shut me out."

With a finger she traced a fishtail in the quilt. "When we make love I have to run pictures in my head. Sometimes I can remember when sex felt like love, all by itself. But that was years ago."

"Whose fault is that? Whose fault? You're the one who changed. I want to hear you apologize for that, and for all this pain"—he clutched his shirt, the skin of his belly—"and I don't hear apologies, I hear excuses. You destroyed what we had, you tried to destroy me. For something cheap." His mouth turned stingy. He shook his head. "I deserve more respect than that."

"More respect than I deserve?"

He clenched his teeth. "*Fucking around,*" he said.

She tried this story aloud on the bedroom ceiling. Tried it on the high chair, the dismantled sleigh bed. She looked at

Will. "Those aren't the words. They're your words, not mine. And they smear over anything I need to tell you."

"You pick the words. You live with them. One thing I want is a wife who's faithful to me. Who takes an interest, who doesn't wreck everything I need to be happy."

"I want that, too. In a husband."

He shot her a look and then turned to leave.

"Will, I'm sorry—" she spoke to the back of his head—"about the pain. All this pain, I'm truly sorry."

He stopped, shoved his hands in his pockets. His back stayed toward her. "You could have told me yourself."

"I could have, and you could have asked. Anything."

He put his hands on his hips, looked at the floor.

"Would you have told me?"

Be honest. Her breath stopped in her chest. "I don't know."

He snapped his head up as though snapping free of the last thread that connected them and walked out the door.

As his feet pumped rapidly down the stairs Aspera followed to the top. She saw him meet Dena coming up. He stopped short, seized Dena by the shoulders and kissed her roughly. Aspera watched. He lifted his eyes to her as he finished, then pushed past. Dena tottered where he left her, poised on a stair step. Aspera slipped back inside the bedroom. Seconds later she imagined she heard the back door shut, imagined what she felt was the sensation of air pressure in the winter-sealed house force in against her eardrums.

Dena came into the bedroom. "I just had the most extraordinary birthday greeting from Will," she said. "Where was he going in such a rush?"

"It's been a terrible night." Aspera looked up, but Dena had turned away and with her hand was smoothing the scalloped edge of the quilt over the pillows.

"There is such delicate work in this pattern." Dena spoke with emphasis. "I've always admired it. Double wedding ring, is that right?"

"Pane at the Window."

"I love handmade things." Dena withdrew her hand, smiled. "I found the most lovely hand-painted glass ornaments this year. I meant to bring one for your tree."

Aspera's thoughts reeled. Dark green, light green, red; pop and crush.

"I just came up to see what was keeping you," Dena said. "Several people are looking for their coats."

"My impulse is to try to protect you," Aspera said. "Amazing how I think I can."

"Protect me?" Dena blanched. "That was Vicky on the phone, somebody said. She knows I'm here with Kevin?"

Taken by surprise, Aspera shook her head. Dena whooshed a sigh of relief, a hand laid to her bosom. "Life is too complicated."

"Dena," Aspera said, "this won't be easy for you to hear. Kevin and I were lovers."

Dena's blue eyes flooded with black. She shifted her weight twice. "Poor Will," she finally said. "No wonder. How hard for him."

The ache began again high in Aspera's chest. "Maybe you'd rather not know, Dena, I couldn't work that part out. But I have to sweep the board clean. No more secrets."

Dena's hand made three spasmodic brushes at the quilt fabric. "I think you could have spared us some pain. I think people deserve some protection when facts are brutal. I'm sure you did what you thought best, but I for one am not grateful and I doubt Will is."

At the door she turned. "You know, I could hardly comprehend when Will called me today, on his birthday, that you'd force him to arrange his own party. I couldn't imagine you'd be so callous. And now this—" The tears started, Dena's voice quavered. "I think you've done irretrievable harm to your marriage."

When Aspera looked up she was gone.

After time and silence had been sustained in the house—the needle off the last record—Aspera went downstairs to find it nearly empty of people. Misery and discord were telepathic. Party guests had disappeared like waxworks rolled off display. Stragglers in the front hall wished her cheerful ordinary good nights.

When she had closed the door, Aspera was alone in the house. Which was dimly lit but restored to ordinary light, and nearly ordinary in other respects. Tidy. Some thoughtful guest—please

God, not Bunny or Dena—had seen to the major share of clearing up. All the paper cups and pizza boxes were bagged in two plastic yard bags in the kitchen. Two extra-long twist ties lay handy on the kitchen table.

She opened the cupboard, poured two saucers of vinegar. She carried these in her hands, walking carefully through the passage. She set one on the dining room table, one on the bookshelf in the living room. Vinegar to mask the scent of staling cigarette smoke. Things she had learned, traveling the labyrinth. She'd followed false leads, had seen light at the end of a tunnel, light which proved to be a hard surface reflecting the beam she herself carried. By that light she was to find her way out again; she hoped batteries lasted.

The front door chimed. She looked through the glass and saw Kevin. She opened the door.

"Is Dena all right?" she asked him.

"Don't worry about Dena," he said. "You have to learn that. Here. Present for you." He took her hand and into it dropped a length of chain.

She looked at the small rusted links, looked at him.

"Your birches," he said.

She looked out where the white mottled trunks swayed, separately now, at the wind.

The green eyes took in her stunned expression, and he left. She shut the door again and this time leaned against it. She looked at the living room, the dining room as though she had lost her connection with them. A dance of black and white swans on dining room walls. A living room as cluttered with odd shapes—extra things. She walked to the hearth, bumping a corner of an end table with her hip as though she'd forgotten it was real. She picked up the ashtray, the bronze and copper lighter from the coffee table. Heavy objects, beautiful, but freed of their weight the oval of the table surface floated up. She turned and from the mantel removed a crystal paperweight, pewter candlesticks. Her hands could not hold these things; she made a cradle, a vise of her elbows against her body to secure them. She stood back to see. Will's voice, when it made its path to her brain, did not startle because it harmonized thoughts gathered there.

"Moving out?"

She felt the strangeness of the figure she cut, candlesticks jutting, the flat side of the ball of crystal packed under her breast. She faced him, felt her face flash pale.

He stood at the living room threshold, hands jammed into jacket pockets. "Taking a few things with you?"

Awkwardly she stood, silenced by crosshatching of what there was to see, what there was to say. His voice was not harsh, as she had expected; nor was it broken. A tenderness in it made tears spring to her eyes. She wanted to touch him and stood instead with her hands full, her arms occupied.

Lacking faith she sat down, backing gingerly on to the sofa. She might have been a very old woman as she let the defunct lighter, candlesticks, paperweight tumble onto the sofa cushions. As they left her grip her stomach registered a loss of ballast, and she began to cry.

Will came round the corner of the sofa where she leaned. Scarcity pressed in upon them, of time, of place, of love enough to go round. He sat on the edge and they leaned toward one another, in the slow bending that trees adopt when their roots are overwhelmed by the approach of water. When she flung her arms about his hips, he rested the weight of an arm about her shoulders. His own crying loosed itself, hoarse and rusty. He slipped down into the sofa beside her, scarcely noticing the cigarette box lodged beneath one thigh. They held to one another in tears and fastness among the hard objects of their living.

CHAPTER TWENTY

Watching was of great importance. They kept eyes on one another as though sight could keep them safe from the predation of thought. They made love in their bed with the reading lamps on, watching one another as carefully as if they met in a dark sea as strangers. Touch was important, touch insured against loss, against disappearance. Beside the bed they kept emergency candles and safety matches, and they lit one of the candles, let it burn even while they slept so that neither would risk waking up to grapple with history in the dark.

"Every time I walk out of the house like that," Will said during a time when they rested, exhausted and wakeful, candlelight flickering on the yellow diamonds that surrounded them, "I'm always so surprised. I had it in mind that I would get to dance with you tonight. Then there I was by myself, when what I wanted was to be with you."

The first waves of galvanic fervor passed, those first twenty-four hours in bed broken when Aspera left for her job in Minneapolis and reinstated when she returned. In a sustained violence of lovemaking they'd tried to scour one another's flesh of any trace of taint, of otherness. Strenuous effort; a few days later the bedroom took on more familiar proportions.

"If you want to change something," he said to her Sunday morning, sitting up in bed, "how about the wallpaper in this bedroom?"

She looked at the pattern on the walls. "I thought you liked it for sentimental reasons."

"Me? This was my parents' room. I told you, those yellow diamonds always looked to me like eyes watching."

She struggled up against the dynamics of the waterbed. She folded her arms on her knees. "The paper always went well with the quilt."

"I could do without that, too," he risked.

She looked at him, then down at the quilt. "All right," she decided. "But then I want big swashes of pastels, something in here that makes it oceany-feeling, like the walls could just float away."

"You're sure about that?" he asked. "When I wake up in the morning, the bathroom's already so far down the hall."

She shook her head, sighed. "Should have got you that bed-pan on your birthday."

Good bedroom cheer. The proximity of loss had done it, had produced this altered state. Big threats called for consolation, old World War II secret of the baby boom. At the hospital across the river from where they lay together, September's bumper births tattled every year on the seeds of dread citizens of Bracken found in their pockets in the dead of winter. This could be explained. Morning had arrived in the dark and faith was required.

One-flesh could console for lack of faith, Aspera knew. What was troubling was that it could be achieved only intermittently. Resolve and relief and gratitude, too, had intervals that grew more widely spaced, and before dawn of the third day of unconditional lovemaking, Will was in a mood for facts. When, where, how, how far, how often, why?

Aspera clutched a pillow to her chest, folded her arms around it.

"I don't see how we start over," Will said. He had found that most avenues led to precisely this point. "Are we supposed to just start trusting one another?"

Seconds wore by. "Maybe we earn that if we do the other stuff right."

"What other stuff?"

She considered. "Saying what we mean out loud. Saying it more than once. *Not* doing the other things we do—covering up, faking each other out."

"We must have had some very good reasons," he said, "for

going to all the trouble of doing things backward."

"Is fear a good reason?"

"Are you trying to finger me?" he asked. "Because I don't think I'm the only one at fault here, I'm not the one who—"

"I'm not saying you."

"What am I supposed to think? I think you mean me when you talk about fear."

"*I'm* afraid I'm supposed to be everything to you. I'm afraid you'll find out I don't *want* to be—I try to keep you from finding out. Then I'm furious with you for asking and needing."

"I recognize that part."

"Well: I don't get to refuse you anything, before you want *signs.*"

"You can't refuse me anything?" his voice cracked. "That's all you have been doing. The books, the store, weekends, goddamn Sunday breakfast—!"

"—a birthday party you *said* you didn't want!"

"I still think you could have figured that one out."

"Why should I have to?" she exploded. "When you could have told me?"

Will made a wry face. "My mother would have known what to do."

She'd gathered herself for another outburst when she saw he meant this as a joke.

"Will." She tapped his leg, a slow rhythm that gave her heart time to slow. "Two years from now that might be funny. Right now—" She stopped.

"Things don't need lightening up yet?" With his thumb Will made several slow, rising gestures toward the ceiling. "I always think things need lightening up; I think of myself as trying to help."

Against her wish she could see the bobbing ribbon-striped balloons of his gesture. With her hand she grounded his. "Maybe you could wait till I get both feet in the basket before you throw the last sandbag."

He grinned. "This could be tough. I like the sight of people's feet dangling." The skim of a smile faded as his eyes probed her face. "But it's not reassuring, I guess. It's not *friendly.*"

"It's not friendly."

He rubbed his chin. The furnace clicked off in the basement;

the sound traveled through the hollows of the ducts. Will took a ragged breath. "Is this the kind of thing—when you needed somebody else—a friend?"

She flinched as sheet lightning played about her stomach wall. So this was how they would talk about it. "I tried dividing things up. So I could risk being angry, and not also have to risk losing you."

Will looked away, set his teeth. "I don't want to understand that. It makes me—god*damn*!" He slugged his fist into his other palm. Then sat silent, holding on. He let out a breath, and when he spoke the anger had gone out of his voice. "It probably worked for you as well as booze did for me."

When their eyes met, he said, "I felt so cut off from you all the time. If you'd made one gesture—"

She shook her head. "Nothing I did could touch you—that's how I felt—so it seemed like nothing could hurt you, either."

He stared dully at the far wall. "I thought I was proving something, making you run the store by yourself. So stupid! Then I thought I could make it up to you if I was a big success, I thought you'd fall all over me. I *wanted* you to fall all over me, but that's when you left!" He rubbed his chin, a light rasping of whiskers. "I was just so wound up making things go, I couldn't tell exactly *when.*"

Aspera shut her eyes. "Sometimes I think we're living two different lives completely," she said. "Or we're stuck in some time warp."

"I'm sure it doesn't have to be like that."

"You're lucky, then."

"Am I?" he asked her.

She saw that it was a real question, that he was waiting. "For a while if I was loyal to you I felt crazy," she said at last. "Any move I could make that felt sane also felt disloyal, like living two lives." She turned to him. "I don't know how anyone survives, divided like that."

Will folded his hands, superintending the motions with his eyes. "I have to ask you this," he said. "Are you going to see him again—Kevin?"

The name, never an easy one between them, heaped the space between their bodies with fine, jagged crystals.

"I don't know how people find out the difference between two and one. Find the *balance,*" she said carefully. "I was trying to learn. Kevin was a friend to me in that way, but he"—she took a shallow breath—"he thinks everything can be divided and divided again, and again."

For a long moment nothing in the room had life.

"Talking about him," Will said, "makes him too real."

Her mouth dry. "He's real. Was real. I don't like talking about him in here."

Will slowly shook his head. He let his eyes wander the walls of the room. "Where do we go to start over?"

"Maybe we don't."

When he didn't say anything she leaned back on the pillows. There was a word they were both afraid of. "Maybe we should get divorced," she said. "At least then we'd have a right to know what we know. Divorced people are privileged that way."

"I don't want a divorce," Will said.

"Me either," she sighed with relief. "Then I guess we start from here."

"But in this much pain? Arguing about who did what?"

"Talking," she said. "Like we're doing."

He shrugged. "Not much difference."

She chewed her lip. "Well, you waiting for me to finish a thought, that feels different. Not destroying the connections, not jumping to some other place." She glanced at him. "Me saying what I think when I know you don't want to hear it."

He pulled a very deep sigh, so like one of Dena's that for a second he caught her eye to offer the joke, then shook his head, made a detour. "I think I have things to figure out." He pushed his palm down his thigh once, twice—a nervous gesture she remembered from civics class. "Like why I was so sure you ought to love me if I was finally a good boy and ran the store for you. Like why I thought I had to be such a hard guy." He made a crooked mouth. "I'm glad you shut me down on the second store. After I do this remodeling—it's going to be splendid, I can't tell you how *good* it felt ripping that old stairwell out—anyhow, once I get the new space organized and Interiors back on its feet, maybe I could just draw patio plans for a while." His eyes stole over to see her face. "I mean, designing some of these small jobs the contractors walk in with. There I am, point-of-purchase advantage, I could keep my hand in, you know?"

"I do love you, Will," she said.

He held very still. "Here's the part that bothers me," he said at last. "About love, you either decide everything somebody does is OK, or everything they do is horseshit. Isn't that the way it is? I know how it feels not to be able to do anything right."

She looked at him. "Both of us know."

"Well, I made sure *you* couldn't do anything right, just to feel like we were even."

They eyed one another. Habits of combat.

"So," he said, "whose turn is it to get even now?'

She closed her eyes, tried to think how it might begin. You could walk through walls, she wanted to believe it; a slight shift in frequency, and you could find the molecules flung wide for passage. Still, this matter of beginning.

"I love you, Will," she told him, "but this is conditional love. You have to love me back. And I have to be able to feel it, and be able to say so when I don't feel it."

He thought it over. "Sounds fair," he conceded. "Doesn't sound too romantic."

They looked at one another.

"OK," he said. "Let's start where we belong, try and dig ourselves out. But I have to tell you." He slipped his arms around her. "This stuff scares me."

She held on to his arms.

He pressed his cheek tight against hers. "How'd we ever get here? I'm a decent guy, we're both so basically decent—"

"Every last one of us," she broke in, "is decent and sane except when we get into pairs! Then the pathology leaps out, Dena's right about that much. We marry our homework—I really think that's true. Running away doesn't work for you and me because our homework is our homework, our pathology is our pathology."

Will rubbed his chin, tested the stubble of copper beard. "I don't know about this hospital library job," he said. "Talking to you I never know if we ought to be in love or in medical school." When she laughed he relaxed some, let his arms bracket her more comfortably. "I'll tell you how I feel," he said. "My pathology is, I don't want to go to medical school, but I want to survive the operation. And I'll be your pathology if you'll be mine."

A wariness in the look they exchanged then, a look that caught and held.

CHAPTER TWENTY-ONE

Each weekday morning in December Aspera drove to the VA Hospital in Minneapolis. All day she breathed books and dating ink. She came home to Bracken tired, buoyant. Some evenings, the Christmas rush upon them, she spent with Will at the store. Not that her help was needed, but some gesture was, if only to forestall the questions they tried not to ask each day: Did you see Kevin? Did you go through my desk? Are you really there for me?

Christmas, they selected brave gifts from elsewhere. Will surprised Aspera with silk underwear, made in France, as he'd done after they were first lovers twenty years ago. But this time the brassiere's cups were set too wide apart and the effect was not at all sexy, the wire circles missing her breasts and deforming their contours, rose lace pulling to the sides in taut folds. She promised to exchange it; he would exchange the fine cotton nightshirt, made in India, that she'd chosen for him and which stretched tight over his chest for all the size claimed Extra Large.

He ordered shelves made for the small room upstairs. Together he and Aspera placed Elvira's books on them. Aspera opened a volume to show him the three slips of onionskin, and Will listened to the story of the pearls; he had a strong impulse to leave the room, but he stayed.

"I don't know what to do," he said, folding his arms and rubbing his chin. Without confidence he opened his arms to her, and she leaned against his chest. He held her cautiously. "I could send away for new pearls," he said. "Do you want to start over that way?"

She put her fingers to the necklace she wore. Seven pearls—she knew them now, four and three, and this felt settled, felt just. She shook her head. She sighed and rested her cheek on Will's soft shirt, sensed the heat of his body through the cloth. High in her chest was an aching that she recognized. She thought about what she wanted now, what she knew about wanting things.

Toward evening the two of them put on coats and boots and hats and mittens. The carillon sounded from the hospital chapel across the river, and while "Faraway Places" and "Lady of Spain" rang across the frozen Mississippi, Aspera and Will waded through snowdrifts in their front yard to break from the cold trees a handful of twigs. In one of Elvira's books, Aspera had come across a mention of a custom the ancient druids had for honoring the new year—birch twigs gathered and offered to the chosen lover, the giving itself an invitation: you may begin.